J J Holland is the pseudonym for Jane Holland, a Gregory Award-winning poet and novelist. She has published six collections of poetry and dozens of thrillers, historicals, romcoms and feel-good fiction under various pseudonyms, including Victoria Lamb, Elizabeth Moss, Beth Good and Hannah Coates.

Her first thriller, *Girl Number One*, hit #1 in the UK Kindle store in 2015, catapulting her into a life of crime. She currently lives with her husband and young family in South West England, and enjoys encouraging new writers.

You can find her on Twitter as @JJHollandSavage and @janeholland1.

IN HIGH PLACES

J. J. HOLLAND

Quercus

First published in Great Britain in 2019 by

Quercus Editions Ltd
Carmelite House
50 Victoria Embankment
London EC4Y 0DZ

An Hachette UK company

A CIP catalogue record for this book is available
from the British Library

PAPERBACK ISBN 978 1 78747 636 3
EBOOK ISBN 978 1 78747 637 0

www.quercusbooks.co.uk

Typeset by Jouve (UK), Milton Keynes

Printed and bound in Great Britain by Clays Ltd, Elcograf S.p.A.

ða com of more   under misthleoþum
Grendel gongan,   godes yrre bær;
mynte se manscaða   manna cynnes
sumne besyrwan   in sele þam hean.

Beowulf

*Then Grendel came stalking from the high moors, down
misty slopes, the mark of God's anger on him. Rapacious
destroyer, determined to ensnare one of the race of
men in that great hall.*

PROLOGUE

The last thing Lina had said to him was, 'Find Jarrah for me, Aubrey. Find my brother.'

Savage couldn't move his legs. The stench of burning rubber and metal was thick and vile, clogging up his throat, scouring his lungs with every breath.

Something floated down through the debris-filled air, still partly alight, a wavering red line against a dusty, smoke-filled sky. A shred of some bright material. Silk, perhaps, from one of the dozens of glorious bolts of silk on display in the nearby bazaar, their colours a vivid temptation for women in the ubiquitous black hijab. They had stopped by a cloth seller's stall after finishing their morning coffee, ducking under the low awning to admire its array of fabrics out of the scorching Afghan sunshine. The smiling cloth seller had greeted them in Arabic, suggesting a foreigner's price for the tall, blond Englishman in his jeans and white, short-sleeved shirt, then instantly lowering it under Lina's dark scrutiny.

The burning shred touched his cheek and Savage lifted an instinctive hand, brushing it clumsily away, as yet unaware of pain.

Find Jarrah for me, Aubrey. Find my brother.

Memory came back slowly, piecemeal, and with it a creeping sense of dread.

Savage had been leaning inside Abdul Walid's van, keeping

his head below the level of the dashboard so as not to be seen, hunting through tatty documents in Arabic, and empty snack packets and drinks cans in the glove box and on the filthy floor of the van. He'd been looking for evidence that Jarrah had been there, that he had met with Abdul in Kabul, perhaps even worked as a courier for him as part of his cover. That was what they'd heard from their sources: that he and Abdul had been thick as thieves in the months before he disappeared. Any evidence would have been useful. But Savage was hoping for a handwritten note or document, anything with Jarrah's name on it.

Then he'd felt an enormous, soundless impact.

It had lifted Savage off his feet, and the van with him, flinging them both several feet away, joined together in a tunnel of unholy fire. He'd watched the van – or what was left of it – roll silently over him inside a burning cloud that had obliterated the dazzling azure of the skies above Kabul. Like some unspeakable apocalypse straight out of the Old Testament.

That was roughly when he'd lost consciousness.

How long had he been out?

Blood ran down his cheek and bubbled into his mouth, the iron-rich taste baffling. It took Savage another moment to realise it was coming from a wound high up under the hairline. There was something embedded there, he realised, fumbling at the wet, jagged edge of the wound. Some kind of metallic shrapnel.

He knew that smell too. The familiar stink of exploded ordnance.

'Bomb,' he mumbled through bleeding lips, and slowly began to pick himself up out of the hot, smoking wreckage of Abdul Walid's van.

The marketplace had been obliterated.

The leather goods stall and its nearest neighbours no longer existed. Where they had stood was a thick cloud of dust and debris. And scattered, burning bodies.

CHAPTER ONE

Aubrey Savage noticed the scarecrow first, drenched and bowed on its wooden stake, its shambolic straw head hanging low. And so nearly missed the woman in the lay-by a few hundred metres further along, bent over the open bonnet of a classic MG in the pouring rain. Passing, he caught a glimpse of a wild, pale face, dark hair streaming bedraggled down her back, and thought at once of a romantic line from Keats that made him feel like a nineteen-year-old student again.

I met a lady in the meads, Full beautiful, a faery's child . . .

The car had drawn his attention before the woman, of course. Its ghostly gleam was impossible to miss on a moorland road at dusk.

Diamond White.

Early-1970s from the partial registration, and almost exactly like the classic MG he'd owned in his pre-army days.

A fantastic little car, but increasingly unreliable with age. He was not surprised to see it broken down in this near-horizontal downpour, either. Those old MGs hated the rain. Distributor cap had got wet, in all probability.

An easy fix, Savage thought, peering back at the car in his rain-flecked wing mirror. A two-minute job, if you knew what you were looking for.

But did *she* know?

As the woman straightened to stare at him, he checked the wing mirror again, and then laughed, astonished.

Savage was not given to helping damsels in distress. Too much bloody trouble, in his experience, and he was not in a mood for interaction with the opposite sex. Not today, and certainly not given where he was headed, a meeting too-long avoided. But this woman intrigued him. Enough to make an exception to one of his rules. At first glance, he had missed what she was wearing, her outline lost against the white car under a rain haze. But her outfit, in this remote location, a lonely spot on the moorland road between Postbridge and Princetown, coupled with this appalling weather, made a Good Samaritan response almost obligatory.

He turned his beast of a camper van in the opening to a five-bar gate marked Private, and headed slowly back to the lay-by – if it could be called a lay-by; a mere semi-circle of gravel at the side of the lonely road, surrounded on both sides by grasslands and high, rolling moor to the horizon. He had been planning to park up in Yelverton again that evening. Maybe grab some fish and chips for supper.

But at the back of his mind, he was dreading what lay ahead. Anything that might put off his visit for even half an hour was a welcome distraction.

The driver stood there in the gloom, backed up against the open bonnet, hands behind her back, staring at him through the rapid flick of his windscreen wipers. He guessed her to be somewhere in her early twenties, heavily made-up, her mascara running.

She looked scared.

No, Savage thought, studying her face more closely. Not scared.

Terrified.

Of him?

It was possible, he supposed. He was a big guy in his thirties, drastically short hair a hangover from his army days, out on his own. He might well seem a potential threat to a woman alone, especially on an empty moorland road like this.

Smile, he told himself.

Savage turned off the engine and jumped down from the cab, forcing his mouth to crack into that unfamiliar grimace he called a smile. The ground was boggy and waterlogged, despite the dry weather they had been enjoying in the South West for three days previously. He had come down the motorway from Bristol to Exeter, spent a day looking round the cathedral city, then driven in a leisurely fashion around the lonely side roads and lanes of Dartmoor.

He'd been drifting, in other words.

Putting off a long-delayed visit that part of him was reluctant to make.

But today, rising with the sun in a fuel station car park near Yelverton, he had drunk a strong cup of coffee, and admitted to himself that the day had finally come.

It had been nearly a year since Lina had died. He had made her a promise. A promise that her death had done nothing to diminish. It was time to keep it.

'Hello?'

She watched his approach, wide-eyed, silent.

Was he so intimidating? He was a stranger, of course, and a man. And the light was failing around them. Dusk fell rapidly on Dartmoor. He recalled that from previous visits. Soon it would be full dark.

'Engine trouble?'

He had spoken mildly enough. But the woman continued to stare at him as though in fear for her life, and said nothing in return.

'Best not to keep the bonnet open too long. Not in this

weather.' Blinking away rain, Savage glanced past her into the engine cavity. 'Do you know what the trouble is? Would you like me to take a look?'

'It just stopped.' She had a thick, Devon burr, the sort of countrified accent he associated with cream teas and long, sunny afternoons spent outdoors. 'I didn't know what to do.'

He could not resist. 'On your way to church? Or did you change your mind?'

Again, the wide-eyed stare.

'Sorry?'

He nodded to her sleeveless white dress. It was sodden, and see-through in places, and could have been a clubbing dress, he supposed. But its simplicity of styling, and the discreet sequins on the bodice, both suggested a more symbolic purpose. The sleek white silk clung to her slender frame, stopping just above the knee. Her tights and white shoes were splattered with mud.

'That's a wedding dress, isn't it?'

She didn't answer his question, her eyes evasive. 'Look, if you can get it started again, I'd be dead grateful.' Her wary gaze kept shooting back the way she had come, as though expecting someone else to appear. But the road to Princetown remained empty under the glowering skies. 'I'm in a hurry.'

There was a fine black tattoo on the inside of her left wrist. It looked like a letter, elaborately drawn.

P?

He tried to see but she clasped her hands behind her back, her look suddenly defensive. Not his business, anyway.

'OK,' he said. 'I'll check it over for you. It could be the distributor cap. Sometimes they get dirty or crack on these older models. But you should wait inside the car. You're getting soaked.'

'I'd rather not, thanks.'

The young woman made a face, rubbing her bare arms, and

he could see now that she was shivering. Her close-fitting dress had been ripped open along one side seam, and recently too, white threads still hanging down.

There wasn't much room in an MG. Had she torn her wedding dress deliberately, to make driving easier?

That certainly suggested she was in a hurry.

Desperate, even.

'Why not wait in my camper, then?'

'I'm wet.'

'I don't mind. There's a clean towel in the back if you want to dry your hair while you wait.' He stuck out a hand, trying not to stare at the sodden clinging silk of her dress. 'I'm Aubrey, by the way.'

'Dani.'

They shook hands in a perfunctory way. Her grip was loose and slippery.

'Go on, honestly. This could take a few minutes.'

'Thanks.'

Dani wrapped both arms about herself and dashed to the passenger side of the van, climbing inside out of the rain.

Savage bent to inspect the engine, wishing he had a torch. Daylight was already fading under the dark clouds.

He ran a hand over the cooling engine, looking for the most obvious faults. But everything seemed to be in its rightful place, and the oil was at a good level when he checked it. It was a pleasure to see an MG engine again, after all these years. And so well-maintained. Not her car, he guessed. *It just stopped.* Not what he'd have expected to hear from the knowledgeable and conscientious owner who had kept this classic car in such excellent condition. The groom's car, then? Or was it hired for the day?

Had she stolen the wedding car itself to make her getaway?

None of your business, he reminded himself. You stopped to

help restart a broken-down car, not get involved in some love story gone wrong.

He fiddled about under the pouring rain. It was not the distributor cap. The inside of the cap was clean, as were the contacts, and there were no cracks to let in water and cause a possible engine misfire. He lowered the bonnet two-thirds of the way, and then gently dropped it so it clicked shut.

Going round to the driver's side, he stooped to adjust the seat setting to his rangier build, then climbed inside the MG and closed the door.

Rain streaked the windscreen and pattered noisily on the roof, the car interior a gloomy little cave. The dashboard was clean and tidy too, as were the vinyl seats and foot wells. Directly opposite, the brunette was sitting stiffly in the passenger seat of his camper van. Her head was bowed, hair falling down to hide her face. Dani – perhaps short for Danielle – was staring at her lap. Probably trying to make a phone call.

Then he realised her mobile was still poking out of her handbag on the seat next to him, beside a zipped-up sports holdall.

So what was she doing over there with her head bent?

Crying? Praying?

He heard the rumble of a diesel engine coming flat-out along the moorland road, and waited. A moment later, a dirty white Ford Transit flashed past at speed, the long-wheelbase version, and the diminutive MG shook in the wake of its passing. White Van Man, and a typical example of his species. Doing somewhere in the region of eighty miles per hour, at a rough guess, on a country road barely fit enough for sixty.

Savage shook his head.

The key was still in the ignition. He turned it, listening for the familiar roar.

Nothing.

He waited a moment, counting under his breath, then tried

again. The engine turned but did not start. Was it flooded? That did not seem feasible. She had been here a while. Only then did his gaze rise to check the fuel gauge.

The needle was flat to the red.

Gathering up her things, Savage climbed out and locked the MG. Then he ran back to the camper van through the rain. Handing over her handbag and sports holdall, both now glistening with raindrops, he said, 'Mystery solved.'

'Did you get it started?'

'Not yet.'

He passed her the MG key too, then started the camper van engine. She looked at him anxiously but there was really no need. His van ran on diesel and was therefore unaffected by the damp weather. It started first time. He set the windscreen wipers going again, peering ahead through the gloom, then over his shoulder. A few cars had passed while he was checking under the bonnet, but now the road was clear. No other headlights in view.

'Don't worry,' he said easily, 'it's a simple enough fix. When did you last fill her up?'

'I'm not sure.' Her expression was carefully blank as she took a moment to consider the question. 'Last week?'

Definitely not her car.

'Is that fuel gauge accurate?' He knew the gauges on those older models often stopped working. 'Or does it always read as empty?'

'I . . . I think it works OK.'

'Then you've run out of fuel, that's all.'

He glanced at his mobile on its dashboard mounting. It was slightly askew, as though hurriedly replaced. Had she taken his phone and tried to make a phone call with it? Unlikely she'd have got through the password. He wondered who she had been hoping to call.

'There's a filling station down in Yelverton,' he said. 'Unless you know of a nearer one?'

She looked uncertain. 'I don't think so.'

It was a long, winding drive back to Yelverton through narrow country lanes. But he could hardly leave her stranded at the roadside in this appalling weather, with night coming on. And he seemed to recall, from studying the maps online, that the next fuel station in the other direction was even further. Dartmoor National Park was an excellent place to visit. But it was not known for its wide selection of filling stations. Hence the need to keep an eye on your fuel gauge, he thought drily.

'I can't lend you a spare fuel can, I'm afraid. Mine's been used for diesel. But the garage is bound to sell them. You can fill it up at the pump, then I'll drive you back here. Shouldn't take more than half an hour. Forty minutes, tops. How's that?'

'Thank you,' she said.

She was plucking at the damp hem of her dress with nervous fingers. Her voice was husky, tinged with reluctance. Dani did not want to return the way she had come.

Scared of being caught?

But why?

Who might be coming after her?

Dani didn't look like the sort of woman who would have any difficulty telling a man she no longer wanted to marry him.

In fact, she looked like trouble.

Savage checked his mirrors, then pulled out onto the lonely road in the dark. The van shuddered, coughed and then roared as he moved up through the gears, gathering speed. Her handbag was clutched on her lap, he noticed, the sports holdall lodged safely down beside the gearbox. She had one foot on the holdall, as though afraid it might slide about when he cornered. Which was always possible.

They passed the scarecrow again, unlikely in its field of rough, moorland grass. This time, he barely glanced at its bowed figure.

'So, Dani,' he said, 'want to tell me why you're running away from your own wedding?'

CHAPTER TWO

'I'm not running away.'

Savage said nothing. Not because he was impolite, though his sister might have disagreed with that, but because he knew that saying nothing was often the best way to get information out of a reluctant informant. And there was something about Dani that suggested there was more to this than a simple lovers' tiff. He needed a good story to take his mind off the important visit he had still not managed to make, but which loomed ahead of him like an obstacle in an otherwise clear road.

'I had second thoughts, that's all. Not a crime, is it?' Pulling down the sun visor to check her reflection in the mirror there, she wiped streaks of mascara off her cheeks with unsteady fingers. 'I'll be fine once I ... After I've had a break from him.' There was stress in her voice that did not match her words. 'A breathing space, that's what they call it. Some time away.'

'In his car?'

'It's not his car.' She glared at him, then her shoulders slumped. 'It's my dad's, OK? I was in a hurry, so I took it. Dad won't mind. So long as I don't bang it.'

'He must be very understanding.' Savage thought of his own father, and his hands unconsciously tightened on the steering wheel. He pushed the thought aside, focusing instead on the dark, low-hanging clouds ahead, shot through with the last vestiges of dull rainy light. Dartmoor was brooding on every side of the narrow road, its broad, bare expanse slipping inexorably into night as they drew closer to Yelverton. 'So you had second thoughts and drove off in your dad's MG, leaving your man at the altar?'

She had found a tissue in her bag and was making hurried repairs to her make-up. 'Something like that, yeah.'

But in fact nothing like that, he interpreted.

What was she leaving out?

'What's his name?'

She did not answer for a moment, then said in a cold, determined voice, 'I don't really want to talk about it.'

'And I don't really want to drive back to Yelverton. I was on my way to Princetown for a night's rest off-road. Maybe some fish and chips while I listen to the radio. I'm planning to visit someone tomorrow morning and want to be fresh for that. But I was brought up to be helpful, so here we are. Alone together on a dark road.'

Now it was her turn to be silent. Considering, perhaps, that she knew nothing about him. That she had run from one difficult man to one who could turn out to be something worse. A rapist, or worse. Out of the frying pan into the fire. And with no other cars in sight, possibly for miles.

He softened his tone. 'Look, it can get lonely, living in a van. I understand perfectly if you don't want to tell me what's happened. It's none of my business, I get that. But I'd appreciate a little conversation, at least.' He glanced at her, but she had turned her head, looking out of the side window. 'In return for the ride?'

'OK.' Her voice was muffled. 'If you put it like that.'

'Thank you.'

She rubbed a little porthole on the misted-up side window with her fist. 'Terry.' Her tone was flat, matter-of-fact. She did not sound very excited. Perhaps she really had changed her mind about marrying him, and it wasn't just a case of last-minute nerves. 'His name is Terry Hoggins.'

'Your boyfriend?'

Again, she hesitated. A split-second. The liar's hesitation. 'Yes.'

He thought about the letter P tattooed on the inside of her wrist. Was that the initial of her real boyfriend, perhaps? Or perhaps he was reading too much into a simple preference for keeping her business to herself.

'And your dad? What's his name?'

No hesitation this time. 'Geoff.'

'No second name?'

'Geoff Farley.'

'Into classic cars, is he?'

'Sorry?'

'Your dad. Geoff. You said that was his car. It looked pretty well-maintained to me. Which is a labour of love with those old MGs. So I'm guessing he must be interested in classic cars.'

There was something off about her responses. About the whole business. He was not sure he wanted to pry too much, though. His stomach rumbled. He was still thinking about supper. There was a good chippy in Yelverton. He remembered it from last time he'd visited the moor. The kind with freshly cooked fish and a large glass jar of pickled eggs on the counter. If it was still there, of course, and being run by the same people. It was some years since he'd been to this part of the world, after all.

Peter had taken him to the chippy with Jarrah, the three of them eating their chips afterwards on a town bench. The Three Musketeers. Watching the world go by, with a paper wrap of chips. As much world as could be found on a quiet evening in a small Dartmoor town, that is.

'I guess.' She shrugged, considering the question without much interest. 'We're not that close.'

'You live with Terry, is that it?'

'That's right.'

'Except you decided you didn't fancy being Dani Hoggins.'

Dani did not answer.

She had found a lipstick and was applying it with deft, automatic strokes. Coral pink. She made a face at herself in the mirror like a goldfish, then looked satisfied, tossing the lipstick back into her bag.

'What about you?' she asked suddenly. 'You married?'

Savage stared straight ahead into the dark curtain of rain, saying nothing. And not merely because he didn't like any of the options available to him in response to that particular question. There were lights coming up the other side of the hill. Another car, moving fast through the empty landscape. Its headlights dipped as it crested the hill, then suddenly switched to full beam, dazzling him through the pouring rain.

He swore, braking and instinctively half-closing his eyes.

'Idiot!'

He flashed his headlights, but it made no difference. He was being deliberately blinded, the cab of his camper van almost floodlit as the other driver came on at speed. The car looked like an old Land Rover Defender, sandy-coloured. It was wobbling all over the road.

Savage hugged the verge, wondering if there was going to be a collision. Not a head-on. But a glancing blow, perhaps.

Fleetingly, he caught a glimpse of a furious face behind the wheel.

Round-framed glasses, reflecting his own headlights. Ginger hair, possibly. Hard to say if it was male or female, but if pushed, he would have guessed a young male. Though that could simply have been down to the suicidal pace and uneven driving.

There was someone else in the car, a dark formless shape in the passenger seat. Perhaps wearing a hoody. Certainly there was no face visible.

Dani moaned and sank her face in her hands.

The car shot past them.

Savage blinked and shook his head, the halo of those blinding lights still ghosting in his vision. There had been some wording on the back of the Defender, an advert of sorts. But he hadn't been able to make out what it said in that swift, dark glimpse.

He checked his wing mirror, and frowned.

The driver had slammed on the brakes. He'd stopped a few hundred feet beyond them, and was now attempting to turn his Land Rover on the narrow road.

'Friends of yours?' he asked, slowing his own pace. He was not interested in racing a couple of Dartmoor locals, especially given that the driver looked drunk. Drunk or high. Whichever, it was probably best to pull in to the side of the road and have an actual conversation with these guys, let them get whatever it was out of their system.

'What do you mean?'

'Whoever they are, they're coming back.'

'Don't stop.' She sounded terrified again. 'Keep driving.'

'Look, they're not going to—'

'Please don't stop.'

Something in her voice made him slacken off the brake. But it made no difference. Thirty seconds later, the Land Rover Defender roared past them again, engine straining, loud in the night.

Was he hoping to taunt Savage into racing him?

Fifty feet ahead, the driver braked violently, just before the bend. Red brake lights lit up the near-horizontal rain, and a rough expanse of moorland grass beyond the road, picking out the eyes of some startled pony in the distance. The Land Rover shuddered to a halt, finishing slewed halfway across both carriageways, effectively blocking the path ahead.

Savage swore, braking hard.

The camper van skidded on the wet road, the wheel nearly wrenched out of his control as he fought to keep it from colliding with the other vehicle. He was vaguely aware of the Land Rover's passenger door opening, and a tall figure getting out. Then the van was bumping along the sodden verge, missing the Land Rover but crashing instead against thorn bushes and other unseen obstacles as it slowed, eventually subsiding into a boggy stretch which, thankfully, did not turn the van over as he had feared.

He threw off the seatbelt and fumbled with the door handle, jumping out into the relentless downpour.

'You bloody fool,' Savage began, striding back towards the Land Rover. But the car was already moving again, straightening up as it headed for him, its headlights on full, blinding him again. 'What the hell . . . ?'

He jumped back onto the verge behind the van to avoid being hit, and the Land Rover accelerated past him. A few seconds later, he heard it stop. A door opened, and he thought he heard a muffled noise. A shout of some kind? Not a man. It had been too high-pitched for that. The door shut again with a thud before he had even rounded the back of the van. Then the engine revved violently.

He stared after the car as it roared off towards Yelverton. It rounded the bend at an insane speed, then its red tail lights vanished as it headed down the hill. With astonishing swiftness, the road became quiet again, insistent rain the only sound audible for miles in both directions. As though nothing had ever happened.

Going back to the driver's side of the van, Savage furiously wrenched it open. 'Some friends you've got,' he began, then stopped, staring at the empty space where Dani had been sitting.

Her door was hanging open, rain pouring down beyond it. She was gone.

CHAPTER THREE

Savage stood there, fists clenched impotently, staring at his passenger's empty seat. Then he ran round to the other side of the van. There was no sign of her there either. He walked round the van again, stared up and down the desolate, black, rain-drenched road calling her name, then realised he was achieving nothing.

He went back to the cab for a torch and his raincoat.

Kitted out for a search, he walked along the verge for some ten minutes, his hood up, the raincoat affording him little protection against the driving rain, and shone the torch beam across the barren moorland on both sides, calling out, 'Dani?' at intervals. Then he reversed his steps, doing the same in the opposite direction, in case she had become scared and run away despite the dark and the rain, heading back towards the remote pull-in where they had left the MG.

He gave up the search, which had been perfunctory anyway.

Dani had been desperate enough to ignore the weather conditions and make a run for it across the moors, of course. He'd seen terror in her eyes when the Land Rover appeared over the hill. Then she'd hidden her face in her hands, like a fugitive ducking the beam of a prison searchlight.

But that was not what had happened.

One of the doors to the Land Rover had opened while he was standing about outside in the rain like a fool.

He had heard it clearly.

Then the door had slammed shut again.

And somewhere between those two sounds, he'd heard a muffled cry. The kind of angry, frightened cry someone might make if they were being bundled into a car against their will.

Savage returned to the camper and shone the torch over the road surface in front of the bumper. If there had been any signs of a struggle here, the relentless rain had erased them. Or perhaps he was wrong. Perhaps she had taken one look at her boyfriend and all had been forgiven between them.

Perhaps those guys had been rescuers. Not aggressors.

But why disappear into the night afterwards in that loud, dramatic way?

Rescuers would have stopped to interrogate him. To ask why he was picking up random women in lay-bys. Maybe to warn him off too. Or to thank him. To shake his hand for having saved their errant bride from a drenching by the side of the road. For being a Good Samaritan and stopping to help, rather than passing by on the other side.

He crouched down, rain dripping down his face, to survey the damage to the front and nearside of the camper. There were scratches and a bad dent to the front bumper, and the lower part of the van was mud-black in places, fragments of thorn bush caught underneath. It looked cosmetic though, nothing serious. His only problem might lie in coaxing the lumbering camper van off the soft verge, which had become part-marsh under all this rain, and back onto the road.

Standing beside the open passenger door, Savage looked at the empty seat again. He was filled with impotent rage at his own stupidity.

Whoever had been in that ancient Land Rover Defender, they'd driven out along this desolate road in search of Dani, the missing bride. Like tracking down a piece of lost property.

And as soon as they had discovered their runaway, they'd taken her back again. Without so much as an introduction, or a conversation about the rights and wrongs of it. Lost property found and reclaimed, thank you very much.

Their retrieval of Dani Farley had been almost contemptuous in its ease.

And he had done nothing to prevent it.

He slammed the passenger door shut, and squelched round through the muddy puddles to the driver's side. It took him a few moments to negotiate the camper van back onto the road, the tyres spinning angrily at one point, tossing up mud and grass tufts. But eventually he was free of the boggy verge, and back on solid tarmac.

Deciding not to turn back and spend the night in Princetown as planned, he drove on slowly in the direction taken by the Land Rover, back towards Yelverton.

There was always that chippy, after all.

Parked up in a muddy lay-by on the outskirts of Yelverton, he bent to put the wet torch back into the glove box. Which was when he realised Dani had left something behind.

Her sports holdall.

It was tucked in under her seat, still zipped shut.

That decided it.

It was unlikely a runaway bride would have transferred to the Land Rover of her own accord, yet failed to take all her possessions. Even if she had been overwhelmed with joy at the sight of her groom-to-be, and forgiven him instantly, she would never have abandoned her bug-out bag to a stranger.

Which was what this holdall represented, by his reckoning.

A bug-out bag.

A bag packed long in advance, specifically in anticipation of this moment, of the need to escape at a moment's notice. It would contain a clean change of clothing, some toiletries and personal effects, plus enough cash to survive up to a week on the run, if she was sensible. Debit and credit cards could be tracked, and accounts blocked. But cash was both anonymous and universal.

Dani would almost certainly not have had time to pack at the point of deciding to run. Such drastic decisions were like lightning strikes, and had a similar effect on the brain. Everything narrowed to the immediate and overriding need for escape, all thoughts of fresh underwear or 24-hour protective deodorant forgotten. So the sports holdall would have been packed on a previous occasion, and then hidden away in an obscure corner of a bedroom. On top of a wardrobe, perhaps, or in a closet.

For Emergency Use Only.

Turning off his headlights, he swung through from the cab into the seating area of his van, carrying Dani's holdall. The bag was lighter than he had expected. Unevenly balanced too. As though it contained only a few items, one or two heavier than the others.

He could hand the bag in to a police station without ever opening it, of course. That would be the good citizen way of doing things.

But there might be something inside the sports holdall that would help locate her without needing to involve the local constabulary. An address book, for instance, though that seemed less likely now that everyone kept such details on their phones. She'd taken her mobile with her. He recalled Dani clutching her handbag as they bumped across the muddy verge. The phone had been inside it.

But there might be a photograph with information scribbled on the back. Or some official letter, perhaps mentioning her current address.

Besides, he was curious now.

What did a bride-to-be pack in her bug-out bag?

Savage sat at the table in the back of his camper van, the sports holdall sitting in front of him. A truck passed on the main road beside the lay-by, the driver going too fast for the wet conditions. Late getting home from a haulage job, perhaps. The camper van swayed in the slipstream of its passing. Glasses and pans rattled in the cupboard above his head. The dusty blind screens on the windows shook.

Savage waited.

The sound of the truck died away in the distance.

The road into Yelverton was silent again.

He unzipped the holdall.

At the very top was a blue cotton dress, folded neatly. He put it to one side, trying not to disturb the folds. Beneath that was a scrap of paper.

A greyish scrap of paper, about two inches long, folded in half. Rough texture. Thin, cheap paper. Like something torn from the blank edge of a newspaper.

He unfolded the scrap of paper.

Someone – presumably Dani, but not necessarily – had scribbled 'may day' on the paper. Nothing more. All in lower case letters.

May Day?

It was nearly the end of April. May Day was the 1st of May, a traditional English celebration of spring. Some called it a pagan ritual, some saw it as an excuse to sing songs and dress up in odd clothing. Some never bothered.

The two words seemed cramped together though, the space between the final y of 'may' and the d of 'day' barely discernible. It could have been written in a hurry, of course. Or perhaps the note more properly read 'mayday' – a universally acknowledged expression of distress, normally given at sea or in the air.

Usually 'mayday' had to be repeated three times to distinguish it from other call signs.

Mayday, mayday, mayday. I need emergency assistance.

This was only one word: *mayday.*

Did that rule still apply when the call sign was written down, though?

Alternatively, perhaps there was an entity or even a person named Mayday, and she had made a note of the name before leaving. But that made the name vitally important to remember. Otherwise, why stop long enough to make this note and slip it into her bug-out bag?

Unless it had already been in her bag. Packed away for future reference.

Mayday, though, with a capital M?

Perhaps it was a business organisation. A company called Mayday, for instance.

Or Dani was the kind of person who disdained capital letters and never used them, of course, or perhaps had not bothered to use one in her desperate need to be gone. The former was possible, but the latter unlikely, given the simple fact that, if she had been in such a rush, why bother stopping to write a one-word note in the first place?

Which brought him back to the distress call.

Mayday, mayday, mayday. I need emergency assistance.

Something clicked in his head. Was 'mayday' a secret code, perhaps to be given to someone at an agreed rendezvous later? A word to differentiate between friend and foe? *Mayday. I'm on your side. Let me in. Give me shelter from the enemy.* Or was he putting too much of his own history onto a perfectly simple case of last-minute jitters at the altar?

Giving up, he refolded the note and put it in his wallet.

For future reference.

He heard voices outside. Two people at least, about to walk

past the van, front end to rear. A man and a woman. Devon accents, the woman giggling.

Leaning across, he peered out of the slats of the blind cautiously. The man came first: unshaven, wearing a grey, rain-stained hoody and a black woollen bobble hat with neon pink lettering. K A R was all he could read. Karl, presumably.

As Savage watched, the man spat at the side of his camper.

'Effing tourists.'

The woman laughed again, saying something Savage didn't catch. She had a blue woollen bobble hat and a round, red-cheeked face beneath it.

Savage listened to the couple as they sauntered on along the road, no doubt headed for the pub he had passed a short distance back, of which there were all too few on Dartmoor. He resisted the urge to get out and give Karl a damn good kicking for spitting on his van. But he was likely to need information later, and Karl looked like the kind of man who would have friends in that pub. Friends who liked nothing better than putting the boot into tourists. Getting arrested for affray might not be useful in the long term, even if the exercise gave him short-term satisfaction. It was still raining slightly, and the spittle would soon wash off anyway.

He returned to Dani's holdall.

On top of the pile now were an unopened pack of black, elastic-top stockings and two pairs of underwear. One pair plain white cotton knickers, high-waisted. Very prim. One pair neon pink see-through lace panties, with a thong back. The opposite of prim.

Savage grinned, shaking the knickers out in case of more hidden notes. There were none. He put those and the black stockings to one side too.

Pervert.

Then he put his hand back into the bag, still grinning, and

felt something hard and oblong. A familiar enough shape. But not one he had expected to find in Dani's bag.

Savage stilled.

His fingers closed about the object, resting there a moment while his brain ticked through the possibilities. He could not see it yet, but knew perfectly well what he had found.

A handgun.

Slowly, he drew the gun from the bag and examined it.

It was a Glock 19.

The makers called it a 'Compact'. For good reason. It was slightly smaller than the Glock 17 he'd used in the army. Perfect for concealed carry.

He doubted this was a legitimate possession. Dani hadn't struck him as special forces, or an undercover firearms officer with the police. So this was almost certainly a black market weapon, obtained illegally.

The grip had been taped.

Black tape.

It was not new. Not even newish. There was a deep scratch on the barrel. Scuff marks on the underside of the butt. It had seen action. Rough-and-tumble, even. And it was loaded. He checked the magazine. Three 9mm Parabellums left.

So she'd meant business.

An empty gun, that was for show. A deterrent on the road. An empty gun would keep difficult people at bay without risking an accusation of attempted murder.

But not a gun that was loaded.

Bullets were there to be used. For firing into things as a warning – or people's heads, for closure to an issue. No bullets, no shooting. Yet here she was, armed with – not only a handgun – but a Glock with three cartridges in the magazine.

So who had she been planning to shoot? And why?

And where the hell had she got a handgun?

This was Dartmoor, not inner-city London. A vast, remote National Park in the South West of England, mostly home to farmers and countrymen, and the occasional green-loving professional with a laptop and a high-speed broadband connection. Difficult to get hold of a black market handgun on the moors, he'd have thought.

He weighed the Glock thoughtfully in his hand, then set it down on the table in front of him.

Exhibit A.

A concealed carry like that didn't belong to a farmer or a countryman. Farmers who liked to shoot things typically owned bloody great shotguns: noisy, double-barrelled weapons intended for bringing down rural pests like rabbits and foxes. This was a slick, professional weapon. A killing machine for humans, not rabbits. Or it had been, once upon a time. No farmer was likely to be granted a licence for a weapon like this.

Dani was trouble. He'd known that as soon as he saw her in his wing mirror. But she had not struck him as a particularly dangerous person.

It was possible he had misread her. Just as it was possible that everything she'd told him had been a lie. That she was not a runaway bride. That she was not about to marry a local named Terry Hoggins. That her dad's name was not Geoff. That 'Geoff' was not a classic car enthusiast whose Diamond White MG she had pinched in a moment of distress, in order to dump an irksome groom at the altar.

Mayday, mayday, mayday. I'm on your side. Give me shelter.

It was a professional weapon. Serviceable, but not new. And not replaced by a more up-to-date weapon, in which case this would have been relinquished. Which suggested the original owner of this Glock could be ex-military. Or more likely secret service. Someone who needed a discreet, concealed carry weapon.

And had already used most of the rounds in the magazine, with no spare clip in evidence.

Nothing like Dani Farley.

But exactly like the man he was looking for.

Savage had come to Dartmoor for a very specific purpose. It was surely too much to hope this gun might be connected to his mission here. But without Dani Farley to explain the presence of this gun in her bag, he was in the dark.

He had to get her back.

But first, there was someone he needed to visit.

CHAPTER FOUR

Rowlands Farm stood on a lonely ridge of land, overlooking the moors. From the main road it looked grim and uninhabited, possibly even derelict. But on closer approach, a thin plume of smoke was visible above one chimney, and although the cows he remembered from the main enclosure were long gone, a few scrawny hens still pecked at the mud ruts beyond the gate. An even scrawnier goat bleated at him from a side pen. Not so much a farm now as a smallholding, he thought, studying a broken-down tractor rusting beside the track. He decided not to dig too closely into what had gone wrong, however. He knew better than most how the most ordered lives could unspool with astonishing rapidity.

Savage drove the camper van with painstaking slowness over the cattle grid, wincing as everything in his cupboards clinked and rattled. Something made of glass broke. An unsecured frying pan slid off the cooker top with a crash. It was like a war zone back there. But he kept his eyes forward, the hens scattering in front of him with only desultory alarm. Presumably they had to put up with the postman's visits too.

The door to the farm house opened, and a man came out, followed almost in the same instant by two black-and-white sheep dogs.

Peter Rowlands.

He was tall and lanky in dirty jeans and green wellingtons,

wearing an open-necked white shirt, mostly unbuttoned, over a grey T-shirt. The shirt sleeves were pushed up to the elbows and folded over several times, as though to keep them up. The poorly tucked-in shirt served to disguise his waistline, which seemed swollen under the gathered material. But his forearms were thinner than they ought to be, faint tattoos showing bluish-black against the pale skin.

Even in his university days, Peter had always seemed slumped, one shoulder permanently lower than the other, never showing his true height – despite being the tallest out of the three of them. Now though he looked genuinely beaten-down. And more unkempt than ever. Was he growing a beard or had he simply tired of shaving? His fair hair was longer too, brushing his shirt collar, limp and unwashed.

The dogs ran forward, barking furiously at the camper van.

Perhaps he ought to have rung first.

But that would have given Peter an opportunity to change his mind and say no, to turn him away before he even arrived.

Turning off the engine, Savage got down into the farmyard. He was instantly mobbed by the dogs, leaping up at him and sniffing his crotch enthusiastically, though they had fallen silent at a whistle from Peter.

'Hello, boys,' he said calmly, and bent to pat their heads. Never show fear. It was the same with horses. 'Good dogs.'

He was smiling, but secretly he was unsure of his reception. It had been just before Christmas when he contacted his old friend about a visit, saying he'd drop by sometime in the New Year. No doubt Peter had given up on him ever arriving. But life was complicated. And he'd had a few issues of his own to work through before the trip down to Dartmoor was possible. He had got there as soon as he could.

'Peter,' he said, thrusting out his hand.

'Aubrey.' Ignoring his outstretched hand, Peter dragged him

close in a surprisingly fierce hug. He smelt of whisky, and other less pleasant odours. Stepping back, he looked him up and down. 'You haven't changed.' His voice was unsteady, his blue eyes watery and bloodshot. 'Jesus, look at you. You could be twenty years old still. You bastard.'

'You always did know how to flatter a man. Silver-tongued Pete.'

'Elegant Aubrey.'

He had forgotten that nickname. Well-deserved once, perhaps. And sustained to a point during his army career.

'Once, maybe. Now I'm happy if it fits and is clean.'

Peter gazed past him at the camper van, his look one of disbelief. 'When you said you were living out of a van, I thought you were pulling my leg.'

'Do you like her?'

'Her?'

Savage laughed. 'It's a lonely life. You make do . . .'

'I bet.' He shrugged, rubbing at one ear. 'Yeah, she's . . . very nice. What is it, a five-berth?'

'Three.'

Peter snorted. 'A three-berth camper van. Bit of a comedown for you, isn't it? Don't you have some vast ancestral pile to look after?'

'Not yet.'

'Dad still going, is he? I saw he'd had another stroke recently. Sorry.'

'Yeah, he's still ticking.'

Savage glanced around the farmyard, reluctant to continue with that particular topic. He hadn't come here to talk about himself. Grass was sprouting between cracked concrete slabs, debris and nettle patches everywhere, ironworks overgrown with brambles. It looked like Peter had given up. Not merely farming, but living day-to-day.

He felt uneasy, as though all this neglect was down to him not having kept in touch. Which was ridiculous as well as arrogant.

All he said though was, 'So how are things down here?'

'As you see.'

'Got any help yet? Last time we spoke—'

'It didn't work out.'

'How's that, then?'

'Too expensive, hiring help. And this place is too far from . . . Well, from anywhere. Nobody wants to travel all the way out here just to shovel shit. Nobody wants to travel at all, these days. It's all laptop jobs round here now. Work-from-homers. Commute-refusers. That, and the bloody second-homers, sucking the life out of the moor. Here for a few weeks in the summer, then leaving their houses empty all winter.' Peter turned on his heel and looked out across the moorland, a greenish-brown expanse glinting sharply in the spring sunshine. There was a loud rushing of water close by, presumably an unseen stream on its way downhill to join the River Dart. Still swollen from last night's rain, tumbling noisily over stones. It ought to have been a reassuring sound, yet somehow it was intrusive. 'Everything's changed since my granddad bought this farm back in the fifties. It's not the same place.'

Dartmoor didn't feel like the same place as yesterday, Savage thought, let alone seventy years back. The weather was almost mild now, the sky bluish-white, the sun breaking easily through the clouds, as though yesterday's dramatic downpour had never happened. Apart from the evidence of deep puddles, that was, and roadside verges that were more water than mud.

'So you're still trying to manage the farm on your own?'

'And failing.' Peter made a face. 'Christ, I sound like an old man.'

He whistled for his dogs, who were busy exploring the outside of the camper van. The smaller dog came back immediately. The other stopped to cock his leg against the front driver's side tyre, then ran back, wagging his tail as though proud of himself.

Peter studied the camper, his watery eyes blinking in the sunlight. 'One of those might do for me if I have to give up the land. It looks snug enough for one man and his bottle.'

'Looks can be deceptive.'

The thin lips curled back off the teeth again. 'Is that so?' Peter stuck his hands deep in his pockets. 'Must be hard, I suppose, wanting a drink when you're in charge of a vehicle.'

'That's why I make sure I never want a drink.'

'Wasn't always the case.'

There was a short silence between them. A silence charged with unspoken anger. Only to be expected, of course. But he had hoped Peter would have forgotten by now. It had been years . . .

'People change,' Savage said lightly. 'Like places.'

'Do they? Do they really change?' With one wellington boot, Peter rubbed at a spiky patch of grass thrusting up out of a crack in the concrete. 'When you rang, months back, and then never showed, I thought . . . Well, you know what I thought.'

'Sorry about that.'

'No, it's . . .' Peter was hiding something. He could hardly meet his eyes. 'I'm glad you turned up in the end. Though your timing isn't brilliant. Never was, of course. Your special skill, some might say. But you're welcome to stay a day or two.'

'Problems?'

'A local issue. Nothing I can't handle.' Peter cleared his throat, and then straightened. He ran a hand through dirty hair. 'Look, I was just about to make a brew when I heard the van. Shall we go in?'

*

The inside of the farmhouse was even more ramshackle than the outside. The black slate flags in the hall were mud-encrusted, there were old boxes and crates kicked to one side near the door, mouldy coats and clothing lying here and there, and stacks of newspapers on each wooden step of the staircase, leaving only a narrow channel for getting upstairs. The whole house was silent, and stank of muddy dogs and booze. Savage glanced into a few rooms on the way to the kitchen. They were in much the same state as the hall, cluttered with random debris, the living room probably the worst, the sofa grimy with age, with the remnants of late-night drinking bouts strewn across the coffee table. Beer cans, whisky bottles, a few cloudy glasses. The windows were dark with grime, threadbare curtains drawn across most of them.

Savage remembered a bright, pleasant house, sunlight streaming in through open windows, and music on constantly. The place was unrecognisable. It needed a sign on the door: Under New Management.

He wandered into the kitchen after Peter. Same deal here. Unwiped surfaces cluttered with bottles and a few empty food packets, the kind for heating up in the microwave. The sink was piled with dirty plates and bowls. A bluebottle buzzed restlessly at the window that overlooked a small back garden, hemmed in by a low stone wall. More burgeoning nettle and bramble patches instead of the neat vegetable rows he recalled from his previous visit. Beans and peas climbing up sticks, stately alliums and soft-headed potato plants. The whole cottage garden thing.

Maura had been the gardener, probably. A country girl from rural Ireland. Growing vegetables had never been Peter's bag, despite his rural upbringing. He hadn't even liked eating them, as Savage recalled. Chips with everything, that had been Peter. And given the dearth of chip shops on Dartmoor, it was easy to see why he'd embraced urban living once it was offered to him in Oxford.

Peter began to make some vague attempt to tidy up, clearing a newspaper off a kitchen chair, then washing up a couple of mugs in a slapdash fashion.

'Do you ever hear from Maura?' Savage asked.

Peter had his back to him, rinsing out an old china teapot in the sink. He stiffened, then said, 'No,' in a way that sounded angry and defensive. As though that question should never have been asked. And perhaps it could have been more sensitively put.

'So you don't know where she is?'

'I don't know, and I don't care much anymore.' Peter glanced round at him, defiance in his look. 'That probably sounds harsh to you, after what happened to you with Lina. But it's been two years since Maura left. And she chose to end our marriage, not me.'

'Fair enough.'

'Anyway, I've got used to being alone. It suits me. I wouldn't have her back even if she turned up on the doorstep tomorrow.'

'You never said why you two split up.' Savage took off his jacket and slung it over the back of the kitchen chair. 'I always thought you were happy as a couple. Contented, even. That this was your little paradise.'

'Maura was the polar opposite of contented. Or she was with me, at any rate. She wanted something I couldn't give her, you see. And her need got corrosive. It ate away at us, until one day . . .' Peter peered into the teapot, then made a rough noise under his breath. 'Shit, this thing is disgusting. I can't serve tea out of this.'

'I'm happy without.'

'Well, I need a drink. If you don't mind not having a glass. I think most of them are cracked.' Peter reached down a new bottle of whisky from the shelf above the fridge. Grabbing the two freshly-cleaned mugs from the draining board, he sat down at the table and nodded to Savage to join him. 'Straight up, or with mixer? There's a can of ginger ale somewhere.'

'I'm fine.'

Peter sneered. 'Teetotal now?'

'I've fallen out of the habit, that's all.'

'Because of the camper van.'

'Something like that.'

'Well . . .' Peter poured himself a generous four or five fingers of whisky, and slammed the bottle down without bothering to replace the cap. Whisky sloshed out onto the pine table but he didn't even glance at it, picking up his mug instead in a mock salute. 'To absent friends.'

Savage said nothing. He waited while Peter drank, then said, 'Talking of absent friends, this isn't a casual visit. I was hoping you might be able to help me.'

Peter stared at him over the rim of his mug. 'Come again?'

'I'm looking for Jarrah.'

Peter said nothing for a moment, then took another swig and set the mug on the table. He wiped his mouth with the back of his hand. 'I told you back when Jarrah first disappeared and you called, saying you and Lina were trying to find him. I told you then, if Jarrah's gone, my bet is he's dead. Topped himself, probably.'

'Why would he kill himself?'

'That business with your mum. The car accident, all that shit. Hardly surprising he cut his ties with your family and disappeared. The guilt must have done his head in. I told you back then to let it go, that Jarrah was a lost cause.'

'I can't let it go. I made a promise to Lina.'

Peter picked up the bottle with an unsteady hand and

dashed another few fingers of whisky into his mug. 'Well, if that's the only reason you're here, you might as well get right back in that fancy van of yours, and keep driving. Because you won't find him on Dartmoor.' He stared into the mug. 'I don't like the truth any more than you do. But there's no hiding from it out here.'

'Until I see proof—'

'I'm telling you, Jarrah's dead,' Peter said flatly. 'As dead as your Lina.'

CHAPTER FIVE

As dead as your Lina.

Savage jumped up and began to pace the kitchen, staring down at the slate floor with an effort. It was either that or smash his fist into Peter's face. He fought to control his temper. To think of something else, to distract himself. Since Lina's death, he'd struggled with anger in a way that he had never experienced in the army, regardless of the provocation.

Just his wife's name was enough some days . . .

He stopped in front of the Welsh dresser. There was a cheaply framed photograph at the back, dusty with neglect, half-hidden behind cups and old bottles.

He lifted it out and studied the photo.

It was him, Jarrah and Peter, lying on the perfect grass of their Oxford college quad, a bottle of champagne standing prominently beside them, along with plastic cups and the remnants of a picnic. Behind them stood other undergrads in summer frocks and smart suits, mingling with tutors and family members. It had been some kind of party, he recalled. Possibly to celebrate the end of their first-year examinations. A rare privilege for them, being permitted on the quad grass, an honour normally only accorded to Fellows of the college.

His father had not turned up to the party. Neither had Peter's. And Jarrah's only relative within easy train distance had been Lina, his younger sister. Who had probably been sitting her A Levels at boarding school.

So they had decided to celebrate together.

Savage replaced the photograph where he had found it, at the back of the dresser, careful not to knock anything down.

'You can't know for sure that he's dead.'

'If he's still alive, then where is he? Jarrah was never the type to drop out of sight for so long. Six months, maybe. But how long has it been since any of us heard from him?' Peter shook his head. 'The only possible explanation for such a long absence is that he's dead. And given his job, that was always a danger.'

His job.

Jarrah had been recruited by the British Secret Service during his final year at Oxford. He'd been reading Politics, Philosophy and Economics. The ideal hunting ground for recruits. MI5 had approached Aubrey too, who had been reading English, but he had politely declined. 'I'm not sneaky enough for a spy,' was what he'd told Jarrah at the time, only half joking, 'not like you.'

He had concentrated on Anglo-Saxon and Middle English for his degree, then gone into the British Army instead. Within two years, he'd found the army too limiting, and applied for the SAS instead. He had not expected to last the selection process. But to his surprise, the harder he was pushed and punished, the more resilient he became. He also discovered a new talent. He might not be sneaky enough to be a spy, but he was rather good at covert work. Black ops. Even now, several years out of the army, the need for that rush of sheer adrenalin had still not left him. He craved it, the way other people craved drugs or alcohol. And hated that side of himself. His inability to let things lie.

That was what had got Lina killed.

Him.

He was the one who had got his wife killed. He might not have detonated the bomb, but he was the one who'd taken her to that marketplace in Kabul, looking for Jarrah.

They'd heard the ghost of a rumour a month before. Probably nothing. But possibly something. The rumour went that an unspecified third party had seen Jarrah in the market earlier that year, talking to one of the stallholders, a massive, bearded Arab called Abdul Walid, an expert in ancient handicrafts, specialising in quality leather goods, belts, bags, travelling cases, even camel saddles. Also known for his contacts within Islamic State.

It had surprised both Savage and Lina that Jarrah might be in Kabul. As an MI5 agent, the main focus of his work would normally have been within British territories. But since the British government had been openly disavowing Jarrah as their man by that time, it was also possible that he'd travelled to Afghanistan for other reasons, as yet unknown.

Savage had sent Lina to buy a handbag from the leather goods stall while he checked out Abdul Walid's van, parked on the other side of the marketplace. There'd been the blinding light and air punch of a massive detonation, the truck had been thrown in the air, and him with it, knocked unconscious. When he opened his eyes and struggled out of the burning van, he found a scene of carnage to rival anything he had ever seen as a soldier.

Lina had been killed instantaneously.

Among twenty-seven others, including other women and children.

Abdul Walid had also died, though not until five days later in a central Kabul hospital, having lost both legs in the explosion. He had never regained consciousness. Any information he might have held about the whereabouts of Lina's brother died with him.

Savage himself had been lucky, according to the doctors in the emergency room where he eventually took himself that night to be stitched up and have his burns treated. Shrapnel had also peppered his right side and back. Painful but easily removed, though the scars they'd left behind were a constant reminder of his mistake.

He had survived, though.

Lucky.

Islamic State terrorism had been the official explanation on the Afghanistan news bulletins that night. Spreading fear and panic through an arbitrary bombing campaign, though IS had never claimed responsibility for that particular bomb, despite the impressive death toll. And if IS had been behind the bombing, they'd killed their own man in the blast. Which suggested that Abdul Walid had been playing a dangerous double game with Islamic State. That perhaps he'd been working secretly with the British government since Jarrah's visit. But not secretly enough.

If he had not sent Lina to distract the stallholder . . .

'I hear what you're saying. And you're probably right. Given his job, the likeliest scenario is that Jarrah's dead. But I gave Lina my word, and I'm not ready to give up yet. Not until I have absolute proof that he's dead.'

'Such as?'

'A body would do it. But failing that, some indication of what Jarrah was working on before he died. So I can piece together what got him killed, and why.'

Peter nodded without saying anything, and pushed the whisky bottle away.

'So you'll help me?'

'I'll try.'

'Good.' Savage leant his elbows on the table, regarding his friend steadily. 'I know Jarrah was planning to visit you before he vanished.'

Peter's expression became defensive.

'He mentioned it to Lina in a phone call. He was in Germany at the time, or so he claimed. But there'd been some kind of trouble, so he was being recalled to London.'

'Trouble?'

'He didn't elaborate and Lina didn't ask. Anyway, Jarrah promised to call in and see us once he was back in England. Said he had something to tell us. Something interesting. But we never heard from him again.'

Peter was gazing towards the kitchen window. 'What did they say at his work? MI5 or whatever it was.'

'What they always say in these cases. They had no knowledge of his whereabouts, and they wouldn't tell us even if they did know.'

'Bastards.'

'We hung on for months after that phone call, hoping to hear from him again. But there was nothing. No more calls, not even a text message. Absolute silence. Eventually, his personal effects were returned to Lina by the Home Office, which was when we drove up to his London flat and discovered it was being rented by somebody new. It seemed clear that MI5 believed him to be dead, even if they weren't prepared to say so officially.'

'Did you find anything among his things? A diary? An iPad?'

Savage shook his head. 'We checked through the boxes, of course, but it was always a long shot. If there had been anything of interest there, it would have been removed long before his possessions reached us.'

'Right, of course. That makes sense.'

'After Lina died, I went back to his bosses, asking questions.

Only I went in harder, less politely than before. Finally, they sent someone senior down to talk to me. He intimated that Jarrah had no longer been working for MI5 at the time of his disappearance. That he'd been sacked, in fact.' Savage thought back to that conversation, and was unable to keep the bitterness out of his voice. 'In other words, whatever really happened to Jarrah, MI5 were keen to distance themselves from it.'

'But you think he may have come here? To Dartmoor?'

'Did he?'

'Not to my knowledge.'

Savage studied him. That was an odd turn of phrase.

'You sure about that?'

'What the hell is that supposed to mean?' Peter got up, moving jerkily. Now it was his turn to pace the kitchen. 'Is that why you came here today, Aubrey? To accuse me of . . . Christ, I don't even know what you think I've done.'

'I haven't accused you of anything.'

'But you think I had something to do with Jarrah's disappearance.'

'Did you?'

'I don't know who you are anymore, Aubrey. You're clever. You always were. You and Jarrah, you were both smarter than me. First class material. More adventurous too. You wanted to change the world, to make a difference.' He paused, breathing hard. 'But you're wrong about this. Dead wrong.'

Savage, who had shared a flat with him and Jarrah during their second year at university, could tell that Peter was hiding something. But it was unlikely he would give it up voluntarily, and Savage had no intention of forcing it out of him. This was his friend, not an enemy suspect.

He got up, and put a hand on Peter's shoulder. Felt him flinch.

'You say you don't know who I am anymore. But I'm your

friend, Peter,' he said quietly. 'Every bit as much your friend as Jarrah was. Or is, if he's still alive. That's why I'm here. Because I hope you might be able to shed some light on what he was doing in the weeks before he disappeared.'

'Well, I can't.'

'Maybe. But maybe you know things, only you don't know you know them.'

'Sorry, you've lost me.'

Savage smiled. 'I always thought you were the smartest out of us, actually.'

'How's that?'

'You didn't make a mess of your life. You came back here, to Dartmoor, where you were born. To build something new with Maura. Yes, we wanted to see the world. Well, we saw it, and it saw us. And Jarrah is . . . who knows where. And I'm living in a van. So which of us looks cleverest now?'

Peter didn't respond.

Savage looked out of the window over Peter's shoulder. Beyond the stone wall of the garden lay moorland, a rolling sunlit wilderness of rough grass and bracken and heather, dotted with clusters of trees and overgrown walls where men had tried to claim the land for their own, and failed. The land out here was uncompromising. It broke people, and continued on regardless as though nothing had ever happened.

In the distance was a tumbledown ruin beside a gnarled, wind-bent tree.

It had probably been a smallholding or an attempt at a new farm once, or something even more humble. A shepherd's hut, perhaps. Whatever it was now, it had been an outlier on the fringes of the wild west once, a place where someone in the distant past had tried to scratch a living from this inhospitable soil or from the few hardy sheep that could graze here. Except its owner had failed, as they all failed sooner or later, and nobody had wanted to try again. Not in that exact spot, not with that building. So the house had been abandoned. It had fallen into disrepair, then into a crumbling ruin. Now it was a dilapidated collection of stones, leaning together in the shade of a low, twisted tree. Barely any roof to speak of, and its four walls had long since buckled under a tangle of brambles and greenery. Yet there was something inviting about its sunlit ruins. Even beautiful.

A place of peace, he thought, recalling one of Lina's favourite phrases.

'Let's get out of here,' he said abruptly.

'What?' Peter looked round at him in surprise. There was a thread of panic in his voice, as though he were half-expecting to be frogmarched into the farmyard and shot. Which merely reinforced Savage's suspicion that he was hiding something. 'What do you mean?'

'Let's go for a walk on the moors. Show me the boundaries of your property. We can take the dogs with us, if you like. I need some fresh air.' Turning, Savage screwed the lid back onto the whisky bottle, as tight as it would go. Then he plucked his jacket off the back of the chair. 'Come on, Peter. Some fresh air wouldn't do you any harm either.'

CHAPTER SIX

They walked across the moors in the sunshine, following the line of the stream. The running water, tumbling over stones and through narrow gullies, sounded like voices constantly hissing and whispering. Savage could see why there'd been so many stories about the moor over the years, especially after the persistent downpour yesterday, more like smoke than rain at one stage. More rain had fallen during the night too, thundering down on the camper roof during the early hours and keeping him awake. Nothing unusual about that, of course. He was often awake in the night these days, unable to sleep. But there had been something about last night's rainstorm that had bothered him in particular.

It could have been the possibility that Dani was out there somewhere, stumbling about in her silk wedding dress, on her own in the dark. Or if she had been snatched from his van, the awareness that he had not been able to protect her.

Just as he had not been able to protect Lina.

They climbed towards a steep and sparsely wooded ridge, where Peter said they would have a good view of the moors. The ground near the stream was boggy, and as the incline grew steeper, it became increasingly hard to find a safe foothold there. By mutual consent they shifted away from the stream, instead following a dirty ribbon of a track through a thicket, possibly made by deer, from the damage marks left behind on the lower bark of trees they passed.

They stopped halfway up at a natural ledge backed by a massive boulder set into the slope. Peter leant against the boulder and took a swig from the hipflask he'd brought. He offered it to Savage, who shook his head.

'Suit yourself.' Peter took another long swig, then tucked the flask back into his inner jacket pocket.

Savage studied the view. From here, the old ruin he'd seen from the kitchen window was more clearly visible. Approximately one quarter of a mile from Peter's farmhouse, it was a rectangular building in two distinct parts, one long rectangle, plus a square, the back gable end facing them. It had been constructed on a slight rise, far enough from the stream bed to avoid flooding in winter, yet close enough for the physical fetching and carrying of water on a daily basis. How old? Hard to estimate at a glance, but he would guess sometime in the early nineteenth century. A rustic cottage, perhaps. A place of retreat. Though it looked more practical than that.

It wasn't entirely roofless, he realised. That had been an illusion. From the kitchen window he had seen wilderness invading tumbledown walls. But from this vantage point, he could see a partial roof covering the back square of the building. Probably an annex tagged onto the original cottage in later years, and more sturdy. There had been a chimney – he could see remains of the stack along the back wall – but it had fallen in at some point over the years. Now wilderness was encroaching on that end too, creeping through broken windows and along the base of the house from the front end, where two walls had long since collapsed into rubble, and the others were inexorably headed that way.

There did not seem enough rubble to account for an entire

house at the front end. But perhaps scavengers had come and gone since its abandonment, removing a few loads of stone at a time for their own building projects, and so contributing to its inevitable decline.

Savage was reminded of a fragmentary Anglo-Saxon text he'd studied at university, a poem speculating on the vast ruins they believed had been left behind by a race of giants. The Romans, more likely, who had packed up and headed back to Rome, leaving their towns and villas to fall into disrepair.

Hrofas sind gehrorene, hreorge torras
Hrimgeat berofen ...

'The roofs have fallen in,' he quoted, '*the towers tumbled to ruins, the broken gate lies caked in ice ...*'

'Sorry?' Peter was staring at him.

'Those ruins.' Savage nodded towards the cottage. 'Some kind of shepherd's hut? It's too far from the stream to have been a mill.'

Peter followed the line of his pointing arm, squinting into the light. His hair drooped over his eyes, and he flicked it back, a familiar impatient gesture that took Savage back to their undergraduate days.

'That's Agnes's cottage.'

'Agnes?' Savage lowered his arm. 'Who was Agnes? And how or why did she let her cottage get into that unhappy state?'

'It's a local legend. I'm not entirely sure of the facts.' Peter scratched his forehead, looking distracted. 'She was a woman, named Agnes ...'

'Not a difficult leap to make.'

'She was the wife of the landowner's foreman, or bailiff, or something like that. It was a long time before my grandfather even bought this place. The story goes that the husband was old and not much to look at, but fairly well-off, as bailiffs go.'

'Don't tell me,' Savage said drily. 'Agnes was young and attractive?'

'Of course.'

'So she had an affair.'

'Not hard to guess, is it? Except that Agnes got pregnant.'

'And the bailiff wasn't very happy.'

'Well, he didn't know if it was his child, or this other guy's. So he killed Agnes in a fit of jealous rage. He confessed, and was hanged. End of story.'

'What happened to the lover?'

'Nothing, I imagine. Probably continued banging the good wives of Dartmoor, undetected. Perhaps Agnes kept quiet about his identity. To protect him.'

'When did all this *Sturm und Drang* take place?'

'Back at the turn of the nineteenth century, I think.' Peter brought out his flask again, had another quick swig, glanced at Savage, then pushed it back inside his jacket. 'The cottage belonged to the farm in those days, of course. But nobody wanted to live there after the murder. Local people said the cottage was haunted. That they'd seen Agnes there, walking up and down in the dusk, wringing her hands.'

'So it fell down. And now nature is reclaiming it, stone by stone.' Savage studied the overgrown ruins for a moment. 'Poor old Agnes.'

Peter straightened up. 'Shall we keep climbing? There's a better view from the top, I promise. Right over Dartmoor.'

'Not your favourite place?'

'Maura liked walking out here in the summer.' Peter glanced back at the cottage, then ran a hand through dishevelled hair. 'Never seen the attraction, myself. Bloody place is an eyesore.' He shrugged. 'Now she's gone, I ought to knock it down properly. Build something useful in its place. A winter shelter for the sheep, perhaps.'

They began to climb again, keeping more or less side by side, since the track was less visible here. More a swathe of mud and flattened grass where climbers had presumably veered from side to side at each ascent, depending on the conditions.

It was bloody steep.

'Talking of unhappy marriages,' Savage said, 'an odd thing happened to me on the Dartmoor road last night. I met a girl.' He stopped, wryly correcting himself, 'Sorry, a *young woman.*'

Peter half-smiled at the political correctness. 'Go on.'

'It occurred to me that you might know her.'

'How's that?'

'I think she's in trouble.'

Peter raised his eyebrows. 'So I must be involved?'

'The thing is,' Savage said, breathing harder as the slope became sheer, 'this woman had a tattoo on the inside of her left wrist.'

This time Peter made no comment, which was telling.

'A tattoo that looked like the letter P.' Savage looked at his friend sideways. 'As in, P for Peter.'

CHAPTER SEVEN

Peter denied knowing any woman with a P tattoo, of course. And it was possible that he was telling the truth. P need not stand for Peter, after all. And Savage had not seen the tattoo clearly.

It might not even have been a letter P.

Dropping that line of enquiry, Savage detailed his encounter on the moorland road with the runaway bride instead. He left out the part about the Land Rover Defender, and the sports holdall and what he had found inside it. It was clear that Peter was nervous about something, and he didn't want to spook him upfront.

He described the Diamond White classic MG instead, thinking it could be a well-known car locally. That Peter might even know the owner, who was possibly either Terry Hoggins or Geoff Farley. Or an unknown third party, if Dani had been lying about where she got the car. That would have given him a good place to start looking for the missing woman. But there was no sign of recognition on Peter's face.

'The woman said her name was Dani,' he finished.

Peter looked round at him, startled.

'Dani? Skinny blonde, about five-five?'

Savage stopped, staring at him. 'That's the one. So you do know her?'

'Yes.' Peter paused too. He was struggling with the climb.

'That is, not well,' he said more slowly, seeming distracted, focused on the damp ground ahead. 'I've met Dani a few times. She's a local. Never noticed a tattoo though. Maybe she had it done recently. Or prefers to keep it covered. But you said ... She was wearing a *wedding* dress?'

'White. Like the car.'

'You're sure? That's strange. I always thought ...'

They had reached the top of the ridge.

Peter was breathing heavily from the climb, as though unused to any exertion that did not involve lifting a bottle.

He stopped, not finishing his previous thought, and turned, looking back the way they had come. 'There,' he said, nodding to the view. 'What do you think, Aubrey? Worth the climb?'

Savage turned too, and stood beside his friend, looking down from the ridge. It had indeed been worth the climb. It was nearly midday and the sun was overhead. Dartmoor stretched dusty brown and green below them to the horizon, a broad, undulating swathe of moorland alternating with narrow strips and diamonds of grazing. Besides these occasional pockets of dingy whitish sheep, there were a few strips to the far right of the ridge containing prehistoric-looking cows with shaggy hides and vast, horned heads.

His heart rate slowly began to return to normal.

'*Earth hath not anything to show more fair,*' he quoted from Wordsworth. 'Except for those huge cows, perhaps,' he added, pointing. 'They look like something out of Jurassic Park.'

'My neighbour's herd,' Peter said, not sounding very enthusiastic. 'It's a rare breed. Highland horned cattle. They used to be everywhere on Dartmoor a couple of centuries ago. There's been an effort to bring them back.'

'There don't seem to be many fences or walls. Don't they wander off on their own?'

'There's not enough good grazing on the open moor, so cows

tend to graze together, in roughly the same spots. Makes them easier to find.'

'Big beasts, aren't they? I bet your neighbour never runs short on steak.'

Peter said nothing. He turned away, and kept heading east, taking longer strides now. 'Come on,' he said over his shoulder. 'You wanted to see how far my land extended. We're nearly at the eastern boundary. It stops at the road. Then we'll head down along the fence line, and back to the house. It's an easier walk on the way home.'

Savage studied the shaggy cows a moment longer, then caught up with him. 'I seem to remember more land last time I was here. Didn't you own that field where the cows are now?'

'I did, yes.'

'But you sold the land.' It wasn't a question.

Peter shrugged, keeping his gaze on the uneven ground. 'Needed the money. And I wasn't using that field. It was in bad shape, too boggy for livestock, and I couldn't afford to have it drained.'

'But your neighbour could, I take it?'

'The Reverend Barton.' Peter sounded bitter. 'He's American. From somewhere insanely remote like Wyoming. He came to England about three years ago. But he was born here. And I literally mean *here*, on Dartmoor. Two miles in that direction.' He flung out an arm, indicating an area beyond the trees ahead, roughly north-east. 'Barton's Farm. He founded the Green Chapel on his land. There's a spring of some kind.' Peter rubbed his forehead with the back of his hand. 'They claim it has healing powers.'

'And has it?'

'No point asking me. I've never been a member of his church. Though cult is a better word for it.'

'Sounds worth a look.'

'I'd steer clear if I were you. You're an outsider too, remember?'

Savage thought of the couple who had walked past him in the dark last night. The man in the bobble hat who had spat on his van.

'The locals don't take easily to outsiders, then?'

'Your family has to have lived here for at least three generations before you get so much as a hello in the street. Though they all love the Reverend Barton now.'

'How did he manage that?'

'Good bloody question.' Peter was breathing hard again, though the track had levelled out as they hit the trees, and the walk was no longer strenuous. 'Because he makes damn sure of it, is the simple answer. The man's untouchable.'

They were nearing a road, tarmacked and in good condition, bordered on the far side with low trees, nothing but a tangle of bracken and grasses on their side. In a town, it would have seemed impossibly narrow. On Dartmoor though, it was a generous size for a tractor, a few passing places visible where the road eventually wound into a shallow valley below.

A few yards ahead, a roadside sign was mounted on a rough wooden stake.

The sign was a bright, unnatural green with a white border. It stated in a florid, Ye Olde-style font, *THE GREEN CHAPEL. Revd. Barton.*

Below that, in stately italics, was an invitation to, '*Come thou, believer, and be healed.*' Beside those words was a thick black P, a Facebook page address, and a white arrow pointing east along the ridge.

The sign was relatively new-looking, no sign of rain damage, and with fresh splinters sticking out of the stake. The ground around its base was muddy and well-trampled. If Savage had to guess, he'd say the sign had been installed today.

'What the hell . . . ?' Peter halted in front of the sign, his face contorted with rage. 'I don't believe it. How many times do I have to tell him? Not here, I said. Not on my land!'

Peter grasped the sign in one hand, then kicked the wooden stake. His booted heel came down exactly halfway between the sign and the ground.

The whole thing juddered but stayed upright.

'I'll kill him.' Peter lifted his foot again, and kept kicking until the stake cracked, then snapped under the next blow. 'I swear, one of these days I'll bloody kill him.'

'That's right, get it all out of your system.' Savage watched Peter stamp on the fallen sign, swearing loudly, then grind the smashed pieces into the mud under his boot. 'Who exactly is it you're planning to kill, though? The Reverend Barton? Aren't we meant to love our neighbours? Especially when they're religious types.'

'Don't, Aubrey.' Peter's fringe had flopped in his eyes. He knocked it back, panting, still stooped over the broken sign. 'You have no idea who this man is, or what he's capable of. He's not human. He's a demon.'

'I thought he was a clergyman?'

'A *Reverend*. At least, that's what he calls himself.' Peter brought down his foot on the word *healed*, obliterating it. 'But it's bullshit, trust me.'

Savage turned. A diesel engine was barrelling fast up the road behind them, unseen in the dip for now. It had come from the direction of the Green Chapel, whatever the hell that was.

'Car,' he said shortly.

Peter straightened guiltily, like a kid caught breaking a school rule. For a second, it looked as though he might make a dash for it back down the ridge. Then he stopped, took a deep breath, and waited.

'The Reverend Barton?' Savage asked quietly.

'Unlikely.'

'How so?'

Peter bared his teeth. 'Barton doesn't come down from his stronghold very often. He lets other people do his dirty work for him.' He stared at the point where the track emerged from between rocky bushes at the top of the slope. 'It's usually his men, on this back road. Not many other people go to the Green Chapel this way. It's a single track road, too many twists and turns.'

'I thought this guy was a preacher, not a mountain chieftain.'

'You should go back to the farm. They won't bother you.'

'They?'

'Big Swanney and the others. They work for Barton.' Peter cast about the rough ground as though hunting for some kind of weapon. But there was nothing obvious to hand, only thorn bushes and a few unwieldy rocks. Catching Savage's eye, he grimaced. 'I've run into them before. Not a friendly bunch. And very territorial.'

There was a quick flash from behind a screen of scrawny trees near the brow of the hill. Then another flash. Sunlight reflecting off a windscreen.

Finally, the car appeared, accelerating noisily towards them. It was a sandy-coloured Land Rover Defender.

CHAPTER EIGHT

There were at least five men inside the Land Rover. Three on the front bench, and two in the back, roughing it on the folding seats. The driver was short, wearing a dark hoody that obscured his face. Savage would have laid bets he was one of the men from last night. The man in the middle front passenger seat was bald, lean-faced and incredibly tall. He was holding his neck at an odd angle, as though the top of his head was brushing the interior roof of the vehicle. The man next to him was broad and red-cheeked. Swathed in a black anorak, he was crushed against the side door, and pushed slightly forward too, glaring at Savage and Peter as though he blamed them personally for his lack of space.

The red-cheeked man pointed at the fallen sign, and began gesticulating angrily.

The precipitous pace of the vehicle began to slacken off.

'Looks like they're stopping to investigate,' Savage said. 'Better let me do the talking.'

Stooping, he selected the largest fragment of the wooden stake, and picked it up. It was only about a foot and a half in length, so not exactly a spear. But the business end was jagged and sufficiently threatening. Besides, holding it ought to create the illusion that he'd been the vandal, not Peter.

'You don't need to get involved, Aubrey.' Peter sounded

desperate, which surprised him. 'I'm telling you, these men don't mess about. And it's not your battle.'

'Maybe not, but I'm already involved.' Savage nodded to the Land Rover Defender. 'That's the same vehicle that ran us off the road last night. Which means some of those men, at least, are the ones who took Dani away. Probably against her will. Probably to hurt her. So I've got a few questions I'd like to ask them. About who and why, and where Dani is now.' He weighed the splintered stake in his hand. 'And if they think I'm the one who knocked down their nice chapel sign, the conversation may go a little quicker.'

The occupants of the Land Rover Defender were all peering out at them now.

And the broken sign.

Inside the car, there was a brief exchange of words. It became heated. The fat guy was pointing, jerking a thick finger in Peter's direction. The tall guy seemed unmoved. The car continued past them, but braking now. Finally, it skidded to a halt a few yards past their position, half on the road, half on the grassy verge, throwing up damp sods of turf.

At the rear of the Land Rover, there was an advertisement on the spare tyre cover of the Land Rover. Tastefully picked out in white paint on the black cover was a sketch of a man in a flat cap apparently pointing a rifle into the sky. To bring down a game bird, perhaps. Or shoot a peasant climbing a tree.

It said, DARTMOOR GUN CENTRE: *Quality Guns Bought & Sold.*

The driver and the fat guy on the end got out first, leaving their doors hanging wide open. The two men in the back climbed out too, through the back door, shrugging their shoulders and rolling their arms and cracking their knuckles. Limbering up for a fight was presumably the required inference.

The incredibly tall man in the middle stayed put.

Perhaps he was stuck.

The driver and the two from the back had some kind of muttered confab, heads together, in front of the vehicle. More exaggerated shoulder shrugging and arm rolling, accompanied by nods.

The fat guy swaggered on alone towards Savage and Peter.

Though, to be fair, it would have been hard for him to walk without swaggering, given his girth.

Beer belly, Savage diagnosed at a glance. His stomach rose over the top of his jeans like a small mountain, a narrow strip of pinkish-white flesh visible where his T-shirt had parted company with his waistband. The rest of him wasn't too bad. Though his thighs were quite generous too. They would need to be, of course, to support his weight.

'Who's this?' he asked Peter under his breath.

'Mike Cooper.'

'Not a friend of yours, I'm guessing.'

Peter shook his head. 'Gun dealer, local low-life,' he whispered, leaning towards him. 'One of Barton's top cronies from the start. I wouldn't trust Cooper an inch. He always goes where the money is.'

The fat guy called Mike Cooper stopped at the broken sign. He looked down, studying it for a moment. Then he looked up at Peter, saying in a thick Devon accent, 'You did this.'

Peter said nothing.

'You did this,' Mike Cooper repeated, disbelief in his voice. 'Broke the Reverend's sign. Destroyed his property.'

Behind him, the three men waited. In a row. Like dominoes.

'No, I broke it,' Savage said, stepping forward with a smile. 'I'm sorry. Was it yours? I couldn't help myself, I'm afraid. It's a medical condition.'

'A what?'

'Religiophobia.'

'Relig—' Mike Cooper gaped at him. 'What the hell are you talking about? Come on, enough of this crap. Which of you broke Rev Barton's sign? You?' He jabbed a fat finger in Peter's direction. Then hesitated, and jabbed the same fat finger at Savage, who was still holding part of the wooden stake. 'You?' Finally, the finger was jabbed down towards the splintered board, in a gesture of accusation. 'Don't think you can get away with it, Rowlands. Not this time. He's let you off before, but you've crossed a line here.' From the way Peter shrank back, it was clear there was some unpleasant history between him and this Reverend. Serious enough to keep him silent now. 'Barton may be a Reverend, but he's not a forgiving man. And this here is sheer vandalism.'

'Quite right,' Savage said agreeably. He dragged his mobile out of his back pocket, and showed it to the man. 'In fact, you should call the police. Have me arrested. Shall I do the honours?'

'Now, hold on there a minute.' Mike Cooper retracted his finger. He glanced round at the three men with a doubtful expression, as though looking for guidance. They did not say anything, but shifted awkwardly. He made a face and turned back, glaring at Savage. 'OK, I know Rowlands. I've seen his ugly face before. But who are you?'

'A friend of his.' He indicated Peter with his thumb.

'I meant, what's your name?'

'Aubrey.'

'Aub – Are you making that up?'

'That's what I said about *your* friend's name.'

'*My* friend's name?' Cooper looked blank. 'Who you talking about?'

'The Reverend Barton.' Savage shook his head. 'What is he, Church of England? Does the Archbishop of Canterbury know what your Reverend gets up to out here? Or is he a Catholic? All smells and bells, that kind of nonsense. I suppose they report to the Pope.' He turned to Peter. 'Do priests still get unfrocked for lewd behaviour? Do priests even wear frocks? Or do they get *decollared* these days? I don't know much about the modern church, I'm afraid. Never been a believer, myself.'

Cooper's face twitched in annoyed disbelief.

'Look, it was an accident.' Peter sounded angry. 'The sign shouldn't have been here, anyway.' He nodded to the opposite verge. 'Next time, put your sign on the other side of the track. Not on my land. That was the agreement I made with Barton, and I expect him to respect it.' He paused. 'You can tell him that from me.'

Mike Cooper laughed. 'You can tell him yourself. We were on our way to pick someone up. But that can wait. The Rev's going to want to know what you've done here. Straight away.' He looked to his right, a gesture the driver took as encouragement to join him. 'Billy, put them both in the back.'

Billy started forward.

His friends, two fresh-faced lads in black hoodies that so uncannily matched Billy's, Savage wondered if it was some kind of uniform, shifted behind him in perfect unison.

Backing singers, one on each side of the lead vocal.

The taller one looked well-built, in good physical condition. Probably a runner. His mate on the left had a slight limp. He wasn't up for a fight, wavering already.

'Don't bother, Billy,' Savage told him. 'We're not going anywhere. Not with you and Coop here, at any rate.' He tightened his grip on the wooden stake. Short as it was, it would still make an effective weapon. 'But now you've finished asking me questions, it's only fair I should get my turn.'

Billy stared, then looked back at Cooper, who nodded him to keep going.

Savage sighed.

He tossed the wooden stake to his left hand.

Billy watched it.

The lad was about the same height as Dani, and not much bulkier. He had the physique of a dancer, and moved like one too. He came forward, fists half-up like an old-time boxer, which was embarrassing and a little sad.

Savage waited until he was closer, then feinted with the wooden stake, watched the guy's eyes predictably follow the move, then punched him flat in the face with his right. His follow-through took him further than intended, the ground being uneven, making it hard to regain his balance. But that was OK. Because the other two lads were already charging him, and that slight edge of momentum helped him duck the taller one's first punch, then chop up sharp into his belly with the wooden stake. Not too sharp, as he didn't want to kill the idiot. But it did some limited damage. The guy's abdomen was surprisingly soft, despite his muscular-looking build, and he doubled up, wheezing like an old man.

Before his wavering friend knew what was happening, Savage had leant the other way, kicking out with his left foot. The kick smashed into his right knee, sending the lad down in agony. One look told Savage he would not be getting up again any time soon. Not through injury, but sheer lack of will.

By this time though, Billy was up and dancing again. Blood was streaming from his nose, but he was a game lad. 'Come on,' he said thickly, waving his fists about, 'come on, you posh bastard.'

Savage gave him a sporting chance. Fists up, a few blows exchanged. Back and forth, swaying, ducking. Proper old-style. Then he heard swearing and saw the taller guy struggling back into the fray, some kind of weapon in his hand.

Of course.

The guy was clutching a foot and a half of vicious wooden stake, which he'd recently taken to the stomach.

A gentlemanly boxing bout, all very sportsmanlike and Marquess of Queensberry rules, was acceptable when it was one-on-one. But not when there was a second opponent wading in, looking for revenge and armed with a pointy stick.

No, that was definitely not cricket.

CHAPTER NINE

Savage waited for his chance, pressing the boy harder, left to right, right to left, until he saw confusion in his eyes, and knew he'd wrong-footed him. Then he dipped under Billy's guard and jabbed hard at his bloodied nose again.

Roughly in the same place.

This time the crack of cartilage was audible.

Nasal fracture.

Not pleasant. Especially twice.

Billy swore, staggering back, left hand covering his nose, right fist flailing wildly. Like he was directing traffic. He slipped on the damp grass, and down he went, groaning, the look on his face almost thankful.

Savage spun, eager to avoid being staked like a vampire, but found Peter had got there before him. He'd already disarmed the taller guy, wrestled him to the ground beside the broken chapel sign, and was now smacking him in the face with the splintering stake.

Rather too vigorously.

'You OK there, Peter?' He waited, then repeated his name. Several times. 'I think he's done now. Let's leave it.'

Peter released the guy and sat back, panting.

'Now,' Savage said, taking a step forward, at which Mike Cooper retreated, no longer so brave without his crew, 'I'd like to ask you some questions. We've been open with you about the chapel sign. I hope you'll be just as open about Dani.'

Peter staggered to his feet. 'Aubrey, no . . .' He shook his head, a warning note in his voice. 'Let it go.'

Savage ignored him.

'Dani?' Cooper looked nonplussed.

'Miss Farley.'

The men glanced at each other without speaking.

'Aubrey, I'm serious.' Peter's voice had dropped to a hiss, unmistakable fear in his eyes. What did he know that he wasn't sharing with Savage? 'We're done here. We've made our point. Now drop it, would you?'

'Only once I've had an answer to my question,' Savage said coolly, and turned his attention back to Cooper. 'Dani Farley was in my camper van last night on the road between Post-bridge and Yelverton when your Land Rover nearly ran us off the road. When I stopped and got out, someone took Dani from my cab against her will.' Savage looked down at the short guy, still kneeling on the grass, his face a mess of blood. 'I think it was you who took her, Billy. You were in the passenger seat. I saw you in the headlights. And one of your other friends here was probably driving.'

Billy said nothing, but glared up at him impotently.

He was probably considering whether he should ask to be taken to hospital, or if that would make him look even weaker in the eyes of his boss.

There was no reaction from the other two either. Peter's victim was sitting up now, nursing a red-streaked face and hands, possibly laced with wooden splinters. The lad who had wavered had already begun crawling back towards the car, clutching at his injured knee. He didn't appear to be paying any attention to the conversation.

The incredibly tall man in the Land Rover shifted slightly. One shoulder slipped upwards, the other one went downwards. Then both returned to their original positions.

Perhaps his neck was aching.

Mike Cooper blinked, then said, not unreasonably, 'OK, so let's say something like that might have happened. I'm not saying it did, mind you. But let's say there was a young woman in your van last night. This Dani. And someone else came along, and let's say she did get into their car instead. How do you know it was against her will?'

'Trust me, she didn't want to go with them.'

'Did you hear her scream?'

'I heard . . . a cry.'

'A cry of recognition, perhaps.' Mike Cooper rubbed his large belly. 'Like, erm . . . *Hey, hello there, thank God you've found me.* That kind of thing.'

'I don't think so.'

'Did you hear what she actually said during this . . . cry?'

'No.'

'Aha.' Mike Cooper wagged a finger at him. 'So did you see her struggling, then?'

'I didn't see anything at all. It was dark and raining hard, and I was standing behind the van when they took her.'

'OK, so you didn't hear what she said, and you didn't see her struggling. So how can you be so sure she didn't want to go with them?'

'Intuition.'

'Intu—' Mike Cooper stopped. 'You just love those long words, don't you?' He shook his head. 'OK, question time's over. Now, Mr . . . August, or whatever your name is, I'll tell you what I think, shall I?'

Savage raised his eyebrows.

'I think you found Dani exactly like you said, at the side of the road. Only nobody took her away from you. I think you took her somewhere in your big van. And raped her.' He paused. 'Killed her maybe.'

Peter said angrily, 'That's bullshit.'

'Is it? Who knows what these upcountry folk do at night, when nobody's looking?' Mike Cooper nodded. 'Maybe that's what I'll be telling the police. Soon as I've taken Billy and his boys to be checked over. Happen they've broken some bones. The Reverend won't like that at all.'

'I won't keep quiet this time.' Peter's chest was heaving. 'I may have kept my mouth shut in the past. But this is different.'

'Is that so?'

'What would your daughter say if she knew what you were doing?'

'You leave Carrie out of it.' Mike Cooper was no longer looking at Peter, his gaze shifting restlessly about. 'This ain't none of hers.'

'She'll hear soon enough.'

'You'd best not bring my girl into this. I'm warning you—'

'And I'm warning you.' Pete shook his head. 'I won't stand by and let you pin the blame for Dani onto one of my friends. Not this time.'

'Now you shut your hole and listen to me, boy.' Mike Cooper spat on the ground beside the fallen chapel sign, and his strip of exposed belly quivered. 'Don't be no fool. This is Dartmoor, not the big city. Things get lost here. People too. Some folk can lie hidden for a hundred years or more, so nobody even remembers their name. You were born on Dartmoor, you know the way of it. Maybe tell your friend with the fists, so he knows too.'

'I'm right here,' Savage said.

'OK, Mr Right Here.' Mike turned to him, arms folded across his chest. 'You want it straight, I'll give it to you straight. You and Pete should toddle off back to Rowlands Farm, and stop asking questions about things that don't concern you. That clear enough?' His smile was unpleasant. 'Otherwise, Big Swanney may have to pay you boys a visit.'

At those words, as though they were the signal he had been waiting for all this time, the incredibly tall man unfolded himself from the Land Rover.

Everyone turned to watch as he exited the passenger side slowly and with delicate care, limb by limb, like a butterfly emerging from its chrysalis. Or, more accurately, like a retractable ladder being opened to its full height. Once safely free of the vehicle, the man straightened, and took a few lurching strides towards Savage and Peter. He was deathly pale, staring down at them from dark, deep-set eyes above jutting cheekbones and sunken cheeks, his bald head adding to the cadaverous look.

Big Swanney.

Savage craned his neck to look up at him. Talk about a misnomer. The man wasn't just *big*. He was vast. Maybe seven foot, or thereabouts. Like a scion of that lost race of giants whom the Anglo-Saxons had envisaged building all those enormous amphitheatres and aqueducts and forums actually left behind by the Romans.

Except this guy was real. He wasn't the stuff of legend or folk tale. He wasn't a superstitious misinterpretation of material evidence.

Big Swanney was an actual flesh-and-blood Gogmagog, striding the moor in jumbo-sized hiking boots. He was wearing the longest pair of blue denim jeans Savage had ever seen, and a long-sleeved black sweatshirt that actually managed to stretch beyond his waistband. It must have taken three times as much cotton and Lycra to make as a regular sweatshirt. The sheer acreage of his socks didn't bear thinking about. It was unlikely the poor sod had arms long enough even to cut his own toenails.

And he didn't look too happy about it.

CHAPTER TEN

'I don't blame you,' Peter said for the third time. 'I would have walked away too.'

'I needed more information.'

Peter nodded. 'He was a big bugger.'

'I could have taken him. Size isn't everything.' Peter held out a mug of coffee, fortified with a generous slug of whisky, and this time Savage accepted it without demur. 'It was simply that, at that moment, I didn't want to jeopardise Dani's position.'

'A tactical retreat.'

Savage grinned. 'Precisely.'

It was late afternoon. Dusk was still another few hours away, yet there was a shadow over the moors. Looking out through the window of Peter's kitchen, he thought the landscape looked darker and more inhospitable than ever. Clouds gathering overhead. Or maybe his view was coloured by the fact that Dani was still out there somewhere, probably in danger, and he had failed to get any information out of those men.

'You said Barton was an American preacher,' he said, studying the high ridge beyond which the Green Chapel lay.

'Allegedly.'

'So what's an American preacher doing on Dartmoor, and why is he employing thugs like that? Is it to protect himself, or whatever's up there at this mysterious Green Chapel?' He frowned. 'You told me it was more of a cult. Do you know what actually goes on at the chapel?'

He looked round when Peter didn't respond.

'Peter?'

His friend knew more than he was saying, that was obvious. Which got under his skin. He could appreciate a certain amount of caution, especially when one of their opponents had been the size of a small mountain. But somebody here was going to have to start talking. And Peter was the likeliest candidate.

The only candidate, in fact.

'Come on, Pete, stop stalling. What's this about? And don't tell me people round here have suddenly got religion, because I won't believe it.'

Restlessly pacing the room, Peter said nothing.

'There was nothing even remotely spiritual about that Cooper character,' Savage continued. 'Or Big Swanney. And that was definitely the same Land Rover from last night. Those men have got Dani. Or they know where she is. And I intend to get her back.' He was quiet for a moment, mulling over his next move. Then returned to his original question. It seemed the key to this mystery. 'Why does a preacher hire outside muscle to keep people away from his church?'

Peter stopped pacing and leant back against the kitchen table, arms folded, clearly too restless to sit down. There'd been a decided air of tension about him ever since their walk. Savage guessed it had nothing to do with not having had his usual quota of whisky by this point in the afternoon.

'They're all locals,' he said, 'except for Swanney. I think he's Serbian. Or possibly Russian. Swanney's short for some unpronounceable Slavic name.'

Savage knew some Russian, though he hadn't used it in a long time.

'Savanovic?'

'That's the one.' Peter blinked. 'OK, maybe not completely unpronounceable. But they weren't hired to keep people away from the Green Chapel. Barton started recruiting his little army a couple of years back, after things got nasty.'

'Define nasty.'

Peter pushed a hand through limp hair. 'God, where do I start?'

'You could always start with God. Since he seems to be involved.'

'Aubrey, I know you like to joke about stuff. But this is complicated like you wouldn't believe. Dangerous too. There are things I can't tell you. Or don't want to. Not yet, anyway.' Peter looked away. 'Difficult things.'

'Give me the highlights.'

'OK, I can do that.' Peter gulped at his coffee-whisky mix, which was probably considerably stronger than the one he'd handed to Savage. 'This Green Chapel . . . It's not how it sounds.'

'As in, not green? Or not a chapel?'

'Neither, actually.' Peter made a face. 'I mean, it's both. Green and a chapel. But what goes on there, the religious cult stuff? That's not what you might expect. You saw the sign.'

'*Come thou, believer, and be healed.*'

Peter nodded.

'And a Facebook page. I have to say, that was impressive. Even God is online these days.'

'It's a group, not a page. That's how they get the word out, via the Facebook group. The chapel doesn't have regular Sunday services like ordinary churches. They only operate on certain days. Or rather, nights.'

'They hold services at night?'

'They don't like people seeing what they're up to. Sometimes the services are . . . Well, they're held outside.'

'Surreal.'

'Anyway, the Facebook admins post up the latest news and instructions to chapel members. Including the dates and times of special services.'

'What are these special services? Like a mass, you mean?'

'Not at the Green Chapel. It's a place of healing. That's what *they* call it, at any rate. The Reverend Barton. The admins. They hold special services for healing named people.'

'What do you mean by "named"?'

'People come to them with a particular problem. So the special service is held in their name. Then if other people want to come and support their ... healing process, then they know which service to attend.'

'Seems innocent enough. Though it would be good to take a proper look behind the scenes. They're obviously up to something else at this Green Chapel, and I'm betting it doesn't involve candles and incense.' Savage scratched his ear. 'So, can we look at this Facebook group? See if there are any special services coming up?'

'It's a closed group. You need to apply to join, and then two of the admins vet you. Check who you are, if you live in the area, if you're a believer, et cetera.'

'So they'd spot me a mile off. I'm guessing you're not a member?'

'What do you think?'

'That's unfortunate.' Savage examined his grazed knuckles, which were still stinging slightly, though he'd run his hand under the tap as soon as they got back. 'But look at that. I could do with a spot of healing. Would minor injury count towards getting a special service, do you think? Or is it one of those miraculous "we cure cancer" places?' He grinned. 'How forgiving is this Barton guy? Would he agree to heal injuries sustained while breaking his henchman's nose, do you think? Twice?'

Peter smiled at last. 'It was a good punch.'

'It felt good too.' Savage looked at him. 'Thanks for jumping in, by the way. Your help was appreciated. Though I understood why you held back at first. You have to live here. I'm only passing through.'

'And I wasn't in the SAS.'

Savage laughed.

'I want to help you find Dani,' Peter said abruptly. 'I'm no expert at this kind of thing. Not like you. But I feel partly responsible.'

'How's that?'

'I've kept quiet about what they do up there. Haven't asked questions like you. If something has happened to Dani ...' Peter shook his head. 'I don't like her husband, but I wouldn't wish that on any man.'

'Sorry, her *husband*?'

'Terry.'

'I thought she ditched him at the altar. Wasn't that why she stole a car, and ran away? Because she'd got cold feet about marrying the guy?'

Peter was silent a moment. Then he said, 'It's not as simple as that. Most of these special services ... They're for couples. Well, wives. Barton calls them "rededication" services.'

'Oh, I get it. Like renewing your vows.'

'Not quite.' Peter stared down into his now empty coffee-whisky mug. 'It's more to do with healing.'

'Marriage guidance, you mean? To address problems in the relationship?'

'Sort of.'

'Serious problems?'

'Fertility.' Peter grimaced. 'Or lack of it.'

'You're kidding.'

'It's their speciality. You know what women are like when

they can't get pregnant. They'll try anything, however wacky. That's who the chapel caters for. Barton claims the water from his spring is . . . holy, that it increases fertility. They get desperate couples flying in from all over the world for what they call their "Spring rites". It's a kind of pilgrimage, I suppose.'

'And I imagine the Reverend Barton charges for this treatment?'

'Oh God, yes. Through the nose. It used to be free, in the early days. Then he launched the website and . . . Now, wealthy couples turn up and pay some phenomenal sum for a dip in the holy spring, hoping to be made fertile. It's a goldmine.'

'Where do these people stay? Dartmoor's not exactly crawling with hotels.'

'They have a retreat lodge beside the chapel. It's very exclusive. They only allow a few couples up there a month. But every now and then, to keep the locals happy, Barton gives someone a freebie.' He paused. 'The full fertility service, I mean.'

'Like Dani.'

'I guess so, yes. Except she obviously changed her mind.'

'Would that have pissed Barton off?'

'Massively.'

'Enough to kidnap her? Force her to go through with it anyway?'

'I don't know. Maybe.'

'Could it have been her husband? What was his name again? Terry. Which of them wants a baby most? Her or Terry?'

Peter shrugged.

'*Come thou, believer, and be healed.*' Savage shook his head. 'Christ. No wonder she took a gun with her.'

Peter stared at him. 'What?'

'Didn't I say?'

'No, you missed that little detail out.'

'Wait here.' Savage went out to the camper van, retrieved

the gun, which he had locked in the glove box, and took it back into the house. Peter was standing by the window, staring out. He looked over his shoulder, and then turned in disbelief when he saw the Glock. 'She left a holdall in my van when she disappeared last night. The kind you might use for sports gear.' Savage placed the handgun on the kitchen table. 'There were some clothes in there, personal effects . . . and that.'

'Where the hell did Dani get a gun?'

'Good question.' Savage paused, watching Peter's face as he handled the Glock. 'Careful, it's loaded.' Peter put the handgun down on the table again, but reluctantly. As though he wanted to keep it for himself. 'Seen it anywhere before?'

Peter said nothing, but shook his head. He sat down at the table, still staring at the Glock.

'There was a note with it, inside the holdall. Just one word scribbled on a piece of paper. *Mayday.* All one word, all lower case.'

Peter blinked. 'Like the emergency signal?'

'That's what I thought at first. But it could be the traditional First of May celebrations. A date which happens to be coming up soon. She may have written it in a hurry and missed out the space between the two words.' Savage paused, studying Peter's distracted expression. 'What does "mayday" mean to you?'

'Dragging myself out of bed at half-four in the morning. College choir warbling away at the top of Magdalen Tower. Jumping into the River Cherwell in my tux.'

'Good to see we both have similar memories of university life.' Savage grinned. 'But I don't think May Day celebrations in Oxford are going to be even roughly equivalent to whatever happens here on Dartmoor. In fact, I wouldn't be surprised to discover a connection between her note and the spring fertility rites you mentioned. Maybe Barton is planning something big this year. Or something new. And Dani didn't like the sound of it. So she bolted, and he sent his goons after her.' Savage frowned. 'What is it? What's the matter?'

'Nothing.'

'Come on, I'm not stupid. We've known each other for years. I can tell when you're holding something back. What is it you're not telling me?'

'I can't, Aubrey.' Peter buried his face in his hands, his voice muffled. 'I wish I could. But I can't.'

'OK, calm down.' Savage folded his arms and looked down at the slate floor. There were dips and smoothed-out hollows in places, where feet had continually crossed and recrossed the kitchen over the years. 'You said you wanted to help me find Dani.'

'I do.'

'Then this is your chance.' Savage looked up at his friend. 'I need to get to one of these special services.'

'You? Go to the chapel?'

'I need to find out what Barton is up to. And to see if he's got Dani stowed away somewhere. Maybe in this retreat lodge you mentioned.'

Peter suddenly jumped up, muttered, 'Hang on a minute,' and left the room. A moment later he could be heard upstairs, banging about as though hunting for something, the floor-boards creaking as he moved from room to room.

What the hell had happened to him over the years they'd been apart? Savage shook his head, staring at the open kitchen door. Peter had always been a nervy sort. He would never have made it in the army or the secret service, for instance. He wasn't a natural fighter, and he took things too personally. But this fear was a new thing.

Savage turned back to the window.

Dani had been afraid too. Was she out there somewhere on her own, or did Barton have her? He hoped for the former, but his instincts told him the latter was more likely.

The moors were so grim and inhospitable. He did not fancy anyone's chances for long, stranded out there on their own. The sun had shone today though. That was something.

'Here you go.' Peter returned, carrying an open laptop. He was breathless. 'I didn't think I'd be able to get in. But the password was easy to crack.'

'You forgot your own password?'

'Not mine. Maura's. The laptop belonged to her. She forgot to take it when she left.' He set the laptop down on the table. 'See?'

Savage frowned. 'What am I looking at?'

'The closed Facebook group for the Green Chapel.' Peter bent forward, fiddling with the laptop, tilting the screen to avoid glare from the overhead fluorescent light. 'I've never been a member, but Maura was, almost from day one. She was obsessed with the bloody Green Chapel. Healing, laying on of hands, all that cult crap.'

'So you've signed into her Facebook account?'

'And hey presto.'

'Nice work, Peter.'

'Thanks.' Peter enlarged the browser screen, then stood back so Savage could see. 'There's a special service scheduled for tomorrow evening. And look who it's for.'

Savage pulled out a chair and sat down, examining the Facebook page that was open on the screen. The group profile photograph showed no people, only a cluster of mossed, sunlit boulders with a narrow cleft at the centre, leading through into what appeared to be a green enclosure. The entrance to this enclosure had been dressed with white and red ribbons, below a beautifully handwritten sign that proclaimed, *The Chapel In The Green. Revd. Barton.*

He read out, 'A Special Service for Rose. 9pm sharp. Only believers welcome.' He looked at Peter. 'Sorry, who is Rose?'

'Billy's girl.'

Outside in the farmyard, a dog barked suddenly. A warning bark. Then the other joined in. Soon they were both barking hysterically.

Peter took a few steps towards the open kitchen door, then glanced round at Savage. He looked tense, ready for a fight. 'We've got company,' he said.

CHAPTER ELEVEN

They both listened to the sound of a vehicle bumping unevenly over mud ruts on its approach. It was loud, though still some way off yet. Maybe three or four minutes out, depending on speed and how well it was handling those mud ruts. But it had definitely turned off the main road – over a mile to the south – and was headed for Rowlands Farm. There were no other turn-offs, no other possible route it could be taking.

Savage closed the laptop and stood up. 'Expecting a visitor?'

'No.'

'Postman?'

Peter frowned. 'Wrong engine note. And wrong time of day.' His hair had flopped into his eyes again while he was studying the laptop. He straightened, flicking his fringe back irritably, then gazed around the kitchen as though hunting for a place to hide. He seemed almost scared. 'This is my fault. I shouldn't have smashed up that sign. It provoked them, and now I've got you in trouble as well.'

'Two.'

'Sorry?'

Savage stood still, listening with his good ear. 'There are two of them. Two vehicles. Coming fast.'

'Barton's crew, for certain. With reinforcements this time.'

Peter turned, starting towards the Glock, his expression wild. Savage put a hand on the barrel and drew it away.

'No guns.'

'You think they won't have weapons? They know about you now. And what you're capable of. They'll be after revenge. They may have brought rifles. God knows what else.'

'Picking up a gun is asking to have a gun used against you. Or be forced to use it yourself. Opening a dialogue is the best first option in most situations.'

'Not with this lot. You don't know what they're like.' Peter nodded to his grazed knuckles. 'Besides, talking didn't help us before, did it?'

'That was different. We were out in the wilderness, and you were standing over the remains of their sign. We're on home territory here.' Reaching for yesterday's newspaper, he laid it over the gun, and then headed for the door. 'We keep the gun in reserve. OK? A back-up. Just in case things go cock-eyed.'

They waited in the doorway to the farm. Peter whistled for the dogs and they came at once, sitting beside him with their tails wagging and tongues lolling. Savage checked the time on his phone. It was nearly a quarter to six.

Late April.

Sunset was another two hours away, by his estimate. But the sun, so inviting earlier, had become trapped behind heavy clouds thickening from the north-west. Now the gathering gloom could be mistaken for dusk. Certainly the world felt colder and darker than when they had walked over the moors that afternoon.

There was a silence.

The approaching vehicles were almost at the gate to Rowlands Farm. Two sets of four tyres splashing through puddles and over mud slurries. Two sets of four tyres slowing at the sharp bend, but only momentarily. The lead vehicle was already accelerating. The one following copied its example. A clutch slipped. The second engine roared, then settled again. Nerves?

Excitement? Aggression, maybe. Two vehicles coming in hot, their occupants perhaps tooled up, perhaps not. Perhaps clutching pitchforks and crosses, for the burning of.

This was Dartmoor, after all.

Savage caught flashes of white through the gnarly tree screen. The second car was white. Clean-looking too. Unlikely to be farmers, then. And definitely not a post van. Postman Pat always came in red. Did hellfire preachers drive white cars? It was possible. The purity-preaching type, perhaps. To match their spotless white robes and even cleaner souls.

They were at the gate.

No lessening of speed.

Perhaps the lead driver didn't know about the cattle grid.

Or didn't care.

The first car was a silver Volvo.

The second car had a smart white roof and sides, with increasingly visible yellow and blue neon decals.

Both cars looked incredibly clean for moorland vehicles.

And they were coming in *very* hot.

'Who's chasing who, I wonder?' he said under his breath. Glancing over his shoulder, he peered down the dimly-lit, untidy hall. Dani's gun was still on the kitchen table. Hidden under the local news rag, sure. But a tell-tale bump, nonetheless. Not exactly inconspicuous. 'Or are they together?'

It was not his gun, of course. He had not immediately handed it in to the authorities though, and possession was nine-tenths of the law. The full tenth when it came to illegal possession of a firearm. And not just any firearm.

He still had thoughts about that Glock. Thoughts he was not yet ready to articulate even to himself. But they were part of the reason he had not handed it in as soon as he'd found it. Because there was a puzzle there, a nagging suspicion still hidden in the dark.

'Police.' Peter sounded baffled. 'It's not Barton's men. It's the police.'

'And two cars at once. It's practically a posse.'

'But why? What do they want?'

'How should I know? It's your farm.'

'I haven't done anything.' Peter seemed uncertain. 'There hasn't been a police car up here in years. Then you turn up at the farm, and . . .'

'And suddenly you get two at once. Like buses.' He looked at the Volvo. The gloomy early evening light was reflecting off the windscreen, making it impossible to see who was driving. 'Assuming they're both police cars.'

'Who else, driving like that?'

'The police car could be chasing the Volvo.'

But he knew it wasn't.

That Volvo was too clean to be a getaway car. It was also a standard issue vehicle for police detectives. Volvos, Mondeos, all those sturdy, high-performance cars. And who would cut across the open moors in an attempt to escape a police car?

Only a fool, when the narrow side roads, the truly oblique ones without signposts, were little better than goat tracks in places, and any one of them could end in a quagmire or a tourists' car park.

Or a farm like Peter's.

'Don't talk rubbish, Aubrey.' Peter was staring fixedly at the approaching cars. 'They must be here for you. But why?'

'Maybe they want to know why I'm going round breaking people's noses.'

Peter stiffened. 'I'm going to hide that gun.'

'Probably better not. If they decide to turn the place over, they'll soon find it and that will only make matters worse.'

'They won't find it.' Peter grinned. 'Wait here.'

Peter ducked back inside.

His gaze on the approaching police vehicles, Savage rolled up his sleeves. Consciously trying to appear hard-working; more like a farm hand, less like a vagrant. Then glanced at his tattoos, and rolled them down again. Probably not the right impression.

Peter reappeared almost immediately.

Savage stared at him, baffled. 'That was quick.'

Breathless, Peter winked at him. 'They won't find it, trust me.' He flicked a glance at the police cars. 'Anyway, look, Mike Cooper won't have reported us for that brawl up on the ridge. He wouldn't risk attention from the police. Not even to get his own back on me.'

'Maybe not. But perhaps one of the others did. Billy, for instance. He looked pretty pissed-off. And there was a lot of blood. Perhaps his girlfriend freaked out when he went home covered in blood, and picked up the phone. Women do that occasionally. Take matters into their own hands.'

Savage smiled, thinking of his sister. Margery would have picked up the phone straightaway. Hell, she'd have called the police even if it had meant getting her own brother arrested. Margery was a stickler for the rules.

'What, Rose? She's not the sort to call in the coppers.'

'So maybe Rose called her mum instead. Or Billy's mum. And somehow, between all that, the police got involved.'

'But why two cars? And why is one unmarked? That's a detective's car.' Peter shook his head. 'They've closed most of the rural stations these days. So this lot must have come from one hell of a distance. Coming in mob-handed too. It doesn't make sense. Why not just send PC Plod out to caution us on his next rounds?'

'I don't know. But it could have been classed as an affray. Three of them, two of us. Some blood was spilt. Maybe that lad's kneecap was dislocated. Police tend to take a dim view of that kind of thing. Even rural police. Anti-social behaviour, I believe they consider it. Back in the SAS, we called it a necessary corrective. Effective in most cases.' He sighed. 'But I guess that explanation won't wash on Dartmoor. Especially given what's in your kitchen. Besides all those unwashed dishes, I mean.'

The Volvo hit the cattle grid, still accelerating, and the bonnet bounced violently in the air, then smacked down hard. All the occupants' heads hit the roof, and then wobbled. The rear section followed the same pantomime a second later.

'Ouch,' Savage said.

The second driver, belatedly spotting the issue, slammed on his brakes. But it made little difference. The police car also hit the cattle grid hard. Bounce, smack, wobble.

The Volvo accelerated past his camper van, followed closely by the police car. The car's occupants were staring straight at them. The hens scattered, wings held wide, frantic in their hurry. The bigger dog barked again, excited and aggressive, and Peter caught him by the collar, shushing him. The other dog stood, tense and alert. Two sheep dogs. Two carfuls of police. Not much good against Her Majesty's constabulary, but still reassuring to have them there.

Savage had often wondered if he should get a dog. Company for him in the camper van, and a deterrent against thieves while he was asleep or out of the vehicle. But life on the road wasn't necessarily good for a dog. Too unsettled, too stressful. Besides, he'd have to clear up after a dog. And it was bad enough having to empty the septic tank without taking on responsibility for animal waste too . . .

The Volvo skewed to a halt a few feet away, just as the Land Rover had done on top of the ridge. He could see the driver now. And the other occupants.

A young man was behind the wheel. Keen, focused, proud of his driving ability. In a dark suit.

The front passenger was a woman.

Short black hair, minimal make-up, a severe expression.

Almost certainly a plainclothes detective.

She had been clutching the hanging strap as the car jolted and swayed into the farmyard. Now she released it, and sat there staring at Savage. Not Peter.

She was speaking into a mobile phone.

The police patrol car stopped behind the Volvo. Two uniformed men got out. Both in body armour. One with a beard. One holding a single-shot carbine. Probably a Heckler & Koch MP5SF, by the look of it.

Savage was surprised. Which didn't happen often.

This shout was definitely not about a reported assault. Even where blood had been shed, and a potential dislocated kneecap involved. Not unless the Devon and Cornwall Police Constabulary were considerably more hardline than elsewhere in England.

The officer with the Heckler & Koch leant it on the roof of the Volvo and pointed the barrel directly at Savage. At his chest. Greatest mass, harder to miss.

'Armed police!' the bearded officer shouted, running round the car to shelter beside the man with the carbine. 'Hands up! Where I can see them!'

Savage said nothing, but put both hands in the air.

No point getting shot.

Peter released the dog, whose collar he had been holding, and raised his hands too.

The bigger dog shot forward as soon as he was released, barking fiercely.

'Call off your dog!' the bearded officer shouted.

Peter whistled, and the dog fell back to his side, still barking, but less aggressively.

There was a moment of silent appraisal.

No combatant weapons in sight.

Suspects cooperating.

Hands in air.

Dogs seemingly under control. For the time being, at least.

'Clear, ma'am,' the officer stated loudly.

CHAPTER TWELVE

As one, all the occupants of the Volvo opened their doors and exited the vehicle, leaving the doors open.

The driver hung back. His eyes were darting all over the place, scouting out possible hidden enemies. Perhaps he felt evasive manoeuvres might be required and wanted to stay with his vehicle.

The woman was small and dark.

She wore a black Pashmina-style scarf draped over one shoulder, and beneath that a black jacket, unbuttoned over a white blouse. Her trousers were black, well-cut, above plain boots with modest two-inch heels.

The other two men, in cheap, functional work suits like the driver, followed the woman, flanking her in a way he recognised. Clearly, she was the ranking officer.

Which suited Savage's theory.

She walked briskly forward, studying the farmhouse, the outbuildings, the two men in the doorway with their hands in the air, careful all the time not to walk between the carbine and Savage.

She was wearing a wedding ring. A plain gold band.

'I'm Detective Inspector Paglia.'

An Italian name. That potentially accounted for her Mediterranean looks. Though she was married. So was it her husband's surname?

Perhaps they were both Italian.

She glanced at the camper van, then at Peter, then finally looked at Savage. Sizing him up. Trying to decide on her play. She looked tired, pale with dark circles under her eyes. Yet she kept fidgeting with her hands, adjusting her scarf, her gold wedding band, as though on edge. As though she half-expected trouble but couldn't really rouse herself to take the threat seriously. She was experienced, but not necessarily with these officers. She had not met anyone's eye since exiting the vehicle, which told him there was no rapport between them. No 'I've got your back, you've got mine' understanding. No nods, no winks, no funny hand signals. No camaraderie, in other words. Whoever she was, regardless of her status with these men, she was alone. Which made her vulnerable.

Paglia said, 'Which of you owns the camper van?'

She already knew the answer to that question. He could see it in the way her gaze had turned naturally to Savage as she spoke. The van documents were all legal and up-to-date. Registered, taxed and insured in his name.

A quick PNC check would have given the police his name and personal details as they pulled into the farmyard. In a matter of seconds, perhaps.

Unless they had not bothered. Unless they were there for Peter, after all.

Before Peter could reply, he said, 'Why do you ask?'

Never volunteer information. Not until you know how it's likely to be used.

Paglia's gaze, which had lowered to his mud-covered boots rose slowly to his face. She had a very direct stare, Savage discovered. A 'don't even think about messing with me' stare. He could see why she had risen up through the ranks so quickly. What was she, thirty? Maybe early thirties?

No older than him, at any rate, unless she was using excellent face moisturiser.

'And who are you, sir?'

'Aubrey Savage.' He saw a slight flicker of surprise on her face, and was surprised himself. So they hadn't checked his van registration yet. 'Again, why do you ask?'

Paglia flicked an irritable glance at one of the men behind her, and he turned away, lifting a mobile to his ear.

Definitely no love lost between this crew.

She looked at Peter. 'Sir?'

'Peter Rowlands. This is my farm, I live here.'

'Could we possibly lower our hands now?' Savage asked, feeling a little annoyed by this major over-reaction. 'As you can see, we're not armed.'

She glanced sideways again, and the other man came forward. He had them turn and lean against the wall, then patted them down. The man shook his head at Paglia, who said, 'OK, you can lower your hands.'

Savage stuck his hands insolently in his jeans pockets. It was a gesture that had always annoyed his father, so he imagined it would probably have a similar effect on a detective inspector.

'So,' he said sweetly, 'any chance you could explain why you lot came racing down the farm track like this is Hot Fuzz? What were you expecting to find?'

Paglia had narrowed her eyes on him. The hands-in-pockets thing was working.

'We had an anonymous tip-off,' she said coldly. 'A man with a gun was reported as having been seen at the farm.'

'You came out here mob-handed on the strength of a hoax caller?'

'Shots were heard.'

'Bloody nonsense,' Peter said in a snarl. 'There are no guns here.'

'Not even for rabbiting?' Paglia asked him.

'I like rabbits,' Peter told her.

'So you won't object to us taking a look around?' one of the other officers said.

Peter glared at him. 'You got a search warrant?'

The officer hesitated, glanced at Paglia, then said, 'Not yet. But it's in hand.'

Peter laughed and folded his arms, not budging from the doorway to his farmhouse. 'I've got nothing to hide. But you're not going in without a search warrant.'

'What about the van?' The officer flicked a look at the camper, then turned to Savage. 'What will we find in there, I wonder?'

'Nothing more sinister than last night's takeaway and some unwashed socks,' Savage said calmly. He took his keys from his pocket and tossed them across. 'Take a look if you like. I've nothing to hide.'

Paglia nodded her permission, and the man headed across to the camper with one of the other police officers.

'Given the circumstances,' she said to Savage, a little less tense now that he appeared to be cooperating, 'I'm sure you can see why we had to be sure.'

'Circumstances?'

She studied him coolly, still no embarrassment in her face despite the signal absence of a gunman here. Which was interesting. There must be something else to this business besides the anonymous tip-off, he guessed.

'A camper van like yours was described by a witness as having been involved in a serious incident yesterday. Today's anonymous caller also mentioned a camper van. So naturally we decided to take precautions.' She held his gaze. 'Perhaps you could account for your movements yesterday?'

Savage digested that information in silence, his expression carefully blank.

'What kind of incident?'

'First, tell me where you were.'

'No thanks.'

'You want me to arrest you?'

'For what? Refusing to play twenty questions?'

'As I've already informed you, there was a serious incident on the moor last night. Your van was seen in the vicinity. So I need to ask you some questions. Urgently.' Her gaze had not faltered, holding his. 'We can do that here or at the station.'

'You said you had a witness.'

'That's right.'

'And this witness gave you the registration number of *my* van?'

'We were given a good description of the vehicle. It matches your van closely.'

'But no registration number.'

She shrugged.

Savage looked past her at the man with the carbine. It was still pointed straight at him. 'So why the marksman? It must have been a very serious incident.'

'It was.'

He met her gaze again. Something in her voice. 'How serious?'

'We recovered a body.'

He felt Peter stiffen beside him and knew what he was thinking. A body? That wasn't what either of them had expected. And it changed things. Not least his view of the Reverend Barton's chapel. Perhaps these guys weren't the rank amateurs he had assumed them to be. Perhaps they knew only too well what they were doing.

Barton's boys had lured him into that fight this afternoon, to make him look aggressive and adversarial. And now this dead body had been laid on his doorstep. That told him he was being set up to take the blame for their actions.

Dani.

That gun in her sports holdall had been for protection, he realised. Not blackmail or revenge, as he had originally suspected. Simple protection. Against men who were a danger to her. Only she had left the holdall behind when they dragged her from the van. Unwillingly, he was sure.

And now she was dead.

He had to get them away from the farm, give Peter a chance to hide the gun off the premises before a search warrant could be issued. If they went inside right now, however confident Peter was of his hiding place, odds were high they would discover the Glock. And then Peter would be arrested too.

He had never intended to bring that kind of trouble to his friend's door. So there was only one thing for it.

'In that case,' he said, 'I'd like a lawyer present.'

He should never have got out of the camper van last night. Never have left her alone, not even for a few minutes. He ought to have known, even from that hesitant, piecemeal account of her situation, that whoever Dani was running from would try to take her back.

This was his fault.

'That can be arranged.' Paglia's mouth flashed a microsmile, then returned to its more natural compressed state. Her working face. She was relieved that he was playing along, yet still wary. What else was she hiding? 'You can call your lawyer from the station. Sergeant?'

The sergeant came forward, but Savage was already heading for the cars. Paglia fell back at his approach, deliberately keeping her distance. The carbine continued to train on his chest. No way to miss at that range. They were taking no chances. It still seemed like overkill, given that he was clearly unarmed. The whole thing was a puzzle, and there was at least one large piece missing. Possibly more than one.

We recovered a body.

Dani.

And presumably the police were treating it as murder rather than suicide or accidental death. Otherwise they would hardly be frogmarching him out of there at gunpoint.

But how had Dani died? Had she wandered off into the dark and fallen into one of the many marshes or ponds scattered about Dartmoor? Or had Barton's men taken her back to his place last night, as he suspected? Perhaps she had resisted, or threatened to tell the police, so she had to be silenced. For good.

What the hell was he supposed to have done?

CHAPTER THIRTEEN

It was a long drive to the nearest police station. And a silent one too. Savage had been put in the back of the patrol car, hemmed in by three officers. Dusk fell abruptly over the moors. Just like last night. One minute they were bowling along the narrow moor-top road in the gloom. The next it was almost full dark, the silhouettes of trees like figures pointing, or old men in the distance. The headlights of the patrol car picked out the number plate of the Volvo, driving about a hundred feet ahead of them, and occasionally the backs of heads in the car itself. Paglia was the shortest, seated in the front passenger seat again, so he couldn't see her.

Paglia was an attractive woman, he thought.

Intelligent too.

He had seen the expression in her eyes as she questioned him. A gleam of humour through the weariness. Darkly ironic, but humour nonetheless.

Stupid people rarely had a sense of humour, he found. Especially not when it clashed with the demands of their job. He had met plenty like that in the army. Jobs-worth types. Following orders without thought or question. For many that was the reason they had chosen an army career. It was an uncomplicated choice. They had happily relinquished control to a greater power, and so never had to wrestle with an ethical question or a philosophical point. The army was about following orders.

'Shoot,' your superior officer says, and you had to shoot, regardless of the situation. Simple as that.

That was why he had never quite fitted in with the army. He had sometimes stopped to ask why, and to suggest there might be a different way. A better way.

Eventually there was a town, though in the dark he missed the name. It was not busy. A few cars crisscrossed the streets. Even fewer people hurried home under the street lights, or to the pub, or the cinema. The Volvo drew into a car park behind a concrete and glass police station. The patrol car followed at the prescribed distance. Police cars everywhere, green and blue high-vis strips glowing in the headlights.

Inside the station, Savage was led to a small interview room that smelt incongruously of boiled cabbage, and left there in the care of a sturdy police constable. The constable, who was in uniform and looked like he spent most of his spare time in the gym, studied him with a mixture of curiosity and contempt.

We recovered a body.

What had those bastards done to Dani before they killed her?

For the first time, Savage felt a slight edge of concern. But he pushed it to one side. He had not touched her. Dani had been alive and unharmed when he last saw her. And nobody could prove otherwise.

Though she had been in his camper van. Forensics would tell the police that soon enough.

If it got that far.

After about ten minutes sitting around pointlessly in the interview room, wondering why the hell it smelt of cabbage, another young, more fresh-faced constable came in. The boy looked about nineteen, but keen to get on. He offered Savage a cup of tea and his phone call. Very civilised. Savage accepted both, refused sugar, and was brought lukewarm tea in a polystyrene cup, and a plastic-covered telephone handset.

He checked the number on his own mobile, and a minute later was on the telephone to his lawyer, watched by the contemptuous police officer.

'Faith? It's Aubrey.' He listened to her astonished outpouring for a moment, then interrupted with, 'Yes, I'm sorry. I know it's been ages. All right, years. But listen, I'm in a spot of bother.' As briefly as possible, he outlined his issue, gave her the postcode of the police station, and then asked how soon she could get there. 'I know it's very last minute, and you're miles away, but I don't trust anyone else with this.'

Faith was annoyed and flattered in equal measure. 'Aubrey, you're such a pest. What on earth were you doing on Dartmoor anyway?'

'I told you, visiting Peter Rowlands.'

'Oh, come on. There's got to be more to it than that.'

'Will you help?'

'Hang on a tick.' He heard her typing something. Probably checking her schedule. Then she came back and said, 'Very well. It means shuffling some things around. Bloody Devon though. I'll need to pack wellies, I suppose.'

'De rigueur.'

'I feared as much. And I've just taken the Merc through the car wash. Normally, I would say no, straight out. But since it's you . . .'

'Thank you, Faith.' He smiled at the barely disguised curiosity in her voice, and turned his back on the police constable, who was still staring at him in a hostile fashion. 'I won't forget this.'

She hesitated. 'Won't you, Aubrey?'

'What does that mean? Of course I won't.' He frowned. 'Look, I'm genuinely sorry for not keeping in touch. Since Lina died, things have been difficult. Not just for me, but at home. My father, you know . . .'

The door to the interview room opened. It was Paglia, her black pashmina gone, looking rather less tired. Had she reapplied her make-up? Yes, she had. Her lipstick was stronger and her eye shadow was green now, instead of brown. And her hair had been brushed, gleaming smoothly under the strip lights. She was holding a manila file, still studying the documents inside it as she came to the table.

Faith was apologising, soft-voiced, for having needled him about his long absence.

'Sorry, I have to go,' he said into the phone.

'Try not to answer any questions until I get there, OK?' Faith sounded concerned. 'I'll do what I can, but I'm in Oxford. It'll take me at least five hours to reach you, and it's already early evening. Can you hang on until after midnight?'

'You want me to sit in silence the whole time?'

'If that's what it takes.' She paused. 'We'll talk privately when I get there, I promise. You can bring me up to date then. Meanwhile, just stick to your name and address, and deny everything else.'

'Understood.'

He ended the call and passed the handset back to the constable. 'Thank you.' The man merely glared at him without saying anything. Charming manners. He stood up and smiled at Paglia. 'Hello again, Detective Inspector.'

Paglia seemed surprised. 'Please, sit down. I'd like to talk to you.'

'Of course.' Nonetheless, he remained standing until she had drawn out the plastic seat opposite him and sat down, placing the closed manila file in front of her. Then he sat too. 'I'd love to chat. But I'm afraid my lawyer has advised me not to answer any questions until she arrives.'

'I see.' Paglia looked irritated but resigned. It was no doubt a response she had heard many times before. She glanced at the wall clock. It was coming up to half past seven. 'How long will it take your lawyer to get here?'

'Not until midnight,' she said. 'At the earliest.'

Paglia was startled. 'Midnight?'

'She's coming from Oxfordshire.' He folded his arms. 'Bit of a hike down to Devon, and I'm sure you wouldn't want her to break any speed limits.'

'But presumably we can have an informal chat until she arrives?'

'I suppose so.'

One of the men from the Volvo came into the interview room and took his seat beside her. He was young but already balding, with a stubbly, gingerish beard, prominent blue eyes and an untidy look. Dropping a file noisily onto the table, he opened it and began abruptly rustling through paperwork.

Paglia seemed to stiffen, as though disturbed by the noise he was making, but all she said was, 'This is Sergeant Franks.' She hesitated. 'Ready, Sergeant?'

'Ready, ma'am.'

Sergeant Franks withdrew a notepad and a ballpoint pen from the file. He clicked the pen a couple of times, looking at Savage with the same hostility he'd encountered in the constable's face. Then he flicked through the notepad to the first blank page and wrote a heading. Date and time, presumably.

DI Paglia glanced round at the muscular-looking constable, who nodded and left the room.

Savage watched the sergeant writing out his sheet. He unfolded his arms. 'I thought you said an informal chat.'

'Oh, it's only for my memory. You're not under caution. Not yet.' She glanced at the polystyrene cup. 'You got a cup of tea, I see.'

'Yes, thank you.'

'Polite, aren't you? First thing I noticed about you, in fact. Do you always stand up when a woman comes in the room?'

'Not *always*. But in general, yes.'

'Why?'

'Training.'

'In the army, you mean?' She indicated the manila file in front of her. 'I've been reading about you. An officer in the SAS. Impressive stuff.'

'God, no.' Savage sampled his tea. It tasted soapy and was almost cold now, but he knocked it back anyway. Habit, really. In situations like these, you never knew when the next drink was coming. 'The army did many things for me. But good manners? I have to lay the blame for that squarely at Jemima's door.'

'Who's Jemima?'

'She was my nanny.' He saw her eyes widen in surprise. 'Yes, rather embarrassing for a grown man to admit. But I was blessed to have a nanny as a young boy. Several nannies, in fact. But Jemima was the one who lasted longest. And made the deepest impression on my boyish psyche.'

'So what, she made you stand up whenever a woman entered the room?'

'When any adult came in. But that habit went by the wall as I got older. Standing for women seemed to stick.' Savage pushed away his empty cup. 'Perhaps you could tell me more about this incident. At the moment, I know very little, except that you've found a body, and I'm supposedly involved.'

'All in good time. Could we start with your name?'

'You know my name. You looked me up.'

'All the same.' She crossed her legs, smoothing out the black material of her trousers. 'In case I mispronounce it.'

'Savage,' he said. 'First name, Aubrey.'

'And your title?'

He met her gaze drily. 'You have been doing your research, haven't you?'

'For the record, please.'

'I'm Aubrey Savage, Viscount Chiche.'

'So you're a peer?'

'It doesn't work like that. My father is Earl Redvers. He's a peer. We have an estate in Oxfordshire. But I'm assuming you know all this.'

'Pretty much, yes. I didn't check your credentials in the Who's Who of British aristocracy, but what we have on file for you is quite revealing.' Her mouth twitched. 'What should I call you?'

'Savage is fine. Or Aubrey.'

'Not, *my lord*?'

'Thankfully, no. I told you, I'm a viscount, not an earl.'

'But one day?'

He shrugged and left that question unanswered, unwilling to discuss his difficult family dynamics with a stranger.

Paglia sat back and studied him. The amusement in her face gave way to something more sombre. 'Where were you yesterday?'

He hesitated. Faith had told him not to answer any questions until she was there. But what harm could it do to tell the truth? He had nothing to hide, after all.

Nothing except the Glock.

'On the road, mostly.' He gave her details of where he had parked the camper van the night before, and the route he had taken down through Devon and across Dartmoor. The man with the stubbly beard took notes, glancing up at Savage occasionally, as someone might look at an exotic creature in a zoo. 'I was on my way to Postbridge for the night when I passed a classic MG in a lay-by, facing the other direction. Bonnet up in the rain. I used to drive an MG myself, back in the day. So I stopped to offer assistance.'

Something flickered in her face. 'An MG?'

He described the car in more detail, and Dani Farley herself.

'Sergeant?' She looked at the man with the stubbly beard, and he delved into his file, producing a folded map of Dartmoor. He opened it up to roughly the correct area, and spread it out across the table. Paglia said, 'Can you show me where this lay-by was?'

He studied the map for a moment, then pinpointed the place. 'Here.'

'You're sure?'

'I was in the army, remember? I can read a map.'

'Is that a yes?'

'Yes.'

'What kind of time would this have been?'

'Around dusk.'

'Did you get her car going again?'

'Impossible.'

Her eyes narrowed suspiciously on his face. 'Why's that?'

'She'd run out of fuel. It's easily done in those old MGs. The fuel gauge was probably faulty.' He sat back and crossed one leg over the other, mirroring her body language. An old trick to make the listener feel like he was a sympathetic person, someone to be trusted, someone just like them. 'I offered her a lift to the nearest garage. I'd passed a little place on the road. It was almost dark by the time we set off.'

Again, the odd flicker in her eyes. 'So you're saying you left with this woman?'

'That's right.'

'And you took her to the garage for fuel?'

'No.'

'Why's that?' she said again.

'Another car came along. A Land Rover Defender. Bloody

lunatic of a driver, practically ran me off the road.' He explained exactly what had happened, giving them all the details he could recall, and ended with, 'I have no idea if Dani left of her own accord, or if the occupants of that car took her away with them forcibly. All I know for sure is she was gone by the time I got back in the camper.'

She glanced at her sergeant, who had been scribbling fast. They exchanged looks, then she asked, 'Number plate?'

'I didn't see.'

'Not even a partial?'

'Sorry.'

'You were in the army, and you didn't catch the number plate?'

'The driver stopped across the road directly in front of my van. Diagonally. And when it pulled away, I was round the back of the van.' His smile was dry. 'Plus, it was raining heavily. Poor visibility in that weather, as I'm sure you'll appreciate.' He hesitated. 'But I saw the same Land Rover earlier today.'

'You're sure?'

'It looked like the same vehicle. And I have reason to believe the occupants may have had a connection with Dani.'

'So did you get the number plate that time?'

Again, he hesitated.

Faith would tell him to shut up. That adding multiple assaults to a possible murder charge would do him no good at all.

But Faith was not there.

Not yet.

He gave them the number plate of the Land Rover.

The sergeant wrote it down.

'We'll need to speak to this Dani, see if she can corroborate your story.'

'Good luck finding her.'

'Leave that to us. We'll also need to search your camper van. Which means involving forensics. I'm afraid you may not get it back for a few days.'

'That van is my home. Where am I supposed to sleep?'

'Maybe we'll be keeping you here.'

He raised his eyebrows.

'I don't know. But there are plenty of bed-and-breakfast places round here. I'm sure you'll find somewhere suitable.' Paglia held out her hand. 'Keys?'

Reluctantly, he handed them over.

'So you see,' he said, 'I can't have had anything to do with your body. I spent the night in Yelverton last night. Had a take-out for supper, then grabbed an early night.'

'Oh, it's not last night we're interested in. It's earlier in the day.' Paglia nodded to the sergeant, who produced a few photographs from his file. She slid them across the table. 'This is what we're interested in.'

Savage pulled the first photograph towards him.

It was a scarecrow.

The scarecrow he'd passed just before spotting the MG in the lay-by.

Only now, close up, he could see that it was not a scarecrow.

It was a young man, wearing a flat cap, his clothes dishevelled, his body fixed to a wooden post in the middle of rough grasslands.

There was a bullet hole in the middle of his forehead. A neat, round hole, washed clean of blood by the heavy downpour that day.

Exactly the kind of hole a Glock 19 would make.

CHAPTER FOURTEEN

It turned out that estimated time of death had been lunchtime or early afternoon. Unable to provide an alibi for that time window, having been mostly on the road, Savage had decided to say nothing further, but to wait for his lawyer to be present before answering any more questions. He'd been escorted to a holding cell, and had been there roughly four hours when he heard footsteps in the corridor.

The grille in the door slid open.

The duty sergeant's face looked in. He checked that Savage was lying on his bunk, then unlocked the door. 'Up you get,' the sergeant said, gruff but not unfriendly, and then added, with a wink, 'my lord.'

He preceded the sergeant down the corridor, hoping Faith had finally arrived.

They had taken away his phone.

'For your security,' the duty sergeant had said, smiling at him comfortably.

It didn't look good.

A young man had been shot, probably with the Glock from Dani's holdall, as it seemed unlikely there would be a large number of such handguns at large on Dartmoor. Possibly by Dani. Possibly by some person known to Dani, who had later absconded with the weapon. The deceased had then been hung up like a scarecrow within sight of the road, like a dead rabbit on a gibbet.

And a witness had seen a camper van similar to his own nearby, possibly around the estimated time of death, possibly later, but definitely putting him in the frame for murder.

If it had been the height of the summer season, he would have been in a better position to deny everything and walk away. But there were fewer campers than usual around, largely due to the atrocious weather they'd had recently. He'd heard someone say so in the chippy last night. Plus, he himself had pointed usefully to the location of the lay-by where he had stopped to help Dani.

No, it didn't look good.

The only thing in his favour was that the Glock was no longer in his van. Bringing his van in for forensic examination was bound to be next on Paglia's list, and that would not have helped his case. Hopefully, Peter would have hidden the gun properly as soon as the police had gone. Wiped it down for prints and concealed it well away from the farmhouse, if he had any sense, before the threatened search occurred.

The analogue clock above the duty desk showed a quarter to one in the morning. There were a couple of spotty, pasty-faced youths in the waiting area, and one middle-aged woman in a hooded coat, head bent, weeping silently into a handkerchief.

The woman looked up as he went past, studying him with red-rimmed eyes, and then returned to her handkerchief.

Mother of the dead boy, perhaps?

Another corridor took them further into the police station.

Paglia came out of a side room.

She looked tired, a faint speckling of mascara under her eyes, as though she'd rubbed at them with her fist. He wondered how long she'd been on duty. Longer than she ought to have been, by his reckoning. But maybe she was doing a double-shift so she wouldn't have to hand over his interview to another detective.

'Hello again,' he said. 'Did you manage to find Dani?'

Paglia shook her head. 'We tracked your missing "bride" down to an address, but there was nobody home. And her father said he hadn't seen her in days.' She paused, looking at him steadily. 'He told us he knew nothing about any visit to the Green Chapel, or a marriage rededication service.'

'Then either he's lying or she told as few people as possible. What about the MG? Was it his?'

'No sign of it. Are you sure that was where you saw it?'

'Positive.'

The detective inspector shrugged, then looked at the sergeant. 'You taking Mr Savage to see his brief, Sergeant?'

'Yes, ma'am.'

'Very well.' Paglia stepped back into the room. 'We'll speak later,' she said to Savage, and nodded goodbye.

Savage continued down the corridor. The sergeant said, 'Right here, sir,' knocked at the door to another interview room, then threw it open.

'Your brief,' he said shortly, nodding Savage inside.

Faith was seated behind a table in the sparsely furnished room. She stood up at once, smiling broadly. 'Aubrey.'

He went in, and the door was closed behind him.

They embraced, then he stepped back, grinning. 'You haven't changed.'

'Liar.'

She did look older, in fact. It was the clothes, so different from the relaxed look he remembered. A designer skirt suit, the white shirt a little crumpled after hours on the road. Brown leather high-heeled boots. A brown leather briefcase to match.

Very professional.

They had met at university, appearing in the same student production of *Hamlet*, though she had gone to a different college and had barely known Peter and Jarrah. She had played Ophelia to his rather gloomy Hamlet. In those days, she had been lovely, if a little kooky. Now she was still stunning but with the harder edge of experience.

Not too hard though, he was glad to see.

A few wrinkles, perhaps, but fundamentally the same soft brown eyes. The same honey-blonde hair, artfully arranged to tumble over her shoulders. The same smile, warm but guarded. There had been a fling during rehearsals for the play. Three or four dates, several ending very pleasurably in her narrow bed at Lady Margaret Hall. Then her stern-faced girlfriend had found out, and the dates stopped.

'Thank you for coming at such short notice,' he said, and drew out the chair opposite her. He sat down, and watched as she did the same. 'How was your journey down?'

'Tiring.'

'I'm sorry.'

'No need to apologise, Aubrey. You've done nothing wrong.' Faith had some papers on the desk in front of her, and had been scribbling notes in a legal pad. 'Unless you've been less than honest with me, I can't see that you had any connection with the deceased.'

'I was entirely honest.'

'The only thing that links you is location.'

'The lay-by.'

'Which is circumstantial. Anyway, the timing is all wrong.'

'Time of death doesn't match up?'

'Precisely.' She checked her notes. 'Time of death has been established within a two- to three-hour window, sometime early yesterday morning. And your van was seen in the area some twelve hours later, from what I've been able to glean. So they've got nothing, in other words.'

'That's a relief.'

'The only worrying factor is that death is likely to have occurred elsewhere, according to the preliminary report.' She met his gaze. 'Just to check my facts, you came down to Devon in a camper van?'

'My home.'

'Right.' Faith opened her mouth to ask about that, then shut it again. Again, she checked her notes. 'They're arranging for forensics to examine your van.'

'They think I shot this young man, possibly somewhere totally different, and then conveyed his body to its final resting-place via my camper?'

'That's the theory, I'd guess. They've already appropriated your camper van and sent it for a full forensics check. So unless they find evidence that the deceased was there—'

'They won't. Find evidence, I mean.'

'Because he wasn't there.' It was a question stated as fact, he realised belatedly, when she frowned, adding, 'Was he?'

'Absolutely not.' Savage saw her hesitation, and decided more was required. A fling at university did not result in lifelong trust, it seemed. 'They showed me a photograph of the deceased. I've never seen the poor bastard before in my life.'

She smiled, and he could see relief in her face. Had she really believed him guilty? It had been a long time, he supposed.

'Then all you need do,' she said, 'is establish an alibi for early yesterday morning, and you can walk away.'

'Ah.' He laced his fingers together and studied them.

'Did you know him?'

'No.'

'Recognise his name?'

'They didn't tell me his name. Perhaps they don't know who he is yet. Perhaps they were hoping I'd know and give it away.'

'The police jump to absurd conclusions from time to time, of course. But even the most imaginative officer couldn't believe a murderer would return to the scene twelve hours later.' She played with her pen, knocking it rhythmically against her legal pad. 'I mean, why would anyone do that?'

'To gloat?'

'Don't even suggest it.'

'To take photos and post them to Facebook?'

The pen became still.

'Aubrey . . .'

Savage ignored the warning note in her voice, leaning forward. He did not want anyone who might be listening to overhear him. He waited until she had done the same, then he whispered, 'I'm half-serious.'

'I can see that. Unfortunately.'

'Listen.' Briefly, he explained about the Green Chapel and its closed Facebook page. The aggressive crew in their Land Rover, again leaving out the part where he broke Billy's nose. He touched on Dani's involvement, explaining about the broken-down MG and ignoring her amusement. 'Yes, entirely my fault for playing the knight errant.'

'I didn't say a word.'

'You didn't need to, trust me. Anyway, I'm sure it was the same Land Rover that chased us on the Postbridge road. Nearly turned the bloody van over. I got out to speak to them, but they weren't hanging about for that. And I'm certain they took Dani. The door was open when I went back, and she had gone.'

'Willingly?'

'Not a chance.' His gaze met hers. 'For starters, the girl was terrified. And on top of that, she left something behind. Exactly as she would do if someone had snatched her from the van.'

'What did she leave behind?'

He was very aware that someone could be listening in. 'That doesn't matter right now. Get me out of here first. Can you do that?'

Faith shuffled her papers, frowning. 'I think so.'

'I'll need somewhere to stay until I get my van back. A bed-and-breakfast place on Dartmoor. Somewhere near where the victim was found. Not too expensive.' He ignored her surprised stare. His finances were no one's business but his own. 'And some new clothes. Everything I own is in the camper.'

'I can arrange that.'

'The police took my wallet when they put me in the cell. But I guess I'll get it back when you spring me.'

'Absolutely.'

She was writing something in her notepad, her handwriting small and precise. *Cheap B&B???* he read upside-down. *Change of clothes. Wallet?*

He studied her averted face. There was something there. Something that troubled him. 'I didn't have anything to do with that young man's death. You believe me, don't you?'

'Of course.' Her voice was hollow though.

'Faith?'

She looked up, catching his hesitation, and smiled, repeating more firmly, 'Of course I believe you. And from what I can see, they have no reason to hold you while forensics are working on your van. But to establish that, you'll need to be formally interviewed first. With me in the room, to make sure everything goes smoothly.'

'Of course,' he said too.

'So let's go through what happened again. In proper detail. Then I'll help you with your answers.'

'Coaching? Is that legal?'

'Call it professional advice.' Faith sat up straight. 'And this isn't *Hamlet*, OK? Don't screw up and forget your lines.'

He grinned. 'Oh, get thee to a nunnery.'

CHAPTER FIFTEEN

Faith was on top form, Savage thought.

She listened to everything Paglia had to say, instructed Savage in a whisper to reply, 'No comment,' to most questions, and then calmly pointed out the police had only circumstantial evidence at best. After agreeing to return if the forensics search of his camper van – which she insisted had been illegal and premature – turned up nothing, she finally got him released with textbook efficiency.

Even so, by the time they got out of the police station, it was close to dawn and would have been pointless trying to get into a hotel.

But they were both starving.

Faith drove them in her mud-spattered Mercedes to a service station with an early-opening diner, a few miles from the desolate moors road, and they sat down to breakfast together.

The Lucky Diner was a cheerful moorland restaurant, loud pop music being piped out of every corner and torn red seating in most of the booths. But the waitress was friendly, and the food smelt good. Savage ordered a big cooked breakfast with a pot of tea. Everything twice, with an extra round of buttered toast. Faith was pickier, ordering poached eggs on toast, and asking first if the eggs were organic. They weren't. But she had them anyway.

The restaurant looked out over the car park, beyond which

was a busy A-road. While they waited for breakfast, Faith read through her notes again and Savage looked out at the passing traffic. It was still early but the Devon commute was well underway. It included tractors and at least one milk lorry.

DI Paglia had been reluctant to release him. Without Dani's corroboration, the police only had his word that he wasn't involved in that young man's death. But Faith had made it clear the police couldn't hold him any longer unless they planned to charge him. He had signed a statement, then his possessions had been returned without further argument and he had walked free.

One useful thing had come out of that second chat with Paglia, though.

A patrol car had driven out to take a second look, Paglia had said, just in case he'd mistaken the place, but there was no Diamond White MG in that lay-by, or any lay-by along the moors road. Which meant someone with a can of fuel had gone back after they'd left, and got the car started again.

Maybe Dani's husband, Terry Hoggins.

Or her father, Geoff.

The police had contacted Geoff, unable to get hold of Dani or her husband, Terry. Apparently, Mr Farley knew nothing about the car, nor his daughter's plans for a rededication service. And he claimed the couple had 'gone away' for a few days. Not terribly helpful, Savage thought. But he intended to pay Geoff Farley a visit. See if he could find out more than Dani's father had been willing to tell the police.

'Nice car,' he said, nodding to the Mercedes parked outside the restaurant window.

'That's why I bought it.'

Savage grinned at her.

The tea arrived, and he thanked the waitress, who looked to be in her early forties, heavily pregnant and beaming with joy.

Her name badge said *Phyllis*. A good, old-fashioned name. It suited the functional cut of her smooth white-blonde hair and lack of make-up.

When she'd gone, he asked Faith politely, 'Shall I be mother?'

'Please. No milk.'

He poured them both a cup of tea, then added a dash of milk to his own cup. He hated weak tea. If he wanted a milky drink, he ordered coffee.

'So you've done well for yourself. Expensive new Mercedes. And that looks like a Rolex.' He smiled when Faith pulled down her sleeve to cover the gold watch, her expression suddenly self-conscious. 'Success is nothing to be ashamed of. You were always intelligent, and a hard worker too. More power to your elbow.'

'What about you?' She took a handful of paper napkins from the table dispenser and wiped the area clean in front of herself. 'You said that camper van was your home.' She was frowning. 'Did you mean that, Aubrey? Or was it one of your little jokes?'

'No, I live there.'

'You mean, on the road?' When he nodded, she made a noise under her breath. 'But what on earth happened? Why aren't you at Redvers House anymore?'

'My father kicked me out.'

She stopped and stared at him, mid-wipe. 'What? Why?'

'Take a wild guess.'

'Not over what happened with . . . with your mother, surely? But that wasn't your fault.'

'I was responsible for bringing Jarrah into the family,' he said lightly, 'by marrying his sister. And look how that turned out. Jarrah murdered my mother.'

Faith was shocked. 'That's not true, and you know it. What happened that night was an accident. The verdict was man-slaughter, wasn't it?'

'So the judge said.'

'Well, that's all that matters, legally speaking.'

'I don't think my father sees it the same way. Especially as it came out during the trial that Jarrah had been sleeping with my mother.'

'That was never proved.'

'I saw them together myself.'

That silenced her.

'All that aside, he'll never forgive me for introducing Lina and Jarrah into his cosy little world. To him, it must look as though my marriage destroyed his. And he's not completely wrong.' He shrugged. 'I deemed it best not to argue with him. So I bought the camper and went on the road.'

'Perhaps if you go home and try reasoning with him—'

'He had a second stroke at Christmas. More serious this time. According to my sister, it's hard to have anything but a one-sided conversation with him now.'

'Oh, Aubrey.' Faith started arranging the soiled napkins in a pile, her expression distracted, a sheen to her eyes. Was she on the verge of tears? Over his tortured history? She'd always been a big-hearted girl at university, but he'd thought the law would have soon knocked that out of her. It seemed Faith was less tough than the slick, professional exterior might suggest. 'Look, I should have said before ... I was sorry not to make Lina's memorial service. I was genuinely unable to get there. I wasn't even in the country that day.'

'Don't worry about it.'

'That whole thing ... What happened to Lina in Kabul ...' Her voice faltered. 'It was just dreadful. I'm so sorry, Aubrey.'

He did not know what to say. Or perhaps the wound of Lina's death was still too raw to be discussed in an off-hand manner. Either way, he kept silent.

Breakfast arrived a few minutes later, Phyllis apologising

profusely for the wait, though it had only been a few minutes. Obviously an apologising vibe was in the air.

Once the pregnant waitress had bustled away again, one hand supporting her rounded belly, Savage started to eat immediately. It had been a long night, and he was eager to get some hot food inside him. Looking across, he was amused to see Faith stop to wipe her knife and fork first, as though afraid they might have been infected by some previous diner.

'You know, I'm sure they put the cutlery through the dishwasher.'

'I like to double-check, that's all.' She sounded defensive. 'No harm in making sure.'

The sausages were slightly overcooked. Savage enjoyed them, all the same. He had got used to meagre breakfasts in the camper recently. He could rarely be bothered to cook so early in the morning, and even cereal was a challenge, given that he was always forgetting to top up the fresh milk in his mini-fridge.

The sound of women's laughter drew his attention. The pregnant waitress had stopped to talk to a red-head eating alone in one of the booths near the entrance. The customer was petite and shapely, dressed all in black, a baseball cap clamped over her red hair as though trying to conceal it, which was impossible.

The woman in the baseball cap slid out of the booth a moment later, on her way out of the diner, and glanced briefly in his direction.

Their eyes met, she smiled, and he smiled in return, then felt an odd shock.

She was wearing a dog-collar.

A vicar.

The real deal, this time.

She left the diner, pausing on the threshold to wave a cheery farewell to the counter staff as though a regular customer there. Savage watched, even more curious when she blew a kiss to Phyllis before banging the door shut.

He wondered if she knew the Reverend Barton, and if so, what on earth she made of the American preacher and his bizarre Green Chapel.

The thought made him grin.

'So,' Faith said, moving her poached eggs suspiciously off the toast to examine them, 'your dad didn't like Lina very much.'

'He was unsure of her. And Jarrah, of course.' It hadn't been so much his wife's partial Iraqi descent that his father had objected to, but that he simply didn't understand what he considered to be a different culture. And disliked the effort involved in trying to understand it. 'Until the accident, he treated them both like curiosities. Spoke to them politely enough, but that was as far as it went. My mother, on the other hand, thought they were both wonderful. Especially Jarrah.' He smiled. 'You met my mother, she was always so . . .'

'Vibrant?'

'I was going to say, flirtatious. And she loved new people. To the point of nearly devouring them.'

'I remember. She scared me half to death that time at university.' Faith smiled back at him. 'But your dad didn't try to stop you marrying Lina, did he?'

'Not overtly. He just made it clear he didn't approve of my choice. The fact that Lina was half-Scottish as well as half-Iraqi wasn't any help either. He's always hated the Scots. Ever since his first proper girlfriend dumped him for a Scots Guard.' His smile broadened. 'Lina could put on a pretty good Scots accent when she wanted, courtesy of her dad. When my father was being particularly annoying, she used to start rolling her Rs. It drove him mad.'

'I wish I'd known her better. The two of you were so perfect for each other.' Faith put down her knife and fork, and took a few sips of black tea instead, frowning. 'Living in a camper van though. That's not what I expected to find you doing.' She hesitated. 'Do you need help?'

'Help with what?'

'Money,' she said bluntly, picking up her cutlery again.

'I'm good, thanks.'

'OK.' She finally began to eat, as though unable to put off the awful moment any longer. He could see how she had managed to keep her figure all this time. 'But don't you ever . . . I don't know, get cold?'

'Frequently.'

'So what do you do?'

He shrugged. 'Put on a jumper. Turn up the heating.'

'You do have a heater, then?'

'It's not a tent halfway up Snowdonia, Faith. It's a camper van. A little the worse for wear in places, to be fair. But with electric sockets and a petrol generator to power them. I even have a cooker and fridge.'

'But what about washing, and so on?'

'There's a shower cubicle in the back. And a WC, for so on.'

At his dry tone, Faith looked up from dissecting the second of her poached eggs. 'Sorry, you probably think I'm interfering.'

'Only because it sounds like you are.'

They ate for a while in silence, then Faith finished her food and pushed the plate aside. Savage felt her gaze on his face, but continued eating, taking his time, glancing out of the window occasionally. He was waiting for her next question though. It was obvious his old friend was perplexed by his lifestyle and was not about to let it go.

'How's your dad doing now, if it's not too much like interfering to ask?'

'My sister Margery's been looking after him since his last

stroke. Along with a private nurse she's brought in, for the medical side of things. Between the two of them, he seems reasonably comfortable.'

'You've visited him?'

'Of course.' Savage too pushed aside his plate, unable to finish his black pudding. Not the best breakfast he had ever eaten. But it had filled a hole. 'I'm not an ogre. We quarrelled, but he's still my father.'

'Was it a bad stroke?'

'Bad enough.' He drank some tea, not meeting her gaze. Discussing his father made him uncomfortable. 'He's bedridden. Can't speak. Can't swallow properly. All his food has to be puréed or cut into tiny portions, and hand-fed to him.'

'God, I'm sorry.'

'We hoped the worst of it would be short-lived. But the longer it goes on, the less likely he is ever to recover.'

'You should go home to him.' She saw his face and added again hurriedly, 'Interfering again, I know. It's none of my business.'

'I did go home. My father didn't want me there. He was quite adamant about that. He may not be able to speak, but he can communicate with hand gestures just fine.'

'I'm sorry,' she said again.

'We never had a great relationship. My father always resented that my brothers both died young. That meant he was landed with me as heir to the title.'

She looked surprised. 'What's so wrong with that?'

'I'm not peer material. Too flighty, apparently. Couldn't stick the proper army. Married an unsuitable woman. Was the cause of my mother's death. And now I'm basically living in a van at the side of the road.' He smiled tightly. 'As far as my father's concerned, one of his dogs would make a better earl than me.'

'What about Margery, then?'

'A woman can't inherit the title. Not under British law.' Savage shrugged. 'Crazy as it sounds in this day and age, but you can't have a female Earl Redvers. Not unless Margery declares herself male,' he added, grinning, 'and there's no way that would ever happen. Besides, my sister isn't interested in the title. All Margery cares about is my father and racing.'

'She's an athlete?'

'Race horses.' Savage laughed then, genuinely amused. 'She owns a racing stable. Quite successful too. Her boyfriend manages the place for her. Out of all of us, Margery's the only one who's making a reasonable living.'

'And how are you earning your living these days?'

'I'm not.'

'Then how on earth—'

'Remember my cousin Sara?'

'The mad one?'

'She may have been mad. But she was an only child, and my uncle Dickie left her a bloody fortune. Then Sara died too, within a year of him. Childless. Left most of it to me. Plus a few hundred thousand to a local cat shelter.'

'Good God, you jammy bastard.'

'Hey, I worked hard for that jam. Her favourite cousin, Sara called me. All those years of stopping my older brothers yanking on her pigtails ...'

She laughed, her eyes bright with humour, and after a few seconds Savage joined in. It felt good to laugh with a friend after the year he'd had. He should do it more often. And would, if he got the chance. First though, he had to sort out this mess that he'd somehow become tangled in.

'Though you're right,' he continued, sobering, 'I can't stay on the road forever, even with cousin Sara's money behind me. And I won't. But I made a promise to Lina, and I intend to keep it.'

She searched his face. 'A promise that brought you to Dartmoor.'

'I came looking for Jarrah.'

Faith's eyes widened. 'Even after . . . after what happened?'

Some days it made little sense to him either, Savage thought. Much as he disliked admitting it, he agreed with his father. Jarrah had behaved appallingly towards his family, first by seducing his mother behind his father's back, and then causing her death through nothing short of reckless stupidity.

But Lina had loved her brother. And she'd begged Savage to find him.

'I made a promise,' he repeated doggedly.

'Well, I admire your commitment. Especially under the circumstances.' She frowned. 'Didn't Jarrah end up working for the government in some capacity?'

'SIS.' He saw her confused expression, and clarified. 'Secret Intelligence Service.'

'Bloody hell.' She paused. 'But wouldn't they know where he is?'

'If they do, nobody's talking.'

'So you came here. You think he's on Dartmoor?'

'Remember Peter Rowlands?' He drained his tea cup down to the bitter-tasting dregs. Force of habit from the army. 'I suppose you didn't mix much with my other friends outside theatrical circles. But Peter was at Oxford at the same time as us. Reading PPE, same as Jarrah.'

'Shambolic type, always drunk?'

'That's the one. He hasn't changed much, I'm afraid. Always had this bucolic dream about the good life. After Oxford, he got married almost out of the gate, and then tried to make a go of running his dad's farm here on Dartmoor. Only the dreaming spires don't prepare you for a life of rural hardship.'

'Not the best career choice, I'm guessing.'

'Well, he's still got the family farm. But he's clinging on by his toenails.'

'And his wife?'

'Maura. She left him a couple of years ago. Got sick of his drinking, by all accounts.' Savage thought about it for a minute. 'Though I've a hunch there may be more to it than that. Possibly a fertility problem. Peter said she had connections with that weird Green Chapel place. Belonged to their Facebook group. Sounds like a cult, if you ask me.'

'Good God. So what's the link between Peter and Jarrah?'

'We were inseparable at one stage. The Three Musketeers, that kind of thing.' He saw a ghost of a smile on her lips. 'It meant a lot to us in those days. Male bonding, and all.'

'I didn't say a word.'

'Shortly before Jarrah disappeared, he called Lina. Claimed he was going to visit Peter in Devon. Only he didn't go into details. Jarrah was always tight-lipped.'

'And what did Peter say?'

The waitress stopped beside their table, smiling down at them both. Not a false smile, either. Phyllis looked gloriously happy, he thought. There was an evangelical glow to her face, and she seemed to glide rather than walk.

'If you don't mind me asking, when's it due?' Faith asked, nodding to the woman's rounded belly.

'I don't mind.' The woman stroked her belly almost gleefully. 'I've got another five weeks to go before the big day.'

'Is it your first?'

'She'll be my one and only.' Phyllis beamed with pride.

'Oh, congratulations. Though you look as though you ought to be at home, taking it easy. Don't they give you paid maternity leave here?'

'I finish next week. I shouldn't say so, but I can't wait.' Laughing again, the waitress bent to check the teapot, which was empty. 'More tea? Another round of toast?'

Savage shook his head. 'You could tell me about that woman. The vicar?'

Phyllis's smile froze. 'Sorry?'

'I saw you talking to her earlier.' He pointed towards the booth seating near the entrance. 'Dog collar. Baseball cap. Red hair.'

Her manner had become wary. 'What about her?'

'I'm just curious. You don't see many woman vicars. Church of England, is she?'

'I wouldn't know.'

He raised his eyebrows. 'She blew you a kiss on her way out.'

'Did she?' Phyllis cleared the plates and hurried away. 'If there's nothing else, I'll get your bill.'

Faith watched the waitress go, then looked at him in surprise. 'What was that about?'

'I'm not sure.' He filed that exchange away under 'interesting' and leant forward on his elbows, answering Faith's previous question instead. 'Peter denied that Jarrah ever came to see him. Point-blank. He got almost angry when I pressed him about it. So I backed down.'

'You think Jarrah used Peter as an excuse for going off-grid for a while.'

'Either that, or he travelled down to Dartmoor as arranged, and something happened to him. Something Peter dare not admit, even to me.'

'You think he never left.'

'That's my fear, yes.' Savage reached into his jacket for his wallet. 'Trust me, I don't want to be right about that. But if I am, I owe it to Lina to find out what happened to her brother. And why.'

'I can understand that.' Briefly, she laid a hand on his arm. 'But first, you need to clear your name over this young man who's been shot.'

'Agreed.'

She looked relieved. 'So we'll wait until the forensics team comes back to us about your van. Which shouldn't be too long, with any luck.'

'Meanwhile, I need to find Dani. I'm worried about her.'

'As your lawyer, I have to advise against it. She's not your concern. Leave that to the police.'

'The police have nothing to go on, and no missing person report has been filed. Paglia said the police spoke to Dani's father, who claimed his daughter was fine and had gone away for a few days, and that she had no connection with the Green Chapel.' The waitress approached with the bill, and Savage stood up. 'Let's go and see if we can jog his memory.'

CHAPTER SIXTEEN

A few discreet enquiries at properties along the road to Post-bridge led them to Geoff Farley's place. From what they had been able to find out, he was a farmer. Yet his property was more of a glorified smallholding than a farm, comprising one cottage and some ramshackle outbuildings set back from the road behind a turf bank, a couple of rusting farm vehicles in the yard, no obvious livestock in sight beside a desultory-looking tabby, and a For Sale sign, its wooden post sunk deep into the front bank.

The For Sale sign was sagging and faded. It looked as though it had been there a long time.

Faith, who had been reluctant to drive him anywhere but to a hotel or bed-and-breakfast place, parked on the road beside the turf bank and turned off the engine.

'What kind of farmer is he, do you think?'

'Hard to say.' Savage studied the farm vehicles. One was an elderly tractor, the other some kind of covered trailer, though neither of them appeared to be in good working order. 'Though he can't be farming the land with any success, I wouldn't have thought. Not here on the high moors. The weather can't be good enough to sustain a crop.'

'Looks warm enough today.'

She had a point. It was sunny again, and considerably warmer than yesterday. Dartmoor stretched away to their right, a rolling green expanse, almost hospitable in the sunshine. But he thought back to that sudden violent downpour on his first night here, and could easily imagine the winters must be a thousand times harsher.

'You coming?' he asked.

Faith looked at him with raised brows. 'What do you think?'

He grinned, and got out of the Mercedes. There was hammering coming from an outbuilding, so he picked his way across the muddy yard towards it. A mangy-looking dog of indeterminate breed wandered out from the cottage to stare at him, but did not bark.

Savage stopped outside the door to the outbuilding, which stood partly ajar, and called, 'Hello?'

The hammering stopped.

Someone pushed the door fully open and came out, an oily rag in his hand. This had to be Geoff, he decided. He was a large man in orange overalls, with frizzy hair riddled with grey, a red-cheeked face and bloodshot eyes. He looked Savage up and down, then his gaze moved to the car parked on the other side of the turf bank.

'I'm not interested,' he said flatly. 'Whatever it is, I'm not interested.'

'I'm not selling anything.'

'God, then, is it?' The man sneered, rubbing the oily rag between his fingers. 'Told you, I'm not interested.'

'I'm here about your daughter, Dani.' Savage watched that sink in. The sneer disappeared, the small, bloodshot eyes contracted, and the red-cheeked face became tense. As he had suspected, the man was afraid of something. But of what? 'I believe you told the police you don't know where she is.'

Geoff glanced towards the car again, wary. 'You police?'

'No.'

'Then who are you?'

'A friend of Dani's.'

The sneer reappeared. 'I know all Dani's friends. I never seen you before in my life. You must think I'm stupid.'

'Not at all.'

'Go on, get lost.' Geoff raised his voice, waving the oily rag, his manner blustering. The dog ambled forward at last and barked, somewhat belatedly but with enthusiasm. 'Get back in your fancy car and don't come back.'

'Do you know the Reverend Barton?'

Geoff fell silent.

'Did Barton tell you to lie to the police?' Savage continued.

'I ain't lied to nobody.'

'You're lying to me. Right now. Where is she, Geoff? Where's your daughter?' Savage met his uncertain gaze. 'Or don't you care what happens to Dani?'

Geoff licked his lips. He looked Savage up and down again, this time more carefully. 'You're a stranger. You wouldn't understand.'

'Then explain it to me.'

'Her husband's with her. He'll look after her just fine.'

'Terry?'

Geoff looked even more surprised. 'That's right.'

'Dani was running away from Terry when I met her. She was on the run, Geoff. From her own husband. That doesn't sound like a very happy marriage to me.'

'You don't know what you're talking about.'

There was a car coming fast along the uneven side road towards the farm. Unless the driver always drove at that speed, something was wrong.

Savage glanced towards the cottage. 'Shall we go inside? Is your wife in? Perhaps I could talk to her instead?'

'You'll have to speak up, then. My wife's dead. Fifteen years now. Cancer.' Again, the sneer. 'Shows how much you bloody know.'

'I know Dani had a gun with her when she ran away.'

Geoff said nothing.

'A young man was shot dead. And I think Dani might have been involved.'

Now Geoff was scared. He shook his head wordlessly.

Savage was listening to the high, strained engine note. Not a Land Rover. Something smaller and infinitely less powerful. Behind them, the car braked as it approached the farm, skidding on the muddy road. Geoff half-turned that way, a helpless look on his face.

Savage continued urgently, 'Maybe Dani didn't kill him though. I'd like to think that. She didn't strike me as the sort of person who could shoot a man, even in self-defence. But maybe she knows who did.' He paused as Geoff turned back to stare at him. 'Maybe that's why Dani ran. Because she saw what happened and was afraid she might be next.'

'What the hell are you talking about? What young man?' Geoff backed away, still shaking his head. The dog started to bark again. 'Who . . . who got shot?'

There was no deception in his face now. Only fear.

Savage turned at last.

The car had slithered through the muddy gateway into the farm, past the silver Mercedes parked beside the turf bank, and was headed straight for them.

It was a Renault Clio, a hatchback. A young man's car. And there was a young man behind the wheel, his pace barely slackening as he gunned towards them. Early twenties, Savage guessed. Sunk down low behind the wheel, so unlikely to be particularly tall. Celtic-looking face, short dark hair, intense eyes. From his complexion, the kind of guy who worked outdoors most of the year. His hands were clenched tight on the wheel. The sun glinted off a ring on his left hand. A wedding band?

His face looked grim and furious.

Frenzied, even.

As though he intended to run them both down.

CHAPTER SEVENTEEN

Beyond the turf bank, he caught a flash as the driver's door opened and Faith got out of the silver Mercedes.

'Stay where you are,' he shouted across to her, and lifted a hand, partly in warning, partly as an order to stop. He didn't want Faith involved in this business any deeper than she already was. Especially if the young man in the car really meant them harm.

But it seemed the driver was here to talk. Not kill.

Not yet, at any rate.

The Renault Clio slammed to a halt a few feet from the mangy old dog who, suddenly galvanised into action, skipped out of the way and stared up at the bonnet with accusing eyes. The young man jumped out of the car and ran towards Geoff, ignoring Savage as though he didn't exist.

He had a cut lip and a black eye.

'Callum. They've killed Callum. Do you hear me?' He grabbed Geoff by his oil-smeared work overalls and shook him. Hard. Like a rag doll. Frizzy head snapping back and forth, arms flailing. 'He's dead. Bloody dead. Did you know they had him? Did you know what they were planning to do to him?'

Geoff's eyes were wide. Panic and horror. No pretence there. 'Callum?' he repeated, then looked towards Savage. 'That was who . . . Callum was the one who got shot?'

'You old fool. Did you think they wouldn't go that far? Men

like that? Oh God . . .' The young man let go at last and half-collapsed, bent double, retching onto the muddy concrete.

Geoff stood silent, but shocked. There were tears in his eyes.

Savage checked, but Faith was standing beside the car, not coming any closer. She looked worried though.

He gave her a brief wave, hoping it would reassure her. Then he turned back to the young man, who was leaning against the wall of the outbuilding. He appeared to have finished retching, anyway. Which was good.

'I take it you're Terry Hoggins?' Savage said gently.

The young man straightened, belatedly becoming aware of Savage's presence in the farmyard. His breathing slowed and he wiped his mouth on his sleeve. His face grew wary. 'Who are you?' He glanced sharply at the older man, eyes narrowed. 'He one of them, Geoff? Thought I told you to keep your nose out of my business?'

'I don't know who he is,' Geoff told him. 'He just turned up.'
One of them.

Savage stuck out a hand. 'Aubrey Savage. Pleased to meet you. And I'm very sorry for your loss.'

The young man stared at his hand. Then at his face. Then glanced towards the silver roof of the Mercedes. He took a quick step backwards.

'That your car?'

Savage shook his head. 'My friend's car.'

'Then why don't you get in the bloody thing and drive away? This is nothing to do with you. This is family business.'

'You mean it's to do with Dani?'

Terry stared. A muscle jerked in his cheek. 'What d'you know about Dani?'

'Less than I'd like.'

'I don't understand. Why are you here?'

'To talk to Geoff.'

'And what d'you want from Geoff?'

'Answers.'

Geoff muttered something in his ear, and Terry stiffened. He glared at Savage, openly hostile now. 'Look, get lost, all right? Whoever you are, whatever you want, we're not bloody interested. So you can sod right off. This is private property.'

'Understood.' Savage held up his hands. An open, unthreatening gesture. No weapons. 'But this Callum. The man who got shot. He was a friend of yours?' He saw the shock register in Terry's face at his mention of the dead man, swiftly replaced by grief. The kind of overwhelming grief he understood only too well.

'My brother.'

'I'm really sorry.' And he was. Genuinely. He looked away, waiting while Terry battled to control his tortured expression. 'For what it's worth, I've lost two brothers.'

'Not like this you haven't.' The young man's tone was bitter. 'Not shot in the head.'

'True,' he said, 'but I lost my wife to a bomb blast. Nothing prepares you for that horror, trust me.' He saw the young man's eyes widen, and paused. 'Where's *your* wife, Terry?'

Both men fell silent.

'Right,' Savage continued in the same tone, 'then let me tell you where I think Dani is. If I had to lay odds on it, I'd bet she was up at the Green Chapel, a guest of the Reverend Barton and his boys. Am I close, do you think?'

The two men looked at each other warily, more or less confirming his guess.

'Is that who you work for?' Geoff asked hoarsely. 'Barton?'

'No.'

'Then who?'

'I don't work for anybody. I'm here because of Dani.'

'What the hell?' Terry stepped forward, his hands clenched

into fists, jealousy in his eyes. His mouth worked silently, then he studied Savage again and seemed to change his mind, his manner suddenly deflated. As though he had thought for a wild moment that Savage and Dani had been involved, then dismissed it as impossible. 'How do you know my wife?'

It was best to be honest with them, Savage decided. Otherwise they were unlikely to be honest with him. So Savage explained about the Diamond White MG, and the relentless downpour, and the bride standing forlorn in the lay-by next to an open bonnet. Then his visit to Rowlands Farm, and his unexpected arrest.

Again, he left out the part about the Glock in the sports holdall.

He suspected Terry had no idea that his wife had last been seen carrying the weapon that despatched his brother from this earth. And telling him would only confuse matters. Not to mention laying Savage open to attack as the bearer of unwelcome tidings. The young man was in a mood to murder someone himself, that was clear. If he decided that someone should be Savage, he was unlikely to be successful.

All the same, best not to inflame the situation unnecessarily.

Geoff and Terry listened in silence to his account, tense and suspicious. But he could see they believed him, perhaps because of the flash Mercedes parked a few feet away, or his unaggressive air, or simply because he didn't look like someone the Reverend Barton would employ. Though he had not had a chance to shave yet today, his chin already rough with stubble. But maybe that made his story all the more credible. A night in the cells was almost a marker of integrity.

Besides, Terry looked like he had not managed to grab much sleep himself recently. And who could sleep, with his wife and brother missing?

'Who told you about your brother?' he asked. 'That he was dead, I mean?'

'The police.'

'I thought they'd been to your house but couldn't find you?'

Terry hesitated. 'I was out looking for Dani. They pulled me over on the road.'

'You spoke to DI Paglia?'

'Who?' Terry shook his head. 'I've got a friend in the police. He knew my car. Knew about Callum too. What happened to him, I mean.'

Savage looked at the swollen, bloodied lip. 'And how did you get that?'

Again, Terry hesitated. He ran his tongue over the cut lip, wincing slightly. 'Fell down the stairs, didn't I?'

'Clumsy of you.'

'Why don't you mind your own bloody business?'

'I told you, I'm worried about Dani. Just as you should be. She is your wife, after all.'

The young man looked at Geoff again, who shrugged.

Terry swallowed. 'Dani's fine. She's staying with . . . friends.'

Savage studied his face. He was flushed now, and the way he had said *friends* had sounded more like *enemies*.

'So I was right. Barton's got her?'

Terry said nothing.

Savage asked delicately, 'What does this Barton character have on you? Why not just go up there and take her back? She's your wife, not his.'

Now the young man hung his head.

Savage looked at Geoff instead. 'Dani's your daughter, for God's sake. And she's in trouble. Don't you want to help her?'

Geoff opened his mouth, then shut it again. But there was a dark red in his face, and his eyes were tortured.

Time to try another tactic.

'Geoff, your son-in-law seems to blame you for what happened to his brother. How's that, then? Did you put the two of them together? Barton and Dani?'

That got a reaction. From both men.

'I told you, get lost!' Terry looked furious, like he was ready to throw a punch at him. 'You don't know nothing about it.'

Savage sighed. 'If I don't know nothing, then technically that means I know something,' he pointed out.

'What?'

'It's obvious you're terrified of Barton and his crew. That's why you're not willing to go up there and intervene. But how about if I help you to get Dani back?' He paused. 'I can help, you know.'

Geoff was wavering. 'He was different before. When he first arrived.'

'They always are.'

'I trusted him.'

'No one's blaming you, Geoff. This Green Chapel business . . . It's some kind of a cult, right?'

Geoff looked at Terry. Then he nodded reluctantly.

'These cult leaders are experts at deception and control. They're also very good at making you want whatever they're selling. Immortality, forgiveness, love. Even power. They project an image of utter perfection that deceives people into joining their organisation. Then they make bloody sure you can't ever leave.' Again he paused. 'Not without a fight.'

Terry was cracking. His face crumpled. 'We only wanted . . .'

'A baby?'

'Rev Barton said if she went through the ceremony, she'd get pregnant for sure. He promised. But then Dani changed her mind.'

'And Barton didn't like that.'

'He said it was too late, that we didn't have a choice. That the bargain was struck.' He stopped, writhing in self-hatred. 'I didn't know what to do. He said we had to bring him Dani straightaway, or else. Callum got all worked up. Said he was going to drive up there to confront him. Dani ran out the back of our house while I was trying to stop him.'

'And neither of them came back?'

Terry nodded, rubbing wet eyes.

'So why didn't you tell the police? That the Reverend Barton killed your brother, I mean. Or had him killed, at least.'

Terry said carefully, 'We wanted to tell them. But my mate in the police, he warned us to keep quiet. He said Barton was untouchable. That he owns top people in the police, judges, all that.'

'What top people does he own? Do you know any names?'

Terry hesitated, then opened his mouth. But before he could give Savage any names, Geoff burst out with, 'Don't tell him anything else, Terry.' He looked Savage up and down. 'Why should we trust you? Maybe you're working for Reverend Barton. Testing us, like. To see if we'll crack.'

'Do I look like one of Barton's crew?' Savage inclined his head towards the silver Mercedes. 'Does that look like a car one of his men would drive?' There was silence. He looked at the young man. 'Right, Terry, I want names. Who does he own? Unless you're happy to let Barton win?'

'I don't know names. My mate goes up there sometimes. For the meetings. But so do lots of people our age. Billy, Rose, Shaun, Chris, most of our friends at one time or another. The ones who haven't gone off to find work in Plymouth or Exeter, that is.' There was self-loathing in Terry's voice. 'And we went to the Green Chapel too. Me and Dani. It was good at first. The church stuff wasn't too heavy. And there were some cracking all-night parties. As much drink as you wanted, drugs going round on big plates like they was sandwiches, and the women ... I'd never seen women like that before. Walking about in next to nothing, sitting on your knee, real beauties too ...' He looked embarrassed. 'But that was before we realised what Barton really wanted.'

'What did he want?'

Again, Terry fell silent. But he looked ashamed.

'OK, now your brother's dead, and the Reverend Barton has taken your wife. And according to your mate in the police, the man's untouchable. Nothing you can do will make any difference. *Apparently.*' Savage looked at him hard. 'So, Terry, the real question becomes, are you willing to let all that go? To let Barton murder your brother and rape your wife? Or do you want to go up to the Green Chapel tonight, get your wife back, and do something about this American preacher?'

There was a flash of hope in Terry's face, swiftly extinguished by thought. 'Barton will never agree to let her go. Besides, we couldn't get in. He's got that huge Russian, for starters. And a dozen men or so. With guns and all. The place is a bloody fortress.'

Savage looked at Terry and Geoff, assessing their strengths and weaknesses. As he had once assessed men in the SAS. The prognosis wasn't great. He was not dealing with the cream of the crop here. Geoff was past his prime and none too fast on the uptake. Terry was younger and fitter, but afraid of his own shadow.

Nonetheless, they were the best he'd got.

'Point taken,' he said. 'So we're going to need a plan.'

CHAPTER EIGHTEEN

The Green Chapel was a vast complex surrounded by a wooden stockade fence, like some ancient hill fortress, exactly as Terry had described it.

The wooden fencing was honed to spikes, roughly six foot high, with a large gate opening onto the main track up there. The gate itself was open but guarded by a tower alongside it. There was a man on guard there, pacing the small tower top, wearing what looked like army fatigues, and armed with what looked like a rifle of some kind. A pair of binoculars hung about his neck, and he lifted them occasionally to stare out into the gloomy dusk.

Very Christian and welcoming, Savage thought, studying the man and his rifle from a distance through his own set of binoculars.

From his vantage point on the high moors opposite the stockade, Savage panned the binoculars slowly across, keeping low on his belly among scrub bushes.

There was a main house – the old farmhouse, presumably – with five vehicles parked outside. Three cars and two vans, but no sign of the sandy-coloured Land Rover Defender. Some activity there, he noted. People coming and going. Some of them had rifles slung over their shoulders, but were at ease, seemingly not expecting trouble. Or not without adequate warning. Perhaps from the guard on the gate tower.

He recognised Billy, directing people to unload one of the vans. The van did not seem to have a British number plate, but there was a large, rust-brown Springer Spaniel standing directly in front of the van, wagging its tail excitedly back and forth, so he had no chance of making it out. He couldn't see what was being unloaded, either, as the van was backed up to the large double doors of the hall, and there was no way to see properly from that angle. Billy was laughing and grinning with the other men. There was no urgency in his body language. Yet it was clear from all the activity that they were preparing for some event.

The 'special service' at twenty-one hundred hours, no doubt. The service they had been discussing on the Green Chapel Facebook page.

For someone called 'Rose'.

Who was, according to Peter, Billy's girlfriend.

A number of outbuildings surrounded the main house, some sturdy new builds, some mere dilapidated sheds with fallen-in doorways and rusting corrugated iron roofs. About a hundred feet beyond the last of those stood what looked like a long, high-roofed barn, with small, narrow windows set at intervals into thick stone walls, and a large chimney stack at one end. Set apart in a marked way, like a gathering place.

The chimney was belching greyish-white smoke into the cool spring twilight. More smoke than was entirely natural. Green or wet logs, perhaps. Though even from that distance, he could smell the smoke; it was sweet and heady, as though more than just green wood was being burnt.

He turned and whistled low, like a moorland bird call.

Terry shuffled forward through the bushes, looking pained. 'What do you see? Is Dani there?'

'I haven't seen her. And nothing's happening yet. There's a big barn with a chimney. Is that the Green Chapel?'

'That's the Green Hall. Most of the meetings are held there.'

'So where's the chapel itself?'

Terry pointed to the far end of the stockade, where it dipped out of sight of his binoculars. 'The ground falls away at the back. Like a mini-ravine? There's a kind of crack in the rocks, and the chapel's down there.' He was talking too loudly. There was a danger his voice could carry across the moor in the quiet dusk. Savage hushed him, holding up a hand, and Terry lowered his voice to a hoarse whisper. 'It's not a real chapel. It's just grass and rocks.'

'An outdoor chapel?'

'That's right.'

A memory stirred in him from an old Middle English poem, 'Sir Gawain and the Green Knight': *And ouergrowen with gresse in glodes aywhere, And al watʒ holʒ inwith, nobot an olde caue, Or a creuisse of an olde cragge.* Riding through wilderness for months, Gawain had finally reached the infamous 'Chapel in the Green', and was disappointed to find nothing but a rocky crevice among the crags, overgrown with grass and hollow inside like an old cave.

He trained his binoculars on the far end of the stockade. But as with Gawain, there was nothing to see there. Not in this poor light, at least. Only a shadowy gleam of exposed rocks, and then darkness.

Savage signalled Terry to back up, then shuffled out of the bushes backwards after him, keeping low on his belly. Once they were out of sight of the guard on the stockade tower, he scrambled back down the slope to where Geoff was waiting with his rusting tractor. That had been the only mode of transport possible without approaching by road, where they would have been too easily visible.

He was glad Faith was not there.

She had used her mobile to book a local hotel – from Terry's description a glorified pub with a few rooms, situated just off the moorland road – and retreated there for a shower and a sleep. Faith was game for most things, what his father might have called 'a good sport', but even she was unlikely to be up for a spot of breaking and entering. Not when getting caught could mean an end to her legal career.

Whereas Savage had little left to lose.

Geoff was smoking, the red end of his cigarette a fiery point in the dusk. He dropped the cigarette to the ground as they appeared, crushing it under his wellington boot.

'Well?' He sounded nervous.

'You were right to bring me here.' Savage patted the binoculars round his neck. 'And thanks for these. I got a pretty good look at the place. There's a guard on the gate, and probably more inside. They're gearing up for something. The nine o'clock service mentioned on the Facebook page, I expect.'

'Guards?'

'Nothing I didn't expect.' He paused. 'I saw Billy unloading crates from a van. What's that about?'

'Don't rightly know.' Geoff looked shifty. 'Food supplies, most like. There's a handsome number of 'em in there. And they all need food and drink.'

Savage could tell he was lying. Or not telling the whole truth, at any rate. But he let it go. He had other things to worry about than the contents of a van.

'So what's the plan?' Terry asked.

'I want to get a closer look at this Green Chapel. That's where this so-called healing happens, isn't it?'

'I guess so.'

'Is it guarded?'

Geoff and Terry glanced at each other.

Terry said, 'I don't think so. No one goes there except during ceremonies.'

'So what's the big hall for?'

'They meet in the hall before a special service and Barton gives a sermon. About following the old ways.'

Savage frowned. 'The old ways? What old ways?'

'I don't know. I never understood half of what he said. All New Age mumbo-jumbo about eco-warriors and the Green Man, that kind of stuff. Then he takes the bride down to the spring.' When Savage raised his eyebrows, Terry stumbled on with his explanation, looking uncomfortable. 'There's a spring under the hall. Like a well, you know. It's been there forever.'

'The hall was built over it,' Geoff said, interrupting. 'Specially, like.'

'That's right, it was.' Terry looked more confident. 'Barton calls it the Sacred Spring because it's meant to be holy water, or something. "Pure from the source," he always says. Only he's the only one allowed down there. Him and the big Russian. Anyway, he takes the bride down there and anoints her with the water.'

'Bride?'

'That's what she's called. The woman that's got a fertility problem. She's the bride.'

'So who's the bridegroom?'

Terry bared his teeth. 'Barton, of course.'

'OK,' Savage said, deciding not to press that sore point. 'So the ceremony starts off in the big hall. Then what?'

'Once it's dark enough, everyone walks down to the Green Chapel in a procession. It's an open-air chapel, just rocks and stuff. They light flaming torches. Barton goes first, then the bride, then everyone else.'

'Why flaming torches?'

'Barton calls it the Flame of Life. Says it's part of the healing process. Like going down to the sacred spring.'

Geoff nodded. 'Earth and water,' he said helpfully, 'then fire and air. That's what the whole ceremony's for. Barton calls it . . .' He hesitated.

'Summoning the elements,' Terry finished for him.

'That's it. Summoning the elements.'

Terry had not been far off the truth when he called it New Age mumbo-jumbo, Savage thought. This special service sounded very much like an elaborate smokescreen for something else. But he decided to keep that conclusion to himself. It was clear these two believed Barton to be genuine, if deluded, in his beliefs.

'So how does it work once they get into the Green Chapel?' Both men looked at him blankly in the gloom. 'The fertility treatment, or whatever it is.'

Geoff shuffled his feet and hung his head.

Terry looked away.

'Come on, one of you has to tell me the rest.' Savage held out the binoculars to Geoff. 'Here, these are yours.'

'Keep them. I hardly ever use them.'

'Thanks.' He hung them round his neck again. 'Come on, Geoff, let's hear it. I presume there's an altar in the open-air chapel?'

Geoff nodded.

'And does the bride have to lie on this altar, by any chance?' When Geoff nodded again, he said, 'With or without her clothes on?'

'Without.'

'Right. Yes, I think I get the picture.' He glanced at Terry, who was still staring at the rocky ground, shame-faced. 'So, does everyone get to watch this "special service"?'

'The congregation have to watch the first part, where the bride is taken to the altar. Then they get led back to the hall until it's over. Only Barton and the bride stay in the chapel, and sometimes the big Russian too, if . . .'

'If the bride's unwilling?'

Terry nodded. 'But everyone knows what's going on, even if they can't see. Everyone can *hear*.'

'Presumably that's why Dani ran. She changed her mind, didn't she? Dani decided that she didn't want to be his bride.' Terry did not answer, but there was guilt in his face. Savage looked back at Geoff instead. 'Only nobody wanted to cross Barton and help her escape. Am I right?'

Geoff dragged off his flat cap, ran a hand through his short grey hair, then fitted the cap back in place. 'You don't understand. It wasn't that simple. We all take a share in what the chapel brings in. That was the arrangement from the start.'

'A share? What do you mean?'

'Barton said people would pay for the treatment. Rich people. Americans. And they do. They come here and pay through the nose, and we all get a share.'

'Who's "we"?'

'Those of us within a few miles or so of the Green Chapel.' Geoff shrugged, his tone defensive. 'There's not much of a living up here on the high moors. The chapel share keeps our farms going.' He raised his chin. 'And most of them women get pregnant. It works. It really works.' He hesitated. 'But in return . . .'

'In return you have to keep quiet about *how* it really works. Not with holy water and prayers, but Barton having his way with these women. Am I right?'

'The Reverend says . . .'

'Yes?'

'Special seed.' Geoff's voice lowered to a whisper, as though afraid the men in the stockade could hear them. 'That's what he's got. He told us when he arrived and set up the chapel. Special seed from God.'

Savage threw back his head and laughed. 'Special seed from God?'

The two men were silent.

'And you believed him? Seriously?'

CHAPTER NINETEEN

'It works,' Geoff repeated, his face set in stubborn lines. 'Women get pregnant. Women who couldn't get pregnant before. And not just rich Americans. Our women too. Some locals are chosen to get the treatment for free.'

'Whether the woman likes it or not.'

Nobody spoke.

They believed the 'treatment' was real, even if the whole thing was impossible. There was nothing supernatural going on here. Men making money from people's fears was one of the oldest con tricks in the world.

But there was no point offending them.

Savage looked up at the sky. It was nearly dark. 'You said it works. That these women get pregnant. Every time?'

Geoff said reluctantly, 'Not every time, no. But that's just the way of it, Barton says. You can't get what you want every time.'

'How many times, then? How often?'

'I don't know.'

'As a percentage?'

'I told you, I don't know. Nobody knows. Barton keeps that kind of information to himself. But them rich women, they keep coming back for more treatments. Month after month, sometimes.'

'Is he good-looking?'

Geoff stared, baffled. 'Who?'

'The Reverend Barton. Is he an attractive man?'

'How would I know?'

Savage looked at Terry. 'Is he good-looking?'

Terry struggled in silence for a moment, disgust on his face. At last, he shrugged, muttering, 'Some women might say so, I suppose.'

'Did Dani say so?'

'Sod off.' Terry glared at him, angry then. 'She ran away, didn't she? You said it yourself. In the end, she couldn't go through with it.'

'Your brother tried to help her, didn't he?'

'I told Callum not to come up here. Stupid, stubborn bastard. But he was set on it.' His voice wobbled. 'Said he was going to tell Barton once and for all to keep his filthy hands off our women.'

'Only someone shot him.'

Terry said nothing. He looked away, and ran his sleeve across his cheek. It was hard to tell in the thickening dark, but Savage guessed that he was crying.

'Do you know who killed your brother?' he asked softly.

Terry stayed silent.

'Do you think it might have been Barton himself?'

'What, do his own dirty work?' Terry's mouth twitched in contempt. 'Not him. One of his men, most like. That big Russian, maybe.'

'Swanney?'

'That's what they call him, yes.' Terry eyed him with sudden suspicion. 'You know a lot about it. For a stranger, I mean.'

'Not really.'

'You've met Big Swanney though?' Geoff had turned the tractor headlights on, since it was getting so dark they could hardly see their hands in front of their faces. Now he turned, staring at Savage with the same narrow-eyed look as his son-in-law. 'How's that, then? Mike's always about the place, sticking his nose into other people's business. But the Russian . . . He don't come out of the stockade too often.'

They were beginning to doubt him.

Briefly, Savage told them about his encounter with Mike Cooper and the others in the Land Rover Defender. He explained how he and Peter had wanted to avoid a fight, but it had been forced on them.

The two men nodded, understanding in their eyes. They looked grimly pleased at the description of him breaking Billy's nose. Possibly in two places. They listened intently to what Mike Cooper had told him. And they admitted to knowing Peter up at Rowlands Farm, but it was clear they didn't have much to do with him.

Peter had always been a loner though.

In fact, he was still a loner.

Savage had tried to ring the farm several times since leaving the police station, but there was no answer. Peter was probably out on the moors, or about the farm. He had a mobile, but wasn't answering that either. So he'd been unable to ask if Peter could put him up for a night or two. He didn't like asking. It felt awkward. But it was only until he got his camper van back from the forensics team. Assuming they found nothing.

'So how did you get that?' Savage nodded to Terry's cut lip and bruised cheek, even more sickly-looking in the bright gleam of the tractor lights. 'The truth this time.'

'When I realised Dani had gone too, I knew at once where she'd be. That she'd followed him up to the Green Chapel. She probably thought she could persuade him to come back.' He swallowed. 'Callum was like her own little brother, you see. Dani doted on him.'

Savage nodded, remembering how distressed and scared

Dani had been when he found her in that lay-by. She must have just come from witnessing her brother-in-law's murder.

'I caught up with him at the entrance gate. He was yelling and shouting the odds at Mike Cooper. Threatening to call the police.'

'Where was Dani?'

'He said they'd taken her inside. Callum was wild, I'd never seen him so angry. Billy was furious too. He decked Callum, so I . . . I decked him. Then everyone started laying into the two of us.' Terry touched his split lip, and winced. 'That's when Barton came out, with Big Swanney behind him.'

'Barton stopped the fight?'

'He said we were hooligans, that we'd interrupted his prayers. Callum told Barton to get out. To leave Dartmoor and never come back, or he'd tell the papers what the Reverend had been up to.'

Geoff looked uncomfortable.

'I told Callum to shut up,' Terry continued, 'but he wasn't in a mood to listen. He was out of control. It took three of Barton's men to hold him down.'

'What happened?'

'I didn't want Dani to get into trouble, so . . .' Terry fell silent.

'So you walked away.'

'Only because Barton said he wanted to talk to Callum,' Terry said quickly. 'Alone.' He shook his head. 'He said he was going to explain everything, and that after that, Callum would understand. How was I to know Barton was planning to kill him?'

Savage decided it was dark enough.

'Right,' he said, 'I'm going in.'

They looked at him blankly.

'Going in where?' Terry asked.

'In there.' He nodded towards the fortress-like stockade, its fencing rising unseen behind them. 'The Green Chapel.'

'What?' Geoff looked horrified.

'You heard me. And in case I don't get back tonight,' he said, getting out his mobile, 'let's swap phone numbers.'

Dani wasn't his responsibility. No argument there. But Savage had been last to see her before she disappeared, and he wanted to satisfy himself that she wasn't being held against her will. Which she almost certainly was. But making sure was important.

Besides he was curious to get a glimpse of this Barton character. What kind of man went about the place impregnating women in the name of God?

CHAPTER TWENTY

Savage soon saw why the stockade fencing was not as high and impenetrable at the back as the front. The ground to the rear of the Green Chapel compound formed its own barrier against intruders. First came a thicket of spiny shrubs he could not identify in the darkness. After tearing his way through them, he found himself walking with even more difficulty as the slope grew steeper and more hazardous. Long, matted clumps of moorland grass concealed outcrops of rock, sharp to the touch and split by fissures, all of which slowed his progress. Eventually though, he reached a stretch of low wire fencing, designed more to keep out wandering sheep than people. As though to confirm this, several damp wisps of white wool clung to the wire where sheep had rubbed themselves against the fence.

A few judicious kicks lowered the fence to where he could easily climb over it. Having done this, he stood a moment and listened.

On approaching the rear of the stockade, he'd heard occasional bursts of singing from within, as though a door into the great hall had been opened and then rapidly closed. But the singing had stopped now. A mist had begun to creep up through the grassy rocks, masking the upper slopes of the Green Chapel and deadening sounds from above. The air was damp and chill, despite the bright spring day they had enjoyed earlier,

The silence was eerie.

There was a rocky fissure above, with some kind of misty light above it. Outdoor lanterns? Scrambling up through the gap, Savage emerged on a rough, flat area of grass bordered by shrubs and low trees.

Was this the Green Chapel?

Odds were good that it was. There was a long granite slab, supported by two stone plinths, set in the centre of the clearing and lit by four lanterns on poles, with thick, church-style candles burning in each. Possibly an outdoor altar, though it was unadorned and looked too low. Unless Barton was a very short man, five foot or thereabouts, it would involve a lot of stooping during services. Not terribly good for the back. Besides, it was more bed height, by Savage's reckoning. Which suggested this was where the deed was done when women came to the Reverend Barton with infertility problems.

He strolled up to the granite slab and examined it. The stone was about five and a half feet long, ancient, cracked across at one end, and pitted with tiny indentations. It didn't look particularly comfortable.

He grinned.

Maybe Barton brought cushions, though. Or at least a pillow for the lady.

Suddenly, there were noises from above. Voices penetrated the quiet, misty air. Not speaking though. They were chanting. And in Latin.

There was an acrid taste of smoke on the air too.

Something was burning.

For a wild moment, Savage was suspicious that the Reverend Barton was burning someone at the stake for witchcraft. But it was nothing so barbaric. Seconds later, the night sky lit up with flickering torchlight, its orange glow deepening as what was clearly a ceremonial procession drew closer to the outdoor chapel.

Savage hesitated.

He had hoped to encounter Barton and his 'bride' alone. That would have been the simplest scenario. But given that a large number of people were heading in his direction, by the sound of their footsteps, it was probably best to be cautious.

Heading back towards the fissure in the rocks, Savage ducked behind a spiny hawthorn tree. From his vantage point, he could see the mouth of the path leading from the buildings above. He'd moved out of sight just in time too. As he crouched down below the hawthorn, a man in an ankle-length red robe came into view, holding aloft a burning torch.

Could this be Barton?

Not much of a looker if he was. This guy was bald and stockily-built, with a baby-face not helped by a faint ring of stubble.

Somehow he had envisaged the charismatic alternative priest rather differently.

Then others came, chanting and filling the small clearing with light and noise. More flaming torches, more people in red robes. Or no robes at all, but everyday clothes. People huddled up against the chill of the mist, wrapped in hoodies and jackets, staring about themselves with pale faces and wide, superstitious eyes.

And in the middle of this throng came a veiled woman.

This had to be the bride.

No red robe.

But no everyday clothes either.

The woman was wearing a gossamer-thin robe. Some silky, transparent material that clung like parachute silk to every curve of her body.

Underneath, she was naked.

And gorgeous.

Savage did not want to stare. But it was inevitable. And he

was not the only one. All the men there were stealing covert, sideways looks at this stunning young woman, standing more or less naked among them. Naked, that is, except for a bare scrap of see-through material, more cling-film than robe. He was hard-wired to stare, given the circumstances. Beautiful naked woman in front of him? Brain says, stare. Among other, even less politically correct responses.

Besides, it was also about intelligence gathering.

The 'bride' was in her early twenties. And not Dani, by his guess. Dani's build was slight, almost boyish. This woman had a nipped-in waist, but generously proportioned hips.

This must be Billy's girl, he reckoned.

Rose.

He could see Billy now. Bandaged nose, bandaged knuckles, following the small group shuffling into an untidy pack towards the left of the clearing, all of them in ordinary clothes. They seemed to be separating out from the men in red robes and carrying torches. The ones chanting in Latin.

'. . . *benedixitque illis Deus et ait crescite et multiplicamini et replete terram . . .*'

It was a familiar piece of scripture, straight out of the start of the Book of Genesis, and easy enough to translate from the Latin Vulgate edition of the Bible.

Savage knew it off by heart, thanks to his father's zealous insistence that he attend the parish church's Sunday Club every week from a tender age until he was old enough to be packed off to boarding school, where he learnt even more biblical verses, only this time in Latin, as well as any number of what his mother, who had been a closet Catholic, would have called venial sins.

And God blessed them, and said unto them, 'Be fruitful, and multiply, and replenish the earth . . .'

Billy stood, not chanting, towards the far edge of this pack of non-robed onlookers, who made up the congregation, presumably. He did not look happy, and not just because his nose had been well and truly broken. His hands were pushed deep into the pockets of his padded jacket, and his body was tense, like a coiled spring, ready for action. He reminded Savage of men waiting for the order to attack.

Billy wasn't doing anything though.

Except staring.

And not at Rose, like all the other awestruck men there.

Billy was staring at the dark mouth of the path up to the stockade, as if waiting for someone to appear.

The chanting, which had continued throughout this strange, shuffling assembly in the clearing, abruptly stopped. The crowd stirred, also turning to look at the path. Billy looked even more tense, if that were possible. The bride did not move, the only one there who was looking the other way. Rose did not look any happier to be there than Billy. Her hands were twisting together in tiny, nervous movements in front of her chest, her veiled head turned towards the long, low jut of the granite slab, whatever function it served there. Barton's altar/bed. The latter didn't really bear thinking about. Yet what else could it be, given what Terry and Geoff had told him?

Silence fell.

A hooded man in a green robe appeared at the mouth of the path, holding a flaming torch, and halted there, smiling at the congregation.

The veiled bride stiffened in the silence. Her clasped and twisting hands stilled, and her chest suddenly stopped rising and falling, as though she were holding her breath.

Fear, almost certainly.

Savage tore his gaze from Rose and studied the newcomer instead.

The man in the green robe was at least six foot tall, maybe slightly taller. He was white and in his early thirties. The robe aside, he looked like a possible former rugby player, with broad shoulders, broad chest, and a ruddy complexion. Plus the kind of swaggering, wide-legged confidence as he walked that suggested not only natural authority, but incredible health and vitality too.

No, not confidence.

Arrogance.

The man pushed back his green hood, and curly fair hair sprang free above a high, smooth forehead like the head of some Greek god. His eyes were brilliant blue, large and expressive, shining in the torchlight.

This had to be the Reverend Barton.

'Where is she?' he called out in a southern American drawl, his voice strong and deep. He repeated the question, and the three words rang about the clearing, bouncing off the mist with a faintly sibilant echo. Then he asked, his tone ritualistic, 'Where is my bride?'

Nobody moved or spoke.

Rose gave a muffled sob, then began breathing again, her chest heaving, her whole body visibly shaking.

Barton held out his flaming torch to the nearest red-robed man, who stepped forward smartly, taking it with deference. The Reverend stood straight in the long green robe and spread his arms wide, everything about him bold and magnanimous, and somehow theatrical.

'Let my bride be brought to the Green Altar,' he insisted, raising his voice along with his arms, 'that she may receive the gift of new life.'

Two of the men in red robes moved at once, heading for Rose. Each man took one of her arms and led her to the granite altar stone. Rose did not resist at first, walking as though in a trance. But she began to struggle when they tried to lay her down on her back on the stone slab, her panting cries audible in the silence.

Which was when Savage decided they'd had enough fun.

CHAPTER TWENTY-ONE

Savage stepped out of hiding.

'Hello,' he said.

Everyone turned to stare, including Barton, who frowned and lowered his arms. Rose stopped struggling briefly, then kicked out even harder. No doubt she was hoping the cavalry had arrived. Or, in this case, a lone infantry man.

'Bit of a damp evening to be out of doors. Especially in those robes, I'd imagine.' Savage strolled towards the altar, studying Barton's 'bride' with feigned interest. 'Am I interrupting a wedding ceremony? Sorry about that. The bride doesn't look too keen though.' He stopped in front of the two red-robed men, who were still holding tight onto the struggling woman. 'Rose, isn't it?'

Rose stopped struggling at the sound of her name, then her head jerked sharply.

'I'll take that as a yes.'

Out of the corner of his eye, Savage saw Billy start forward, presumably intending to get his revenge for last time they'd met. That bandaged nose looked painful, he had to admit.

'What the hell do you think you're doing?' Billy said, baring his teeth. 'You can't be here. This is our place.'

Reverend Barton held up a hand, and Billy fell silent. 'No need for anyone to get upset, Billy. It's just a momentary interruption, that's all.' He studied Savage intently. 'Is this the gentleman you were telling me about?'

Gentleman?

That's a first, Savage thought.

Billy clearly thought so too, his face screwed up with contempt. Nonetheless, he grunted his assent.

'Well,' Barton said, his southern drawl intensified, 'I'm sure Mr Savage isn't here to interfere. He merely wants to know what's going on. Isn't that so, Mr Savage?'

'In a manner of speaking.' Savage studied the man in much the same way he himself was being studied. 'So you're Barton?'

'*Reverend* Barton, please.'

'No offence, but does that title come with a certificate? Do you have to pass an exam to be called a Reverend? Three years in a cult seminary or something? I'm asking for a friend.'

Barton said nothing.

Keeping one eye on Billy, in case he decided to make another fight of it, Savage turned his attention back to the two men in red robes. To his surprise, they weren't ashamed to have been discovered manhandling a woman against her will. Part of their job description as henchmen in red robes, presumably. They did seem baffled by his appearance though. He guessed strangers didn't often penetrate the fortified stockade.

Though the unfortunate Callum had pushed his way in, hadn't he?

And ended up dead.

'All right, lads?' He smiled at both men, deliberately cheerful, and then nodded to their unhappy prisoner. 'Why don't you let her go? I'm no expert on pre-wedding nerves, but it looks like Rose may have changed her mind.'

'Get lost,' one of them growled at him.

The other looked towards Barton, who hesitated, then nodded his permission. The man released Rose's arm, and was followed, with obvious reluctance, by the other guy.

'Here you go,' Savage said to Rose, taking her arm to help

her up off the stone altar. She stumbled, seeming weak and disorientated, but he caught her before she fell. Wanting to see her face, Savage removed the veil and threw it aside. She shrank from him at first, then seemed to notice that he wasn't leering at her. No doubt that was unusual in this place. Billy snarled somewhere behind him, but Savage ignored him, keeping his gaze on Rose's face.

'You OK?' he asked.

'Yes, thank you.' Her voice was a whisper. She looked up at him, intensely pale, her eyes red-rimmed. 'Though I do feel a bit . . .'

Rose dropped abruptly to her knees, retching violently.

'That's right.' Savage crouched beside her, touching her shoulder. Just a light touch. Enough to reassure her that she wasn't alone. 'Get it all out of your system. There's no hurry.'

She shuddered, not looking up. Her body convulsed again, one long spasm of horror and disgust.

Savage straightened, meeting Barton's fixed stare. He was so angry, it was hard not to let it show. But the most important thing was to get Rose out of there and to safety.

'What did you give her?'

'Give her?' Barton pretended not to understand. 'What are you suggesting? Like you said, pre-wedding nerves. She's a nervous bride, that's all.' His smile was benign. Indulgent, even. 'Excited, but nervous.'

Savage suppressed his desire to break Barton's nose too.

'I'm taking her out of here,' he said.

Barton smiled then. 'And how do you intend to manage that?' He looked mildly about at the people watching them. 'The numbers aren't quite on your side.' He paused. 'Though that didn't stop you and Peter Rowlands, did it?'

Savage stilled, watching Barton. He didn't like the way he had said Peter's name. With an implied threat.

'Unusual of Peter to intervene in my business,' Barton

continued smoothly. 'Unusual and not altogether intelligent. No doubt he wanted to impress his friend. I only wish I'd been there to stop things before they went too far, and my boy Billy here got hurt. Fighting is just so . . . unnecessary.'

'Not always.'

'Well, you would say that. You're an ex-soldier, aren't you? Not just some blue-blood with a silver spoon up his ass.' Barton looked about at his followers, some of whom sniggered as though on cue. He quirked a smile, and then gave a shrug. For their benefit, presumably. 'Y'all have to forgive my vulgarity. I wasn't born into privilege like Mr Savage here.'

Savage kept quiet.

Barton studied him thoughtfully. 'Yes, I looked you up. You're not hard to find online. That's quite a career you've had. Rugby School. Oxford. The British Army. SAS. Officer class, of course. Only the best for the British aristocracy.' His mouth twisted. 'Which tells me you know a thing or two about strategy. Battle tactics, and all. That there are always times when retreat is a better option than advancing.' When Savage said nothing, he went on, 'This is one of those times, Mr Savage. If you leave this place now, nobody will try to stop you. You're a free man and the United Kingdom, so I'm told, is a free country. But you're not taking Rose with you.'

'Because she's not free?'

'Because she's mine.'

Billy made a noise under his breath at that bold statement, but did not contradict the Reverend.

Right on cue, Savage's phone rang, loud in the silence.

Everyone looked at each other.

Then at Barton.

Then at him.

'That sounds like my phone.' Shrugging as though embarrassed, Savage dragged his phone out of his back pocket. The screen was lit up with one word. He answered the call, mouthing to Barton, 'Sorry, this'll only take a moment.'

'Aubrey?'

Faith sounded breathless. But he could tell she had not only received but understood the text he had sent while still lurking behind the hawthorn bush.

'Hi, Faith. Can I hand you over to the Rev?'

He threw the mobile to Barton, who caught it one-handed, looked at it suspiciously, then put the phone to his ear.

'Hello? Who is this?' Barton stiffened at the reply, then listened in silence for a moment. He threw the phone back to Savage as though it had stung him, his face furious. Then the Reverend took a step back, raising his voice. 'Friends, it seems Mr Savage will be leaving us. Billy, perhaps you and Mike could escort him to the gate?'

Billy's lip curled again. But he didn't argue.

From the back of the crowd of onlookers, Mike Cooper appeared, a smart wedding-guest shirt dragged down over his large belly. One of the robed men handed him a flaming torch, and he held it at arm's length, blinking at the brightness and heat, clearly uncomfortable.

Savage looked down at Rose. 'Want to get out of here?'

She did not even look at Billy.

'Yes.'

'Come on, then.' Savage got Rose carefully to her feet, then hooked a supportive arm about her waist. Billy looked ready to kill him, but still said nothing. 'That's it. Now, lean on me. One step at a time, nice and easy does it.' With a reluctant Mike Cooper leading the way, they began to walk up the steep slope back to the main buildings. Billy brought up the rear, walking lightly, a few steps behind them the whole way. The others watched their progress, a few muttering, most standing silent and astonished. He could feel Rose shaking, and said quietly in her ear, 'It's OK. No one's going to stop us.'

Her head turned towards him, eyes wide. 'Barton won't let us go.' Her voice was a whisper, meant only for him. 'You don't know him.'

Savage glanced back.

The men in red robes were following Billy, and the others had fallen in behind them. He could not see Reverend Barton, but guessed he was unlikely to leave the Green Chapel. Not immediately. It would be too much of a personal defeat for his followers to see him bringing up the rear in a procession like this.

Unless he intended to have them jumped before they reached the gate.

No, Faith's phone call had taken Barton by surprise. That much had been obvious. With more time to plan, the Reverend could probably have found a way round the situation. He was cunning, good at finding solutions. But not caught off balance like that, suddenly faced with exposure of his personal fiefdom for what it really was. A man like Barton would loathe and fear the glare of outside interest, and do anything to avoid it.

Even if it meant relinquishing a prize like Rose.

Besides, Billy might not enjoy seeing his girl being taken away by the man who had broken his nose. But secretly, part of him had to be glad, even if he was hiding that right now, afraid of a confrontation with Barton.

'He'll let us go,' he said confidently.

But Rose did not believe him. She shook her head almost imperceptibly, looking paler than ever in the misty torchlight.

'Trust me, OK?' Savage gave her a quick smile. It probably wasn't a very comforting smile. But it was all he had under the circumstances. 'I'm sure you know who I am by now. But we haven't been properly introduced. I'm Savage.'

Again, the wide-eyed look.

'Aubrey,' he added.

If anything, her eyes widened. 'That's a girl's name.'

'So they used to tell me in the army. Most days, in fact. But sadly, they were wrong. It's a boy's name.' He risked another smile. 'I'm living proof.'

They had reached the main compound. More people spilled out of the hall to stare at them. Faces appeared at the lit-up windows of the old farmhouse to stare at them. Mostly older women, younger men, children. The kind who would be unlikely to act as witnesses to the ceremonies of the Green Chapel. No doubt someone there had been alerted by a phone call from Barton, or one of those following Savage and Rose.

Nobody tried to stop them.

They were nearly at the stockade gate, which stood closed. There were two men waiting by a vehicle parked right in front of it, their faces lit up by its headlights. It was the same battered, sand-coloured Land Rover Defender he and Peter had met on the moorland road.

One of the men was cradling a shotgun. Another was holding a large axe in both hands, like he'd been called away from chopping wood. A third, unseen man was perched on the front passenger seat of the Land Rover, long legs outside the vehicle, torso inside, the door yawning open in the darkness. As Savage and Rose approached the gate behind a silent Mike Cooper, the legs shifted, the door opened to its full extent, and a huge figure reared up out of the Land Rover.

Big Swanney.

Rose gave a gasp, almost stopping at the sight of him. 'Oh my God. Not him. Not the Russian.'

'Don't stop. It's OK.'

Savage, his arm still about her, gave Rose a quick reassuring squeeze, and they continued walking towards the gate. But it was slow progress now. She kept trying to pull back, shaking her head.

'That's Swanney. You won't get past him.'

'Leave him to me.'

'He's huge.' Her whisper was frantic 'What are you going to do?'

'Whatever it takes.'

Rose stared at him. 'They've got guns.'

Ahead of them, Mike Cooper had a mobile phone to his ear now. He was nodding, listening, but saying nothing in return. He stopped to let them pass, then took Billy aside, muttering something in his ear.

'Having a gun isn't the same as using it,' Savage said, glancing about the compound. 'Trust me, Rose, we're leaving and nobody's going to stop us. I won't let them keep you here.'

'But Big Swanney . . . Look at the size of him.'

'Size isn't everything.' He quirked an eyebrow. 'Or so I've been informed.'

Savage wasn't looking at the Russian anymore though. He'd turned his head to scour the windows of the old farmhouse, hunting for one face in particular. And found it, at last, at one of the highest windows, narrow and dimly-lit. An attic room?

There was a man there too, looking down at him.

A man he recognised.

Then Big Swanney took a step forward.

Savage looked round at once, on alert. The huge man lurched rather than walked, his upper half moving substantially after his leading foot, the whole structure swaying precariously. From the look on his face, it was obvious he had something to say to them.

Savage had never heard the Russian speak. He was curious to know what he sounded like. He imagined some great booming voice floating down to them, like a prophet speaking out of rolling clouds . . .

The reality was very different.

'Let the girl go.' Big Swanney's Russian accent was exactly as expected, yes. Clipped and guttural at the same time. But there was no great booming voice to accompany his enormous frame. He spoke in more of a whisper, though perfectly audible, the whole effect somehow theatrical on the dark, misty air. A stage whisper, in fact. A Russian stage whisper. And he repeated those four words in exactly the same intonation, as though following a script. 'Let the girl go, and nobody needs get hurt.'

Savage stopped in front of the three men, keeping Rose slightly behind him. He was about to try out his rusty smattering of Russian when Mike Cooper intervened, both hands in the air like he was surrendering.

Probably just as well, since the only Russian phrase that had come perfectly to his mind had something to do with goats. He'd encountered a Russian goat farmer once, while on deployment in Afghanistan, and there'd been this long, heated discussion about the man's mangy-looking livestock . . .

'The Rev wants them untouched,' Cooper told the huge Russian, craning his neck to look up at him. He sounded nervous. 'Just open the gate, OK? Barton's orders.'

Savage looked at Big Swanney expectantly.

There was a pause.

Big Swanney seemed baffled. No doubt he was wondering why his boss didn't simply order him to crush this interfering stranger. He scratched his head and studied first Mike Cooper, then Savage himself. Having exhausted his thoughts on the matter, he tilted his head at a sharp angle to look down at the man with the shotgun.

'Gate,' he said shortly.

To Savage's ears, the single truncated syllable sounded a bit like 'goat'.

The man with the shotgun appeared to understand him though. He shrugged, and nodded to his mate, who sloped reluctantly towards the gate to open it.

A four-man order. Henchman hierarchy in action, Savage thought. One man to take the boss's call, another to issue the order, a third to mediate it, and down at the bottom of the pecking order, a fourth man carried it out. With an axe in hand.

The man with the shotgun threw his weapon into the front of the Land Rover Defender, turned on the engine, revved it hard and loud like a boy racer, then backed up out of the way of the opening gate.

Big Swanney watched this procedure in silence. His large lower lip began to quiver. It rose to cover the upper lip, and then his whole chin squashed upwards, his eyes squinting at the same time. Like he was sulking.

The gate was nearly fully open now.

Mike Cooper looked relieved that everything had been achieved without violence. His gaze met Savage's. 'Go on, then. You wanted out, you've got out. No need to hang about over it.' His gaze flicked to Rose, suddenly resentful. 'This isn't the end though, Rose. You swore an oath, remember? He won't let that go.'

Swore an oath? To Billy, presumably.

Savage looked round, but Billy had disappeared. That didn't bode well for his relationship with Rose. He wasn't even there to see his girl taken away by a stranger. Unless he'd decided he couldn't bear to watch. Or perhaps he didn't give a monkey's. Billy had been prepared to do nothing in the Green Chapel while Barton impregnated her, if Savage was right about what this 'wedding' ceremony entailed.

Then he recalled that the young couple weren't married, unlike Dani and Terry.

So what oath was Mike Cooper talking about?

There was a car waiting on the narrow track outside the gate, facing away from the stockade. The front passenger door was standing open in invitation. Its engine purred, headlights streaming away into the misty darkness.

It was a silver Mercedes.

Perfect timing.

Not least because the man with the shotgun was climbing back out of the Land Rover, already tooled up again, and Big Swanney was only a few feet away, staring at them both with a look of brooding intensity.

Savage made for the Mercedes, Rose's hand still trembling in his, just as a familiar voice growled through the open passenger door, 'Aubrey? Get a bloody move on, would you? I'm like a sitting duck here.'

CHAPTER TWENTY-TWO

Savage bundled Rose into the back of the Mercedes, then jumped in the front. Faith took off before he had even pulled the passenger door shut.

'Don't ever do that to me again,' Faith said, accelerating fast away from the stockade, and craning over the wheel to peer through thickening white mist. 'I was in bed, Aubrey. In bloody bed!'

'Sorry about that, darling.'

'And who's this?' She shot a rapid glance over her shoulder at Rose. 'Another of your waifs and strays?'

'This is Rose.' Savage turned to give Rose a reassuring smile. He could barely see her face in the dark interior of the car but knew how badly she'd been on edge. The last thing he wanted was for her to wrongly believe she'd escaped from one set of grim bastards only to land herself with another. 'Rose, this is Faith. An excellent lawyer, and an old friend of mine from uni days. She sounds tetchy, but that's only because I texted her at an awkward moment.'

'Don't presume too much on that friendship, Aubrey,' Faith said. 'Especially not when you ask me to drive out into the bloody middle of nowhere when I've just got into my pyjamas.'

He studied her. Thankfully, she had changed back into day clothes before heading out into the night. 'I'm really very grateful, Faith,' he said. 'I wasn't sure you'd find it.'

'I can read a map.'

'Of course you can. You're a star. Thank you for saving me from a very difficult situation.' He could see Faith was angry, but was too curious not to ask, 'What did you say to Barton?'

'I told him I had photos of everything he'd been doing at the Green Chapel, and my finger was on the Send button to the newspapers. Unless he let you go.'

He laughed. 'I wish we had photos. Some of those outfits . . . They deserve to be on the front page.'

'Don't act the fool, Aubrey.'

'Sorry.' But he was still grinning as he looked round at Rose, sitting silent in the back seat. 'I'm glad you were able to help Rose though. You don't want to know what would have happened if we hadn't got her out of there.'

'We?'

He could tell by her voice that Faith was calming down.

'I'd call it a team effort, yes. Especially the all-important getaway. Walking into the mist would have been a lot less easy to pull off than driving away at speed in this extremely comfortable Mercedes.' He touched Faith's arm briefly. 'Without your phone call, there's no way Barton would have let either of us go.'

'Now you're being melodramatic.'

'They had guns.'

Faith slammed on the brakes, and not simply because the narrow road ahead was twisting in a tight left-hand bend. She turned her head to stare at him, breathing fast. 'Excuse me? What do you mean, *they had guns*?'

'Maybe a rifle on the gate. And at least one double-barrelled shotgun.'

'A shotgun? Are you sure?'

'I know a double-barrelled shotgun when it's being pointed at my head, yes.' She continued to stare at him. Savage glanced back at the distant glow from the stockade. 'Keep driving, OK? This would be a bad moment to stop.'

She drove on automatically, but her face was distracted.

'They have other guns as well,' he added, 'according to local rumour, but that was the only weapon I had eyes on. I'm aware of one other gun in particular, though I didn't see it tonight. A handgun. Almost certainly the same one used to shoot the young man whose death the police just tried to pin on me.'

'Legally-held weapons?'

'The shotgun's probably legit. For rabbiting and keeping down vermin. At least, that will be the official line. They may have several shotguns among the community. Maybe the odd air rifle. I imagine the rest are illegal.' He checked behind them, but nobody seemed to be following. 'The handgun will be, for sure.'

'But they're in the middle of nowhere. Why have guns?'

'To enforce Barton's rule there?'

'You make him sound like a king.'

'He's not far off that, from what I could see. The whole compound is like his personal kingdom. Heavily fortified, and protected by foreign mercenaries with guns. It's a sex cult of some kind, posing as a fertility treatment for barren couples. Not quite sure what else is going on up there, but I witnessed part of one of the supposed "wedding" ceremonies he conducts, and it wasn't pleasant.'

'And nobody's tried to stop him?'

'I think that's why Callum Hoggins was shot.'

'Oh God.' She thought for a moment. 'Well, it's simple. We need to tell the police. Get him arrested.'

'Others have tried and failed, apparently. He's the Reverend. Nobody would dare.' He paused. 'He's not just a priest, either. They treat him like a god round here, and not a particularly benign one.'

'Then why—?'

'Why let him get away with it? For starters, Barton's a good-looking bastard. I have to admit, he has a certain charm.'

'Seriously?'

He gave a wry smile. 'He rules by fear, though. Fear and the promise of financial gain, among other perks. I haven't got the full picture yet, but one thing's for sure.' He lowered his voice. 'No woman's safe there. The man's a serial rapist.'

'You mean . . .' Faith glanced back at Rose.

'I got there just in time.'

'That's appalling. I don't know what to say.' Faith kept driving but her expression was horrified. She swore under her breath, then said, 'OK, so much for my hot chocolate. We've got to go straight back to the police, tell them everything. Others may have tried, but they probably didn't have *prima facie* evidence of wrongdoing. We have Rose, and she needs to make a formal complaint against him.'

'Hang on there.' Rose leant forward, speaking for the first time since getting into the car. 'I'm not saying nothing about the Reverend Barton. Not a word.' She sounded terrified, much as Dani had done when he stopped to help her in the lay-by. 'Not to the police, anyhow.'

Faith looked at her in the mirror. 'Why not?'

'You wouldn't understand.'

'Then help me to understand. A man attacks you – nearly rapes you, according to Aubrey – and you don't want the police involved?'

Rose fell silent.

Faith looked at Savage helplessly. 'Aubrey?'

'Give her time.'

'You know as well as I do that the longer she delays, the less likely a conviction will be. Especially for an attempted rape. Were there any other witnesses apart from you?'

'At least a dozen.'

'Good God, then why not press charges?'

Rose interrupted them. 'Not one person there will back me up, that's why not. Said you wouldn't understand.' She made a noise under her breath, half sob, half laughter. 'You city folk. You've no idea what goes on here. The things that can happen to a person out on the moors.'

'Help me, Aubrey,' Faith said.

'I'm sorry, you know I can't force her to make a complaint if she doesn't want to. It's her choice. Not ours.'

They had reached the main road over the moors. Faith stopped at the crossroads and sat there, engine running, her hands clenched on the wheel.

The moorland road was dark and empty in both directions.

He thought of the young man, Callum, shot in the head and hung out in the rain, his body tied to a post like a scarecrow. As a warning, perhaps. Cross the Reverend Barton, and this is what happens. Or could his murder have been part of something darker and more ritualistic? Perhaps the occasional human sacrifice was required to make the 'seed' take. According to Barton, at any rate. It would be a useful cover for hushing up his enemies. Death as a necessary part of life-giving.

Anything was possible after what he'd seen down there in the Green Chapel.

Savage checked his phone again. The signal had returned after a brief period where all the phone said was No Service. But Peter had still not returned any of his calls. And there were no new messages.

The long silence was beginning to worry him. Peter was flaky, yes. But he usually answered his phone eventually.

Faith began slowly, 'But if there were witnesses—'

'Witnesses aren't any good unless they're going to back up her story. You heard her. Barton's got that place sewn up. She goes to the police with this story, he's more likely to come back at us with a counter-accusation. Trespassing, for instance. Which would actually be true.'

'Hardly on the same scale, though.'

'That's not the point. Barton's too clever to let himself be caught like that. Or it would have happened by now.' He shook his head, remembering the faces he'd seen at the farmhouse window. 'Besides, at least one local police officer is part of his fold.'

'What?' Faith was genuinely shocked. 'Who?'

'Some bobbie I saw down at the station. A constable.' He turned to Rose. 'Dani's in that farmhouse, isn't she?'

Rose hesitated, then nodded unhappily.

'With her own private guard, I'm guessing. What's his name? The PC who's keeping an eye on her? Nasty scowl, not much of a charmer.'

Again, Rose hesitated. 'Petherick.'

'PC Petherick?'

She nodded, the gesture barely discernible in the darkness.

'First name?'

'Charlie.'

'PC Charlie Petherick. And how long has Charlie been part of what goes on at the Green Chapel?'

'Dunno.'

'Since Barton came here?'

'Maybe.'

'Charlie must think a lot of Barton to risk his career like that. Or is getting well-paid for his loyalty?'

She shrugged.

Faith tapped her fingers on the wheel, impatient. Missing her hot chocolate, no doubt, now all the drama was over.

'Where to now, then?' she asked, confirming his suspicions. 'If we're not taking this to the police, I'd rather like to get back to my hotel. If that's not too much to ask.'

He glanced at the clock display on the dashboard. It was quarter past eleven. Definitely past her bedtime, given the long drive she'd endured last night. Hence the acid tone.

'I need to get back to Rowlands Farm. Can you drop me there?'

'At this time of night?'

'Peter's not answering his phone.'

'I imagine he's asleep. Some of your friends occasionally do that, you know. Sleep, that is.' The acid tone again. 'I take it you'd like to wake him up too?'

He smiled, acknowledging her irritation, and she flashed him an infuriated look.

Savage turned in his seat again. He could only see Rose in profile now. She was biting her fingernails, staring out of the back window as though worried Barton and his boys would be coming after them.

'Can we drop you somewhere, Rose?' he asked. 'At home, maybe?'

She shifted, staring round at him. 'Are you kidding? That's the first place they'll look for me. My Billy's probably there right now.'

He wanted to reassure her. But he couldn't deny that Billy had disappeared before they left the compound. While checking out the general layout of the place, he'd spotted a side door to the left of the main gate. If Billy had slipped out through there, and taken a vehicle parked outside the stockade, she was right. He could already be home, waiting for her. And though Billy had obviously been unhappy about Barton's role in the 'wedding' ceremony, he had kept quiet and made no attempt to halt proceedings. So he was unlikely to support Rose in her refusal.

'OK,' he said. 'Then come with me. I can put you up for the night. Or rather, my friend Peter can.'

'The one who's not answering his phone?'

'Like Faith said, he's probably just asleep,' Savage said, and knew at once that wasn't true. She knew it too, by her face. But she shrugged and said nothing, which he took to be acceptance. 'Anyway, the place is never locked. Even if he's not there, we can let ourselves in. Peter Rowlands is a good man. He won't mind another house guest.'

'A good man?' Rose made a snorting sound. Disbelief. 'I met his wife. That's not what she called him.'

He said nothing.

'So,' Faith said into the silence, still impatient, 'which way?'

CHAPTER TWENTY-THREE

Faith turned off onto the torturously winding mud track towards Rowlands Farm, driving slowly and cautiously over the ruts. 'How far away is this place?' she asked suspiciously, peering at the dark landscape ahead.

'A few miles, that's all.'

'Oh, is that all? A few miles? On this bloody sheep track masquerading as a road?' When he didn't answer, assuming that to be a rhetorical question, Faith made a growling noise under her breath, and then muttered, 'This is going to kill my suspension. And then I'm going to kill you, Aubrey.'

'You'd better get in the queue, then.'

She threw him a wry look.

The mist was thinner now, a few wisps still clinging to grassy hillocks here and there, but the night sky slowly clearing over the moor. There was no moon, and stars were visible above them now. Not just one or two of the usual suspects, but a whitish sprawling cluster of pinprick stars that seemed to fill the skies, a dark blue canvas blurring to black at the far edges. He couldn't remember seeing a display like that in years. Not, in fact, since a night memorably spent under canvas with Lina in the Syrian Desert, in the company of a small group of pastoral Bedouins.

'Look,' he said softly, pointing upwards. 'You won't see a night sky like that anywhere in Oxfordshire.'

Faith peered up, and then let out a sigh. 'Beautiful.'

Even Rose looked up out of her window at the stars, though she said nothing. Hardly surprising, of course. He wondered how she was going to cope with the aftermath of what had happened. Perhaps hc had made the wrong decision, offering to let her stay at Peter's. But what else could he have done? As soon as he'd stepped out of hiding at the Green Chapel and interrupted the ceremony, he had put her in even greater potential danger. So it was up to him to make sure Rose wasn't simply abandoned to her fate now. Which meant finding her somewhere safe to sleep tonight. Though what tomorrow would bring was less clear.

They had been on the rough farm track for about three or four minutes when Savage sat up straight, having caught the flash of something above the dark hedgerows.

Another car?

'Slow down,' he told Faith.

He could hear the high-pitched whine of an engine now, coming fast towards them. Too high for a car, surely?

'If we go any slower, we'll stop,' she pointed out drily.

At that instant, a single headlight blazed round the corner ahead of them, bouncing about on the uneven track, flooding the car with blinding white light.

A motorbike.

Faith swore and slammed on the brake, wrenching the steering wheel sideways at the same time. But there was no room for manoeuvre in the narrow lane. Not in a Mercedes, at any rate.

The front passenger tyre dipped into some kind of ditch, and the bumper crunched against a stone wall buried beneath thick undergrowth. The motorbike headlight wavered impossibly for a few seconds, passing the Mercedes on Faith's side with only an inch or two to spare as it skidded and bounced over the mud ruts. Savage caught a glimpse of wide, startled eyes behind a darkened visor. Then the bike was gone in a burst of pure throttle, its high-octane whine fading across the moors.

Faith slammed the wheel in frustration. 'What the hell was that biker doing? Trying to kill us? I bet we're stuck now.' She struggled with the door. 'If that was your friend—'

'It wasn't.'

Savage tried his door but it was jammed up against the spiny hedgerow, partly lit up by the headlights. 'I'll have to get out your side.' He waited while she climbed out, then clambered across, glancing back at Rose briefly. 'You OK back there?'

She did not respond, a frozen terror in her eyes.

'Rose?'

She blinked at her name, then shivered, seeming to snap back into awareness. 'Yes, yes. I'm fine.'

Savage looked up the road towards Rowlands Farm.

He had a bad feeling.

'I'm going ahead on foot,' he told Faith. 'You and Rose stay here.'

To his surprise, Faith did not argue. Instead, she bent and glanced into the back of the Mercedes. Rose had still not moved.

'OK, what's going on?'

'Maybe nothing. But just in case, it's probably best that I check out the house first. Given the state she's in.'

Faith looked at him sharply, then nodded. 'Be careful.'

Savage had no intention of being careful. But there was no point sharing that thought with Faith. She would only fret. Setting out at a trot, he covered the short distance between the car and Rowlands Farm in less than five minutes, despite the blackness and the unfamiliar terrain. After the first few minutes, his eyes adjusted to the dark, and by then the farmhouse was in sight.

There were lights on downstairs, which partly reassured him. But he was still uneasy.

Peter's long silence, the unanswered calls and texts, these were not entirely uncharacteristic. But even if Peter had been in a drunken stupor for the past twenty-four hours, he was still not the kind of friend to ignore increasingly concerned texts. Not when he knew how much concern his silence must be causing.

The black-and-white sheep dogs came running out of the house at his approach, barking wildly just as they had done when he first arrived.

But something was wrong.

He had seen traumatised dogs in war zones, mute witnesses that wore their suffering in their eyes, and these dogs were definitely frightened. One snarled, belly low to the ground, but kept its distance. The other snapped at him, and he used his army voice, which seemed to reassure the animal.

The dog stopped barking and turned, running back to the front door. His companion followed. Both sat down on the grimy doorstep and stared at him, panting.

Like an invitation.

Perhaps they remembered him being there earlier with Peter. Or perhaps they just wanted him to go inside.

On the threshold, Savage paused briefly. He crouched to stroke both animals, murmuring, 'It's OK, good dogs.' Then he straightened and entered the farmhouse.

The dogs did not attempt to stop him, but followed silently behind.

'Peter?'

No answer.

He checked the downstairs, glancing into every room. Nobody was there. The lights were on in the narrow hallway and kitchen. Everywhere else was dark.

One of the dogs gave a sharp bark, sitting at the bottom of the stairs. Its tail thumped the floor noisily. Savage returned and stood there beside the animal, gazing up into the dark.

'Peter? You up there?' He paused. 'It's Aubrey.'

Still no answer.

There was a torch hanging on the hall stand, handy for those evening trips out with the dogs. He unhooked it and switched it on, shining the bright beam up the stairs. The dog ran up the stairs ahead of him. Savage followed more slowly, listening for any sound of movement from above. He doubted there was anyone in the house from Barton's crew. That had been the guy on the motorbike, almost certainly, fleeing the scene. And Savage had given away his presence as soon as he walked through the door, so he hardly needed to be silent now.

But there was no sense in crashing upstairs like an idiot. Not when he did not know what was up there.

And there was definitely *something* up there.

The black-and-white dog came back to the head of the stairs and looked down at Savage, then barked again. Just once. High and sharp. Then he sat, thumping its tail impatiently. Not quite Lassie, perhaps, but there was no mistaking what that bark and the dog's eager posture meant. 'Come and see.'

Reaching the top of the stairs, he nodded to the dog. 'Show me, then,' he said softly, and watched as the dog ran off along the landing into darkness.

The dog nudged a door open. Savage heard it creak, though there was no light. He trod silently along the landing, shining the torch beam a few steps ahead, and came to the room at the end. Peter's bedroom, as he recalled.

The door was ajar.

Inside, he could hear the dog whining, its tail thumping on the carpeted floor. A dull, rhythmic thud-thud-thud.

Quietly, he entered the bedroom. It was dark and chill, and

smelt damp. He caught a faint whiff of gunpowder and checked on the threshold. A weapon had been discharged there, and recently too. He sniffed again, and smelt alcohol too. Whisky, almost certainly. The torch beam picked out the dog first, blinking curiously at the light. Then two muddy old work boots on the floor behind the bed, attached to a pair of legs in faded jeans. Peter's legs.

He wasn't moving.

CHAPTER TWENTY-FOUR

Savage groped for the light switch and flicked it down. He made his way round the unmade bed and stopped, looking down at his friend's body.

Peter was dead.

Single gunshot to the temple. Blackening around the wound in a starburst tattoo. Blood in a dark red pool surrounding his head. His right hand lay with its fingers still partly curled where his grip had relaxed after death.

All the classic signs of a suicide.

The gun had tumbled to the floor a few feet away.

It was the Glock 19.

The gun from Dani's holdall. Presumably also the gun used to shoot Callum Hoggins.

He ought never to have left Peter alone so long. Not once he'd known what Barton and his men were capable of. His visit to the Green Chapel could have waited for another evening. But then he might not have seen what he had. And Dani would be in even greater danger.

The dog barked again. His eyes rolled white and frightened.

'Good boy,' Savage said automatically, and crouched to stroke the distressed animal. The dog nosed Peter's leg, then ran to the door, looking back at him hesitantly. His companion had not even made the ascent, but barked from downstairs, the loud noise splitting the silence in the old farmhouse. Too horrified to come back up into this stink of death, no doubt.

'I've found him now,' Savage told the dog. 'You can go.'

The animal ran down the stairs, no longer barking.

Savage examined Peter silently.

He should call the police.

But the Glock . . .

His own fingerprints would be all over it. Given his recent arrest on suspected murder, that might not go down well with the local constabulary.

Dani's prints would be on it too. And that was a complication she probably didn't need either. Though if he wiped the gun clean, it would look even more suspicious. Unless he wiped it clean, then pressed Peter's hand around it, so at least his fingerprints were on it. Tampering with the scene though . . .

Faith would not approve.

He grimaced.

Better to explain the situation to DI Paglia, perhaps, and hope the over-zealous coppers didn't nick him for murder anyway.

He averted his eyes from his friend's body.

Was there a suicide note?

Nothing obvious on the floor. Or on the bed. There were some disorderly papers and other detritus on the bedside cabinet on the left side of the bed, spilling out of a shoebox. But nothing that shouted suicide note at him. Perhaps he had left a note elsewhere. In the kitchen. Or on a laptop. Did people type suicide notes though? Especially people like Peter, who had never really embraced technology as a big part of his life, no doubt preferring the simplicity of life on the farm.

The bedroom was a mess.

Nothing unusual in that, of course. The whole farmhouse

was in a state of terminal neglect and decline. Yet something else was nagging at him. What?

He studied the shoebox of papers again.

It looked like the lid had been pushed off in a hurry, still lying at an angle, dust on the upper side. Kept under the bed? For several years, it seemed. Old photos, certificates, letters, mementoes . . .

And a short note, written in a smooth, flowing hand he recognised.

Savage walked round to the other side of the bed.

He retrieved the note from among the other papers. Not a suicide note. But his heart beat faster as he glanced down at the signature. It looked like a scrap torn from a larger notebook but was not jagged, the tear edge almost neat, like someone had used a ruler. The note was tatty, discoloured, and had been folded twice at some point in its life. But sure enough, it was signed Jarrah.

He scanned the contents, suddenly aware of a car coming fast along the approach road to the farm.

Peter,

I'm going out for a walk on the moors, clear my head after last night's excesses. Didn't want to wake you. Why the hell did we drink so much? Back in an hour or two.

Jarrah

No date. But it hardly needed one.

So Peter had lied. Jarrah had come here, after all. Why did Peter pretend otherwise? And what had happened to Jarrah when he was here? Because if he had left the place intact, Peter would have had no reason to lie about his visit. Unless there were some other complication at play here.

Beside the shoebox and its scattered contents was an empty glass. A bedside lamp. A crushed beer can. Empty packet of crisps. Food crumbs. A thriller, a paper bookmark marking the place.

He walked back to where Peter lay on the right side of the bed.

No bedside cabinet.

There was room for another cabinet on the right. But instead there was a tall chest of drawers. It was a double bed. No doubt when his wife had still lived here, she would have had a bedside cabinet. Somewhere to put her own glass of water. Her own lamp. Her own paperback novel. But Maura was long gone. And Peter had not moved to the right after her departure. He had rearranged the bedroom furniture, sure. But he had kept the left-hand side of the bed as his own, perhaps hoping his wife would eventually return to give their marriage a second go.

He looked down at his friend again. The still body accused him. He studied the empty right hand, fingers still curled. The hole in the right-hand side of his temple.

Then it hit him.

Peter was left-handed.

So why would a left-handed man have shot himself with his right hand?

Or indeed, how?

The car bumped over the cattle grid at speed and drove into the farmyard. Dazzling blue light strobed through the bedroom window, painting the walls. Savage went to the window and looked out, keeping carefully to one side so as not to be seen from below. The curtains hung open, a grim, dusty dark green.

The vehicle stopped near where his camper had been parked that first day here. It was the Volvo again. A police car. Unmarked.

They must have passed Faith and the ditch-locked Mercedes on the track.

Not only passed but stopped. Maybe left an officer there.

Otherwise Faith would have rung him or texted a warning. Unless there was no signal out there on the track. It came and went over the moorland roads, with long tracts where the signal simply died, especially in dips and hollows.

She would never let it slip that he had gone on ahead to the farmhouse, of course. Watertight, that was Faith. But any police officer would be able to piece that information together, looking at the car in the ditch, its unlikely occupants, both apparently heading to Rowlands Farm at that time of night.

The police would probably arrest him on sight. It did appear suspicious, after all. And more than suspicious once forensics had analysed the Glock. If nothing else, they would want to question him. They would take him to their station headquarters again. There would be more interviews. More waiting around. Yet more long-winded explanations of how he got the gun, when and where he parted company with it, and what his relationship with Peter had been.

They might even charge him this time.

Murder.

He looked at the man on the floor.

Well, perhaps he was to blame. In part, at least. There was guilt there, for sure, like a piece of grit working away under his eyelid, blurring the shadows.

No suicide note though.

There wasn't always a note. But this wasn't the first suicide he had seen. It was his third, in fact. And the other two times the deceased had left a farewell note, with an indication of why they had felt the need to take their own life.

Maybe Peter had been too distressed to bother with a note. Or too drunk. To hell with life, and all that.

Savage took a step back from the window.

If they delayed him, Dani would remain where he had last

seen her, staring down out of an upper window in Barton's farmhouse. He had recognised her heart-shaped face at the glass instantly. Seen her eyes widen as she recognised him in turn. They had exchanged one brief look before PC Petherick pulled her away from the window, but he had thought the young woman looked vulnerable and friendless. And judging by what happened to her brother-in-law, she was right to be afraid. She was almost certainly in serious danger from the Reverend. Captured by the enemy. On his watch too.

Police officers were piling out of the unmarked car.

He saw DI Paglia among them, small and determined, shoulders hunched against the chill as she studied the front of the farmhouse.

He could tell her about Dani.

But then there was PC Petherick. He had seen the young constable in Barton's farmhouse tonight, undoubtedly one of the Reverend's crew, and could not help wondering how far the rot had spread.

Had the police even questioned Barton about that young man's death, given Geoff's story about Callum going up to the Green Chapel and never being seen alive again? Or perhaps Geoff had not been entirely honest either with him or with the police. Savage got the distinct impression that most of the locals hereabouts were in Barton's pocket. That keeping the Reverend on the high moors, oiling the local community in some vile, unspecified way, was more important to them than a few dead bodies.

He folded Jarrah's note and pushed it into the back pocket of his jeans.

He would think about its significance later. There was something he needed to check first. A suspicion that had been nagging at him. Maybe nothing. One of his odd hunches that wouldn't pan out. But maybe something that might explain what had happened here.

He glanced towards the Glock again. Best left where it was.

'Sorry, Pete,' he said under his breath.

Then he went downstairs, let himself silently through the back door, and headed out across the dark moors.

CHAPTER TWENTY-FIVE

The going was slow and frustrating. Savage had underestimated how difficult it would be to navigate uneven moorland in the darkness. But he couldn't afford to walk too slowly. It would be dangerous to be found out there, so near to the place where his friend had recently died. Not only dangerous but obstructive. Because he was on the verge of some kind of understanding. But what exactly he had understood was less sure. It was too misty and far-off in his head right now, and what he had just seen at Rowlands Farm was colouring everything. Another good reason to get clear of the place, empty his head so he could think without that awful, numbing grief and anger hanging over him.

Within a few minutes, he heard shouts from behind him and the busy crackle of police radios. Before long, a powerful torch beam shone out too, picking out spots along the rough grassland.

Hunting for him specifically? Or simply making sure nobody was out here?

He was safe enough by that point, of course. He was too far across the moor to be hit by a torch beam, and the police were unlikely to have any high-spec night vision equipment to hand. All the same, he kept low, and tried not to move too fast or rhythmically. Regular walking movement might be noticed even without night vision. And he did not want them to call out the search helicopter.

Eventually, the inquisitive torch beam was withdrawn. The voices became subdued, barely audible now. They were not looking for anyone else in connection with Peter's death. Not yet, anyway.

A classic suicide.

He felt his phone vibrate in his back jeans pocket, but did not check it in case the screen light gave him away. His eyes having adjusted to the dark, Savage halted on a low, boggy hillock, crouched down, and took a moment to check his trajectory.

He saw at once what he was aiming for. He was close, its dark, shadowy mass easily visible from that distance. A slight course correction was required though. He had been heading too far north.

Savage picked out a line further to the west and kept walking.

He was nearly there. The ivy-clad outline of Agnes's cottage loomed out of the night before him, the roofline ragged, the front windows empty as dead eye sockets. He slowed, finding the terrain uncertain, then a few steps further took him through a narrow gateway. The gate itself was missing, but one wooden post remained, leaning at a drunken angle. Underfoot was what felt like a stone path that led to the shattered remains of the cottage entrance. No door either, only a yawning maw that rapidly swallowed him.

Concealed behind the still intact external wall of Agnes's cottage, Savage stopped at last. He leant back against the wall in the darkness and took a long breath.

He'd thought he had himself well in hand. That he could accept his friend's death with at least a show of cool professionalism until it was safe to grieve, to unpack what had happened without breaking down. But all that shit had been an illusion. Years of hard experience in the field, and he was still shaken by the memory of Peter lying dead in his own blood.

He had seen dead bodies before. Seen his wife . . .

Savage closed his eyes.

There was no point trying to pretend he was still the same person who had walked into that dark bedroom less than an hour ago. Some things bit deep and refused to be shaken loose. Regardless of training, regardless of experience. You had to honour the pain when it hit this hard, to let it in and acknowledge its existence. Or it would break you.

This death would continue to ride him for years, just as Lina's still did.

He should have been there when Peter needed him. Not playing cowboys with Barton. And Barton was playing a game. He wasn't for real. How could he be? Special seed. That was crazy talk, and Barton was not crazy. He had seen the man's eyes as he fielded that phone call from Faith. There had been calculation in his face, a moment of weighing up the odds . . . That look had not come out of craziness. It had been cool, intelligent, cunning.

Of course, the Reverend Barton could be cunning and deluded at the same time. Savage had met a few like that in his time. Usually the religious types too, the ones who believed themselves on a mission from God. Or wished others to believe it. He had not been convinced by Barton's spiel in the Green Chapel, though he could see how others might fall for his patter. The 'chosen one' routine. It had certainly appeared spectacular: the red-robed priests, the torchlit procession, Barton himself . . .

But there was always something beneath such slick, professional-looking tricks. Some need, some desire, some dirty little scheme.

What was Barton hiding beneath those robes? Apart from the obvious.

Savage grimaced.

Who had been on the motorbike that forced Faith into the ditch?

One of Barton's men. Who else?

But why had he gone there? To threaten Peter? To tell him, 'Keep quiet about what you know or else?' Then had found him already dead, perhaps, and ridden away in confusion. Or, a more sickening possibility still, the unknown motorbiker had found Peter with the gun, overpowered and then shot him. Then staged the suicide to throw the police off. Though it may have been at the back of his mind to make it look like murder, knowing that Savage was probably on his way back to the farm.

Framing him for Peter's murder would have been an obvious next move for Barton. But it was likely nobody in the commune knew he had touched that handgun. Not even Dani, though she might have guessed he would find it.

No, the double whammy of his fingerprints on the murder weapon was coincidence, that was all. One of those ironic twists of fate he hated so much. A spit in the eye.

He listened a moment, studying the interior of the tumbledown cottage. The place was eerily silent, riddled with knotted undergrowth, thick brambles up to his ankles. Everything was steeped in shadow.

Sure now that nobody was coming after him, he slid the mobile phone out of his back pocket. The screen gleamed at him and he angled it towards his chest, trying to reduce the amount of tell-tale light.

There was a text waiting. From Faith.

Stay out of sight.

By now she would know what he'd found at the farm, and also that the police had failed to spot him on the premises. *Stay out of sight.* The curt nature of the text, its curious brevity, suggested to him that she had sent it while in someone else's company. A police officer, almost certainly.

He did not reply to the text, but turned off the phone to conserve battery life.

Pushing the phone back into his pocket, Savage slid slowly down the wall until he hit the ground. Then he let his legs stretch out in front, pushing against the tangled undergrowth.

Not exactly comfortable.

But he'd been in worse spots, and it was at least comfortable enough to allow him to sleep. Now that the initial burst of adrenalin had begun to drain away, he felt exhausted. It must be forty-odd hours since he had last slept.

Savage closed his eyes.

Sleep evaded him at first, despite his immense fatigue. Part of his consciousness was listening as more vehicles arrived at the farm, voices spoke, the sound drifting across the ancient landscape, and then doors slammed, loud engines retreating into the night again.

Was it wishful thinking that Peter had not killed himself? Because that depth of despair was something he ought to have noticed and acted upon . . .

As an officer, he had always been mindful of the mental health of the men under his command. It had been part of the job, watching them for early symptoms of stress and depression, and taking action when anyone exhibited worrying signs. A soldier with a mental health problem was a serious danger. But he had left Peter with a loaded handgun, knowing his friend was not in perfect shape, and thought nothing of it. It had never occurred to him that Peter might use that weapon to take his own life.

No suicide note, he reminded himself.

But there had been something dark and terrible about his

despair over the failure of his marriage to Maura. It had come across almost like guilt at times. As though Peter had blamed himself for driving his wife away with his drinking and bad behaviour. And perhaps he'd had good reason for that.

Was that it? The thing nagging at the back of his mind?

Or something else?

The farmhouse was quiet again now. The police had all departed, no doubt having cordoned off the yard first with blue-and-white POLICE DO NOT CROSS tape. Unless they were convinced it was suicide. No doubt Faith would know. She had not sent any more texts, so he would follow her advice and stay low until first light. It was likely she had taken Rose back with her to the pub where she was staying. She would be annoyed with him, and rightly so. But she had a good heart and would not desert that woman simply because he had disappeared on them.

He would text Faith first thing in the morning; find out how Rose was doing, and what the police had told them about Peter's death, if anything. Meanwhile, it was dark and chilly, and he was exhausted.

The logical next step was sleep.

Savage folded his arms for warmth, dipped his chin onto his chest, and gradually allowed his breathing to slow. A fox barked far off across the moors, and somewhere a rabbit screamed in its final throes. But he was no longer listening . . .

CHAPTER TWENTY-SIX

Savage started awake with a jerk, alerted by a noise.

He had slumped sideways in his sleep. Straightening up, stiff from sleeping with his back against the old ivy-covered stone wall, he gazed about the tumbledown cottage. He could hear nothing now. It was still dark, and his jacket and jeans felt damp with dew. He stood up, stretched out his aching limbs, and looked over the moors through the empty window frame.

A faint bleeding of pale light on the eastern horizon told him that dawn was not far off. Less than fifteen minutes away, he guessed. Which meant it must be about five o'clock. He could hear the lilt of birdsong on all sides, and caught a few flutters among the heather where small birds were starting to hop about, looking for food and no doubt warning each other about a human presence on the moor.

He'd been dreaming deeply and vividly most of the night, mostly a series of unrelated military scenarios. The usual seek-and-destroy tropes, like a violent video game running in his head.

But in his last dream, the one just before he woke, Jarrah had been standing over him in the ruins, gun in hand, pointing to something in the darkness behind him. His presence had felt viscerally real, so much so indeed that Savage found it hard to believe Jarrah was not there in the cottage with him now.

Jarrah had been dressed in an old-fashioned flying jacket,

the kind with a sheepskin collar, pulled up tight against his bearded chin. Despite the handgun, the expression in his eyes had not been angry. Yet Savage felt accused all the same. As though his old friend was complaining he'd not done enough to save Peter, or was urging Savage to make some kind of connection between events. To join up the dots before it was too late.

Yet how was that even possible, when he couldn't see the dots clearly? And maybe Peter's death wasn't a dot at all, but a red herring. A coincidence. Bad timing.

Savage was not sure he believed in coincidences. He definitely didn't believe in dream visitations though. The psychological significance of dreams was something few people would deny. But a message from a man who might or might not be dead? The sceptic in him dismissed it, even as his more spiritual side explored that idea as a possibility, however remote and improbable.

The noise that had woken him came again. Not birdsong, he realised, but something infinitely harsher.

A motorbike engine.

It was coming closer. And now that he was fully awake at last, he could hear that it was more than one motorbike. Maybe as many as three.

The high-pitched whine and engine fluctuations suggested off-road bikes.

Savage slipped out of the cottage and stood close to the front wall, staring up towards Rowlands Farm. But everything in that direction was still and silent. The sound must have ricocheted off the stone back of the farmhouse, bouncing back over the moorland. He trod quietly through undergrowth round to the other side of the cottage, and crouched down, keeping low in the semi-dark so he was less visible.

The roar of the bikes was louder now.

A few seconds later, he saw headlights glinting through the thickly clustered trees on the ridge. Then the bikers crashed down the slope, not riding together but separately, a few hundred feet apart from each other but all heading in the same general direction. Almost like a search formation. And now he could hear barking and shouts. Others were following the bikers on foot, by the sound of it, urging each other on with whoops and cat-calls, and accompanied by dogs.

It looked like some kind of hunt.

But who or what were they hunting for? A fox? That seemed unlikely on motorbikes. Unless they were a substitute for horses on this rough, dangerous terrain. And surely most fox hunting would take place during daylight hours, not in the last watches of the night?

It was a man-hunt.

His first instinct was to assume that the Reverend Barton had somehow guessed or discovered his location, and sent out his men in some kind of revenge attack for losing Rose. It was not beyond the bounds of belief that a man like Barton would have heat-sensitive search equipment, which would have shown up his body heat without any trouble in such a remote area. But why not come sooner? It was nearly light now, making it less likely he would be taken by surprise. The early hours of the morning would have been a more effective choice. And their noisy approach would alert even the heaviest sleeper to an imminent attack.

So if they were hunting somebody, it was unlikely to be him. Who, then?

The black-helmeted bikers paused at the base of the slope, and he heard a mobile ring, an eerie sound over the wasteland. They turned and gathered together, conferring over the phone call, perhaps deciding which way to go. Or maybe waiting for the dogs to pick up the scent.

The birds had stopped singing.

He studied the bent heads of the bikers, wondering if one of them was the man who had ridden out to Rowlands Farm last night. But with helmets on, there was no way to be sure.

As dawn began to light the ancient landscape, he saw the first men emerge from the wooded ridge. They were wrapped up against the cold, and most of them were carrying hunting shotguns, some held loosely in their hands, others slung over their shoulders, within easy reach. The bikers were the beaters, flushing out the moorland bushes and bracken. The hunters came behind with the dogs, ready to pin down their prey or maybe pick off a fleeing figure with a firearm.

He counted about ten men on foot. They came out of the trees and crossed to where the three motorbikers were still waiting, engines running. Their torch beams hit and glanced off bent, windswept trees and shrubs as they came on, searching the moor in the half-light. The dogs were milling about the bikes now, tails wagging furiously. They set up a yelping as the bikers revved their throttles. Then all three turned their bikes and headed straight for Agnes's cottage, followed by the rest on foot.

Savage swore under his breath. So they were looking for him, after all. Perhaps if he were to run back to the farmhouse . . .

He froze, hearing something else.

Someone was heading towards the ruined cottage. Someone on foot, panting as he hurtled over the rough terrain. Someone who veered sharply away before the old stone-walled bounds of the cottage to splash through the narrow stream instead.

Someone being hunted.

From a distance, it looked like a young man, wearing a black hoody and dark jeans, head down as he concentrated on not falling. Wiry, light-footed, not particularly tall. His pace slowed, wading through the ankle-deep water as though hoping that would throw the dogs off his scent. He was tired but still running with grace and agility, neat-footed as he dodged across slippery stones in the stream.

As the fugitive closed in on Savage's hiding place, his face became clearer, a pale oval in the dawn light.

It was Billy.

CHAPTER TWENTY-SEVEN

Savage backed round the other side of the ruins and waited there, listening, until Billy had run on, drawing his pursuers away from Agnes's cottage.

The bikes roared across the moor, tearing up the ground. The men ran after them with the dogs bounding ahead, a melee of shouts and excited yelps disturbing the quiet air for several minutes as they passed his hiding place.

One of the dogs came worryingly close, no doubt having caught his scent.

Savage heard panting breath at the back of the cottage, bushes rustling and shaking as a dog's muscular body searched the undergrowth.

He held his breath and kept as still as possible, eyeing the distance between him and Rowlands Farm. It was a long stretch of open countryside, bleak and bare, nowhere to hide, nowhere to stay low and hope not to be shot at. A kind of No Man's Land, only without the barbed wire. And he was still cold and aching from sleeping in such an uncomfortable position. Yet if the dog found him, he would need to leap up and cross that ground at speed, regardless of his stiff muscles, regardless of the rifles at his back.

It was a long way. Nearly a quarter of a mile, by his estimate.

He did not fancy his chances.

But it seemed the gods were on his side. Or maybe Agnes's ghost, as a thank-you for his company during the night.

Just as the dog was nosing inexorably towards his hiding place, one of the men whistled the questing dog to heel.

The animal hesitated, then raced off again, barking cheerfully.

Savage let his breath out slowly.

He waited until the sound of pursuit had faded into the distance again. Then he eased up out of his crouch and edged to the side of the ruined cottage. He looked round the crumbling stone wall, hearing faint shouts and the revving of bike engines far off. But he saw no sign of Billy or those on the young man's tail.

The man-hunt had passed on across the wild moors and out of sight, where the ground dropped away slightly into a kind of hollow.

It seemed unlikely that Billy would escape those dogs, even using the stream to hide his scent. But would those men with guns kill him, or simply capture him and take him back to the Green Chapel for Barton to decide his fate? Savage hoped for the latter, but could not dismiss the former. Not after having seen those photographs of Callum, the young man they'd shot in the head and hung up like a scarecrow along the moorland road. A grim warning to locals to keep silent or face the consequences. What else could it have been?

So what had Billy done to incur Barton's wrath?

Having witnessed the bike hunt, the disparate pack of dogs, the armed men, he could not help feeling sorry for Billy. Yes, he had abandoned Rose when she'd needed him to step up. But Barton must seem like a truly formidable opponent to a young man. Maybe even impossible to defeat, given that so few people in the local community were willing to stand up to him. And why was that?

Last night, Geoff and Terry had hinted at some kind of financial reward for those locals who didn't interfere with Barton's operation on Dartmoor.

But where was all the money coming from?

Barton's dubious fertility cult could not generate enough income to silence so many people. It certainly wouldn't be enough to corrupt a police constable into joining their ranks, or authorise a deadly man-hunt like the one he had just witnessed.

What else was Barton up to at the Green Chapel?

It was nearly light now. He turned on his phone and waited. Sure enough, another text popped up as soon as the signal strengthened.

It was from Faith again. The time stamp told him it had been sent at three minutes past two in the morning.

Where are you? I'm with Rose at the pub. Please call me.

He checked the time.

It was only twenty-five past five. Too early to call her back now. She would still be asleep, and if she was annoyed at two o'clock in the morning, she would be bloody furious with him for having her sleep disturbed only a few hours later. Or else she would be filled with foreboding over Peter's death and want to know his state of mind. And right now, he was not sure what that was. All he felt over Peter's death was numbness. Numbness and a growing anger that was looking for someone to blame. Even if that someone turned out to be Savage himself.

He compromised by sending a text.

Safe and well. Heading for the GC on unfinished business. Will ring later.

Faith would not like that. But she would probably understand.

He did not know what Billy's sudden fall from favour indicated. But there was little he could do about it. He was unarmed and on foot.

What he could do was walk back to the Green Chapel while it was still early, and try to locate Dani. He had seen her at the window in the old farmhouse last night, probably being guarded by that constable he'd met at the station. PC Charlie Petherick. She had been taken from his van, and Savage still resented that. Stupid, perhaps, but it felt like a personal affront, Barton taking Dani away while she was in Savage's camper, ostensibly his guest. Whatever else was happening here, he could not allow that to stand.

He hesitated. Then rang 999.

The young woman on the other end of the line sounded alert and eager to help despite the ungodly hour.

'Emergency, which service? Fire, police or ambulance?'

'Police.'

A click, then the call was answered by a man. This one sounded middle-aged and weary. As though he had heard it all before and was unlikely to be roused to excitement by any reported crime, however unexpected. Especially this early in the morning.

'Could you describe the nature of your emergency?'

Savage described it.

There was a brief silence. Then the man said, 'Is this a hoax call, sir? Because we take time-wasting very seriously.'

'It's not a hoax.'

'You're claiming there's a man being hunted across Dartmoor?'

'I'm not claiming anything,' Savage said. 'I'm reporting what I just witnessed on the moors. As a concerned citizen.'

Still baffled, the man said, 'Could I take your name?'

Savage gave his name. Then added, 'Perhaps you could pass that information onto Detective Inspector Paglia, Devon and Cornwall police, as soon as possible?'

Another brief silence.

'And how exactly do you know DI Paglia?'

Savage rang off.

It had not been a very interesting conversation, anyway.

He turned off the phone and put it back in his front jeans pocket. No doubt DI Paglia would try to get back in touch with him soon. He imagined her expression on receiving that message, and could not resist a wry grin. Or Faith might decide to ring, exasperated by his long silence. Or he might get a sales call, suggesting he might want to invest in double glazing or buy life insurance. Whatever the circumstances, it would not be a good idea for his phone to start ringing while he was breaking into Barton's compound. Even set to silently vibrate, that would be inconvenient. Not to mention embarrassing, given that the phone was in his front pocket.

He stopped at the broken doorway and peered into the ruins of the cottage.

That was where Jarrah had been standing in his dream, pointing urgently behind himself, as though at the empty window frame.

He did not believe in significant dreams.

Did he?

He trod gingerly through the undergrowth to examine the window frame. The glass was long gone and the rotten wood had shrunk away from the stone surround. But the window sill was broad and in reasonable shape.

There were some pebbles lying on the sill. Small stones that looked like they'd come from the nearby stream. The kind with a white marbled vein running through the grey. A few tiny shards of black slate too, one piece lying roughly across the other. A twig of what looked like hazel, a cluster of dried catkins still clinging to it. And several thin green stalks with withered flower heads. Snowdrops?

Someone had left them there deliberately. Stones and wood

and flowers. Like a natural altar. The kind of pagan ritual he had occasionally seen in woods or on the seashore, left behind by Wiccans or druidic types, celebrating nature.

He looked out through the empty window frame.

To one side he could see the stream, to the other the misty edge of Rowlands Farm. Ahead lay the moors, with dark sloping woods in the distance. The Green Chapel was somewhere up there, out of sight on the high ground.

He had counted ten men on foot. Three on bikes. Plus one fugitive.

How many people lived at Barton's compound? Most probably came in during the day when required, or for special services. He doubted there could be that large a number actually in residence at any one time. And with at least fourteen out here on the moors, there was a good chance he could enter the compound without any significant challenge. Though what kind of welcome might be waiting for him in the farmhouse itself was less clear. Barton didn't strike him as the gun-toting type. But he must have guards. Possibly even bodyguards. It was obvious he was hiding something up there. Something worth all those guns and elaborate defences, and the bribing of a police officer – or possibly several police officers – to keep the law at bay.

Maura liked this place, Peter had told him. Had she left these things here? But no, the snowdrop stalks were too green. They could only be a few weeks old. Unless Peter had been keeping up her tradition, out of sentimentality.

The ground beneath the window was a mass of brambles and grass that had invaded the ruins, probably years ago. There was something metal in there too, giving the brambles greater mass. He crouched and parted the brambles carefully, his sleeve snagging on the thorns. Part of an old mangle, by the look of it. All smashed up and in pieces. Some wooden beams too, perhaps fallen from the roof, now half-buried in the encroaching grass. But there was soil down there too, as though the original floor of the cottage had been wood which had rotted, or someone had removed the stone slabs to reveal the ground beneath. Now wild things were growing in place of the flooring. Nettles, bracken, grass.

He did not believe in ghosts.

Not really.

Nor did he believe in dreams.

But he did believe in the power of the subconscious. What had he seen or thought about in the past that had made him conjure up Jarrah in his dreams last night, and have him point towards this window?

He picked another withered flower head out of the tangled brambles, and it fell apart in his hands. Pale petals dropped back into the undergrowth, powdery with age.

White roses?

In the distance, he heard a distinct crack.

A gun shot.

Pushing some of the rose petals into his other pocket, Savage left the cottage and stood listening for a moment. But there were no further gun shots to be heard. Either it had been a warning shot or their prey was down.

He took a line on the wooded ridge where he and Peter had climbed the other day, and where he'd seen the men with guns emerge this morning, and started to walk briskly in that direction.

CHAPTER TWENTY-EIGHT

He reached the compound after a fifteen minutes' walk. The front gate was closed, as expected. But he ignored that entrance, ducking from boulder to tree as he circled the defensive stockade at a discreet distance. It was unlikely that anyone was watching the approach road. But he was not taking any chances. He guessed Barton had not yet secured the stony lower reaches of the Green Chapel after his incursion last night, so decided to approach from that side again.

Sure enough, no new fences had been erected yet or guards posted. No doubt Barton did not think he'd be bold or reckless enough to try the same trick twice. But he was wrong.

It was the work of a few minutes to climb the narrow cleft in the rocky slope. He pushed up hard from muddy foot grip to handhold until he reached the top and the enclave of the open-air chapel.

Everything was quiet in the milky light, and soft mist was rising from the ground, obscuring what was immediately ahead. Savage went slowly through the chapel, listening for any sound of movement. He still half-anticipated an ambush. But the place was deserted. He met nobody in the Green Chapel itself, and the grassy path up to the main buildings was silent and empty as well.

The entire place was so silent that he began to wonder if he had miscalculated and everyone had gone out on that man-hunt. Perhaps Barton himself had been among those men with guns. Which made him even more curious to know why they had been chasing Billy across the moors like an escaped convict.

He found his answer at the top level of the compound.

Reaching the end of the path, Savage checked round the hedge at the top before approaching the main hall. He drew back at what he saw there, tucking himself back out of sight, and then peering cautiously round again.

Three men in padded green jackets and blue jeans were crossing the open space between the hall and the farmhouse.

One of the men was wearing a flat cap too. Mike Cooper, with what looked like a gleaming, elderly shotgun balanced on one generously padded shoulder. The kind of hunting weapon country folk kept hidden away in their attics for generations, sometimes unaware of their existence.

The other was the vast Russian they called Big Swanney, loping along slightly ahead of the other two, though clearly trying to keep step with them. His bald head gleamed in the early light, the collar of his jacket turned up against the cold. He kept glancing at Cooper's flat cap, as though resentful that he didn't have any kind of head-covering himself. Either that or he was a Siberian native, and scornful of the Englishman's need to stay warm.

The third man was Reverend Barton.

As he watched, Mike Cooper stopped, halfway through a conversation, and turned to point back at the main hall. The other two turned with him to look, and Savage kept very still, aware that he might be within the field of their peripheral vision.

Barton nodded as though Cooper was giving him sound advice.

Big Swanney's expression was curiously blank. But perhaps

his English was not very good and he couldn't follow what was being said. Or perhaps the huge Russian was bored. Perhaps he would rather be out there crushing heads than listening to a pep talk from the big-bellied, red-cheeked Mike Cooper, every inch the Devon farmer with that shotgun over his shoulder. Cooper must have missed the Henchman 101 classes which Big Swanney had clearly taken. Twice, at least, going by his lowered eyes and deferential air whenever Barton glanced at him.

None of the men looked like they had slept. But none of them looked particularly anxious about the man-hunt that was possibly still going on or had just concluded in cold-blooded murder. It was inconceivable that they were unaware of the man-hunt, or that they were not being kept informed of its progress. He had heard the phone call out on the moors. Somebody directing their movements from a safe distance. Plausible deniability. Who else was behind the hunt for Billy but the Reverend himself?

Savage didn't know why he would have suddenly turned on the younger man. But he guessed it must be connected to Rose's failed ritual last night. Perhaps Billy had flipped sides after they'd left. Accused Barton of trying to rape his girlfriend. Maybe even threatened to involve the police.

Or perhaps Billy had indeed been the rider on the motorbike out at Rowlands Farm last night.

Perhaps he'd been given an order to go out there and silence Peter Rowland, but had taken it too literally, shooting him with Dani's gun. A mistake like that would have gone down badly with Barton, who might be cocky but surely not so stupid as to think a murder investigation would leave his little empire here untouched.

Or perhaps Billy had been sent to the farm to kill Savage, as the place he was most likely to head for last night, and things had gone badly wrong.

However it had happened, young Billy had fallen from favour.

Savage wondered if Barton would make a push to get Rose back too, as he had done with Dani that first night on the moorland road. After all, Rose could bring down serious trouble on the Reverend's head if she decided to accuse him of attempted rape. And until they brought her back to the compound, they could not be sure of her silence.

He made a mental note to call Faith as soon as possible, and warn her to keep Rose close. Maybe even hidden.

A few words drifted across to Savage on the still air. Cooper was advising Barton to 'keep it on lock-down'. He seemed concerned that they might get an unwanted visit soon, presumably from the police.

But what 'it' was, and why it needed to be locked, Savage had no idea.

The main hall?

That was unlikely, given that their trajectory across the yard would suggest they had just left there, and the large entrance doors were standing unguarded and ajar. Surely Cooper would have closed the big doors behind them if he was so worried that the hall should be kept locked. And if it was just a place for people to gather for special services, why would the hall need to be locked in the first place? To avoid religious pamphlets falling into the wrong hands?

Behind them, beside the large entrance gate, several cars and vans were parked in a straggling row. The Land Rover Defender, of course. He was surprised they had not taken it on the hunt this morning. Perfect for off-road pursuits. But perhaps it was too identifiable a vehicle with *DARTMOOR GUN CENTRE* emblazoned across the spare tyre cover. Besides, the bikes would always be better than the Land Rover at handling the tougher terrain where even grass tracks petered out.

There were two long-wheelbase Transit vans parked either side of the Land Rover. Both white, both dirty, both with plates marked with RUS, and the area number 177. His memory could be playing tricks on him, but he felt sure that was one of the vehicle codes for Moscow.

He also suspected he had seen one of the vans before.

A dirty white Ford Transit just like these had passed him on the moorland road while he was trying to get Dani's MG started. He had not seen the driver's face, the van had been a blur in the dusk. But he'd had his pedal to the metal, for sure. Driving like a man who was late for a very important appointment.

One of the Transits was a little mud-spattered, the other was filthy. On the far end of the row was a hatchback, a heavily battered Vauxhall Corsa. Exactly the kind of car he would expect a young man like Billy to be driving. He wondered if it did in fact belong to Billy, and dug into his pocket for his phone, then took a surreptitious photograph of the row of vehicles, including the Corsa with the dented side panels. The number plates might come in handy later.

Savage quickly messaged the photo to Faith, checking the phone was still set to silent in case of a reply.

Barton and Cooper were still talking, still ignoring the Russian, slightly turned away from him. Big Swanney was oblivious to them, though. He was watching a dark, staggered V of birds climbing towards the clouds, high above the stockade. Possibly swallows, though it was hard to tell at that distance. The Russian seemed entranced, his long neck almost folded back on itself as he followed the birds' flight overhead.

Their conversation was interrupted by a man who emerged from the old farmhouse and came hurrying across the compound towards them.

The newcomer was a muscular young man with stocky

thighs and chest. Quite short too, only about five foot five. No padded green jacket for this one. Maybe they'd run out of henchman uniforms. Or else he liked to stand out from the crowd. He was no Devon dweller, that was for sure. Not in fashionably ripped jeans and a cream-and-brown hoody with *ROCK STAR* written across the back, the *A* of *STAR* replaced by a shiny gold star. Clean-shaven, short dark hair damp as though from the shower, he was zipping his hoody right up to the neck with a pronounced shudder as though he didn't like the cold.

Barton stepped aside from the other two to speak to him. It was only a brief conversation. The young man listened, nodding the whole time, smiling in a cheerful, open fashion. Like they were best friends. Savage could see his face, but not Barton's.

Barton took an envelope from inside his padded jacket and handed it over to this newcomer. Not casually, but with a meaningful nod.

The young man checked inside the envelope.

One cursory glance down at the contents.

A polite, 'I wouldn't dream of counting my payment in front of you,' gesture, 'but you know the form.'

The young man smiled again, folded the envelope carefully in half, and forced it down into the back pocket of his jeans. With a little difficulty, so obviously the envelope was quite bulky. Bank notes? Documents of some kind? Nothing that wouldn't fold in half, at any rate.

He shook Barton's hand, called out a farewell to the other two, and headed without a backwards glance for one of the white Transit vans parked beside the gate. The dirtier one. The one that looked like it had driven a long way through adverse weather conditions.

Using his shotgun like a flag, Cooper waved to the large, ginger-haired man in the guard tower beside the gate.

A moment later the gate was swinging open, the whole structure creaking ominously.

It was only after the white Transit had rattled speedily out of the gate, knocking dirt and gravel sideways under the spin of its tyres, that Savage realised what he had heard.

'Poka!'

The young man had said goodbye in Russian, not English.

Once the white Transit had cleared the threshold, the gate began to close again. More noisy creaking, like a galleon under full sail. By then, Barton and the other two had disappeared into a small outbuilding set beside the gate, and shut the door behind them.

Savage saw the back of the guard's ginger head as he too turned away, presumably to watch the van's progress over the moorland track.

Nobody else was in sight.

He slipped out from behind the hedge and made swiftly for the farmhouse, ducking round the back rather than attempting to enter through the front door. Best to avoid trouble for as long as possible. Though he knew trouble would eventually find him, as it always did.

CHAPTER TWENTY-NINE

The back door was locked, but one of the ground floor windows was unlocked. It was an old-fashioned sash window, perfect for burglars. But he imagined Barton was not too worried about security within the compound itself, confident in the height of his fence to keep out would-be intruders. It was the work of a few minutes to wriggle through the gap and jump down on the other side, narrowly avoiding a tall swing-top bin.

Savage stood still a few seconds, listening, but heard nothing. It was dark but there was enough light under the door to see that he was in some kind of pantry. It had a gleaming slate floor and exposed brickwork, the tail-end of an enormous weight-bearing roof beam protruding through a gap just beneath the ceiling. Very Poldark, he thought, eyeing his surroundings. Two huge fridges sat humming away to themselves, one topped with a sleeping tabby, curled up in a ball. The cat opened one baleful eye to glare at him, but otherwise did not stir. There were tinned and boxed goods on open shelves from floor almost to ceiling level. Several large cans of value olive oil stood in a corner behind the door.

Everything looked neat and well-ordered. No laid-back hippy commune this. Crazed cult leader or not, Barton ran a tight ship.

There were even cleaning rotas on the wall, Savage noted. Teams of two. Male and female. Pippa and George had ticked off their slot at 10.47 last night. Daisy and Andrew were up next. Brooms, feather-dusters, mops were all resting against the wall, along with buckets and a collection of cleaning products, ready for use.

The door was closed. He listened again, in case anyone was in the room behind it. There was no sound. It would be just his luck if it were locked, he thought wryly. But when he tried the handle, it gave easily.

The room beyond was empty. It was a large slate-floor dining room that gave onto a galley kitchen. There was a long dining table of old oak, set with narrow benches. An open hearth completed the picture of rural contentment, stacked with balls of newspaper and twigs for kindling, along with several baskets of logs. A feeling of warmth and the smoky, woodsy smell of the room suggested that a fire had only recently gone out.

He peered through the kitchen door.

Nobody about.

But there was a set of keys on the table. Transit van keys, with a helpful little key fob marked with the number plate. The remaining white van outside.

Beside it was a remote control.

He picked it up and turned it over. No helpful label, unfortunately. But he had seen a few garage door clickers in his time, and he guessed that this one opened the entrance gate. Like a back-up. It was a big gate. Hard to open manually, he was willing to bet. So this was a remote control to get you inside if nobody was in the guard tower when you arrived. A nifty little gadget, in other words.

The clicker had only two buttons.

A large green button, and a smaller red button below it.

Green for GO. Red for STOP.

That was the usual way these things worked.

Except this wasn't a clicker for a set of traffic lights. It was for an entrance gate. So green must mean OPEN, and red was CLOSE.

Savage pushed the keys and the clicker into the two front pockets of his jeans. One in each pocket. He wasn't particularly comfortable on the clicker side, as it was slightly too large for the pocket. But it could prove useful later. His primary plan was to get Dani and take her out the way he had come in. Via the Green Chapel, in other words. That was the exit route with the fewest question marks over it. In and out, sweet and simple. In his experience though, sweet-and-simple plans frequently went awry and needed a back-up plan.

Outside the dining room was a hallway with a flight of wooden stairs leading to the first floor, the stairs carpeted to reduce noise. Savage took them at once, treading as softly as he could. No point hanging about when he could be discovered at any moment.

It was dark on the first floor, the only window curtained.

A few feet away, near the top of the stairs, a man was slumped in a chair. He had a double-barrelled shotgun on his lap, held loosely just above his knees, and a shell pouch at his belt.

Put there to guard Dani's bedroom, almost certainly.

Except he had fallen asleep.

Savage paused, then crept towards the man. As he drew closer, he recognised the man. It was the constable he had seen at the farmhouse window that night, with Dani.

PC Charlie Petherick.

A floorboard creaked under his foot, and Petherick stirred.

There was no time to think.

Savage grabbed the shotgun off his lap as the man rose. He spun it round and pointed the business end straight at Petherick's face.

'Fancy a hole instead of a face?' he said, keeping his voice low.

Petherick froze.

'Good lad,' Savage said. 'Now, get up very slowly. No sudden moves, no loud noises. I have a very twitchy trigger finger. Understand?'

Pale-faced, Petherick nodded.

'Give me that belt.'

Warily, Petherick unfastened the belt with its pouch of shells, then handed it over. Balancing the shotgun against his hip, its muzzle still pointed directly at the bent police officer, Savage wrapped the belt loosely about his wrist.

He tried the bedroom door. It wouldn't budge but there was a key on the low table next to the door.

'Unlock the door, Charlie,' he said.

'Wait,' Petherick began, his eyes desperate, but Savage hiked the gun higher and put a finger against his lips.

'Hush, no talking.'

Suddenly, one of the doors opposite opened.

They both looked in that direction.

A dark-haired woman peered out at them, sleepy and surprised, belting up her pink dressing gown. She had huge eyes in a thin face, with thick brows that drew together as she stared from PC Petherick to Savage, then studied the shotgun. Her hand paused on her belly, unmistakably protective.

The woman was in her early twenties, and heavily pregnant.

Savage smiled at the woman sideways. What he hoped was a reassuring, 'Yes, I'm holding a shotgun, but I mean you no harm,' kind of smile. 'Good morning,' he said, hoping she spoke English. 'Sorry if we disturbed you, but could you possibly go back in your room?'

Without a word, she closed the door as silently as she'd opened it.

He transferred his gaze back to Petherick.

'OK, then,' he said, and nodded to the door. 'Open it up.'

With obvious reluctance, Petherick took the key and unlocked the door. 'Now get inside, and remember . . . This finger of mine is incredibly unpredictable.'

Savage followed him into the bedroom, nudging the door shut with his foot.

The room was dimly-lit, blinds drawn against the morning light. There was a woman asleep in an armchair near the window, swathed in black like a widow, even her blonde hair hidden beneath a black lace cap.

Dani was lying on the bed, tied to the bedposts with rope by both wrists. She half-lifted her head, staring at them both in mute astonishment.

'Dani,' he said.

There was no recognition in her face.

She was very pale, just as he remembered. Her dark hair was tied up in a severe ponytail and her cheek was heavily bruised. The *belle dame sans merci* had been shown the back of someone's hand, it seemed. Unless she'd walked into a few cupboards during her incarceration.

Even if he hadn't instantly known her face, the delicate black letter P tattooed on her forearm would have given her away.

'Have you forgotten who I am?' He came closer, keeping a careful eye on Petherick. 'Aubrey Savage. We met in a lay-by. You'd broken down, and I stopped to help. Someone came along and took you away from me. It's taken me some time to find you again, for which I apologise. But now I'm here to rescue you, OK?'

'I . . . I do remember you.' Dani sounded stunned.

'You left your hold-all in my camper, you know.' Her eyes widened with sudden comprehension, and he knew she was thinking of the Glock. 'Yeah, exactly.'

She said nothing, but glanced at the shotgun trained on Petherick.

'I wish we had time for a proper catch-up, but we don't. Not unless you want us to run into the Reverend Barton, that is.' Savage saw her apprehensive look, and nodded grimly. He glanced towards the window. 'Can we get out that way?'

'Too high.'

Abruptly, the woman in the armchair leapt up and charged towards Savage. She had a vast blade in her hand, some kind of ornately handled hunting knife. She was also far older than he had realised, easily in her sixties.

His brain went into automatic mode.

Eliminate the threat.

Only he couldn't fire on her.

Not only was she a sixty-something woman, if remarkably spry for her age, but the house was steeped in heavy silence. The deafening sound of a shotgun obliterating an old lady would bring everyone running.

Including Barton.

In a split-second, he had spun the shotgun round and slammed the stock end into her knife-hand just as she reached him. The knife clattered harmlessly to the floor. She shrieked, a flash of teeth, furiously grimacing as she lunged forward again. Like she intended to chew him to death. He drew back the gun, then thrust hard with the stock again. A stunning blow to the head this time.

The blonde assassin went down, crumpling in a heap of black material.

Petherick had not moved.

Breathing a little faster, Savage spun the shotgun again and pointed it at Petherick. 'OK, who the hell is that?'

'Mother Barton.'

'Say again?'

'Reverend Barton's mother,' Petherick said, his tone surly. 'She's Russian. They call her Mother Barton.' He looked down at the woman. 'He's not going to be very happy about this. You should know that.'

'One less for the Christmas card list, then.' Savage gestured to the bed. 'Untie my friend. And don't try anything stupid.' While the policeman was wrestling with Dani's bonds, Savage went to the window and checked the height. Definitely not possible to jump it. The only good news was, he couldn't see anyone out there or hear an alarm being raised. When the woman rushed him, making that godawful noise, he'd expected more guards to come running. But it seemed they were cocky enough not to bother guarding the farmhouse as heavily as the gate. 'Good, now tie the other one up in her place.'

He watched as the young man dragged the unconscious Mother Barton onto the bed. Tying her up wouldn't be enough to stop her raising the household, but he could manage some damage limitation, at least.

Savage dragged open a drawer and tossed over an item of underwear. 'Use this to gag her. Come on, hurry up.'

Dani came over to him, rubbing her wrists and looking shaky. 'What now?'

'We'll have to go out the same way I came in.' Savage looked her up and down. The bridal gown had gone, at least. No pyjamas either, thankfully. That would have been awkward. She was in jeans and jumper, but barefoot. 'Where are your shoes?'

Dani grabbed at a pair of boots beside the bed, hopping rapidly into them.

'What are we going to do with *him*?' she whispered, glancing at Charlie Petherick, who had finished his task and was watching them in silence.

Savage studied the room thoughtfully.

It was a good question.

The woman on the bed had begun to groan, coming round.

Her eyelids flickered open and she stared groggily at Savage and his shotgun.

'Sorry about that,' Savage told her. 'I imagine you're going to need a few headache pills. But at least I didn't shoot you.'

Some garbled response came from behind her gag, probably in Russian. Then she rolled about, testing her weight against the ropes.

'You've done this before, haven't you?' Savage said, grinning, and was rewarded with a hate-filled glare from the older woman.

'We need to go,' Dani said.

He turned to Petherick. 'Turn round and kneel down. Hands behind your back.' He grabbed a sturdy-looking bra from the underwear drawer and threw it to Dani. 'Tie his wrists together. Tight as you can.' He walked round and looked into Petherwick's face, using the shotgun to punctuate his message. 'You're going in that cupboard. Gagged like her. And I want you to stay put at least ten minutes.'

A hint of cunning came into Petherwick's face.

'Yes, you could get out quicker and come after us. But if that happens, you're going to have a dental appointment with this shotgun. Police or no police.' He met Petherick's eyes. 'Do I make myself understood?'

Petherwick nodded.

'Shit.' Dani, still crouched behind the policeman, stopped what she was doing and looked up at Savage. 'You need to look at this.'

He came round.

Dani lifted the policeman's jacket, and pointed silently.

'Well, well.'

There was a handgun nestled between his shirt back and the waistband of his jeans. Savage pulled it free, weighing it in his hand. It was a Glock 17, not unlike the Glock 19 he'd found in Dani's holdall, though less compact.

'What, did you forget you had a gun hidden away back there?' He showed the handgun to Petherick, who said nothing, though his cheeks were flushed now, a dull anger in his face. With a grin, Savage tucked the gun in his own waistband. 'That's two I've taken from you now. Pretty careless of you, Charlie.'

He glanced at Mother Barton. She was lying still now, perhaps having given up trying to break free, but her face was alight with fury. Though he couldn't be sure how much of their conversation she understood, it was clear she was deeply unimpressed by Petherick.

Dragging the bent copper back to his feet, he thrust a pair of sheer black tights into his mouth, then shoved him into the wall closet. It was a narrow space, never intended to accommodate a person. Petherick stumbled into a hanging row of women's garments, some of them still in plastic dry-cleaning wrappers, and turned to glare at Savage, his eyes bulging above a nylon-stuffed mouth.

'Stay,' Savage said, and shut the door in his face.

It was dim and silent on the landing. He ushered Dani out of the room, and then locked it behind them. 'Follow me,' he said, and trod softly back towards the stairs, keeping the shotgun level, the pouch of shells jingling as it swayed from his wrist.

As they reached the top of the stairs, a door opened behind them.

'Dani?'

He turned and looked back, primed to shoot if necessary. A warning shot, preferably. But if anyone took a shot at him, he was prepared to defend himself.

No need to shoot, he realised, and lowered the weapon.

It was another woman, staring at them from behind her partly open door, looking at the shotgun first, then from him to Dani.

For a second, he thought it was the woman from before. Same large, pregnant belly. Same frightened look. Only this one was blonde, not a brunette. A blonde with sharp blue eyes, her hair braided to one side, hanging down one smooth cheek like a bell rope. Late teens or very early twenties, he guessed. And as shocked as she was scared.

'Dani?' the blonde woman asked, her voice husky and foreign. 'Where are you going? What's happening?'

'It's OK,' Dani told her in a whisper, and put a finger to her lips when the woman opened her mouth again. 'We're getting out of here. You want to come too?'

The blonde looked at the shotgun again, and then shook her head, clearly terrified. The door closed and Dani gave an unhappy shrug.

'Let's go,' she told him.

'Sure?'

'That was Natasha. She won't say anything.'

Savage hesitated, unsure whether he should be leaving pregnant women in the farmhouse, given the situation with Barton. But they didn't seem to be in imminent danger, and he could always come back for them later.

Natasha.

Another Russian name.

The sound of a man's voice outside in the yard made the decision for him.

Reverend Barton.

'Hurry,' Dani said, panicked now.

Savage went quickly down the stairs, aware of her right behind him at every step. They ran together across the silent dining room into the pantry. As he shut the door behind them, he could already hear Barton coming into the house through the kitchen. He was talking to someone with short occasional pauses, but no audible replies. On his mobile phone, presumably.

Squatting behind the closed pantry door, shotgun in hand, Savage signalled Dani to stay still and quiet.

She rolled her eyes at him.

'That's not good enough,' Barton was saying in that smooth American accent, though with an edge now. The Reverend sounded worried. 'I need to clear the place out by the end of today.' A short pause. 'No, I'm not kidding. There's been a serious issue here. It's resolvable but in the meantime, I've had Konstantin move five out, and I want the rest gone as soon as you can get someone here.' Another pause. 'That can be arranged. Yeah, yeah, whatever you want. You scratch my back, I scratch yours.'

Barton laughed, suddenly so loud, he had to be standing right outside the pantry door. 'Sure thing. I'll be expecting your call.'

Barton rang off.

For a moment, there was silence outside the pantry. Savage waited, unmoving. In the pale light, he saw Dani's eyes gleaming, wide and apprehensive.

Then Barton muttered, 'What the hell . . . ?'

The Reverend headed away, shoes squeaking on the polished floor, making swiftly for the stairs by the sound of it.

Frowning, Savage became aware of a dull, rhythmic thudding from somewhere above their heads. Petherick trying to get out of the closet, perhaps. Or Mother Barton slamming her body up and down on the bed, struggling to be free. No wonder Barton was in a hurry to get up there.

They might have only seconds before the alarm was raised.

'Out the window, quick.' He cupped his hands to help her reach the sill. Her weight was negligible. She was partway through the window when the silence was broken by a man's voice above them.

Barton, shouting frantically for his guards.

Lights came on outside the pantry door.

Dani was already out of the window. Savage followed her, no longer caring about keeping quiet.

He dropped heavily beside Dani, who was crouched on the dewy grass, her face blank. 'Where now?' she whispered.

Two men in padded green jackets were emerging from the narrow path down to the Green Chapel. One had a shotgun, the other was unarmed. Some kind of patrol that must have missed him when he came up that way earlier. The unarmed man stopped, responding to a call on his mobile, and the other halted too, turning to listen.

That would be Barton on the phone. No doubt warning the guards that Dani had escaped, and to look out for her and Savage, or some other accomplice. Barton was unlikely to believe that a woman of Dani's slender build could have broken out of her room and knocked out an armed guard on her own.

The two men were listening intently to the call, both heads bent over the mobile. They were also blocking the path down to the chapel. Not that it mattered. The time to slip out unnoticed was long gone.

He nodded towards the remaining long-wheelbase Transit van.

'We're taking that.'

Dani stared. 'But the gate's shut.'

'Let me worry about that.' He dragged the Transit van keys out of his jeans pocket and handed them to her. 'You just get over there without being caught. Left-hand drive, I'm afraid. It's a Russian vehicle.' He smiled encouragingly when she blinked. 'Start her up and back away from the gate, OK?'

Dani's fist closed about the keys, but she did not move.

'You can do this,' he told her firmly. 'But you need to go right now, Dani. It's now or never. Or Barton's going to take you back.'

That reality check seemed to snap Dani into action. She gave a jerky nod. Then she launched herself across the narrow strip of lawn between the farmhouse and the gravel yard, staying low and not looking back.

The men had seen her.

The one with the shotgun called her name, spinning round with his gun ready. But the other one had also seen Savage. He said something, and his friend hesitated, staring from Dani to Savage. Then the shotgun turned in his direction.

'Stay where you are,' the man shouted.

Savage paid no attention. He straightened and walked towards the men, his own double-barrelled shotgun pointed towards them, the stock lodged hard into his shoulder, a familiar, reassuring discomfort, ready to fire.

'You don't want to point that at me, mate,' he said calmly. 'I know more about shooting people than you ever will. So how about you throw me your weapon and we all get to walk away from this? Or are you prepared to die for the Reverend Barton?'

The muzzle of the other gun wavered but did not drop.

Behind him, the van started up. The smell of diesel fumes filled the cool morning air. Then the wheels were spitting gravel as Dani backed up at speed.

He began to walk hurriedly backwards in her direction, keeping an eye on the two men. Soon he was on the gravel and level with the farmhouse, still pointing his shotgun at them.

To his surprise, they didn't follow him.

He soon found out why.

'You'll never get out of here,' Barton said, coming out of the farmhouse as he passed the doorway. At his back staggered PC Petherick, his face red with fury. He was nursing a purpling bruise on his forehead, which suggested that somebody had already punished his failure. Not necessarily Barton, who looked angry but had it under control. 'You made a serious mistake coming back here.'

'My mistakes are always serious. What's the point, otherwise?'

'You're an arrogant man, Mr Savage, and that will be your downfall.' Barton shook his head. 'I was prepared to let it go before. I'm not merely a preacher, you see. I'm a man of the world. And I can understand you wanting to help a pretty girl.'

'I bet you can.'

Barton managed a half smile. 'I've made helping pretty women my life's work. Nothing wrong in following that kind of natural God-given urge.' His voice hardened. 'But you had to come back for Dani. You had to make this personal. Which means I can't be held responsible for what happens next.'

Savage, shotgun butt lodged in his shoulder, was trying to cover all four men at once. Not easy, but he only had to do it for another couple of minutes, at a guess.

There was the Glock he'd taken from Petherick, of course. But he hadn't had time yet to check how many cartridges were remaining in the magazine.

Besides, while it might look cool in the movies, staggering about with a shotgun in one hand, pistol in the other, it was rarely a useful combination in a combat situation. Not with the kick from a shotgun, where you needed to brace for it, rather than shoot wildly from the hip and end up spraying everything in sight.

'Fair enough,' he said.

With his free hand, he dug into his jeans pocket for the clicker and pointed it in the vague direction of the gate. He only hoped it really was the clicker for the gate, and not something that opened a garage door or operated the television. Because if so, he was about to look very foolish indeed.

Barton frowned, then saw what he was holding up. His eyes widened.

Too late.

Savage pressed the green button on the clicker.

CLICK.

The gate grated protestingly over gravel as it began to swing open.

'Kyle!' Barton shouted, turning on his heel, and Savage suddenly remembered the guard in the gate tower. 'Close the gate at once!'

Kyle must have been watching proceedings below, no doubt bemused at what he was seeing. But he reacted instantly at his boss's command. The heavy gate juddered to a halt, then slowly reversed direction, beginning to close again.

Savage pointed the clicker behind his head a second time.

CLICK.

'Kyle!'

The gate stopped, then creaked the other way again.

Savage held up his clicker to countermand that order, and a shot whizzed past his ear. He dodged, belatedly remembering the guy on the gate tower was armed, possibly with a rifle. He was nearly at the back of the van now, standing in the white smoking diesel as Dani revved the engine noisily, her urgency unmistakable.

He whipped the shotgun round to face the Reverend Barton. His finger caressed the trigger. It was so tempting . . .

'You do that again, Kyle,' he called out clearly, 'and I'll put a hole through your leader's head.' He met Barton's furious gaze and could see him calculating the odds. He pressed the green button on the clicker again, and listened to the gate shuddering open again. 'This has been fun, and theoretically we could do this all day. But I'm on a schedule. So if you want to live, call Kyle off.'

Barton's face twisted, and for an instant there was real malevolence there. Then his ready smile returned.

'Very well, Mr Savage. Since it looks like I don't have much of a choice here.' He raised his voice. 'Leave the gate, Kyle. And put down the gun. It seems our guests are leaving.'

'Thank you.'

Savage backed towards the Transit van, feet crunching on the gravel. Then he turned and ran the last couple of feet, jumping in through the door Dani had opened for him. One step up, and he was in the passenger seat, the shotgun across his lap.

'Drive,' he said, and pressed the clicker for the last time.

CHAPTER THIRTY

Dani drove through the closing gate like the devil was after her.

Before the van had bounced ten feet along the mud rut-ridden track, Savage heard a high-pitched crack. Then another. Then another.

'What the hell . . . ?' Dani sounded panicked.

Savage craned his neck to peer over his shoulder. There was another crack as a bullet impacted the back of the van. The guard in the tower was taking his job very seriously. Kyle. Probably ex-military. The type who never got a proper shot off at anyone in the whole of his career, and was now gung-ho, a willing recruit to Barton's private army.

'Better put your foot down,' he said.

'Is someone shooting at us?'

'Let's not stick around to find out.'

The whine of another bullet overhead. Either the guy's technique was sadly rusty, or that had been a warning shot. *Stop or else.*

Dani didn't stop. She accelerated instead, mud thrown up wildly under the churning tyres. Seconds later, the driver's side wing mirror shattered with an ominous crack. It seemed Kyle was finished with the warning shots, or had finally warmed up.

Dani yelped and flinched, glancing at the large, cracked wing mirror, her shoulders hunched. 'Are they crazy?'

'It's a distinct possibility.'

'Are you always this calm when people are shooting at you?"

'They're shooting at the van, really.' He studied her. She looked paler than he remembered. Deadly pale. Like she was about to vomit. 'You OK?'

Dani didn't reply. Perhaps she had not heard him. Or perhaps she thought it was a ridiculous question, given the circumstances. 'Shit, shit, shit,' she began chanting under her breath like a mantra. Which was fair enough. Whatever helped.

'Get round this next bend. Then we'll be out of range.'

She gripped the wheel like she was strangling it, and stared ahead with a fixed stare. They took the bend at an uncomfortable speed, the van skidding on loose mud, its rear end flying out just after they entered the bend.

'Maybe ease off a touch,' he said helpfully, 'then accelerate again after you hit the middle of the curve.'

Dani swore at him, but eased off slightly. The van drifted back into the correct line, then roared away down the narrow track as she reapplied the accelerator mid-bend. Not pretty, but it had done the job. They were out of sight of the guard tower, more or less hidden behind huge, rambling spring hedgerows. Though he doubted they were invisible. The long-wheelbase Transit van would be easy to spot with binoculars, especially from the vantage point of the guard tower.

He checked his wing mirror, still thankfully intact.

No sign of any pursuit.

'Where now?' she asked, slowing to a halt.

They'd reached the junction with the moorland road. One way led due north, the other south-west. A couple of vehicles passed at speed while they sat there, doing maybe sixty miles per hour in the early morning light, secure in the knowledge that few other drivers would be about yet. One was a holiday-maker, heading south, surf boards strapped to the top of his estate car. The other was a vast, round-bellied milk truck, chuntering along the empty road.

'Sure you're OK?'

Dani was breathing fast, hands still clutched on the wheel as though glued there. 'What do you think?' She turned to stare at him. 'You helped Rose escape too, didn't you? I saw you last night. Who *are* you?'

'Let's get you somewhere safe first. Then we can play twenty questions.' He checked his phone. Several new texts from Faith. Variations on a theme of, *Where the hell are you?* 'That way.' He pointed south-west, back towards the pub where Faith had taken Rose last night. 'I need to check in with my lawyer.'

'Your . . . what?'

'Turn left, please.'

'No.' She was looking the other way. There was panic in her voice now. 'I have to go home. Terry will be waiting—'

'Terry's safe. I think he's with Geoff.'

She blinked, then refocused on his face. 'You saw Terry?' She seemed baffled. 'And Geoff? You spoke to them both?' When he nodded, she sucked in a shaky breath. 'Oh my God. How are they? What did Terry say about his brother? No, don't bother. I'll ask them myself.' She indicated right automatically. 'I'm going to Geoff's place.'

He grabbed at the wheel as she began to turn it. 'No.'

'Now, listen here. I'm very grateful for what you did back there. For me and for Rose. But I don't know who the hell you are, and this isn't your business.'

'Geoff's is the first place they'll look for you,' he said calmly. 'If you go there, you'll only be putting them in danger.' He paused. 'You don't want him to end up like Callum, do you?' Another pause. 'Or Billy.'

That seemed to sink in. Her hands began to shake on the wheel, and now she really did look like she was about to throw up.

'Oh God, Billy . . .'

So he'd been right about Billy. He wanted to know what the lad had done, why Barton had turned on him so vehemently. But that too would have to wait. Sooner or later, he would come after Dani, as his men had done on Savage's first night on the moors. And he didn't want them to be still sitting here in the emptiness of the wilds when that happened.

'But what can I do then? Where can I go?'

'You can go where I took Rose.'

'Which is where?'

'That way.' He tugged the steering wheel in the other direction, and Dani reluctantly followed his lead, turning out onto the deserted southbound lane. He checked in his wing mirror, but nobody was following them. Though that didn't mean they wouldn't be soon. 'It's a pub that, you know, does accommodation.' He took his phone and flicked through to Faith's message, then keyed her inn's postcode into the van's Satnav. Its disembodied voice told them that they would arrive at their destination in sixteen minutes. 'See? Not far at all.'

'A pub, though? Seriously?' She shook her head, her voice rising. 'He's got Mike Cooper, remember. Mike knows all the hotels and pubs on the moors. They'll find us in no time.'

'Maybe. But I doubt they'll come looking for us. Not there, anyway.'

'How can you be so sure?'

'This is Barton's place.' He gestured to the vast, windswept landscape on either side of the road. 'He likes the wide open spaces of Dartmoor. The mists and loneliness of high places. The empty roads that go on forever, especially at night when there are few other cars about. People are at their most vulnerable up here on the moors. They can be frightened and preyed upon. Terrorised. Hunted and killed without interference.' He turned the shotgun over, examining the barrel and magazine.

It was in good nick. 'But nearer the towns and villages, where the people are, where you get schools and shops and guest houses, that's where he can't risk being seen. Or not for what he truly is.'

'And what's that?'

He laid the shotgun down in the space under the front seats, and tossed the pouch after it into the narrow space.

'You tell me.'

'Sorry?'

'It's time for those questions you were so keen on earlier. Only I'm the one who's asking them. What exactly is happening at the Green Chapel, Dani?'

Her foot slipped on the accelerator, and the van jerked forward. She recovered herself with a muttered apology, saying something about wet boots. But he wasn't fooled.

'Don't bother giving me the official spiel either, OK? I already heard all that nonsense about holy water and special seed and infertility treatments from Geoff and Terry, and I don't believe a word of it.' He pressed on, seeing her suddenly tense and wary. 'Come on, Dani. That's two of you I've rescued now. Not that I'm keeping a tally, but I think I've earned the truth. What is Barton really up to at the Green Chapel?'

CHAPTER THIRTY-ONE

For a few moments, she didn't say anything. Then she whispered, 'I can't. Honestly, I want to help. But he'd kill me.'

'Barton?'

She nodded.

'Not if I kill him first,' he said.

'You? On your own?'

He was amused by the surprise in her voice. 'Why not?'

Dani turned her head and looked him up and down in a deliberate fashion. With her face so pale and her hair hanging in dark tendrils about her face, her ponytail having come loose at some point during their escape, she looked more than ever like the *belle dame sans merci* from Keats's poem, the faery's child encountered in the wilderness. Her gaze was brutal though.

'You might be able to handle one or two of his men OK, like you did just now. But you took them off guard. They weren't expecting you. And Barton has an army. No offence, but kill him?' Her laughter was hollow. 'You'd never get close enough.'

'I just did, didn't I?'

'You were lucky,' she said bluntly. 'Rev Barton won't let that happen again. He'll be ready for you next time.'

'He wasn't ready for me this morning. And I took Rose away from him last night. He didn't even set guards on the Green Chapel. That doesn't sound to me like someone who's big on preparation.'

'That was . . . unusual. He was distracted.'

'By?'

She swallowed. 'Billy,' she said, her voice sinking to a whisper again.

'Tell me about Billy.'

Again, she sucked in her breath. This time audibly. 'I can't.'

'So you're OK with what happened to him?'

'God, no.' Her foot lifted slightly off the accelerator. 'Of course I'm not. How can you even suggest that?'

'Don't slow down, Dani. I can't guarantee Barton won't be coming after us. You can drive and talk, can't you? I thought women were meant to be multi-taskers?'

She stared at him, then leant forward to check behind them in his wing mirror, the only one still functioning, before speeding up again. 'You're an annoying bastard, do you know that?'

'It has been said.'

Dani gave an abrupt laugh, then sank back into despondency, her shoulders slumped again. 'I suppose it doesn't matter now. Billy didn't have a chance anyway. Not after what he did. He . . . They'll have caught him.'

'Barton's mob?'

She nodded. 'He calls them his hunters. That's what happened to Callum. Poor bloody sod. He gives you a head start, then sends them out after you over the moors. Like it's a game. Only it's not. Because if they catch you . . .' Her voice faltered. 'When they catch you . . .'

'And then they hang you up like a scarecrow as a warning to others?'

She was shocked. 'You know about that?'

'The police fingered me for it.'

'*What?*'

'I imagine it was a case of wrong place, wrong time.'

She looked perplexed.

'The lay-by,' he reminded her gently. 'The Diamond White MG and a damsel in distress. The young man in the field next to the road, with a bullet through his head.' She blenched, and he felt annoyed with himself. That young man had been her brother-in-law. 'I'm sorry.'

'It's OK,' she said, but she didn't look OK. 'The police thought you did it? Killed Callum? But why?'

'That was where their theory fell down. There was nothing to tie me in that wasn't circumstantial.' He grimaced. 'Hence the need for a lawyer.'

'You mentioned him before. So that's where we're going? To see your lawyer?'

She was trying to steer him away from the conversation about Billy and what he'd done to deserve such a terrible punishment. But he didn't mind a slight detour if it helped her relax enough to be more frank with him.

'Her,' he said.

'Sorry?'

'My lawyer is a woman.' He checked his phone again. 'Her name's Faith. And I've been ignoring her texts since last night. So I imagine she's feeling pretty hacked off with me right now.'

'I wonder why.'

Savage smiled at her dry tone. 'Let's put her out of her misery, shall we?' He hit Faith's number and waited, staring out over the milky brown-green of the moors. The sun had risen and was slowly drying out the night's dampness, a swathe of bright sunshine blazing across the wilderness a few miles ahead of them, like gold spilling down from the massed clouds.

Faith answered at the second ring, her voice breathless. 'Thank God. Where are you? I've been worried sick.'

'Did you get my photo?'

'Of course.' She hesitated. 'Aubrey, how are you?' When he didn't answer, she added, 'I know about Peter. I'm so sorry.'

He stared at the grim landscape ahead.

'Aubrey?'

'I'm OK.' He was aware of Dani glancing at him, and shifted away, looking out of the side window instead. Same barren moorland, different view. 'What was the police verdict?'

'Nothing official yet. But I heard one of them say it looked like suicide.'

'Bullshit.'

She sounded startled. 'Really? You think it was murder?'

'Yes. Unless he shot himself with the wrong hand.'

'I don't follow.'

'The entry wound was in the right side of the temple. Only Peter was left-handed. He would have shot himself on the other side.'

'Oh my God.' Again, she said, 'I'm so sorry.'

'I told you, I'm OK.'

'All the same . . . He was one of your oldest friends.'

Aubrey cleared his throat. 'Tell me about the vehicles in the photo.'

'For God's sake!'

'I'm fairly certain Barton was behind his murder. So the best way to avenge Peter is to nail Barton and his outfit.' His hand tightened on the phone. 'Whichever way we can.'

'Fair enough. But look, I'm not a private detective. So don't expect miracles, right?' He waited, knowing there would be more. Sure enough, she continued more lightly, 'Anyway, I made a few calls to an old friend in the government, and both vans are registered to the same Russian company. I looked them up, and they mostly provide cheap labourers within the building trade to various locations in the UK. That's about it. Nothing sinister.'

'And the cars?'

'Local owners, all of them. Members of his crew, I expect.'

'What about the Land Rover Defender?'

'That's registered to a Mike Cooper. Nothing suspicious there either. And no penalty points on his licence. The man's squeaky-clean. Owns a local gun shop.'

'He's one of the guys who clashed with me and Peter up on the ridge that day.'

There was a strange silence on the other end of the phone.

'Faith? You still there?'

'I'm still here. But my friend in the government was unimpressed. She was asleep. Like most sane people at that hour of the morning. And it was awkward, trying to explain why I needed that information, especially so urgently, without involving you.'

'I hope you told her it was all in a good cause.'

'I don't think Jane cares about good causes, Aubrey. She cares about a good night's sleep. I owe her a slap-up meal now.' Faith made a tutting sound. 'And her husband Jack, who was also disturbed by my call. They're about to become first-time parents too and were trying to get in as much rest as possible. So thank you for that. Nothing like an early call to ruin an old friendship.'

'Sorry.'

'Huh.' She made another noise under her breath, but seemed mollified by his apology. That was another good thing about Faith. She rarely stayed angry for long. 'Now where the hell are you?'

'On my way to you. With a friend.'

Now she sounded suspicious again. 'What friend?'

'Dani.'

'The woman from the lay-by? The one in the wedding dress? But you said she was being held prisoner by Barton. You mean, you took her away from him?'

'Yes.'

'Like Rose?'

'What's the problem? I sent you a text. I said I was going to the Green Chapel.'

'For a look round, I thought. Not to bring out another woman ... Were you seen?'

'Yes.'

She groaned.

'Look, how is Rose? Is she still with you?' He tapped Dani on the arm. They were coming up on a junction and the woman on the Satnav was instructing them to turn off the main road. But Dani did not appear to be listening, driving in a kind of daze, her lips moving but no sound coming out. 'Turn to the right here.'

Dani slammed on the brakes, muttering an apology.

'She's fine. Still very shaken, of course, but that's only to be expected.'

'Good.'

They turned down a leafy, sunlit lane, the scattered roofs of houses and a church tower in the near distance. Civilisation. Or as close to civilisation as they would come on the high moors.

'Stay on this road until we pass the church, then bear left,' he told Dani.

'Sorry, what?' On the other end of the phone, Faith sounded confused. 'Who are you talking to? Are you in a taxi?'

'I'm talking to Dani,' he said, studying the navigation screen on the Satnav. They weren't far off now. 'She's driving us to your accommodation.'

'Oh.' Faith sounded surprised. 'She had a car up at the Green Chapel, then?'

'It's a van. One of the long-wheelbase Transit vans in the photo I sent you, in fact.' He cleared his throat. 'We stole it.'

'*Stole* it?'

'Don't worry, Barton won't report the theft to the police. He's got too much to hide.'

'That's as may be. But the Russian owners might not take the same view.'

'I'm guessing they'll keep quiet too.'

They were passing through a tiny Dartmoor village. A car with trailer was coming the other way, sheep dog sitting up in the passenger seat. Dani squeezed closer to the low stone wall to let the car pass. A weathered-looking farmer in tweed jacket and flat cap was driving, three agitated sheep huddled in the open trailer behind. Savage glanced at the grey stone church. It had a squat Norman tower and half a dozen lichened elms leading to an ancient kissing gate. The gravestones looked ancient too, carved names blurred and illegible even in the early sunshine. Dani drove on past a stagnant-looking village pond shrouded by two vast weeping willows, long branches trailing in the murky green water.

It was the kind of village that had probably featured in the Domesday Book. As had the two old men, probably in their late eighties, seated on a bench outside the tiny one-room shop, which itself did not look as though it had opened for twenty years.

'We're nearly at yours. Speak in a minute.'

He rang off, and checked the shotgun and the shell pouch were still hidden under the seat. Probably best not to get out brandishing a firearm in this quiet village. Dani slowed as they approached the pub on the corner; The Green Man, its sign swinging gently in the wind. The pub was serviced by a tiny lane with a hand-painted sign that announced, *Private Parking At Rear. Guests Only*, in wobbly letters.

'OK, this is the place. Park round the back, out of sight of the road.'

Dani swung smartly into the turn, showing no concern at

the narrowness of the space compared to the broad sides of the Transit van.

Catching his expression, she flashed a grin. 'No need to look so surprised. I drove my dad's van for a year when he lost his licence.'

'I didn't say a word.'

She accelerated up the steep bank into the rear car park, gravel crunching under the tyres. Another hand-painted sign said, *Please Park Pretty*. There was one space left beside the dry stone wall at the far end, next to Faith's Mercedes. Dani reversed the Transit van into the tight space swiftly and without any obvious difficulty, seemingly unfazed by it being a left-hand drive vehicle.

Once the engine was off though, she sat staring straight ahead, no longer grinning, then took a shaky breath and looked down at her hands. They were trembling.

'Hey, it's OK, we got here,' Savage said with a smile, trying to reassure her. 'And in one piece.'

'But what's next? He's going to come for us, you know. All of us. Terry and Geoff too. I've got to warn them.' Dani gave a muffled cry. 'What have I done? Oh God, what the hell have I done?'

'The right thing,' he said. 'That's what you've done.'

Dani swivelled in her seat to glare at him. She was stunning in her wrath, slanted dark eyes flashing, a flush in her pale cheeks. He could see why Barton had tried so hard to keep hold of her. And why Callum had risked his life to get her back. The brother-in-law had clearly had a massive crush. And it had killed him, unfortunately.

'Easy for you to say.' Her Devon accent thickened deliciously when she was furious too. 'Why should you care what kind of hornets' nest you've kicked up? You don't live local. You can just pack up and drive away in your bloody camper. Back upcountry. The rest of us have to live here. With the consequences.'

'Maybe.' He grabbed one of the arms she was waving about in her fury, and turned it so he was looking down at the tattooed P. 'Is that P for Peter?'

'What?'

'Peter Rowlands. Were you having an affair with him?'

'I don't know what you're talking about.'

'You've got the letter P tattooed on your arm, Dani. Your husband's name is Terry.' He hesitated. 'What's Barton's first name?'

'Francis, I think.'

'OK, so that rules him out. But what about Peter? Were you and he in love?'

She squirmed in his hold, saying loudly, 'No, course not,' and he let her go.

'I'm not your enemy, Dani. I simply want to know what's going on.'

'It's just a stupid tattoo, OK? All the girls get them.'

'All what girls?'

She rubbed her thumb across the black etched P on her forearm, then shrugged. 'Up at the Green Chapel. All Barton's girls. The ones he . . .' Dani hesitated, licking her lips. 'The ones who go through the ceremony.'

'Why? What's the significance of the letter P?'

'I don't know. Barton said something about wine.'

Savage stared. 'Wine?'

'Something like that. What's it to you, anyhow? You'll be on your merry way in your camper soon, and you won't have to worry about any of us girls again.'

He gave up trying to persuade her to trust him. She was too angry to listen to reason. And the reference to wine had him baffled. He jumped down out of the van, then looked back up at her. She had not moved from her seat.

'I don't have my camper at the moment. So I can't be on my way. The police took it.'

Dani looked at him, wide-eyed. 'Boozing?'

'Forensics.'

'I don't understand.'

'To check for fingerprints and gunshot residue, I should imagine.'

'Because of Callum getting shot, you mean?' Tears came shining in her eyes and Dani fought them, lips pressed hard together, her chin trembling but still up. 'Poor bloody Callum. He was only trying to help. And Billy too, of all people. I couldn't believe it when I heard Barton had sent the hunters out after him.' The tears fell anyway, but Dani didn't pay any attention, wiping them away with the back of her hand. 'If anyone could have stopped him, it would have been Billy. He wasn't the nicest. A prize bastard to Rose. But people listened to him. Now there's nobody left to stand up to Barton.'

'That's not true. I'll stand up to him. But I can only do it with your help.' Savage paused. 'Will you help me, Dani? Help me stop this.'

Her eyes half-closed, then opened again. 'I can try, I s'pose. Though I'm not going to the police. You hear me? He'd kill Terry if I did.'

'I understand.'

Dani got out of the van and slammed the door, squeezing out of the tight space and walking round towards him. 'Here.' She handed him the van keys. Producing another hairband from her jeans pocket, she twisted her hair into a neat ponytail, tying it up again. 'I don't plan on driving that heap again.'

He studied the grubby van, its mud-encrusted tyres. 'It's done some serious mileage, hasn't it?'

Perhaps because it was rhetorical, Dani ignored that question, continuing, 'Besides, I don't know what possible help I can be.' Her voice was bleak. 'Not against a man like Rev Barton.'

'Leave that to me.'

She said nothing but grunted, seeming unconvinced.

He walked to the back of the van.

The back doors were unlocked.

He swung them open with a creaking sound and peered inside. The interior of the Transit van was clean enough. Too clean, perhaps. It looked like someone had hosed out the floor, roof and walls with disinfectant, and recently too, by the strong, acrid smell. The wood panel walls were dark with damp, and the narrow runnels near the door catch were still gleaming, a tell-tale liquid pooling there. Streaks along the floor showed where it had been mopped out after the hosing.

'Squeaky-clean.' He stood back to let Dani see too. 'Looks like somebody did a comprehensive job on that.'

Dani made a face. 'Smells like a hospital.'

'Bleach, probably.'

The back door of the pub swung abruptly open behind them, slamming into the brick wall behind.

'Aubrey? Why on earth do you have a gun sticking out of your jeans?'

Savage turned.

Faith was glaring out at him, hands on hips, looking tired and exasperated yet somehow elegant at the same time. She was wearing black tailored trousers with high-heel boots, flawless white blouse, and a grey waistcoat that hung unbuttoned and open. Faith had such impeccable taste, it was intimidating. She made him feel scruffy and unkempt. Though after a night sleeping rough on the moors, he probably deserved that description. And smelt pretty bad too.

Maybe her room would have an en suite shower he could

borrow for half an hour. Savage rubbed his chin ruefully. A shave wouldn't go amiss either.

Faith did not look exactly happy, he noted.

'Good morning,' he said, and smiled at her placatingly. 'Sorry about the gun. I picked it up on my travels. Thought it might come in handy.' Pulling his T-shirt loose from his jeans, he let it drape over the back, concealing the Glock he'd taken from PC Petherick. 'I hope you slept well.'

There was no answering smile from his lawyer. 'We need to talk,' Faith said. 'There's been a development.'

CHAPTER THIRTY-TWO

Faith's room was rather more upmarket than he'd expected from modest pub accommodation in the rural wilds of Dartmoor. It was decorated with cream flock wallpaper, with pastel pink curtains and a quilt to match on the double bed, a desk and table lamp, and a large mirror facing the window. The bed had been slept in, but not made, the covers creased, the pillows heaped up as though to support someone reading in bed.

A plasma television screen hung opposite the bed, beside a printed notice apologising for occasional poor reception due to being in the middle of bloody nowhere. Faith had left her laptop open on the desk beside her mobile, alongside an open archive file and a stack of papers, including some photographs. Presumably some other case she was working on.

'Where's Rose?' Dani asked at once, stopping in the middle of the room. Her voice was suspicious, as though she was afraid she'd walked into a trap.

Given Barton's psychotic behaviour, he could hardly blame her for being so cautious. She probably had no idea who to trust anymore.

'The room next door was vacated first thing this morning, so I booked it for her. She's in there now, trying to get some rest.' Faith began tidying the papers on the desk. 'It was an uncomfortable night, the two of us squeezed in here together, not sure whether to sleep or wait for a call. Besides, I didn't know how much longer she'd be staying with us.' She slipped the assembled papers into the archive file and closed the box with a snap. 'I thought it best to give us both some space.'

'I want to see her,' Dani said.

Faith glanced from him to Dani, suddenly hesitant, her law-yer instincts kicking in before she said anything revealing. 'Sorry, you must be Dani.'

'That's right,' Dani said shyly, her accent very Devonish.

'I'm Faith, Aubrey's lawyer.'

The two women shook hands, Dani suddenly uncertain and off balance. She probably wasn't the sort of person who did a lot of hand-shaking. Almost none, in fact. Though Faith did not look much better about the meeting.

'You can trust Dani. She's had a rough few days, that's all.' Savage put a hand on Faith's arm, trying to reassure her. 'Hey, you OK?'

Faith didn't reply, but gave a hoarse laugh.

He frowned, his hand dropping at once. Whatever had hap-pened, she was genuinely shaken up, that was obvious. She had hidden that well on the phone. Trained not to give anything away in her voice, he guessed.

'Faith, what's up?'

'The police found another body this morning,' Faith said. 'Out on the moors.' Dani made an abrupt noise under her breath, and Faith shifted her attention that way. But Dani made no comment, waiting to hear the rest with wide, fright-ened eyes. 'When they first told me, I thought . . .'

'You thought it was me.'

'But then I realised it couldn't be.' She hesitated. 'DI Paglia said it was a local man. Someone already known to the police. And that he'd died in the early hours of this morning. Violently.'

'I see.'

'No, I don't think you do.' Again, the anxious glance towards

Dani. What was she hiding? 'Paglia hinted that it wasn't a very pleasant crime scene.'

'Is there ever such a thing?'

'Aubrey, for God's sake.'

'Sorry.' He thought of Peter, and was angry with himself for that glib reply. That was the army training. Harden up or ship out. But Faith had never been part of that side of his life. 'I might know who Paglia was talking about. You remember the biker from last night?'

'Am I ever likely to forget? If you say it wasn't suicide, then he must have been the one who . . .' Faith took a deep breath. 'OK, what about him?'

'There's a good chance that was Billy.'

She frowned. 'Who?'

'The young man I'm guessing they found on the moors this morning. His name was Billy, and he was Rose's boyfriend.'

Faith closed her eyes. 'Oh no.'

'Exactly.' He felt Dani barge past them, and turned. 'Dani, where are you going?"

'To talk to Rose, of course.' Her face was flushed, and he could see she was on the point of tears. She looked at Faith, who was standing beside the window. 'She's next door, you said?' When the other woman didn't reply, she said aggressively, 'Rose is my friend. She needs to hear the bad news from me. Not you. Or him.'

'Rose is in room number two,' Faith said without turning round. 'It's the next door on the left. Three knocks like this,' she added, demonstrating the rhythm on the wall with her knuckles, 'is the signal that it's safe for her to answer the door.'

When Dani had gone, closing the door behind her, he sat down at the desk and looked across at Faith apologetically. She had still not turned round, and he could only guess at her state of mind.

'I'm sorry about all this,' Savage said.

From the corridor, they heard three rapid knocks.

Rose's door opened.

There was a quick exchange of exclamations. Probably some hugging too. Dani had struck him as a hugger. Rose sounded relieved to see her friend again too. Not surprising, given what the two of them had been through in recent days.

Then the door to Number Two closed again.

Faith left the window. She was playing with one of the buttons on her grey waistcoat, pushing it through the buttonhole, then pulling it out again.

'So that was your bride at the side of the road.' She was not looking at him. 'Well, at least she definitely exists. That's a solid alibi for you.'

'I didn't think I needed one.'

'In an ideal world you wouldn't.' She gave him an exasperated glance, then turned her head away again. 'For Christ's sake, Aubrey ... You storm that man's fortress, then come waltzing back with a blonde on your arm and a gun stuck down your trousers like you're Dirty bloody Harry.'

Savage suppressed the urge to grin; he suspected that wouldn't be the response she was looking for. 'I'm sorry about the way this has gone, Faith. If it's any consolation, I never meant to drag you into my mess.'

'But it's not your mess, is it? That's what I can't understand. You were just passing through. Why get involved?'

From next door, they heard a high-pitched cry of grief.

Rose, learning about Billy's death.

Faith sighed and ran a hand over her forehead. She looked tired.

'I can't just walk away,' he said gently. 'Not now. Not until I've found out who killed Peter. And why that had to happen.' He paused. 'What did Peter know that meant he had to be silenced?'

Faith did not respond. But he sensed her disapproval.

She thought he was imagining that Peter's death wasn't suicide. That it was wishful thinking. And he had to admit to
some doubts himself. Perhaps Peter had been ambidextrous,
and favoured the left hand but wasn't restricted to it.

Or maybe he was right, and Barton had put his friend down
like a stray dog.

'Oh, I nearly forgot.' Faith gave a heavy sigh and sat down on
the bed opposite him. She crossed her legs, a movement he
found mesmerising. 'Paglia said something else. Your camper's
ready for collection from the police pound. She gave me the
Satnav directions. Forensics have finished with it, and there's
nothing to tie you to that boy's murder. Which is great news.
Plus, they're working on the assumption that Peter's death was
a suicide. So you're free to go.'

He said nothing.

Faith took a deep breath. 'You're not leaving, are you?'

'I'm sorry,' he said again.

'Because of Peter?'

'I told you, he was my friend. I don't have many friends.'

'I wonder why,' she said drily. But she did not seem angry.
Merely resigned. 'I'm your friend too, remember.'

'I know.' He smiled. 'Thank you.'

This time she smiled too. 'So you think Barton was behind
Peter's death. That his suicide was faked.'

'Because it was.'

'That's your theory, Aubrey. Wanting something to be true
doesn't make it a fact.' She made a face. 'OK, I'll see what else I
can find out about that.' Faith glanced out of the window. 'You
can't leave that van there, you know. It's stolen property. I can't
be implicated in anything like that.'

'I'll move it once I've had a word with Rose. I'll find somewhere discreet to leave it. Then perhaps you could drive me
over to the pound to pick up my camper?'

'Driving you around is what I live for.'

Neither of them spoke for a few minutes.

The sound of sobbing from the next room was audible through the thin walls. Rose, presumably, mourning her boy-friend. Billy had abandoned her to Barton's sadistic attentions, it was true. But he'd tried to make up for that afterwards, and it had cost him his life. Like Terry's brother, he had stood up to a bully and death had been his reward.

Rose weeping made him angry again.

'There'll be a post-mortem,' he said. 'I'll stay on. Wait for that. Maybe it will shed some light on what happened to Peter.'

An image of Peter's dead body flashed through his mind again, though he tried to repress it. He badly needed more sleep. But there was no time. He thought again about taking a shower. The door to the en suite was ajar, its gleaming white tiles suddenly inviting.

He stood up. 'Do you mind if I grab a quick wash?'

'God, I thought you'd never offer.' She stood too and col-lected a freshly laundered white bath towel from a stack on the chest of drawers. 'I had them bring extra towels. Here, take it.' She handed him the bath towel, smiling. 'There's a bottle of scented gel in the shower. It does your hair too. Please, use as much as you want.'

He was taken aback by her alacrity. 'Smell bad, do I?'

'I would never say so to your face.'

Savage grinned appreciatively, and allowed her to push him into the shower room.

Twenty minutes later, he re-emerged, bare-chested and towel-ling his hair dry, wishing he had some fresh-smelling clothes too. His jeans were good for another day, but he could do with a clean T-shirt. Unlikely there would be anywhere locally to buy one. Though it was pointless being impatient. Once he got the camper back, he would have access to drawers of clean clothes again. It was just a question of time.

Faith was sitting at the desk, talking to someone on her phone. She glanced up as he walked in, a flicker of interest in her eyes.

'Yes,' she was saying. 'I can do that.' She met his eyes, then shifted slightly, turning away, but began to play with her hair. Twirling it round her finger.

Savage cleared his throat.

He finished drying his hair, then threw the damp towel to the floor, not sure what else to do with it and assuming a cleaner would collect it in due course.

Briefly, he took the Glock out of his waistband and checked the magazine.

Fourteen cartridges out of a possible seventeen.

Three rounds discharged.

That discrepancy could be entirely innocent, of course. Testing the firing mechanism. Shooting at vermin. Scaring off rabbits on the moor.

Or executing human beings.

Fourteen were more than adequate to dispatch an intruder though. A lone bullet would have stopped him dead, if placed neatly through his heart or forehead at short range by a trained shooter.

So why hadn't Charlie Petherick reached for his gun?

The question still nagging at him, he checked himself in the mirror, then smoothed down the wilder tufts of his hair until he looked less like a wild man of the moors. He didn't usually bother much with his appearance, though he liked to keep his hair short. But her sideways glance just now had caught him unawares.

Was Faith still interested in him that way?

He wasn't sure how he felt about that possibility. She was very attractive, of course. But it had been a long time. And he was still ... Raw was probably the right word, but he felt awkward admitting that, even to himself. He felt bruised, definitely. Lina's death still hung heavily on him. And why shouldn't it? They had been so deeply in love, and she had been ripped away so brutally, it had taken him a long time just to come to terms with her absence, to understand it and no longer look for her when he turned over in the mornings.

If Lina had lived, he would never have looked at another woman again. Or not the way he had just looked at Faith.

Ending her call, she turned to him. 'Feel better now?'

'Much, thanks.' He pulled on his T-shirt, tucked it into his jeans, pushed the Glock into his waistband at the back again, and then rubbed his bristly chin. 'I could do with a shave. But that can wait. My shaving gear is still in the camper.' He turned back to Faith. 'First, I have to dump the stolen van.'

Faith leant back in her chair, watching him.

'So,' she said lightly, 'how did you know about the dead man on the moors? You said you thought it might be this Billy character. One of Reverend Barton's men.'

'So?'

'So what's your connection there?'

'You think I had something to do with Billy's death?' he asked, frowning.

'Did you?'

CHAPTER THIRTY-THREE

Before he could answer her, somebody knocked on the door.

Faith looked at him, surprised.

'You expecting anyone?' he whispered.

She mouthed, 'No.'

'Better wait in the bathroom,' he said.

Once she had slipped into the bathroom, he crept to the door of her room, keeping to one side out of pure habit, and listened.

There was no spyhole and no sound from the corridor.

The knock came again. Louder, more insistent.

'Who's there?' he asked.

'Mrs Vaughan.'

He had no idea who Mrs Vaughan was. But she didn't sound like someone Barton would send. She sounded friendly and countrified, and a little embarrassed too.

The door to the en suite creaked open, and Faith came out.

'It's the pub landlady,' she told him, and opened the door with a puzzled smile. 'Hello, Mrs Vaughan. Is there a problem?'

'There's no smoking in the bedrooms, I'm afraid.' Mrs Vaughan had powdery blonde hair that didn't quite go with her sixty-something face, heavy green eye make-up, and oddly red cheeks. Broken capillaries, he imagined, from years of peering inside hot ovens. 'There's a sign.' She pointed to a small sign on the writing desk that stated plainly, 'No Smoking Thank You.

Fine £100', and gave them both a harried, apologetic smile. 'Perhaps you didn't notice it.'

Faith stared. 'I don't smoke. And neither does he.'

'Not since I was a rebellious fourteen-year-old,' Savage added, giving the pub landlady his most charming smile, the one that had never failed to work on his mother's friends.

He obviously hadn't lost his touch. Or not entirely.

Mrs Vaughan smirked at him, then abruptly recalled her mission and pointed out into the corridor. 'It's not you that's been smoking. It's your friend,' she told Faith. 'The lady in Room Two.'

'You mean Rose.' Faith nodded. 'I'll tell her. I'm sorry, I didn't know she was a smoker.' She paused, considering the No Smoking sign on her desk. 'You're not going to fine us, are you?'

'Just a friendly warning.' Mrs Vaughan looked uncertain though. 'You'll be picking up the bill for both rooms, I'm guessing?'

'Yes.' Faith turned briskly to her handbag and fished out her card wallet. 'Do you need me to pay now?'

'Well, since your friend's checked out, that might be a good idea.' Mrs Vaughan smiled. 'We can take card payments at Reception.' She glanced sideways at Savage, and smirked again. 'Whenever's convenient.'

Savage frowned. 'Rose checked out?'

'About ten minutes ago.'

Faith had already left the room. They both followed her into the tiny bedroom next door in Room Two. It smelled lingeringly of smoke. The door was partly open and a young woman was stripping the bed. She straightened, clearly surprised to see Faith and Savage squeeze into the cramped space, with Mrs Vaughan a few steps behind them.

There was no sign either of Rose or Dani, and nothing in the room that might indicate where they'd gone.

Faith looked round at the empty room, then made a face. 'I don't believe it,' she told him, keeping her voice low. 'I told Rose to stay put. I was really clear that it was the only way she'd be safe.'

'Not your fault.'

'Can you smell that?' Mrs Vaughan fussed over opening the window as far as it would go, which wasn't more than about five inches. 'Someone's been smoking in here.'

'That's not cigarette smoke.' Savage sniffed the air, then glanced at Faith. 'Wrong kind of smell.'

Mrs Vaughan introduced them to the young woman. 'Clare, my daughter. Did you find any cigarette stubs, Clare?'

Clare was slim but wide-hipped, her hipster tracksuit bottoms flared out at the ankle. Her hair was short and dark with brash red highlights that gleamed in the sunlight now streaming through the open window.

She eyed Savage with interest, but shook her head. 'Only some burnt paper,' Clare said in that same, creamy Devon accent he had come to associate with Dani and Rose. 'In there.' With a jerk of her head, she indicated the waste paper bin, a solid metal cylinder. 'Melted the plastic bin liner when it burnt, too. Bin's going to need a right proper clean out.'

Faith handed the bin to Savage, who reached in gingerly past the molten remains of the white bin liner and withdrew a scorched fragment of paper. The rest was mainly ashes.

'What is it?' Faith asked.

Something had been written on the burnt-edged scrap. He tried but couldn't make it out. A few darkened letters, and a partial number.

'Not sure.' Carefully, he handed the fragment to her, then examined the small heap of grey ashes. But there wasn't much else to be gleaned from the bin. 'Something Rose didn't want us to read.'

Faith asked Mrs Vaughan if she knew where the two women

had been heading when they left, but got little information of use. Apparently, the landlady had been outside in the back garden of the pub, feeding her koi, when Rose had dumped the room key at Reception, telling a deeply unobservant Mr Vaughan she wouldn't be returning.

'Barely looked over his newspaper at her, I bet. He didn't even mention it to me when I came back in. Useless man.' Mrs Vaughan shook her head. 'I wouldn't have known she'd gone if Clare hadn't noticed the open door and smelt the smoke. She came back to find me. That's when my husband told me your friend had checked out.'

'Do you happen to know if Rose was with someone when she left?' Faith asked her. 'Another woman, about the same age?'

Mrs Vaughan shrugged. 'Not a clue.'

'Well, I'm very sorry about the bin. I'll pay for a replacement when I settle up. I just need to have a chat with my . . . erm, friend here.'

Faith herded Savage back into her own bedroom and closed the door.

'Where the hell can they have gone?' She paced the room, restless. 'I thought I'd made it clear to Rose that she needed to stay and talk to you. That if she was seen in the village, we couldn't guarantee her safety.'

'Maybe they'd had enough of being prisoners.'

'That's possible, I suppose. But it still seems strange. After everything those two women have been through . . .' Faith shook her head. 'Maybe they didn't leave here of their own accord.'

'You think someone may have taken them?'

'That man up at the Green Chapel—'

'I doubt Barton is all that bothered about Dani and Rose right now. Not when I've made myself so unpopular. I'll be at the top of his hit list today.' He hesitated. 'Though once Barton's dealt with me, I imagine he'll transfer his attention back to Rose and Dani.'

Faith stopped pacing and leant back against the wall, staring at him. 'Are you going to let that happen?'

'Of course not.' Savage took the scorched fragment back from her and studied it, frowning. 'So what is this? And why did Rose burn it?'

'To stop us reading it.'

'So why not simply take it with her?'

'Maybe she didn't want to be found with it.'

'But needed to write it down while she memorised it.' He nodded slowly. 'Something Dani told her, then?'

'Or somebody else . . . I'll ask the landlady if Rose used the pub phone at any point.'

'Good idea.' He turned the paper scrap round and round, but it still made little sense. 'Numbers and letters. What could that be? A postcode?'

'Or a number plate.'

'Maybe.' He handed it back to her. 'Put that in your wallet for now. We can work it out later.'

'But Dani and Rose could be in danger. What if Barton *has* taken them?'

'Then we'll get them back.' Savage hoped this promise would reassure her, though he suspected the two women would turn up at Geoff's place soon, having grown sick of being told what to do by a couple of strangers. 'But we can't do anything until we know for sure. Meanwhile, I need to decide what to do about Billy.'

'Oh yes, Billy.' Faith raised her eyebrows, waiting. 'The dead man on the moors. You never did explain how you knew about that.'

Briefly, he told her what he knew about the hunt he'd seen,

and how the victim had looked like Billy from a distance. Which was not much. But he had to start somewhere.

Faith made an incredulous face when he had finished speaking. 'That makes no sense. Why would Barton turn on a trusted member of his own crew?' She paused, looking concerned. 'And the police won't be far off thinking the same thing, once all the facts in this case are looked at together.'

'What are you saying?'

'I'm saying Peter's dead. By his own hand, according to DI Paglia. Only you claim he was left-handed, and that the scene will suggest to any competent pathologist that he couldn't have shot himself.'

'Police pathologists have ways of spotting things like that. Left-handed, right-handed, all that. I saw a documentary about it once.'

'So how long before the police work out it wasn't suicide, and decide *you're* the likeliest person to have shot him?'

'Me?' He was genuinely taken aback.

'Why not?' Faith started ticking off points on her fingers. 'Peter was a loner. You'd just come to visit him. There were signs you'd been in a fight recently.' She shrugged. 'Perhaps you went back there after the police let you go, and the two of you argued. Things got heated, out of hand, and you shot him.'

'That's nonsense.'

'But I imagine it's what the police may be thinking.' She folded her arms. 'Aubrey, I know there are things you're hiding from me.'

'For your own good.'

'I'm your lawyer. You should tell me everything you know.'

'I haven't decided what I know yet.'

'Whatever you saw out there on the moors, you need to tell the police.'

'Is that friendly advice or your professional opinion as my lawyer?'

'Both.'

Savage smiled drily. 'Wouldn't do much good going to the police, anyway.'

'How's that?'

'There's no evidence of wrongdoing. Let's look at the facts. I saw a man, who could have been Billy, running across the moors early this morning. A few minutes later, I saw men on the moors. Men with bikes and dogs and torches, who appeared to be following Billy's trail. Or rather, the man, who might or might not have been Billy.'

'So tell the police that.'

'It's too vague. It's inconclusive. We couldn't use it to nail Barton. It would be destroyed in a few words by a good defence lawyer. Besides, like you said, the police already suspect me of involvement with these killings. They'll be looking for evidence that backs up their theory. Not to point the finger at somebody else instead.'

Faith said nothing, and he knew she could not deny any of that.

'Barton's not stupid,' he added. 'I overheard a call he made. Whatever he's been hiding up there, he's trying to move it. Urgently too. One van left while I was watching, possibly driven by a Russian. Others may have left before I turned up. But it was clear he needed those goods gone in a hurry. Before a visit from the police, perhaps.'

'So call them now.'

'Too dangerous.' Savage shook his head. 'He'll be ready for them. Unless the police go up to the Green Chapel right now, mob-handed, with a search warrant, I guarantee they'll find nothing suspicious. And they'll have lost their chance to catch him with the goods on site.' He thought of the constable guarding

Dani. PC Charlie Petherick. 'Besides, they've got themselves a tame copper.'

'I'd forgotten about him,' Faith said. 'Remind me.'

'Some young constable I saw at the nick, then later inside the compound. He was left in charge of Dani, so I'm guessing he must be pretty thick with Barton. Probably passing him information too, about police interest in the Green Chapel.'

'That's appalling.'

'But predictable. Where there's money, there's always corruption. And with this constable in Barton's pocket, it's doubly unlikely we'll catch him with any goods.'

They were standing very close.

Faith seemed restless, a slight flush in her cheeks. She tilted her head back and met his eyes. 'OK, let's say you're right to hold back on contacting the police. What are these goods that Barton's hiding?'

'I don't know.'

'Where did they come from?'

'I don't know.'

'All right. So where's Barton moving them to?'

'I don't know that either.'

Faith closed her eyes, swearing under her breath. She was frustrated, and he could not blame her. He was frustrated too. He looked down at her mouth, and tried not to be tempted. They were barely a foot apart. How had that happened?

All he had to do was bend his head slightly . . .

Faith opened her eyes again and found him staring. Her eyes widened. She shook her head. 'This isn't going to work,' she said.

CHAPTER THIRTY-FOUR

'Isn't it?'

Savage took two steps backwards, creating some much-needed space between their bodies. She was right though. This was hardly the time or place.

'I covered for you, Aubrey,' she said flatly. 'That was DI Paglia on the phone before. She was asking again where you were last night. I said I didn't know, that I was on my way to Peter's place last night when my car went into the ditch, but that I hadn't seen you. Not last night, and not today.' She made a face. 'I had to lie for you.'

'I know, and I'm grateful.'

'The problem is, if the police find out you were with us in the car last night, that I lied to them about your whereabouts, and then later it turns out that you *are* somehow involved in this mess—'

'I'm not.'

'Then that's the end of my career, right there. Down the bloody drain. Lying to the police? Sheltering a person of interest in a murder enquiry?' She met his eyes. 'I love my job. I help people. I don't want to lose that.'

'You're not going to.'

Faith picked up her mobile and held it out to him. 'I'm sick of lying for you. Take my advice and call the police, Aubrey. Tell them everything you know.' She paused. 'Or I will.'

'Give me another few hours.'

'I can't, honestly. I need to finish this and go home.'

'So go home.'

'Aubrey—'

'Leave me to deal with this. I don't want you getting into trouble.'

She said nothing, but watched him uneasily.

Rather than get into a difficult conversation, Savage reached for his jacket. 'I'll go dump the van,' he added brusquely. 'If you're still willing, you can give me a lift afterwards to pick up my camper. Then we'll say goodbye.'

It had been wrong to keep Faith in Devon so long. But he'd been enjoying her company too much to let her go.

Barton was dangerous. The last thing he wanted was for the so-called Reverend to get hold of Faith too. Which was a very real possibility now that Rose and Dani had disappeared. Even assuming Barton hadn't taken them, if his men were out looking for the two women, the chances were high they would soon be recaptured. And once they were back at the Green Chapel, it wouldn't be long before Barton 'persuaded' them to tell him about Faith and where she was staying. If he didn't know already.

'Aubrey, be sensible,' she said. 'You're not in the bloody SAS now. You can't do this on your own.'

'You can send me the bill for your services later. You know I'm good for it.'

'I can't send you a bill if you're dead.'

'I don't think they execute people in this country for murder anymore, Faith. Though I could be wrong.'

'You know what I meant.' She was exasperated. 'You said it yourself. Barton's not stupid. If he can arrange Peter's death and make it look like a suicide, and shoot two young men and get away with it—'

'He's not going to get away with it.'

'Then he can kill you, no problem,' she finished, as though he hadn't spoken. 'If I leave now, who are you? You're a man with no friends. A man on his own in a camper van, out there on the moors where there's nobody to witness what happens. Or nobody who dares stand up to a man like Barton.' She shook her head. 'If what you've told me is true, I walk away now, I'm signing your death warrant.'

'O ye of little faith.'

She didn't laugh. 'What are you planning to do? And don't tell me you haven't got a plan, because I won't believe it.'

'I thought you were going home.'

'Is that what you want me to do, Aubrey? To go home?' She met his gaze. 'For real this time. No kidding about.'

Savage decided to sidestep that question as too dangerous. 'What I want is for you to wait here until I get back, then give me a lift to the police pound. After that . . .' He shrugged, avoiding her eyes. 'First, I need to get rid of that Russian van.'

He drove the stolen Transit van to the far end of the village, looking for somewhere to dump it out of sight, then slammed on his brakes beside a left-hand lane signposted Chapel Only. Not because he felt a sudden urge to commune with his Creator, or to visit a remote out-of-the-way beauty spot, but because he'd spotted something small but highly significant next to those engraved words, 'Chapel Only'. The sign was quite elderly, and the writing looked antiquated. But the symbol next to the words had surely been carved by hand.

At first he thought it was another P, exactly like the P he'd seen tattooed on Dani's forearm. But then his linguist's brain kicked in, and he realised he was not looking at a standard P, but a letter from the Futhark alphabet. The Elder Futhark, not the reduced Younger.

Still a P-like letter, but with a thinner stalk and a top circle pointed like a triangle. Pronounced as a 'w' and meaning something utterly different.

What had Dani told him?

Barton said something about wine.

Of course he had.

Because it was not a P at all.

It was best known as the Old English letter for W. But it had also been widely used by the Vikings in Old Norse as a rune for *wynn*, meaning 'joy' or 'pleasure'. And the 'Wynn' rune was traditionally connected to fertility and pregnancy.

He turned the van down the leafy lane, curious now and wondering what he might find at the end. A good hiding place for the Russian's van, at the very least. And perhaps a clue to the meaning of the tattoo Barton inflicted on all the women who underwent his fertility ceremonies up at the Green Chapel.

Was this place somehow linked to Barton's Green Chapel? Or was the symbol merely a coincidence? But his instincts told him this would be a good place to hide the van anyway, so he didn't fight his curiosity. Two birds, one stone.

And this was certainly off the beaten track.

The lane to the chapel grew narrower and muddier, with hedges higher than the sides of the van, which was both ideal and slightly claustrophobic. The track wound laboriously for about half a mile, growing thinner and more restrictive, until he began to feel he had made a mistake choosing to turn down this way.

The lane ended abruptly in a small car park. Opposite the entrance to the car park was a rough, low stone building he took to be the chapel.

The place looked deserted, possibly disused. On either side of the chapel stood spiny shrubs and clustered trees, thick with buds and new leaves, with an occasional glimpse of moorland beyond their vivid branches.

Perfect, in other words.

Savage parked up against a hedge in the corner of the car park.

Using the edge of his T-shirt, he spent a few minutes assiduously wiping his prints off the two guns. Then he forced the shotgun under the front seat as far as it would go, dumped the Glock in the glove box, and jumped out.

He regretted having to discard the handgun. But Faith was right. He needed to be careful. And it was better not to walk around Dartmoor with an illegally obtained weapon in his possession, especially one whose previous activity he could only imagine.

The ground was bare mud, uneven with stones. Everywhere was silent, except for the cheerful twitter of birds all around, and sheep bleating in the distance. Savage trod softly round to the back of the van. Using his T-shirt to open the double doors, he felt that unpleasant sting of disinfectant at the back of his throat again.

What was it he'd seen in the pub car park? A few odd marks scratched onto the wood panelling towards the back of the Transit van interior.

He climbed inside, feet slipping and squeaking on the still-damp flooring. It was not a new van. There were plenty of random scratches, marks and dents on the wall. He was about to give up when finally he saw it, something etched out like a hieroglyph on the wall behind the driver's side.

It was fairly low down. He crouched and bent close to study it. But even with the double doors open, it was too dark to see the markings clearly.

What were they? Numbers? A picture?

Both, perhaps?

After the symbol on the signpost, he had half expected to find the Wynn rune there too. But this was something different.

Taking his mobile from his pocket, Savage selected the light app, then shone the bright beam on the damp panelling.

The figures had been scratched out with a fingernail, by the shaky, uneven look of each stroke, and the shallowness of each letter. Probably a woman's fingernail, since they tended to be longer than a man's. They were neither numbers nor a picture, he realised, but a single word in Cyrillic. It had been a long time since he spoke any Russian. But he could at least still recognise the language when he saw it.

'*Pomogite*', he read aloud, mentally transliterating the Cyrillic to the English alphabet.

It was the Russian word for 'help'.

Who had written 'help' on the interior wall of the van? And why?

He took several pictures of the handwriting with his phone, then stiffened, hearing a vehicle approaching fast down the narrow lane.

Had he been followed, after all?

Savage pushed his phone back into his pocket, and straightened, listening.

Only one vehicle, the stereo belting out loud rock music that drowned out the sound of birdsong. Iron Maiden, by the sound of it. No doubt the birds had all scattered anyway. Not Iron Maiden fans, he would guess.

Unlikely to be the police. He doubted DI Paglia or any of her colleagues went gallivanting about the countryside in a mobile disco. But the driver was clearly in a hurry, which suggested urgency. Maybe one of Barton's crew, sent to hunt him down and retrieve the van.

Savage hurried back to the double doors, gagging on the smell of bleach.

But the other vehicle had already jammed to a halt some-where nearby, brakes squealing. The engine stopped abruptly, cutting off the lyrics mid-scream. Then a car door opened and slammed again almost immediately.

Too late to get out of sight now.

CHAPTER THIRTY-FIVE

Savage didn't fancy getting caught inside the van, where the new arrival could close the double doors with one good shove and keep him locked up there. He jumped down awkwardly, the sun in his eyes, and so didn't immediately see the figure waiting behind the open doors of the van.

'Good morning,' someone said lightly, walking rapidly towards the van. 'Can I help you?'

It was a woman. About five foot five, in her mid-thirties, and not even looking at him, head down as she tucked a loose black top into her trousers.

'Good morning,' he said automatically, feeling ridiculous now.

He lifted a hand to shield his eyes from the sun and studied her covertly while considering his best reply.

The woman was wearing khaki camouflage-style trousers, though shapely hips and a neat waist were what he noticed first. But it was her hair that really snagged his attention. She had fiery red hair, cropped close to her scalp. Like a furnace burning on top of her head.

He recognised that flaming hair.

And the dog collar.

It was the woman vicar from the diner. The one who'd blown a kiss on her way out. To Phyllis, their pregnant waitress.

'Sorry, am I trespassing?' He said what came into his mind

first, trying not to look too suspicious. He nudged the van doors shut with his elbow, hoping she wouldn't think that strange. But he didn't want to leave his prints behind. 'I just came down here to look at the church.'

'Chapel,' she corrected him, then searched his face. He saw recognition in her eyes too, though she did not say anything. But he was certain she remembered him from the diner. 'Did I take you by surprise?'

'A little bit, yes.'

'I do have a tendency to creep up on people. My girlfriend's always telling me off for it.' She grinned and stuck out a hand. 'I'm Kim. How do you do?'

He shook her hand. 'Very well, thank you. I'm Aubrey.'

Her handshake was warm and friendly, a touch of public school enthusiasm about it. They could have been meeting at a society event, he thought. Not in a lonely car park on the fringe of Dartmoor. Kim seemed to find the incongruity amusing too, because she threw back her head and laughed at his expression.

'You're a vicar,' he said.

'For my sins, yes.' Her hand released his and flew up to the white collar, which was slightly askew, readjusting it with an experienced tug. 'I'm in charge of quite a few churches up here on the moors. Not all of them in active service, as it were. Like this lovely old place. Are you a Christian?' She saw his moment-ary confusion, and shook her head. 'No, don't answer that. Force of habit, sorry. You came to see the chapel?'

When he nodded, Kim smiled and gestured him to follow her. 'You're in luck, then. I can show you round, if you like. I was just about to open her up. She gets an airing at least once a month, though it should be more frequent. I usually say a quick prayer and light a few candles. Care to join me?'

Savage hesitated, aware of Faith waiting for him back at the pub. Much longer, and she'd start to wonder where the hell he was. But he didn't know how to get out of the invitation without seeming suspicious. Not after claiming he'd come down here specifically to visit the damn place.

Besides, he was curious to know more about this woman.

'Thank you.'

As Kim turned away, her gaze fell on the van's number plate. 'Goodness,' she said, stopping. 'RUS,' she read out. 'Is that a Russian registration number?'

He hesitated again, not sure where this conversation would go.

'Yes.'

'Long way from home.' She glanced round at him, her eyes narrowed. 'You're not Russian though. That accent's more Home Counties than Moscow.'

'Oxfordshire.'

'Ah, close enough. Beautiful part of the world.' She smiled. 'Are you here on holiday?'

'Partly that.'

'And partly?'

Feeling a little warm, Savage took off his jacket and hung it over his arm. He had already said more than he'd intended. But something about her made him add, 'And partly looking for a friend.'

'Can I help?'

'I doubt it. But thanks.'

The vicar shrugged and started sorting through a large bunch of keys clipped to her jeans belt, the van's Russian origin apparently forgotten.

'Come on, then. Let's see if any birds are stuck inside. They often are at this time of year. Nesting, you know.'

Savage followed her to the chapel door, surreptitiously checking the time on his mobile. While Kim was wrestling with the rusty old lock, he texted Faith, *Been held up, sorry. Back as soon as I can.*

Kim threw the metal-studded chapel door open and nodded him to go inside first. 'After you.' When he hesitated, she smiled. 'Don't worry. Plenty of light.'

'Right.'

Savage ducked his head to enter the low lintel of the chapel door. Exactly as she had said, the interior was surprisingly bright. Slate floor, most of it badly cracked, some flagstones missing, the ground beneath mere dirt. He wandered a few steps from the door to the central aisle, stepping through dusty shafts of sunlight from the high windows. To his left was a small vestibule, into which Kim vanished with a cheery, 'Only be a minute,' leaving the door ajar. To his right stood the chapel altar, a plain table covered with a white cloth and set with a wooden cross. The cloth had debris on it. Dirt and what looked like plaster fallen from the ceiling. The whole place smelt damp.

Behind the altar, the wall showed some kind of reddish mural, half destroyed by the years and whitewashing. A partial scene with a vast, bearded individual carrying a stick and striding across a plain. Possibly a saint of some kind. It was difficult to tell, the face was so blurry. Though his green tunic seemed to suggest pagan origins.

He glanced down at his phone again. No reply yet from Faith.

Perhaps she was busy packing.

He wondered covertly how long it would take to walk back to the pub. There might be a path that was quicker than the road, of course. From the specialist walkers' map he'd bought before leaving for Devon, the moors were riddled with tiny, barely visible tracks from one point to another. But after the recent rains, he'd probably end up knee-deep in mud if he headed off cross-country. In fact, if he couldn't shake the vicar soon, it might be quicker to walk back to the main road and have Faith pick him up.

'Anything of interest?'

Kim had come back into the chapel, so soft-footed he had not heard her approach, and was looking at him curiously.

He realised that he was not behaving like a tourist.

'I saw an odd symbol on the signpost on the main road,' he said. 'Like a letter P, only thinner. What's that about?'

'I'm not entirely sure,' she admitted. 'But I know what you mean, and it's here in the chapel too.' She nodded to the wall to their left, and now Savage could see a Wynn rune or narrow letter P drawn on the wall. 'There's a useful old guide to all the ecclesiastical buildings in the region. It's huge and a bit old-fashioned, but I have it at home. In there, the author suggests it's some kind of fertility symbol. It's certainly true that people used to regard this entire area as somehow connected to fertility.' She smiled. 'In the pre-Christian era, that is. I imagine the first priests to come here probably appropriated that symbol to keep the locals happy.'

'And who's the big guy in the mural?' Savage pointed up at the wall. 'Looks rather splendid and barbaric, doesn't he? Pity about the whitewashing.'

'Yes, the Puritans made it everywhere with their damn pots of paint, determined to erase the beautiful and the glorious, anything that might interfere with their dour outlook on life. Even up here on Dartmoor, unfortunately. This one was restored about fifteen years ago, and is the only reason we still keep the chapel open, to be brutally honest.' She studied the mural too. 'Accounts vary as to who this is, even among theological historians. It could be Saint Peter on his travels as a missionary, or Saint Christopher, who's rather closer to home.' She paused. 'Though some here in the village would tell you a different story.'

'That sounds intriguing.'

'The old guide book believes him to be a pagan character of purely Dartmoor origin. A fertility god, as the knobbly stick might suggest. Possibly some kind of cross between the Green Man and the Giant of Hele.'

'The who, sorry?'

'The Giant of Hele.' When he frowned, the vicar spelt out the word Hele for him. 'It's an ancient place up on the moors. A spring with an associated cave. Both have been held sacred to fertility for centuries. Maybe millennia.' She shrugged. 'It's always hard to decide how far back these primitive beliefs go.'

Savage stared at the mural, his attention arrested now. That sounded like an oddly familiar story.

'You say it's called Hele, this sacred place on the moors?'

'That's right. Actually, it's the sister chapel to this one. This chapel was intended for the moorland village, a sheltered place of worship. The other is an ancient outdoor chapel, for those in need of sanctuary on the high moors.' Kim hesitated, then added, 'Though these days, most people call it the Green Chapel.'

CHAPTER THIRTY-SIX

Savage stiffened, studying the giant with his vast stick, the enormous, green-clad figure striding through a barren landscape not dissimilar to the wilderness he had just left on the high moors. *Some people call it the Green Chapel.* So there was some substance behind Barton's baby-making empire, even if the ancient story was almost as implausible as the Reverend's spiel. He could see why the locals had not been hard to persuade though. Then something he'd caught in her voice suddenly registered with him, and he looked round at the vicar.

'What's wrong?' he said quickly. 'You don't approve of the new name?' He saw her mouth tense up, lips clamped together, and instantly suspected the vicar knew more than she was saying. 'I've met Barton,' he added, 'and didn't much care for him either, if that's what's holding you back.'

Her gaze met his, keen and searching. Then she came to stand right in front of him, barely coming up to his shoulder, as though to indicate her lack of fear.

'So you know Barton, do you? And are you one of his ... people?'

Despite the aggressive stance, he appreciated her restraint, the delicate way she had paused before finishing her sentence. The vicar was no fool. But no coward either. She had a fair inkling what was going up there in Barton's compound. And didn't much like it, while perhaps having no evidence of any wrong-doing that would allow her to intervene.

'No.'

'Oh.' The vicar seemed relieved by his simple negative, the tense lines about her mouth loosening. 'I see.'

'Tell me, is Barton a real *Reverend*? I mean, technically?'

'That man has nothing to do with the Church of England,' Kim told him flatly. 'Though if he chooses to call himself Reverend, I suppose nobody can stop him. Or nobody dares.' She looked up at the mural, as though it held the answer to some unasked question. 'Barton calls it a belief system. Others call it a cult. But if you ask me, it's a business he's running up there. Like a clinic that exploits unfortunate women who are unable to conceive. A clinic by another name, and one that relies on cult-like practices and local superstitions to hide its true intentions.' Her tone was sharp. 'He even has a giant up there now, people say. The Giant of the Green Chapel. But I've never seen him.'

'I have.' He saw her surprise, and smiled. 'He's no giant though. Just a very tall man. Russian, actually. Big Swanney, they call him.'

Kim nodded. 'Savanovic?'

He was impressed by her understanding. There was more to this vicar than her mild manner suggested.

'Tell me more about this Giant of Hele,' he said. 'The original one, that is.'

She took a deep breath, gazing up at the blurry mural. 'The old myth goes that a giant lived alone up at Hele, tending the spring. He wasn't mean and violent, like the other giants of the moor, always fighting and killing locals, but a kindly giant who had found peace in solitude. The spring he tended had magical qualities, granting fertility to animals and humans alike. Barren women would make the pilgrimage up there on certain holy days, accompanied by their husband and other relatives. Sometimes the whole village would go too, and celebrate the occasion with mead and honey cakes and dancing.'

'Sounds like an excellent excuse for a party.'

'The barren wife would drink from the sacred spring, spend the night alone in the giant's cave, and before the year was out she would be pregnant.'

'Lucky giant.'

'I expect that's why that fertility symbol appears here and there on the moors. The thing that looks like a letter P.'

'Or a penis, in fact.'

To his surprise, she was not offended by his coarseness, but grinned appreciatively. 'I suppose so, yes. The locals used to argue amongst themselves about whether it was drinking the sacred spring waters that made the woman pregnant, or spending the night alone in the Giant of Hele's cave.'

'I imagine they still do.' He frowned. '*Hele* . . .'

'It's quite a common place name in the South West.' The vicar paused, looking at him. 'Connected to the word healing, do you think?'

'Anglo-Saxon.' He stuck his hands in his jeans pocket, studying the mural again. '*Hele*, meaning a secret or hidden place. Yes, that would make sense. The spring and cave in the legend both sound like hidden places.'

'Are you a linguist?'

'A long time ago, yes. Before I heard the call for Queen and country.'

She looked him up and down. 'Army, you mean?'

'For my sins.'

'Snap.'

Now it was his turn to look surprised. 'You were in the army too?'

'I had a few sins to make up for too.'

'Good God.'

'Well, exactly. He moves in mysterious ways, they say. Anyway, I joined up fresh out of school, starry-eyed and looking for adventure. I was in five years, including two tours in Afghanistan.' She saw his startled look, and said quickly, 'FEO, mostly. Enjoyable work, but I have to admit that it was bloody stressful at times.'

He nodded. Female Engagement Officer. Women soldiers and other female army personnel sent in on the ground in Afghanistan to provide a friendly face to the local communities, especially the women, who would rarely speak to male soldiers, even when in desperate need of help. A dangerous position, and not for the faint-hearted.

'Then I heard a call too. Only of a rather different nature to yours.' She described how she had changed her allegiance from the British Armed Forces to a higher power, and sought out a quiet country parish as an antidote to the bruising years she had spent in training and on the battlefield. 'It was a massive leap. But one of faith.'

'A giant's step, in fact. Well, that explains the khaki trousers with the dog collar. I thought it was an odd combination.'

'Old habits die hard.'

'Maybe.' He indicated his own jeans with a grin. 'As you can see, I've found it relatively easy to make the change to civvy street. But then I was never really cut out for army life.'

'How's that?'

Keeping it brief, aware that Faith was still waiting for him back at the pub, Savage recounted his army record, including his years in the SAS. He almost never mentioned that part of his life to civilians. But she didn't really count as a civilian. And he instinctively trusted her not to discuss his army career with anyone else. Something in her eyes, perhaps. A steadfast quality he warmed to instantly.

'SAS?' She whistled. 'You must have worked hard for that.'

'Too hard. Those years nearly broke me. Though leaving was almost as hard. You know how it is, I'm sure. You get used to living a certain way, and then . . .'

She nodded, her expression understanding.

'My wife helped with the transition back to ordinary life. I could never have done it without her. It probably sounds cheesy, but marriage changed everything for me.'

'Me too,' she replied, and winked at his sideways glance before continuing, 'So where is she now? Your wife, I mean.'

'She died.'

The knowing smile vanished. 'I'm sorry.'

'Not your fault.'

'All the same . . .'

He fell silent, thinking of Lina.

'So, if you're not one of Barton's cronies,' Kim said, clasping her hands behind her back and squaring her stance as though back in the army, 'who are you, exactly? And what's your interest in his Green Chapel operation? And don't waste your breath denying it,' she added, seeing him about to protest, 'because I've seen that van out there before. Only it was one of Barton's lot driving it, and he didn't look a thing like you.'

Smart as a whip. Of course. He should have realised she was concealing something when they met out in the car park. The way she looked so closely at the number plate, and then at him . . .

'Was he Russian?'

'No idea. I never spoke to the man. Though he did have that look.' Kim waited, but he didn't add anything to that. 'Look, I'm no fan of Barton's or his cronies,' she said, a touch of impatience in her voice. 'But if that van is stolen, as I suspect it must be, and that man Barton is on your trail, it strikes me you might need a friend soon.'

'You?'

'I might look like a pint pot, but I'm stronger than people realise.'

He grinned at her self-deprecating tone. Army humour. 'I believe you. But I don't need any help, thanks.'

She shrugged. 'The offer still stands.'

It was suddenly cool inside the chapel. The shafts of sunlight that had gilt all the walls earlier had disappeared, leaving only a shadowy chill that felt somehow oppressive. The altar stood plain and dark below the mural. The bearded giant was barely visible now, a vague green figure in the darkness.

He checked his phone again. Still no message from Faith. He didn't like this lengthy silence. It felt ominous.

Kim was watching him. 'Trouble?'

'I hope not.'

She led the way to the chapel door, then locked up after them. The sun had vanished behind a cloud while they were inside, and the skies above were grey. Clouds were rolling in from the north, dark and grim, threatening rain.

'What's your connection with Barton, anyway?' she asked, following him back to the van. 'You said you came here looking for a friend. A woman who needed to visit the Green Chapel, by any chance?'

'I never said a female friend.' Savage half-smiled at her inquisitiveness, then sobered. 'Actually, it was a man. My brother-in-law, Jarrah. He's gone missing. I had to start looking somewhere, and when I last heard from him, he was coming here.'

'Here?' She looked surprised.

'To Dartmoor.'

'Whereabouts, exactly?'

A shiver ran down his back. The grim weather, perhaps. A warning of imminent rain. He looked up at the leaden skies.

'Rowlands Farm. That's why I came to Devon. Peter Rowlands was a mutual friend of ours, you see. I thought he might know where Jarrah was.'

'Peter Rowlands?' Kim drew a sharp breath, holding his gaze. It was obvious that she knew Peter was dead. He saw her face soften and open up, suddenly the vicar again, ready to extend her sympathies. 'He was a friend of yours, then?'

Savage said nothing.

'But you know that he . . . ?'

He nodded.

'How awful for you. I only just heard about his death. The coroner was in touch earlier.' She reached out to touch his arm with her fingertips, a fleeting contact like the brush of silk. 'I'm so sorry, Aubrey.'

She had remembered his name.

Kim looked down at her watch, as though a little embarrassed now. 'Good grief, is that the time? I'd better get back. Phil has her day off today. I promised her we'd go shopping for new carpets. You know how it is.'

'Phil?'

'My girlfriend, Phyllis. I call her Phil sometimes.' Kim ran a hand through her short red hair. 'She hates it.'

'Of course. Phyllis.' Savage grinned at the memory. 'The waitress at the Lucky Diner. I saw the two of you talking. You blew her a kiss.'

Kim said nothing, suddenly watchful.

Abruptly, he remembered Phyllis, pregnant and beaming with joy as she served them breakfast, the neat little black P tattooed on her skin. Exactly like Dani's tattoo. And all the rest of them, no doubt.

'She went to the Green Chapel to get pregnant, didn't she?' His voice sounded loud in the sudden silence. 'She went to Barton.'

Kim stood a moment in silence, her face tense. 'I didn't want her to go,' she said at last. 'But we'd tried everything and Phyllis was desperate.' Her voice dropped to a whisper, as though afraid someone might overhear them, even in that remote place. 'It was almost too late for her. She's older than me, you see. It was always her heart's desire to have a baby, to be a mother at last. So many women who went up to the Green Chapel for treatment seemed to be falling pregnant, and Phyllis couldn't handle it. She had the money, and she wanted to try it too, and I wasn't strong enough to stop her.'

'*That's* why you hate him.'

'You don't understand. Barton did things to her . . . Terrible things.' Kim's face hardened, staring at nothing. 'I wanted to go to the police afterwards. But Phyllis wouldn't hear of it. She said it would come out, what she'd done up there, and she wouldn't be able to look anyone in the eye again. Then the test was positive, and she was so happy. Ecstatic, in fact.'

He waited, knowing there would be more.

'After that, I agreed to keep quiet. For her sake. And the baby's. But I never forgot. And I'll never forgive him for what he did to her. What he probably does to all of them.' Her smile was grim. 'Not very Christian of me, is it? We're supposed to be forgiving, to turn the other cheek. But some things . . . Some things tear the heart out of you. Do you know what I mean?'

Savage thought again of Lina. Finding her body broken and bloodied in the ruins of the marketplace.

'Yes, I know what you mean.'

Then his mobile rang.

CHAPTER THIRTY-SEVEN

When he answered the call, Faith surprised him by saying, 'Hi, Mum.' Though she must have known which number she was dialling.

He waited, frowning.

'Mum? I don't have long, so please listen carefully,' Faith said, speaking very quickly. 'You remember that old friend I was talking about? Aubrey Savage? Well, it seems he's wanted for questioning by the police.'

'Is that so?'

'Yes, it's not looking good for him.' She paused, as though listening to a longer reply. Her imaginary mother, presumably. Then added, with a significant edge to her voice, 'For murder. Two murders, actually.'

'Two?'

'That's right. Anyway, I'm going to have to stay on in Devon for another few days.' Savage could hear a vague buzz in the background, as of many people holding conversations around her. Calm tones, the occasional voice raised in protest. And when she spoke, there was an echo on the end of every word, as though she were calling from inside a sparsely furnished room. 'I hope you don't mind.'

The police station.

'Hang on,' she said, and everything went muffled. He guessed she must be holding the phone against her chest. He heard a man speaking to her, then her acid reply, 'Of course. You're right. I shouldn't have said that. But it's only my mum.'

Seconds later, she was back on the line.

'Mum?'

'Yes,' he said drily, careful to keep his voice low.

'I won't be back tomorrow as arranged. Yes, I know. But it can't be helped.' She paused meaningfully. 'The police are claiming his fingerprints are *all over* the murder weapon.'

Again, someone in the room spoke to her sharply, and again Faith muffled the phone while she apologised profusely for being so indiscreet about a murder inquiry.

Kim was gazing at him with raised eyebrows. He wondered if she had caught any of this bizarre conversation.

Then Faith was back on the line.

'Look, Mum, I have to go. I'm in the middle of something here. I'll ring you later when I have more time to chat. Meanwhile, don't try going out on your own, OK? I don't want you risking a *fall*. So take care, stay indoors, and I'll see you soon.' She took a breath, then added softly, 'I love you,' before the phone went dead.

He stared down at the screensaver. What had she meant by those last three words? Apart from the obvious. Was it part of the act? Or had she genuinely meant it? Perhaps he had misread Faith's decision to stay on Dartmoor after she had sprung him from the police cells that first night. He had thought it was friendly interest. Nothing more serious. But that tone in her voice . . .

'Well?' Kim sounded impatient.

He turned off the screen and put the phone away. 'The police are after me,' he said bluntly, and met her surprised gaze. 'For a double murder, apparently.'

Her eyes widened. 'Your friend, Peter?'

'Him, yes. Plus a young man I never met in my life. Callum

Hoggins. Poor lad got himself shot the day I arrived by Barton or someone inside his organisation. I thought I was in the clear. But it seems the police are determined to pin both deaths on me now.'

'Is that possible?'

'Hard to tell. That was my lawyer on the phone. But she was pretending to be calling her mother. So I'd guess she's with the police right now and can't talk freely.'

He thought of the constable with the hostile eyes who had been guarding Dani. His stomach twisted. There were few things worse than a corrupt officer. If he ever got a chance to deal with that bastard, he'd take it, police or not.

'My guess is that I'm being set up by Barton and his boys,' he said. 'They discredit me in advance, and then my story looks shaky if I choose to tell the police about the operation they're running up at the Green Chapel.'

'You have something on Barton, then? Something concrete?'

He decided to take Kim into his confidence, since she seemed a solid enough person and unlikely to be covertly working for the Reverend Barton. Not when she was a genuine Reverend herself.

As briefly as he could, he told her the whole story, starting with Dani in the lay-by, and the later discovery of Callum Hoggins's corpse nearby. She listened without interrupting, which impressed him. More of that army training. He explained about the police officer he had seen in Barton's employ, and the pregnant women being kept under lock and key at the farmhouse. She nodded silently, her eyes angry, but looked even more interested when he described the two Russian vans, the phone conversation he had overheard, and the man-hunt over the moors. Finally, she exclaimed when he went into detail about the Glock in Dani's holdall, and how Peter had been left-handed, so his death could only have been murder.

'Of course,' she said when he'd finished. 'It makes perfect sense, killing your friend and framing you for his murder. It's quite subtle too, isn't it? They wanted his death to look like suicide initially, because anything too obvious makes you less likely to be the culprit. But Barton must have known about the gun in Dani's holdall.'

'I imagine that's why they came after her so rapidly. Because she'd stolen the weapon they'd used to kill Callum Hoggins, and they needed it back.'

'But when they got her back, and there was no sign of the gun . . .'

'They would have guessed I had it.'

She nodded. 'And thanks to their inside man, they would also have known you hadn't handed it in to the police.'

'So my prints were likely to be on the gun.'

'Which puts you in the frame for both murders. Very clever. A double murder charge will keep the police too busy to investigate any counter-accusation you might make against Barton.'

'Not until it's too late and Barton has shifted the goods. Whatever they turn out to be.'

'I have a hunch about that.'

Savage looked up at the gloomy skies. Rain was on its way, and indeed he could already feel a slight damp spitting against his face. So Barton was going to try to pin his best friend's murder onto him, was he? He was starting to get really hacked off with this so-called Reverend. A prison sentence for fraud would be too lenient. But the alternative would feel too much like revenge for Peter's death. An eye for an eye.

He swayed slightly, light-headed.

Not enough sleep?

Perhaps he could catch some quick shut-eye before he went back up to the Green Chapel again. Not that he had much time left. He didn't have a plan yet, and Barton was aiming to ship everything incriminating out of the compound by the end of the day. And it was already coming up to noon.

Faith could be in trouble with the police because of him. She could be risking her career over his decision to stay and get involved in all this.

The thought made him angry.

'You look awful,' Kim said. 'When did you last eat?'

Yes, that was it. Low blood sugar.

'At the diner, I think. Yesterday morning?'

He was often a bit forgetful about meals. But even to him yesterday morning seemed a long time ago.

'Let's sort you out with a hot meal. An all-day breakfast, perhaps.'

'Not yet.' He thought for a moment. 'Any chance I could talk to Phyllis about what happened to her up at the Green Chapel?'

'I don't think she'll want that. We agreed never to talk about it.'

'Not the bad stuff. What she saw, the layout of the compound, how many guards around the main house, all that. Phyllis might have useful information and not realise it.' He looked at her directly. 'If I'm going to clear my name, I need to prove that Barton's involved in these murders. And to do that, I'll have to get into the compound again. Which means being prepared for whatever's waiting for me up there.'

Kim was clearly reluctant, but nodded slowly. 'I'll ring Phyllis, ask if she can meet us at the diner. But if she says no, I'm not going to force her.'

'Understood.'

Getting out her phone, she saw him glance back at the stolen Russian van, and shook her head. 'Leave it. That's why you brought the van here, isn't it? To dump it out of sight of the main road.'

He couldn't deny that. But he decided not to mention the

shotgun stowed under the front seat and the Glock in the glove box. She was a vicar, after all.

'Come on, we'll go in mine,' she said, and rummaged in her pocket for her car key. 'It's faster than it looks.'

Savage turned on his heel, glanced at her car, and smiled.

Savage had always loved Mini Coopers. There was something about being bounced along in the front passenger seat that reminded him of childhood rides on fairground dodgems. Kim's Mini was striped in classic white-and-red, Victoria Sponge colours as his sister had always called them, with a metallic tint. The car cornered with ease, even careering along the narrow Devon lanes at speed, despite there being no possibility Kim could see what was ahead over these towering hedgerows.

They met a large green tractor first, then a postal van, then a delivery driver on his mobile phone. None of these seemed to faze Kim, even when the vehicles stopped a bare few inches short of her bumper. Each time she merely slammed on the brakes, then either backed up as quickly as she'd been driving forwards, or ducked into the nearest muddy pull-in, usually a farm gate through which he could see sheep staring curiously back at them.

'Sheep seem to be everywhere up here,' he said, pulling a face at one of the woolly white animals pressed up against the bars of a gate.

'Actually, sheep farming is dying out on the moors.'

'Too many vegetarians?'

'That's a factor, yes.'

'I seem to recall reading somewhere that depression and suicide rates among farmers are among the highest in the country.'

'It's a tough industry.'

He thought back to his family home in Oxfordshire, set

among acres of farmland. It had been a long time since he'd been there. Not since the aftermath of Lina's death, in fact. He knew he had to go back at some point. To see his father and sister. To make peace with them, if possible. But he hadn't felt able to face that yet.

There was so much back in Oxfordshire that he was eager to avoid. *Needed* to avoid, in fact, if he wanted to stay sane and whole. Not just the memories locked up in that house, but his family. What was left of it.

'All these changes, they're draining the life out of the moor,' Kim continued. 'I've seen families split up because of it.' The rain was falling heavily now, crashing against the windscreen of the Mini, its windscreen wipers sweeping back and forth at a tremendous rate. Even so, the road ahead was barely visible through the dark curtain of rain. 'I do what I can to keep people together. To provide a sense of continuity, even if it's only through the church and its activities.'

'And how have the locals taken to you?'

She turned her head to smile at him, the two of them cocooned in a warm igloo, rain hammering on the metal roof and sides of the Mini.

'Being a woman vicar, you mean?'

'Amongst other things.'

'Ah.' She slowed for a junction, peering carefully through the rain-streaked windscreen to check for more tractors and vans. 'Phyllis.'

He waited.

'People like Phyllis. Instinctively, I'd guess. She's easy to like. She has one of those smiles that lights up a room.' She paused, then pulled out onto the empty road. 'I try to be open and friendly. It's part of the job description, after all. When you've got a problem, you should be able to talk to the vicar, right? But the truth is, I can be prickly.'

'Impossible.'

She laughed. 'Anyway, the locals took to Phyllis quicker than they've taken to me. I suppose it's the dog collar.' She tugged at the white collar again. 'I'd rather not wear it. But it's like fatigues. You get used to the uniform, and then you feel naked without it.'

'The naked vicar. Now there's an image . . .'

She grinned, taking the joke in good sport. Again, that was the army training coming out. It was how they got through the day, playing tricks on each other and descending into sarcasm at every possible opportunity. He wondered what her particular epiphany had been, when she had suddenly realised the army was not where she needed to be.

Savage was glad when they pulled up outside the Lucky Diner a short while later, finally aware of his hunger after hours of ignoring the signs.

He checked his phone, and found he'd missed two calls on the drive over. There was a voice message too.

This time, it wasn't Faith.

CHAPTER THIRTY-EIGHT

'Do you know Geoff Farley?' he asked Kim, having listened to the rambling, panicked message on his voicemail service.

'Dani's father? Only in passing. I went to visit Terry Hoggins yesterday, Geoff's son-in-law, to see if he needed to talk about his brother's death. To discuss funeral arrangements too. But Terry wasn't in.'

'Geoff wants me to ring him urgently. He doesn't sound good.'

'I'm not surprised. Poor man.'

Kim backed the Mini swiftly into a parking space, then smiled. She waved at a woman with an umbrella who was walking – or rather, waddling – across the diner car park.

It was Phyllis, looking very pregnant.

They got out of the car and hurried out of the rain under the porched entrance.

'Hello again.' Phyllis shook his hand, smiling shyly, while Kim explained that she had met him at the chapel. No mention was made of Barton.

Phyllis's sleeves were rolled up, the tattoo on her forearm clearly visible this time. Savage studied it with interest: the Norse rune P, which stood for *wynn*, meaning 'joy' in Old English.

Why had Barton chosen that symbol for his fertility cult? Wynn indicated fertility, of course. But only if you were an Anglo-Saxonist. Its significance would be lost on most other people. But perhaps that was a clue to Barton's character. He was an intelligent man, well-educated, and maybe he enjoyed having his secret joke, weaving ancient tales of mystery and legend about what was in truth a grubby little scam aimed at vulnerable men and women, for whom his 'fertility treatment' was their last hope of conceiving a child naturally.

Not all of the women who came to the chapel for treatment fell pregnant. Geoff had admitted that, while discounting it as simply the way things were, exactly as Barton intended. No doubt those unhappy couples were sent away as quickly as possible, their failure put down to a lack of faith.

But the victories, the glorious successes . . .

Oh, those had to be paraded in front of everyone, some of the pregnant women kept up at the compound for months, their swollen bellies an outward sign of Barton's virility.

'I remember you,' Phyllis was saying. 'You came into the dinner the other morning. With a woman.' She looked vaguely around the car park, as though wondering what he had done with Faith. 'You left a good tip.'

'You deserved it. That charming smile.'

She bestowed it upon him again, only this time accompanied by laughter. It didn't quite ring true though. The smile, the shyness, the lack of threat.

Her eyes, he thought, meeting them. They were wary. Frightened, even.

His phone rang.

It was Geoff Farley, trying his number again.

'Excuse me, I need to get this.' He turned away while he took the call, his back to the women. He heard them talking softly, just below the range of his hearing. 'Savage here. How are you, Geoff?'

'It's Terry, not Geoff.' The young man was panicked, breathing hard. The line was still hissing, but just audible. 'Have you seen Dani? Or Rose? Are they there with you?'

'Slow down. Where's Geoff? Is he OK?'

'Dad's fine. He didn't want me to call you. But who else is going to help? Not the police, that's for sure. We tried them first time Dani got took and look what happened there. Police went up to the Green Chapel and came away without her.'

'I know.'

'They said she was happy where she was, and no case to answer.' His voice turned bitter. 'Callum didn't believe them, of course. None of us did. But he had to act the hero and get himself shot.'

'It's OK. I got Dani out of there again this morning.'

'I know. Thanks for that. She rang an hour or so ago. Told me she was with Rose.' He paused. 'I couldn't believe the news about Billy.'

'I guess he must have turned on Barton.'

'Maybe.' He didn't sound convinced. 'Anyway, as soon as I could, I drove down to the pub to see Dani. But the girls were gone, and the bloody police were swarming all over the place.'

Savage frowned. 'That's nothing to do with me.'

'Where's my Dani?'

Terry sounded on the verge of tears.

'Perhaps they got impatient and headed off to your place on their own.'

'If they did, they never arrived.' Terry hesitated. 'You think Barton got them?'

'We can't rule that out.'

He exhaled violently. 'I'm going up to the Green Chapel. Right now.'

'You don't know that's where they are.'

'I'm going to kill that bastard. Kill him stone dead.'

'And how are you planning to do that, Terry?'

'We've got a hunting knife,' the young man said, a reckless edge to his voice.

'He has guns. And men willing to fire them at you.' There was a long silence. Relenting, Savage tried reason. He understood Terry's frustration. 'Not to mention human shields. There are still other women up at the Green Chapel, remember.'

'I'm calling the police, then.'

'That worked well for you last time, didn't it?' Savage paused, letting that truth sink in. 'Look, if we're going to get rid of Barton, it needs to be done with cunning as well as force. The police will be involved, I promise. But not yet. Not until we have solid evidence of what he's up to. Something that will get rid of him forever.' He waited, but could only hear heavy breathing on the other end of the phone. 'OK?'

'OK,' Terry said reluctantly.

'I'm at the Lucky Diner. Why don't you and Geoff join me? Do you need directions?'

'I know the place.'

'Meet me here as soon as you can, and bring any weapons you can lay your hands on. Then we can talk about finding Dani and Rose.'

Savage ended the call and turned to find Kim staring at him in consternation. Phyllis had vanished. Gone inside out of the damp, probably.

'Weapons?'

'Best to be prepared.'

'You want my advice?' she said.

He shrugged.

'There's still time for you to walk away.' Kim shook her head when he smiled. 'I'm not kidding. This isn't your fight.'

'Peter Rowlands was my friend. And I don't like the idea that someone can murder one of my friends without me doing a damn thing about it.' He looked her in the eyes. 'Would you stand by and do nothing, if it was a friend of yours?'

'That depends.'

'On what?'

'On the circumstances. The police say it was suicide.'

'The police are wrong.'

'Maybe.' Kim turned her head, looking through the diner window. Phyllis was standing near the service hatch, one hand resting on her large belly, chatting to the other servers. She looked flushed and a little agitated. 'I told Phyllis what was going down. She isn't happy about it.'

'Of course not. What partner ever was before a fight?'

'She's right though. You're not a superior officer. This isn't the army and we're not at war.' She paused, then said bluntly, 'That's Barton's child she's carrying. If we do what you want, people are going to find out about that. People like her parents. This may be a small place. But there are plenty of people round here who don't know a damn thing about Barton's organisation, or what kind of services it offers. And Phyllis would rather it stayed like that.'

'I'm still going up there. With or without your help.'

Kim's mouth twitched. 'I guessed you might say that. So I'm coming too. Only I won't tell Phyllis.' She jerked open the door to the diner, gesturing him to go first. 'What the eye doesn't see, the heart can't grieve over.'

CHAPTER THIRTY-NINE

Savage pushed away his all-day breakfast and stretched out his legs under the table, somehow avoiding kicking either Kim or Phyllis, both sitting opposite him in the narrow booth. Phyllis had already eaten, it seemed, but was picking at a bacon roll to keep them company. Kim had ordered – and demolished in short time – a generous plate of ham, fried eggs and chips. She was still mopping up the remains of the egg with her bread and butter. Pure diner fare.

The waitress came over to take his plate away, a smiling young brunette with freckles, maybe nineteen years old. Her name badge said *Lisa*.

'More drinks?' she asked them, and winked at Phyllis. 'Any desserts?'

He ordered a flat white and a slice of vanilla cheesecake. Kim grabbed another black coffee – she had drunk one alongside her meal – and Phyllis politely asked her co-worker for a herbal tea. Peppermint flavour.

Just as the waitress returned with their hot drinks, an old Renault Clio swung into the car park, windscreen wipers flashing back and forth.

Terry was driving, his face set and tense.

Thirty seconds later, an ancient tractor chugged into the car park behind him, lurching through the puddles and spraying mud over the other vehicles.

Geoff was perched in the driver's cab. It was harder to tell what mood he was in, since the glass was steamed up from the inside. But he didn't hang around once the tractor had come to a halt, turning off the engine and throwing open the cab door before Terry had even jumped out of his hatchback.

Kim put down her knife and fork. 'Talking of the cavalry.'

The two men walked in, shaking raindrops off their quilted jackets and looking about themselves uncertainly. More heads turned, though this time with less interest. A tractor in the car park was like an automatic entrée to the moorland diner. *Pass, friend. You're normal, you're one of us.* Terry spotted them in the booth, and nodded to Geoff. They both squeezed in beside Savage after brief greetings had been exchanged.

Geoff removed his flat cap when greeting Kim, then replaced it afterwards. There was little interest in the smiling Phyllis from either men. They nodded politely enough, but their eyes slid quickly away afterwards.

Like she was somehow untouchable.

That's Barton's child she's carrying, Kim had said, not without distaste. And there was that little black tattoo on her forearm. Like a brand.

'Billy's dead,' Terry said, keeping his gaze on Savage. 'They sent the hunt out after him this morning. Dani told me on the phone.'

'I know, I saw some of it.'

'Can't say as I'm sorry. The way he handed Rose over to Barton.' He caught Phyllis looking at him, and coloured furiously. 'What? All right, I made a mistake with Dani first time round. But I changed my mind. And if I'd gone up there like Callum did, I'd be dead too.'

'Billy must have changed his mind too though,' Phyllis said, glaring at Terry. There was a hint of accusation in her voice. 'He must have crossed Barton. The Rev was planning to get Rose back. Maybe Billy didn't like that. Why else send the hunt out after him?'

'This hunt business seems particularly barbaric.' Savage frowned, draining his coffee cup. Barton clearly fancied himself a feudal lord of the moors. Complete with his very own fortified castle and medieval-style hunters. 'Does it happen very often?'

'Yes, I'd like to know that too.' Kim gave her girlfriend an accusing look.

He guessed Phyllis had kept quite a few things back from her brief time up at the Green Chapel. To protect her girlfriend, he was sure. But Kim seemed unimpressed.

'Only once before,' Terry said. 'It was a while back now. Some bloke came in from upcountry, started making trouble. Barton wanted to make an example of him. So he pushed him out the gate on foot, gave him a head start, and then sent the others out after him. Bikes, off-roaders, dogs.' He shuddered. 'Not me, course. I've never been part of the pack.'

'Pack?' Kim repeated sharply.

'That's what we call the ones closest to Barton. His inner circle. You know?' Terry made a tight circular gesture. 'They get the best money, sure. But the things they have to do to earn it . . .' Again, he shuddered. 'Not me, no thanks.'

Savage looked down into his coffee cup, then took up a spoon and stirred the foamy dregs at the bottom. 'This man from upcountry. What happened to him? Did the hunt catch up with him in the end?'

'Not a clue. I told you, I'm not one of the pack.'

Savage spooned some of the foam into his mouth. It tasted bitter and delicious. Nothing like the pure caffeine hit of Turkish coffee, but strong enough to inject new life into him. He had started flagging earlier. Now he was alert and on edge, keen to get moving. But there were a few things to sort out first.

'What about his name?' He played with the cheap spoon,

pressing the shaft between his thumb and forefinger. 'Do you remember that, at least?'

'I don't know.' Terry looked at Geoff for guidance.

Geoff pushed back his cap and scratched his head. 'Something foreign.'

'Do you mean Russian?' Kim leant forward, suddenly very interested. She glanced at Savage, then back at Terry. 'There seem to be rather a lot of Russians involved in whatever this is.'

Terry shook his head. 'Not Russian. But Geoff's right. It was a foreign-sounding name. Probably Middle Eastern. And he looked it too. Dark skin, dark hair, dark eyes.' He banged his fist on the table, impatient. 'Look, that ain't important now. Barton's got Dani back at the Green Chapel. I know it.'

Probably Middle Eastern. Dark skin, dark hair, dark eyes.

Savage had squeezed the cheap spoon so hard it was bent and misshapen. Guiltily, he dropped the spoon onto the table, then pushed the clamorous past away with an effort.

He had not forgotten his search for Jarrah. Merely pushed a new item higher up his list. He had come to Dartmoor seeking his brother-in-law, and ended up losing one of their friends as well. He would never forget that loss. Or forgive whoever was responsible. But perhaps in solving one problem today, he would sort out another as well. Or come a little closer to the truth.

'You're probably right. Though how he found her isn't clear.' Savage hesitated. 'I was going back up to the compound today anyway. Before dusk. This just makes it more urgent.'

Geoff stared at him. 'Why were you going back?'

'Barton's clearing out his goods. I overheard a call this morning. He wants everything out before nightfall. The whole place clean.'

Kim frowned. 'What are these "goods" he's getting rid of?'

'You tell me.' Savage decided he'd talked around the subject long enough. It was time to get some solid information. He looked directly at her girlfriend. 'Phyllis?'

Phyllis had been sitting in silence throughout, head down, staring at the table top. Now she stirred, looked from his face to those of the others, and shook her head. 'I can't,' she whispered. 'He'd kill me.'

'He'd have to go through me first,' Kim said grimly.

'It's a risk, I get that,' Savage said, not taking his eyes off Phyllis. 'But if you *don't* tell me, more people are going to die. You want that on your conscience?'

Kim made an angry noise under her breath, but said nothing.

Burying her face in her hands, Phyllis rocked back and forth, drawing curious glances from others in the diner. Eventually, she muttered, 'I don't know the whole thing. Just bits and pieces.'

'So tell us what you do know,' he said.

'Bones,' she hissed.

Kim stared at her. 'What are you talking about?'

'There were bones,' Phyllis said, keeping her voice pitched low so only those at the table could hear. 'Buried under the floor in the big hall. I heard the guards talking about it one night. They'd been moving the altar and they found . . . something. Human remains.'

Her voice tailed off into silence.

'Oh my God,' Geoff said heavily, and crossed himself.

Kim put an arm around her girlfriend's shoulders, who was crying now. 'It's OK,' she said, though it was clear she was shocked. 'It's not your fault.'

'I should have told the police, I know that.' Phyllis glanced round at Kim. Her eyes were pleading. 'But I wasn't sure how. Not without endangering you. I couldn't even be sure it was true, do you see? And he's got the local police in his pocket. He'd have found out who told them, and come after us.'

'It's fine, baby. I understand.'

Human remains.

And now Dani and Rose were missing.

What the hell was this cult the Reverend had going on at the Green Chapel? It seemed he was willing to go to any lengths to protect his business, even murder. But what was he hiding?

Savage curbed his impatience to move against Barton. He couldn't risk failure this time. 'Anything else you can remember from the Green Chapel?'

'Well . . .' Phyllis bit her lip, looking nervous. 'There were often vans turning up at odd hours. Nighttime, mostly.'

'Vans with foreign number plates? Russian plates, for instance?'

She nodded, looking surprised. 'That's right.'

'Who was in them?'

'Only a driver, usually. Sometimes two men. He'd reverse the van up to the entrance to the big hall as though offloading something. Or maybe picking up. I could never see properly.' Phyllis sniffed, wiping tears off her cheeks. Kim handed her a handkerchief and she took it with a grateful smile. 'Not from my bedroom window. The angle was wrong.'

'Was Barton around?'

'Always.' She made a face. 'Either him or his mother.'

'His *mother*?'

'Mother Barton. She often went outside to supervise the deliveries.' Phyllis shuddered. 'She never spoke to me, thank God. But the other girls . . . They were terrified of her. Said she's a stone-cold bitch.'

Savage suppressed a smile. 'And now we've got too close for comfort,' he said, 'Barton and his mother will be moving anything that could incriminate them.'

'Moving it where?' Terry asked.

'Another safe house, I expect. He'll be waiting to see if he can bring the goods back once things settle down, or if he needs to move them further afield. If the Green Chapel has been compromised as a hiding place, for instance.'

'*Hele*,' Kim said slowly, looking at him.

'Exactly.'

Terry was confused. 'What?'

'It's what the Green Chapel used to be called in Old English,' Kim explained. '*Hele*. It means a hiding place.'

'Only his cover has been blown. Faith will have told them everything she knows by now. So a search warrant will be issued, at least.'

Terry's eyes widened. 'Faith?'

'She's a lawyer. She's not going to break the law if she can avoid it. Barton has a man on the inside though, who could probably stall things. But only for so long. So he'll move the goods to avoid being found with them on the premises.' Savage smiled grimly. 'But he won't be in a position to move them securely until another van turns up. Because we stole his.'

'You stole his van?' Geoff was impressed.

'Dani and I stole it together, to be accurate. She drove, I rode shotgun. Literally.' Savage pulled out his phone and showed them the photo he'd taken from the interior of the van. 'Take a look at this. It's the word "help" in Russian. It was scratched on the inside of the van with someone's fingernail, for God's sake.' He shifted his gaze to Terry, the weakest link. 'Come on, I know you're withholding information. Explain this.'

He paused, watching Terry in the horrified silence that followed. The young man was worried sick about Dani, that was obvious. A little more pressure, and . . .

'He's going to hurt Dani this time,' Savage said softly. 'You know that, don't you, Terry? To make an example of her. Third time she's flouted his rules, isn't it? However attractive he finds her, Barton's not a fool. He can't risk losing face.'

Terry swallowed.

'What gets transported in these vans?' Savage pressed him.

'It's not a what,' he replied hesitantly. 'It's a who.'

'The only people I saw up there, apart from his guards, were pregnant women.' Savage sat up straight, shocked. 'Tell me it's not babies he's selling?'

Terry looked horrified. 'God, no.'

'Who, then?'

Phyllis, who had been staring unhappily out of the window since her confession, said one word in a husky voice. 'Billy.' She pointed towards the road, her voice growing stronger. 'Billy.'

'What are you on about?' Geoff scowled at her. 'Billy's dead.'

'He doesn't look very dead.'

They all turned to stare out of the window.

Sure enough, there was Billy, surprisingly healthy for a corpse, driving a large, shiny red tractor into the car park.

CHAPTER FORTY

Billy's tractor was followed closely by a sand-coloured Land Rover Defender. Not chased, he noted, but followed. In a friendly, 'we're travelling together' kind of way. There looked to be at least four men in the other vehicle, maybe more. It was hard to be sure through the thick, driving rain. From his position, Savage couldn't see the *DARTMOOR GUN CENTRE* advert on the rear of the Land Rover. But the number plate matched. It was the same one that was registered to a Mike Cooper, local gun owner, according to Faith's friend in the government.

Confirming his suspicions, Savage recognised one of the men in the front of the Defender. A man so tall he had to tilt his head to fit into the vehicle, leaning drastically to one side, his cheek lying on his shoulder, his gaze turned toward the diner.

Big Swanney.

Geoff glared at Savage. 'You said Billy was dead.'

'I didn't actually see him die. What I saw was Billy being hunted.' He recalled the strange man-hunt at dawn with guns and dogs and motorbikes. Why enact such a complicated charade across the moors if they were all still buddies? 'It's puzzling, I agree. But let's not get sidetracked. Dani and Rose are still missing, and their safety hinges on what happens to Barton in the next few hours. We need to make sure he can't move his goods out of the compound before the police get up there with a warrant.' He paused. 'Which means leaving this diner in one piece.'

In the silence, Savage looked about, assessing his surroundings. His heart was racing.

Fight or flight.

Except there was nowhere to fly. And this was hardly a good place for a fight.

They had stainless steel cutlery. But he would soon run out of knives to throw, and he could hardly hurl cups and plates at the big Russian. It would be David and Goliath all over again. Not to mention that any fight here would have an audience. An audience who'd be only too happy to record the entire thing and post it to Facebook within five minutes. Not his style, thank you. The diner was half full. Mostly couples and men on their own, reading newspapers, looking down at their phones and tablets, or chatting quietly. One elderly lady with a walking stick, who was making her pot of tea last as long as possible.

Besides which, they had a pregnant woman with them. He'd already got Faith in trouble over this bizarre business. He didn't want anyone else getting hurt on his account.

He needed to think. And quickly.

'I agree about getting out of here in one piece,' Kim said, also checking the diner with a trained eye. 'But whatever you saw on the moors, Aubrey, it wasn't a murder.'

Terry leant forward. 'Actually, someone did die on the moors overnight.'

'What?' Phyllis stared at him.

'A dog walker found a body first thing. It was all over the news. Didn't you see? I thought they meant a walker. But now . . .'

Geoff was frowning. 'So if it wasn't Billy who died, who was it?'

'Beats me,' Savage said. 'Faith said the body had been

identified. That he was a local man. I assumed she meant Billy. But maybe that's what we were meant to think.'

'But who the hell else . . .' Terry stopped and fell silent.

Savage eyed him sharply. 'Hunch?'

'There's been a few whispers about Charlie recently, that's all.'

'Charlie?'

'PC Petherick, Barton's copper friend. The one who keeps the filth off his back and lets him know when it's safe to move stuff about.'

'So what did these whispers say?'

'Only that he isn't as bent as he'd like folk to think.'

Savage sat back, considering that statement. Then his brain clicked. He remembered how easy it had been to overpower Petherick when he found Dani in the farmhouse, despite that Glock he'd pulled from the constable's waistband. A handgun Charlie Petherick should have used against him, yet somehow failed to. At the time, he'd assumed that was down to careless-ness. Or possibly cowardice. But there was another explanation. And he didn't like how it made him feel.

'You mean Petherick's been working for the police this whole time? Deep undercover in Barton's operation?'

'I didn't say that.' Terry shifted uneasily, watching the activ-ity in the car park. 'All I know is, one minute he's Barton's golden boy. The next they're saying he's a troublemaker and he'd better watch out.'

No wonder he'd got that hostile look from the young man. Mother Barton had been less than impressed by Petherick's performance too. Had breaking Dani out of the compound endangered Petherick? Maybe even blown his cover with the Bartons?

'Brave lad.'

'Stupid too,' Geoff said gruffly, 'double-crossing a man like Barton. That's not a very healthy thing to do.'

Savage transferred his gaze to Billy in his tractor. He knew a sudden furious desire to go out there in the rain and confront him. Maybe break his nose again.

He wondered if Paglia knew about Charlie Petherick working undercover, and suddenly felt certain that she did. She had been hiding something from him, that was for sure. No doubt she hadn't been sure she could trust him. Or was concerned he might inadvertently expose their officer to danger.

Could Petherick be the man he'd seen being pursued on the moors at first light, like a fox with the hounds after him? Was he the 'local man' they'd found dead this morning?

If so, the policeman's death wasn't his fault. But right now, he felt like it was.

'I don't like any of this. What's going to happen now?' Phyllis bit her lip, glancing at Kim, one hand on her swollen belly. 'Kimmy?'

'I won't let him touch you, I promise,' Kim said in a low voice. 'None of them are coming anywhere near you.'

Billy had parked his tractor awkwardly along the verge. There was no room for it in the car park now that Geoff's tractor had taken the last available space for vehicles of that size. He opened the cab door and jumped down into a puddle, much as Geoff himself had done, quickly turning his jacket collar up against the pelting rain.

Mike Cooper, a stout figure behind the wheel of the Land Rover Defender, squeezed his vehicle in beside a white panel van and another car.

There then followed a silent comedy as each man attempted to open the door on his side only to find it could not open wide enough to let anyone out, there was so little space on either side of the vehicle.

Eventually, the rear door was thrown open, and two men climbed out that way. One man from the front clambered over the front seats and also managed to get out via the rear-opening door. Mike Cooper looked at the Russian beside him. Big Swanney could not quite move his neck that far, so merely slid his gaze sideways at Cooper.

There was some kind of exchange.

Mike Cooper apparently gave up at that point, put the vehicle in reverse and backed up a few feet, nearly colliding with the men at the back. Billy ran forward and opened the front passenger door.

Big Swanney unfolded himself from the Defender in much the same way he had done that day on the moorland road, shifting along the seat, then getting a foot out, then a leg, then another leg, then his vast trunk, and finally his head. He reared up in the rain storm, and all the other men took an instinctive step back.

Billy closed the door, then led the others to the sheltered porch of the diner, leaving Mike Cooper to his own devices.

Savage watched the diner door, waiting for it to swing open.

'How did they find us?' Geoff's face was ashen.

'I'm not sure they did, actually.' Savage pushed his empty coffee cup away, and waved at Lisa, the freckled waitress. She came over at once, taking an order pad from the front pocket of her apron.

'More coffee?' she asked.

'Just the bill, thanks.'

The waitress looked at Terry sympathetically. 'I was so sorry to hear about Callum. Such a dreadful thing.' She hesitated. 'Have the police got any idea who did it?'

'Not yet.'

Savage repeated his request for the bill, aware they might need to make a hurried exit soon, and Lisa headed back to the till.

'We should get out of here,' Phyllis said.

Lisa came back with the bill and a handheld card reader. Savage leafed through his wallet, and realised he hadn't been to the cash till in days. The cupboard was bare.

Kim started hunting for her wallet too, but he shook his head.

'I'll pay,' he said.

He forked out one of his credit cards and handed that to the waitress instead, though he preferred cash; it made it harder for people to trace where he was.

Mike Cooper had finally managed to get his door open, and came lumbering through the rain towards the diner. As one, the others turned and pushed through the entrance door together.

Slowly, Savage raised his gaze from the card reader, where he was punching in his four-digit PIN, to witness the men piling into the diner.

Six men.

Billy headed up the group, a white Band-Aid still plastered across his nose. Then came Mike Cooper and three of his entourage, all in their late twenties, dressed in dark blue denim jeans and oddly similar padded jackets. One of the other young men also still bore the marks of their encounter on the moorland road, his left cheek heavily bruised, his lip bulging where it had been split.

Last came Big Swanney with that curious walk, slow and slightly loping, arms swinging by his sides.

Billy saw them first. His eyes widened, and he stopped dead just inside the doorway. The others knocked into him, then stopped too, one after the other.

The huge Russian growled something.

Billy nodded at their booth.

It was impossible for Savage to hear what was being said, but their dazed expressions summed everything up perfectly.

What's up with you, jackass? I nearly went into the back of you. More significant head nods in their direction, accompanied by a confused pointing gesture without any actual pointing. *Shut up and look who it is.* Heads turned. More eyes widened. The battered-looking guy in the padded jacket clenched his fists impotently. *What the hell is that bastard doing here? And those guys? And the vicar and her girlfriend?* Big Swanney bent towards Mike Cooper and words were hurriedly exchanged. *Let's take them back to Barton.* Mike looked shocked. Big Swanney put a hand on his shoulder. Like a vice slowly tightening. *Come on, we can do this. Christ, I could do this one-handed and wearing a blindfold. There are six of us and only five of them, including two women.* Frantic head shaking. *In front of all these people? Are you kidding? Barton said low key . . . There's nothing low key about this place. Look at that old woman. She's staring right at us.* Big Swanney growled again. More gazing about by a worried Mike Cooper. Copious belly and head scratching. *I said, not here. Forget it. Be patient, OK? We'll have to wait until they leave.*

Having finally left her seat, the elderly woman who had been staring at them made her way past, supported by her walking stick. She smiled in gratitude as Billy pulled the door open for her to leave.

Mike Cooper looked straight towards them in the booth.

Savage raised his eyebrows, waiting.

After a moment's sheepish hesitation, Mike Cooper turned and shuffled towards the counter. Lisa came out from the kitchen, a friendly smile lighting up her face like a beacon.

'Hey, Mike,' Lisa said, tidying the menu display. 'Usual order?'

Mike rubbed his large belly uncertainly.

Savage watched the six men in a long rectangular mirror that hung the full length of the counter wall, partly obscured by the till, cutlery trays and a range of sauce bottles. There was a quick muttered conference. More pointing and furious head-shaking. Then they seemed to come to a consensus.

Mike placed both hands flat on the counter, gave the waitress a sickly smile, and said, 'Six bacon baps, five white coffees, and one hot chocolate.'

'Right you are.' Lisa leant forward, scribbling the order on her pad. 'Any sauces in the bacon baps?'

'Red sauce.' Mike hesitated, then added, 'Tomato, that is.'

'And is that a plain hot chocolate? Or one with marshmallows and cream?'

Mike glanced over his shoulder. There was an awkward silence.

Big Swanney leant down to say something in his ear.

Mike's smile turned even more sickly. 'Marshmallows and cream, thank you.'

'To go?' Lisa asked.

Mike Cooper looked round at Savage, as though calculating what he should do. Obviously his calculations came to a dead end. He looked up at Big Swanney instead. Big Swanney nodded, expressionless.

Mike wiped his brow, still glistening with rain, and turned back to Lisa.

'To go.'

He paid for the order, waited for his change, then all six of the men sat down on the circular chrome stools along the counter.

Directly facing Savage in the booth.

CHAPTER FORTY-ONE

'So,' Savage said, to nobody in particular, 'what is it I'm missing about Barton's operation? Whatever it is, my friend Peter was killed for it, and Callum, and now this other local they've found dead. So what's he hiding at the Green Chapel that's worth killing for?' He paused, his gaze steadily on the big Russian opposite, who looked like a giraffe trying to sit on a toadstool, towering over the other five men even in a seated position, long legs splayed awkwardly. 'And if those guards found human remains under the altar, were they old bones . . . or new?'

'Beats me.' Kim glanced at Phyllis, who said nothing. 'I wish I knew.'

'Geoff knows.'

They all looked at Geoff, who swallowed and cleared his throat.

'And I'm guessing Terry does too,' Savage added.

Terry made some kind of instinctive protest, then fell silent. His gaze shot to the six men opposite, who were still waiting for their takeaway order.

Kim leant back and studied both men in turn.

Eyes like lasers, Savage thought with satisfaction, watching the two men squirm under that cold, merciless scrutiny. She must have made a brilliant soldier. Courageous and intelligent. Not to mention resourceful. The kind of colleague he would have been proud to serve alongside.

'OK, I want the truth from you two,' Kim said coolly, 'and I want it now. Terry, you said it's a who, not a what. What did you mean by that?'

Terry opened his mouth, but Geoff laid a warning hand on his arm. 'Careful, son. They might hear you.'

'I don't care if they do.' Terry shook off Geoff's hand, his face flushed. 'I've had enough of this secrecy. Secrecy and lies. That's all we ever get round here since that bastard showed up, splashing his American cash and acting like he's a priest. It's so much bullshit.'

'Terry!'

'No, let me finish.' He nodded to Kim. 'I thought it was a good idea at first. A sex cult on the moor, you know? Liven things up, bit of spare cash, and if things went on up there that shouldn't ... Well, I was happy to turn a blind eye. Until he started picking on our own girls.'

Geoff subsided, looking away.

'First, it was only the ones who wanted it,' Terry continued. 'Mrs Baker, because her husband couldn't get it up anymore. Jodie from the dairy. She was desperate. You, Phyllis, because you wanted a baby.' He lowered his voice even further, shooting a covert look at Barton's men. 'But then he came after the married ones.'

'Like Dani,' Savage said.

'Aye.' Terry nodded, shamefaced. 'I was too afraid to stand up to him. But Callum wasn't. He'd had enough by then.'

'He was a fool.' But Geoff looked tormented.

'Maybe.' Terry swallowed. 'Or maybe if I hadn't been such a coward, we could have done something about him. Done it as a community. But it's way beyond that now.'

'He's too strong, boy.' Geoff too glanced at Barton's crew opposite. 'And we've all taken his bloody money. We're all guilty.'

'But guilty of what?' Kim asked, clearly bewildered.

The loud shrill of Savage's phone made them all jump. The men at the counter stared across at their booth.

Faith's name appeared on the caller screen.

Savage answered at once. 'Faith, I was beginning to get worried,' he said into the phone. 'What's happening? Are you still with the police?' He paused, listening to the crackling silence on the line. He was sure he could hear breathing. 'Faith?'

The phone went dead.

He checked the battery. It was getting low, only ten percent left. He hadn't recharged the phone in several days now. But he hadn't kept it on the whole time either, and he guessed it would still be good for another call or two if he turned it off now.

The signal was low too.

Only one bar.

Except the call hadn't ended because of low battery power or signal strength. It had been cut off deliberately. And not by Faith, he guessed. He had heard someone breathing on the other end, listening without replying. Either Barton had Faith, or he had her phone.

Neither was a particularly comforting thought.

His fist clenched automatically about the greasy knife he'd used to cut up his bacon and sausages. His gaze lifted and met Big Swanney's.

The Russian glanced down at the knife, then up at his face. There was a flicker of something in his eyes. A recognition of danger, perhaps. Maybe even a frisson of excitement. Like the guy was spoiling for a fight, almost hoping Savage would suddenly snap and throw the knife. *C'mon, let's rumble.* But it was only the tiniest flicker. Then the grey face closed up again, carefully neutral.

With an effort, Savage unclenched his fist. Slowly, he released the knife and placed it next to his fork on the empty plate. Meal over.

Too many witnesses here. Too many innocent bystanders. The young couple with the baby. The vulnerable adult who had just walked in with his carer, seated in a booth near theirs. It was part of his training. The basic rules of engagement. Never knowingly target or endanger civilians.

But out there on the moors, with no one to see, miles from civilisation, miles from the nearest police station, miles from anything that wasn't wild and ancient and green . . .

That was a different matter.

'Well?' Kim was looking at him anxiously. 'What did Faith say?'

'Hang on.'

He called Faith back. The phone rang seven times while he waited, aware of everyone watching him. He glanced out of the window. Rain was still falling, though less violently now. A dark, heavy curtain of water endlessly drawn across the grim, rolling wasteland of the moors.

Finally, someone answered.

Again, crackling silence. A faint sound like breathing.

'Who's there?'

Still no answer.

He sat back, staring at Big Swanney opposite, who stared back at him in exactly the same flat way. Dark, lugubrious eyes. A stubbly chin. Large, long-fingered hands clasping both sides of the counter stool he was perched on, as though afraid he might overbalance at any moment.

'Do you know who I'm looking at?' he said softly into the phone. 'Your boys. All six of them. I've got them, Barton. And you're not getting them back. Do you hear me?'

The phone went dead again.

Savage slipped the phone back into his pocket, and looked across at Geoff. 'Guilty of what?' he repeated, picking up from their previous conversation.

Geoff blenched. 'I can't be sure. We only ever heard rumours, nothing concrete.'

'What's he dealing in?'

Geoff looked at Terry, who nodded.

'People,' he said.

Savage locked gazes with Kim. '*People*,' he repeated.

'Shit,' she whispered.

Less than thirty seconds later, Beyoncé's 'All The Single Ladies' rang out jauntily across the diner.

Heads turned.

Five men leant forward and looked at Mike Cooper, sitting on the far end of the row of counter stools.

Mike seemed confused for a moment.

Then he patted his broad chest, and shoved a hand inside his jacket, pulling out a mobile phone. 'All The Single Ladies' continued to trill loudly and insistently as he fumbled to answer the call.

'Hello?'

Savage pushed up out of the booth and was at the diner entrance in a few easy strides. He turned briefly to check the others had followed him. Kim was right behind him, dragging Phyllis by the hand. Then came Terry, still glowering, cheeks flushed with anger. Geoff brought up the rear, fixing his cap back on his head and glancing awkwardly at Barton's men as he passed them.

Mike Cooper was still on the phone, pale-faced as he listened to the boss. He was nodding, stammering something as he stood up too, staring after Savage.

Lisa appeared behind him with the men's order, smiling cheerfully. 'Here you go, lads. Five white coffees, one hot chocolate with marshmallows and cream. Six bacon baps with tomato sauce.'

Utter confusion ensued. Men grabbing food, and hot coffee

in takeaway cups, and arguing over wooden stirrers and the sugar portions at the self-serve island. The big Russian peering into his hot chocolate as though counting his marshmallows.

And above it all, Mike Cooper could be heard shouting, 'Leave the food. We've got to go. Right now. Boss's orders.'

CHAPTER FORTY-TWO

Savage pushed out of the door into the driving rain, and the others came piling out after him. There was a long-handled umbrella beside the double doors to the diner. He picked it up and threaded it through the twin handles, effectively preventing the door from opening. Through the glass, he saw Billy grab the door handles on the other side and tug. Then he met his eyes furiously.

Savage grinned, and blew Billy a kiss through the glass.

It wouldn't hold them for long though. Not once Big Swanney got there.

'Time to get up to the Green Chapel. Before his boys can get there ahead of us.' Savage turned to Geoff. 'I'm going with you in the tractor.'

Geoff stared.

Kim headed purposefully towards her Mini.

'Wait a minute, Kim. I need you to collect something for me.' Savage threw her the keys to the Russian van he'd abandoned in the chapel car park. She caught them one-handed. 'Drive it up to the Green Chapel as quickly as you can. I'll meet you at the gate.' He paused. 'Present under the seat for you, by the way. And another in the glove box.'

Kim nodded her understanding, looking eager now, her face lit up. She turned to kiss a horrified Phyllis on the lips. 'Go home,' she told her girlfriend. 'Keep the door locked and don't answer it for anyone. You hear me?'

Phyllis shook her head. There were tears in her eyes. Tears of anger as well as frustration, by the way she was glaring at Savage. She whispered in Kim's ear, clinging onto her with hands like claws.

Geoff hurried to the tractor, with Savage close behind him.

'I love you too, darling. And the baby.' Kim was gently detaching herself from those desperate fingers. 'But somebody has to do *something*.'

The men were all dragging on the obstructed door handles now. A joint effort, like they were rowing a boat. The muffled, rhythmic thudding filled the air, loud even above the noise of the downpour.

THUD.

THUD.

THUD.

Geoff had already climbed into the cab of the tractor. Savage followed, squeezing in to stand behind him, though there was not much space. The rain sounded thunderous on the roof of the cab as the old diesel engine chugged into life. Savage turned to watch as Terry jumped into his Clio and started her up, gunning noisily out of the car park, mud spraying everywhere as the wheels spun through the deep puddles. Kim followed a few seconds later in her red-and-white striped Mini, no less quickly. Phyllis fumbled into her own silver Ford Fiesta and also pulled away, no doubt aware that a pregnant woman on her own would make an easy target as long as she remained.

The others had all turned left on the main road. But Phyllis's silver Fiesta turned right. Away from Dartmoor, towards civilisation.

She was probably the only sensible one among them, Savage thought.

Big Swanney had pushed the others out of the way. He grabbed both door handles and jerked them towards him, seemingly without effort.

Savage clapped Geoff on the shoulder. 'Head straight for the Green Chapel. Fast as you can. They'll be coming after us. Do you know any shortcuts?'

'Only across the moor.'

The long-handled black umbrella had snapped easily in two. Like a twig under someone's boot.

The double doors opened inwards, causing more confusion. One of the men had fallen in the struggle, or been knocked over, and the others were all stepping over him in their hurry to get out. Only Big Swanney stopped to help him up, reaching down a long arm.

It was Billy who had fallen, Savage realised with a grin.

'Well, we're in a tractor,' he said.

Geoff grunted his assent. Or it might have been laughter. It was hard to tell.

The tractor rolled majestically out of the car park and back onto the main road. Swaying precariously behind Geoff's seat, Savage widened his stance to avoid falling. The engine roared as Geoff pushed up through the gears, deafening them both, the tractor moving much faster than it was designed to do. Luckily the road was empty of traffic both ways. Savage gazed back through the cab window, steadying himself with one hand against the cold, rain-streaked glass.

Six men poured chaotically out of the diner into the rain, in ones and twos, clutching hot coffees and brown paper food bags, making for their own vehicles.

But it was too late.

The good guys were already long gone.

CHAPTER FORTY-THREE

The rain was finally beginning to ease as they came in sight of the stockade, Geoff rumbling his tractor over mud ruts and along narrow, barely visible tracks on the high moors. They had passed within a quarter mile of the outer boundaries of Rowlands farm, the collapsed walls and sunken roof of Agnes's cottage a reminder to Savage of his search for Jarrah. He stared at the ruins until they were out of sight, suddenly angry with himself. He had only driven down to Devon in the first place in search of his missing brother-in-law, finally determined to fulfil the promise he'd made to Lina, and what had he achieved?

Only Peter's death, however that had come about, and a shake-up of the wasps' nest that had settled itself on top of the Hele. Now the wasps were buzzing furiously about his head, and he had no time to stop and make a more thorough enquiry after his brother-in-law.

But perhaps it was a fool's errand. There had been no sign of the man on Dartmoor. Only hints and clues, whispers, vague rumours . . .

Had Jarrah even come here at all before dropping off the radar?

Evidence was scanty, to say the least.

First, there was the mysterious Glock 19 from Dani's holdall. The same gun used to execute the unfortunate Callum Hoggins, and which had later fired the fatal bullet that ended Peter's life too.

Like many secret service employees with a licence, Jarrah had carried a Glock on missions when it was deemed a weapon might be necessary. Was it the same gun, or merely a coincidence? Though if he'd brought a Glock here, on official business, and then disappeared off the map, why had no one from M15 come here looking for him or the weapon? And if Callum had been killed with a weapon registered to MI5, why had nobody from London come racing down here to see what the hell was going on?

Then there was the scrap of paper he'd found at Peter's bedside.

The undated note.

He rummaged in his jeans pocket for the note, and unfolded it, swaying as the tractor climbed a short rise through bracken. *I'm going out for a walk on the moors, clear my head after last night's excesses. Didn't want to wake you. Why the hell did we drink so much? Back in an hour or two.*

He put the note away again.

Jarrah had come here at some point, for sure. And Peter had lied about his visit, denying it had even happened, though it still wasn't clear why. Not the action of an innocent man. Yet what was the guilt Peter had been hiding?

Hints and clues, whispers, vague rumours . . .

That was all he had.

Savage ran a hand through his damp hair, crouching to stare up out of the rainy cab windows at the fortified hilltop above. He'd promised Lina that he would find Jarrah. Or his remains. And he fully intended to honour that promise.

First though, he had to deal with the increasing headache that was the Reverend Barton. He might not have made a promise to Peter, as such. But the two of them had been friends since university days, and it had affected Savage more than he cared to admit, seeing his friend lying in a pool of his own blood. Not a soldier, killed in the line of duty. A struggling farmer, living on the edge of nowhere and trying to get his life back together under difficult circumstances.

Besides, if someone had shot him, or driven him to shoot himself, Savage hoped one of his own friends would take it upon themselves to investigate, and avenge his death if necessary.

Because that's what friends did.

'Look.'

He turned his head, following Geoff's pointing finger.

They were about to cross the narrow hilltop track that led to the Green Chapel. The one where Peter had torn down the sign in a temper, and forced that confrontation with Barton's crew. Barrelling along the track towards them was the sand-coloured Land Rover Defender, followed at a distance of about six hundred yards by Billy, perched high up in his shiny red tractor.

'What do I do?' Geoff sounded scared.

Savage studied the land ahead of their position. Boulders on one side of the road they were about to cross, thick clustered trees on the other.

'Block the road.'

'With the tractor? But what if they crash into us?'

'They won't.'

'But they might. And this is my only tractor.'

Savage crouched again, squinting to see the red tractor through the rainy glass. 'OK, I see why you might be concerned.' Billy's tractor not only had the advantage in size, being larger and heavier than Geoff's older machine, but it also had a large digger at the front. A digger with an earth-soiled scoop and a row of sharp, evil-looking teeth at the front. Like it lived on a diet of granite and hardcore. 'But maybe we could leave the tractor across the road, and then abandon ship.'

'You want me to park my tractor in the middle of the road?'

'And walk away.' Savage scratched his nose. 'Well, run away. Taking the keys with us. But yes, that's the basic gist of it.'

Geoff didn't like that idea either though. 'It's my tractor,' he kept repeating. 'My only tractor.'

'I doubt they'll damage it. Much.'

Geoff shook his head, clinging stubbornly to the vast steering wheel.

'How much?' Savage asked.

'Sorry?'

They were almost at the verge, about to cross the road onto the other side of the moor. But they had been seen. The Defender, which must have been going slow to let Billy keep pace with them on the tractor, suddenly accelerated towards them. Savage could see Big Swanney in the front, glaring at them. Mike Cooper looked stressed and red-cheeked, like he'd been envisaging the end of his cosy agreement with Barton all the way from the diner, and everything such a split might entail.

'How much for your tractor?'

'I don't understand.'

'It's simple, Geoff. I want to buy your tractor. It's a very handsome piece of machinery. I fancy becoming a farmer, and only your tractor will do for me. So how much?'

'Are you seriously offering to pay for my tractor?'

'In a nutshell.'

Geoff turned to stare up at him. 'You're mad, you are.'

'Very possibly. And my late wife would have agreed with you. But let's pass over my mental faculties for now, and focus on the deal in hand. How much for your tractor, Geoff? What's your sweet spot?'

'My . . . what?'

'What's the least you will accept for this fine agricultural vehicle?'

Geoff blinked. 'Two thousand.' He hesitated. 'Or maybe three thousand. Three and a half.'

'I'll give you five.'

'*What*?'

'Five thousand pounds. Not a penny less.'

They had hit the sodden, bumpy verge, littered with rocks and cursed with a steep, horribly uneven bank of grassed-over earth. The tractor lurched viciously from side to side as they negotiated these obstacles. Savage was thrown backwards into the glass wall, then forwards against Geoff's back, throwing out both hands to steady himself.

'Is it a deal, Geoff?' He turned his head, staring at the big Russian and Mike Cooper, only about a hundred and fifty yards away. Not for the first time, he silently thanked his late cousin Sara for leaving him that legacy. Though she could hardly have guessed what he would use it for. 'Say yes. The enemy is almost upon us.'

'How do I know you'll keep your word?"

'You don't.'

Geoff swore under his breath, and scratched his head through his cap, almost dislodging it.

'Is it a deal?'

'Yes, all right, all right.' Geoff swung the tractor onto the wet road, turning the wheel through ninety degrees. 'Though I think you're crazy.'

'Join the club.'

Due to the abrupt change in direction, the old tractor had almost stopped dead. Geoff was accelerating again, but the engine simply wasn't responding. The Defender came right up against them a few seconds later, stridently sounding its horn, the front bumper almost close enough to touch.

Savage partly turned to look at the men in the Defender, which was difficult from his cramped position. Big Swanney had a mobile clamped to his ear. He was saying something into the phone, his dark, mournful gaze fixed on Savage's face. Then he ended the call, spoke briefly to Mike Cooper, and abruptly the Defender swerved away from them.

The other vehicle pulled off the road onto the verge, bumping along towards a boulder at a reckless speed. At first, Savage couldn't understand it. Were they giving up the chase?

Then he saw Billy coming up fast in his digger, and understood the plan.

The Land Rover Defender had moved aside to let the larger, slower vehicle pull in front. Because the Defender was no match for a tractor.

But the digger was another matter.

As soon as Billy had passed them, Mike swung the Land Rover Defender back onto the road behind the digger, braking to adjust his speed down to about fifteen miles per hour.

It was a car chase in slow motion, Savage thought

Now Billy was right behind them in his shiny red digger, grinning malevolently as he lowered and raised the scoop in a menacing manner.

Geoff glanced back. 'He's going to ram us off the road.'

'Keep driving.'

'Did you hear what I said?'

'Keep driving.'

There was a terrible scraping noise as the digger's metal scoop glanced off the back of Geoff's tractor. Savage's tractor now, of course. And already damaged goods.

'Why should I risk my life? You just bought this tractor. You own it now, not me. So why don't you keep driving it?'

Geoff slowed as though meaning to jump out.

The metal scoop scraped the back window, cracking the wet glass, and the whole tractor juddered as Geoff tried to open the cab door while the tractor was still moving.

'Woah, wait a minute. Best not stall with that maniac behind us.' Savage edged round and squeezed into the seat beside him, carefully replacing Geoff's foot on the pedal with his own. 'Now hang on.'

'What?'

'No, I mean . . . Hang onto something.'

Savage glanced in his mirrors and saw Billy grinning back at him. He put his foot down, travelling another fifty yards until they had nearly reached the perfect storm of high boulders on one side, woodlands on the other, and a substantial ditch on the woodlands side, thick with brambles and long grasses.

No way for another vehicle to get past them. Not at that point.

Without warning, he spun the wheel ninety degrees.

The tractor jumped sideways on the gleaming road surface, like a skittish horse shying at a farm gate, and Geoff almost tumbled out of the seat, banging the side of his head against the cab door.

Savage lifted his foot off the accelerator and the tractor stalled, equidistant between two inhospitable verges. A rock and a hard place. Now the road was blocked to traffic in either direction. And the Green Chapel was cut off from this side of the hill, at least. Which would hopefully give them a window of opportunity.

'Come on, time to leg it.'

Savage snatched the key from the ignition and threw open the cab door while Geoff was still clutching his head. He pushed Geoff out first, then jumped down after him into the rain.

'Five thousand pounds,' Geoff said breathlessly. 'Remember?'

'I don't have five grand on me now, obviously. But I'm good for it. You'll get paid. Ask anyone who knows me.' Savage pocketed the metal tractor key and started to run along the rocky verge. He didn't look back at their pursuers. Looking back when running away was usually what got people killed, in his experience. But he did shout back at Geoff, 'Look, you should get behind these rocks. Hide or run, whichever you prefer. But don't wait here or they'll kill you. You got that?'

'I've got it. I'm sticking with ... you.' Geoff followed him, already panting as Savage plunged uphill after the last of the large boulders. 'Where ... are we ... going?'

'Green Chapel. Uphill and cross-country.' There was a fallen beech tree ahead. He hurdled the rotten trunk, and heard Geoff swear as he bumbled into it, probably blinded by the rain. 'Before they can get there by road.'

The Defender's horn sounded several times back on the road below, loud and insistent. Billy's digger was still chugging away as though they hadn't yet understood what was happening. Savage listened as he ran. He couldn't understand why none of the men were coming after them. Then a high-pitched noise tore through the air, like nails down a chalkboard, and he winced.

Metal on metal.

That was the sound of a huge sharp-toothed digger scoop eating into the roof of the old tractor, he guessed. And demolishing it.

But he still did not look back.

'My tractor ...'

Geoff sounded almost tearful.

'My tractor,' Savage corrected him. 'Just keep running.'

His phone rang.

He managed to drag the mobile from his pocket and answer it without slowing his pace, though he didn't have a chance to read the display.

If it was Barton again, he would simply hang up. He wasn't in the mood for another chat with the Reverend. And it would be counterproductive. No point giving away his plans or even hinting that he was on the move. Some vague element of surprise was about all he had left to gamble with.

'Yes?' he said tersely.

'Savage?'

A woman's voice. Not Barton, then.

'Yes.'

'It's Kim.' She paused. 'You sound out of breath. Are you running?'

'Yes.'

'Why aren't you in the tractor?'

The line was crackly again, her voice sounding like it was underwater. He checked the charge on the phone. Less than six percent now.

'Change of plan.' He chanced a quick look back at Geoff. The farmer was over a hundred feet back down the slope, but still gamely picking his way uphill through the wet rocky bracken and heather. 'Did you pick up the van? Where are you now?'

'Waiting for you, of course.' She paused again. 'Thanks for the gift, by the way.'

'You found the guns.'

'I'm not really a Glock fan. But the shotgun's a thing of beauty. Shell pouch too. Whose was it?'

'Petherick's. Give me your location.'

'On the approach to the Green Chapel gates. About three hundred yards back. It's a kind of dirt track. Round the first bend, parked out of sight.'

'There's a tower guard on the gate.'

'Seen him. I got out when I arrived, had a quick recce.'

'Anyone else about?'

'Not a soul.'

'Gates open or closed?'

'Closed.'

'Any activity?'

'Nothing to report.'

He grinned at her formal response, which had only lacked the word *sir*, and resisted the urge to say, *Roger that, Sergeant.*

Instead, he said, 'Sounds like I'm roughly south-south-east of your position. Coming in hot on the ground. I've left an obstruction behind us. But I don't think it'll take them long to get through. Ten or fifteen minutes, tops. Less if they abandon their vehicles and pursue on foot.'

'What kind of obstruction?'

'Geoff's tractor.' He wiped rain from his eyes, dodged another large boulder, then corrected himself. 'My tractor now.'

'Excuse me?'

'I bought it. His tractor.'

There was silence on the other end of the line.

'Kim? You still there?'

'I'm still here.'

'Battery's nearly dead on this thing.' He was almost at the top of the slope, and could see the scrub bushes ahead skirting the dirt track, dark foliage gleaming from the rain. 'I'm about a minute away.'

'Roger that.'

Savage grinned, and ended the call.

CHAPTER FORTY-FOUR

He kept jogging uphill and reached her position just over a minute later, exactly as calculated. The mud-flecked Russian van was parked round the bend from the stockade. Kim had pulled the van in close to the verge, in a spot where it was shielded at the front by a cluster of thorny gorse bushes, blazing with yellow flowers. Behind him, in the distance, he could still hear the crash and whine of the digger trying to shunt the tractor out of the way.

He doubted it would take Billy more than another five or ten minutes to achieve his goal. Which meant they had very little time to make something of their advantage. An advantage that had just cost him five thousand pounds.

Did he actually have five thousand pounds?

Well, too late now.

Maybe Faith would lend it to him.

Assuming he managed to spring her from Barton's compound, that is, which is where he suspected she must be. How else could Barton have got her phone? He must have sent his boys to lie in wait for her, then grabbed her coming out of the pub. Or maybe on a lonely moorland road, one vehicle blocking her at the front, another at the rear.

He could feel anger thrumming through him, like a vibration shuddering up his spine out of the very ground itself, a tuning fork struck by the wilds of Dartmoor. He'd been angry before today, of course. Angry about Jarrah. Angry about Peter.

But now this, with Faith . . .

It was a different kind of anger. Like a higher frequency. It was not that Faith was a woman, but that she was innocent in this situation. She wasn't a player, she was a bystander. And therefore out of bounds. Like a civilian used as a human shield in a war zone. It put a bad taste in his mouth to know Barton had taken her. And he'd done nothing to prevent it.

Had Peter not been an innocent too, then?

Perhaps not.

Or not in the same way.

Something about Peter's ignominious death kept nagging at him. Something he had missed or not considered properly. But he had no time to tease it out of his brain now. All he had for now was this anger churning inside him.

Further along the ridge, he could see Terry's old red Renault Clio parked up behind a boulder. Just the rear end poking out. Invisible from the stockade, yes. But there was no way Terry could walk down the track to their position without being spotted by the guard on the gate tower.

Almost out of breath, he didn't bother getting inside the van but dropped down beside the passenger side and waited for Geoff to catch up.

He was soaked now. It would make no difference to seek shelter.

Kim came round to join him almost immediately, sliding her back halfway down the wet panel wall of the van, still on her haunches and ready for action. She passed him the Glock and he took it without a word.

In her arms, she was cradling the shotgun.

Like a baby at the baptismal font.

He glanced at her black clerical top, which was sodden. 'You going to lose the dog collar, at least?'

Looking down at her top, Kim grimaced. The black material was starting to cling. She shook her head though. 'Could be useful. They might be less likely to take a pot-shot at the vicar.'

'You're enjoying this,' he said, 'aren't you?'

Kim grinned.

'Like old times.' She sobered then, and met his eyes. 'What's Barton really up to? This Green Chapel . . . Looks more like a fortress than a chapel, if you ask me.'

'I don't know. But you heard Terry. He thinks Barton's dealing in people. Personally, I have my own suspicions.'

'Such as?'

'Fertility treatments, pregnant women all over the place . . .' He pulled a face. 'Terry denied it. But I think Barton's selling babies.'

'What?' She shook her head. 'Seriously? Who buys babies?'

'Rich people who can't have them any other way.'

'That's horrific. And I can't believe it. Not even from a man like Barton.' Her disgust was palpable. It was obvious she wasn't convinced. 'So what's the Russian connection?'

'Couriers?'

She glanced behind herself. 'You mean . . . they put babies in this van? And drive them where, exactly?'

'Wherever the buyer is. Or to a holding station. Probably in Eastern Europe. By road and ferry, most likely.'

'I think you're forgetting Customs.'

'I expect Barton has it all figured out. Look, you didn't see him during that ridiculous ceremony. The man's smug to the point of nausea. Totally confident that he won't get caught. Too confident. Maybe there's a well-paid chaperone to keep them quiet. One of the mothers, perhaps.' He recalled the Russian word for *help* scratched on the wall at the back of the van.

Someone in abject despair had etched that out, almost certainly with her own fingernails. 'Maybe there's a change of vehicle at some point. Maybe a private boat, anchored off the coast, with all the crew in his pay. They bundle them aboard, and . . .'

'But that's barbaric.'

'Barton doesn't give a damn about the niceties. This is a well-funded operation, Kim. Whatever he's selling has to be high value. And babies are about as valuable a commodity as it gets.'

Geoff appeared at the top of the steep slope a minute later, stumbling over hillocks and loose stones, red-faced and panting.

By which time Savage, much to his relief, had regained his breath and wasn't feeling too bad. It had been a few years since he'd been anywhere near a battle zone. But he still worked out when he could. Sit-ups and squats most mornings in the camper. Pulldowns from the bunk. Long walks over the moors and cliffs on his travels. The occasional stint in a friendly gym.

Still, he was not in as good shape as he'd been while on active duty. And getting out of breath climbing a hill at a moderate jog was embarrassing.

'OK, what now?' Kim had been examining the shotgun, but now turned her attention to Savage. She looked frighteningly at home with a shotgun for a lady vicar. 'What's the plan?'

Two sets of eyes looked at him expectantly.

What's the plan?

It seemed he was in charge. Well, he didn't mind that. Savage rubbed his chin and squared his shoulders. Another thing army training had been good for. Something to fall back on when plain common sense had gone and you were left with what looked on the face of it like a suicide mission.

'The plan,' he said, 'is to get inside there. Into the stockade.'

'With only this shotgun and the Glock?'

'Hopefully, we won't need them.' Savage half-stood to take another look at the stockade. 'I have a clicker. A remote control to open the gate. But I'm willing to bet they'll have disabled that mechanism at their end by now. Made it so that the gate can only be opened manually.'

'Makes sense,' Kim said.

'So I need to get them to open the gate by guile.'

Geoff stared. 'What's guile?'

'It means . . . Look, it doesn't matter. But we need to move now. Right now. Before Billy manages to shift that tractor and clear the road.'

But Geoff was still frowning. 'Now hang on there a minute, young fella. I think I must have missed something. Why do we have to go in again?'

'Because Dani and Rose are probably inside,' Savage told him. 'And my friend Faith too, I expect. And whoever else they've got hidden in that big hall.' He looked hard at Geoff. 'You know something about that, don't you?'

'I don't know what you mean.' Geoff removed his drenched cap and wrung it out. His tone had become surly and defensive. 'I don't never get involved with any of that religious nonsense.'

He pronounced it *nun-sense*.

'But you are involved,' Kim said. 'And there's nothing religious about what Barton's been doing in his so-called Green Chapel. Calling himself a Reverend doesn't make him holy. You understand that, right?'

Geoff put his cap back on his head and glared at her.

From the road below came the whining roar of a heavy-duty engine at full strain, echoing faintly through the trees. It sounded like Billy and the others were finally clearing the obstruction.

'Come on, there's no time for this.' Savage dragged Geoff to his feet. 'I'm going to drive. Kim, you're in the front with the gun. But keep ducked out of sight.' She got into the passenger side of the van, still cradling the shotgun. 'You get in the back of the van, Geoff. And hurry up. We'll be picking up Terry on the way, so hold the rear door open. He can climb inside as we go past.'

Savage jumped in the driver's seat and started the engine. Briefly, he checked the glove box. There was a clipboard inside, with official-looking paper documents attached to it, including a list of women's names, most of them Russian. And at the back of the glove box was a dark blue cap.

Kim was doubled up in the passenger side footwell, squeezed low under the level of the dashboard, her back hunched. It was just as well she wasn't a large woman. He couldn't see the shotgun but assumed she still had it at her side. The guard's belt with its bag of shells was strapped around her waist.

He started to whistle the theme tune to *The Bridge on the River Kwai*.

'You don't have a plan, do you?' she said.

'Plans are overrated.' He grinned at her expression, and showed her the clipboard. 'Barton's expecting a man in a van. Someone coming to collect his goods. So I'm going to be the pick-up driver.'

'Have you forgotten the tower guard? What if he sees me?'

'He'll be concentrating on me. Besides, from above you should just look like a black mass.' Savage paused. 'No pun intended.'

Kim bared her teeth at him.

He tossed the clipboard onto the dashboard where it would be clearly visible from the front. Then he settled the dark blue cap on his head and tugged it as far forward and down as possible without impeding his vision.

They had maybe three minutes to get inside.

CHAPTER FORTY-FIVE

He had anticipated having to get out of the van when they reached the gates. Possibly shout something in Russian up at the guard, or do his best Russian accent. Maybe even wave his clipboard too in an officious manner and demand entry. Whatever it took to get them past the tower guard with his gun. He'd explained all this to Kim as they approached the stockade, very briefly outlining his plan of attack, such as it was, and what he needed from her once they were inside.

But having collected Terry at a dead crawl, and heard Geoff shout from the back, 'He's in,' he accelerated towards the stockade in what he hoped was a suitably precipitous Russian-van-driver manner, spraying stones and mud everywhere, only to find the double gates opening for him.

Savage slowed down, waiting for the gates to open fully. Then gave the tower guard a cheeky little wave as he drove through into the stockade.

'Well, I wasn't expecting that.'

'What's happening?' Kim asked in a whisper.

'The guard opened the gates for us.'

'That was easy.'

'You thinking, trap?'

'I'm thinking that was a little too easy, that's all.' She poked the shotgun above the level of the seats. Thankfully not pointing the barrel in his direction. 'Feels like they're playing games with us.'

'I don't think these guys are that sophisticated.' He drove slowly past the outbuilding, ignoring the three cars parked near the gate and continuing towards the big hall. 'Besides, let's try to be positive. Sometimes the simplest answer is the right one. I'm driving a van with a Russian number plate. They're expecting a van with a Russian number plate. QED.'

'OK, I buy that.' She paused, still hunched up, her voice muffled. '*Quod erat demonstrandum.* Which is demonstrated by that.'

'*Et tu, Brute?*'

She hesitated. '*Carpe diem.*'

'Enough Latin.' Savage glanced about, trying to decide where to stop the van without looking too obviously like he didn't know what was usual. 'We're through the gate.'

Despite the row of parked cars, the main compound was empty of people, though the large double doors to the hall were standing open.

He hoped that didn't mean the goods had already been shipped out. Not least because that would mean this was, in fact, a trap. And they only had two guns between the four of them, compared to the veritable arsenal that Barton appeared to command.

Not great odds. But he was still hoping for some luck.

Luck was much underestimated, yet often made the difference between winning and losing. Between life and death. Though it was true that in most cases you had to make your own luck. Which he fully intended to do.

He heard shouts.

'What's that?' Kim whispered.

'Hang on.'

Two men with shotguns had emerged from the farmhouse

and were now walking towards them, yelling something. He couldn't catch what they were saying, but it didn't sound very friendly.

Behind them Barton came out of the farmhouse too, casual in jeans and a black jacket. He stopped just inside the shelter of the porched entrance door, staring at the van.

The Reverend was carrying a black sports holdall, similar to the one Dani had left in his camper.

Savage wondered what was in that bag. Overnight clothes? Important documentation that he didn't dare leave behind? A gun? Or a bagful of how-to-run-a-cult textbooks towards his next attempt at a hilltop fiefdom?

'Looks like the Reverend's planning on taking a trip,' he said.

'I told you, don't call him that. He's about as much of a Reverend as you are.'

'What are you saying? That I'm not a good enough person to be a Reverend?' Savage laughed under his breath, aware that he was being watched from the farmhouse. 'Frankly, I'm hurt.'

One of the men pointed a shotgun at the van, shouting, 'Stop.'

'You hear that? They shouted stop. They know you're not Russian.' Kim shifted in her hiding place, restless and primed to go.

'It's the same word.'

'Sorry?'

'Stop.' He smiled and gave the men another little wave, pretending not to have heard the order. 'It's the same word in Russian as it is in English.'

'Are you making that up?'

'Seriously?' Baffled, he flicked her an irritable look. 'Why would I make something like that up?'

'I don't know. To impress me, maybe?'

'Is that all it would take?'

'Stop,' the man shouted again, and started towards them, his whole body language threatening. 'Stop.'

'I don't think so.' Savage put his foot down, accelerating towards the hall. In his wing mirror, he saw the second man also pointing a shotgun in their direction. 'OK, they've definitely rumbled us. Maybe that was an English "stop", not a Russian one.' He grinned down at her. 'Time to come out and play.'

'Thank you, God ...'

Kim sprang up from her hiding place, slightly flushed, her damp black top rucked up, clutching the shotgun as though the two of them had been welded together.

Savage spun the van in a half-circle, tyres skidding on the loose dirt and gravel, stopping just short of the double doors to the hall.

'Right, let's do this,' he said.

Dragging the key from the ignition, he jumped out and made for the hall doors just as someone fired in their direction. Behind him the windscreen of the Transit van shattered with an almighty crack.

He heard rather than saw Kim jump out of the passenger side and start returning fire. Probably from behind the improvised shelter of the van door. A warning shot first, as befitted a member of the clergy, but one that sounded like it had carved a crater in the farmhouse wall. The shot must have fanned out wide at that distance, some of the pellets probably a little too close to Barton's head for comfort.

Savage grinned and checked inside the open double doors of the hall.

Just a quick glance.

Nobody was in sight, and the place was in semi-darkness. A long, high-ceilinged rectangle. No chairs or pews as he had half-expected, just an open space around a central altar-like table. And an iron grille at the far end, like a gate leading into darkness.

Was that the way down to whatever Barton kept hidden beneath the hall?

Savage ran back to the van, keeping low.

Kim had taken another shot at Barton's men, who must have been trying to get round behind them and were now ducked behind a row of metal bins, trying to avoid getting their heads blown off.

The rear doors had been thrown open, and Terry and Geoff were piling out, looking shaken and disorientated.

'Get into the hall,' he shouted to them. 'And keep away from any windows.'

Kim glanced round at him. 'Glad you could join me.'

'Anything for the vicar.'

He took the Glock 17 from his waistband. He didn't like firing an unknown gun without testing it first.

'I think they're planning a charge,' she said, watching through the gap between the open door and the van interior. 'They're idiots. But I'd rather not . . .'

She didn't need to finish that sentence.

Savage rose up slightly and looked too. One of the men was peering out from behind a bin, shotgun held loosely as though about to run with it.

'Mine,' he said.

Popping up from behind the van door like a Jack-in-the-box, the Glock in a two-handed grip, he squeezed the trigger, and dropped down again.

'Ouch,' Kim said, still peeking through the gap. 'Good shooting.'

'Let me see.' She shifted to one side and Savage put his eye to the gap instead. The man had fallen backwards and was now writhing in the dirt, making a kind of gurgling noise. His shot-gun lay a few feet away in the open.

There was no sign of his friend.

'Probably only a flesh wound, from the noise he's making,' Kim said calmly. 'At least they know we're not mucking about now.'

Meanwhile, Barton had fallen back to the safety of the farm-house, perhaps taken aback by the sight of a woman vicar wielding a shotgun. But from what Savage knew about the man, it seemed likely that he'd be back soon. With more men or guns. Probably both.

Savage felt a stab of frustration.

Ever since Terry had mentioned the man with the 'foreign' name whom Barton had set to rout with his bloody pack, he'd been itching to destroy the bastard.

Probably Middle Eastern. Dark skin, dark hair, dark eyes.

Jarrah.

He'd come to the high reaches of Dartmoor, maybe for the same reason that Petherick had been deployed to watch Barton's organisation from the inside, and Barton had smoked him out.

But then what?

The 'pack' had been sent out after him, a man-hunt over the moors with guns and dogs. That seemed undisputed. But whether Jarrah had been caught and killed, or had somehow managed to get away, was less clear.

Perhaps only Barton knew for sure.

He needed five minutes with the man to establish the truth. Before he put a bullet in him. For Peter's sake, if not Jarrah's.

Kim backed behind the van, her gaze on the farmhouse. 'Hey, do you hear that?' She spoke to Savage over her shoulder, shotgun now pointed towards the shadowy guard on the gate tower, who had made the potentially foolish move of appear-ing with his own weapon. 'Sounds like we've got company.'

A heavy diesel engine, strained to the max, was approaching fast on the hilltop track. Or as fast as any digger ever moved. Behind it, he could hear the steadier note of the Land Rover Defender engine. So Billy had refused to move over for the faster vehicle, had he? Or perhaps that manoeuvre had proved impractical once they were past the obstacle of Geoff's unfortunate tractor. The road had narrowed from that point, so perhaps there had been nowhere for Billy to pull in and let the Defender take the lead again.

'Time to fall back,' he told Kim urgently.

'Into the hall?'

'It's the most defensible position. We can barricade the doors from the inside. Besides, we need to take a look in that place. Find out what Barton's been up to.'

'I can't stand the idea that he might have been selling babies to the Russians.' She hesitated, then reluctantly held out the shotgun. 'You want to take this?'

'No, I'll be right behind you. Terry and Geoff are inside. See what the three of you can put against the doors to keep the enemy at bay.'

Kim nodded and disappeared.

The rain seemed to have stalled over Dartmoor, though it was no longer falling as heavily as it had been when they left the diner, just a patchy drizzle that kept running down under his collar. His phone was finally dead, so there was no point checking the time. But dusk was not far off, by the glowering look of the sky.

The gate clicker was still in his front jeans pocket. Worth a try, maybe?

Savage dragged it out, ducked round the rear of the van, and pointed the clicker at the gate, pressing the close button.

To his amusement, the gates began to swing shut. For some reason, nobody had disabled the remote mechanism. But maybe they didn't know how to do it. Or perhaps Barton hadn't imagined anyone would have the nerve to try the same trick twice.

Through the closing gates, he saw the first glimpse of Billy's red digger heading straight for them, headlights gleaming through the rain.

Then the gates shut with a shuddering clang.

Seconds later, the two men emerged from the farmhouse again, dark shadows under the rain, shotguns directed towards him. It seemed the ad hoc council of war was at an end, and a decision had been made.

Because they came out shooting.

CHAPTER FORTY-SIX

Savage held them off briefly with a barrage of shots from the Glock, though the failing light meant only one struck its intended target. But one down was better than none, he decided. But it soon became clear they were not giving up this time, the deafening blast of shotguns echoing about his head, several unnervingly close, one of them blowing the wing mirror off completely. He gave up on holding his position and ran for it instead. He only made it into the big hall without being shot courtesy of the van still parked between him and the farmhouse, though also perhaps because he moved so damn quickly. Force of habit when being shot at, of course. It was harder to hit a fast-moving target, especially at dusk in the rain, with all the compromised vision that entailed. And perhaps poor vision also explained why he reached the hall intact.

It wasn't like they were aiming to miss, after all.

As he dived through the double doors, stray shotgun pellets lodged themselves with a series of cracks in the wall behind his head, the payload knocking the open driver's door off its hinges, less than a foot from where he'd been standing when the shooters re-emerged from the farmhouse.

Inside, Kim was waiting, a large brass key in hand.

She closed the doors, turned the key in the lock, then energetically slammed home three massive bolts at the top, middle, and bottom of the heavy double doors, and stood back, breathing hard.

The hall was locked up tight against the outside world.

Barton must have built this place as a last-stand option, an apocalyptic retreat if he ever found himself under fire. A common thing with those running a cult in the United States, but not something he had expected to find here on Dartmoor, not least because of the planning permission issues he would have run up against. Though it was useful, given the circumstances. And he imagined Barton had found a way round those planning permission rules.

What was it Geoff had said?

He owns top people in the police, judges, all that . . .

Had this monstrosity of a meeting hall been passed with a nod and a wink in return for the Reverend's good favour? Or had Barton simply built the place without permission and no one had yet dared prosecute him for it?

'Now we put *that* in front of the entrance,' Kim told them, indicating a vast and heavy-looking cupboard under one of the high windows. 'Ready? Lift . . . and push.'

Together, they shoved the seven-foot free-standing cupboard against the door. It was massively heavy. Ornate wooden doors, scrolled handles. More cult texts inside, by the weight of it.

'That should hold them for a while.' Panting, Kim stepped back to admire her work. 'It'll only take them a few minutes to push the van out of the way. But these bolts, and this great hefty thing,' she slapped the wooden cupboard, 'I reckon they'll buy us half an hour. Maybe even an hour or two if they're trying to preserve the building.'

'Where on earth did you find the key?'

She pointed to a key rack on the wall beside the door. 'It seems Barton has a conveniently tidy mind. Keys for everything there. Though they're coded with numbers, not names. So unless you have the key to the keys, if you'll pardon the pun, it's a question of trial and error. Or in this case,' she added, grinning, 'pure guesswork. The sod-off huge door looked like it would need a sod-off huge key.' She held up the brass key to the double doors they had just locked. 'And that one wasn't hard to identify.'

'Well done, good work.'

Savage turned on his heel to inspect the hall they had just taken. It was even darker with the door shut, only a few shafts of dying light still streaming in through six high window slits, three along each wall, roughly ten feet up, and the same ten feet apart. Could Barton get his men in that way? Too narrow for an adult body, he decided. But the glass could be smashed and incendiary devices thrown through, or shotguns pointed down at them. Though field of vision would be severely compromised.

'Thank you.' Kim tidied her dog collar, which had become askew, and bent to pick up the shotgun. 'That was fun.'

Geoff had staggered back after moving the cupboard, and was now stooped over from the waist, out of breath. He looked up at her, wiping his brow. 'Fun?' He sounded incredulous. 'Fun, you say?'

Outside they could hear shouting, and a distant grinding sound. Probably the gates opening again to let Billy's digger and the Land Rover Defender inside. Then someone came up to the double doors of the hall and banged on the thick wood with what sounded like the butt of a shotgun. It was impressively loud.

'Open up in there.' A rough voice with a burr. 'There' pronounced as 'thar'. There was a pause. When nobody replied, the man added, his tone menacing, 'You're trespassing, all of you. This here is private land. And we know how to look after our own.' Another few thuds on the door with the shotgun butt. 'Open up and you won't get shot. That's the Reverend's promise.'

Savage glanced at Kim.

She smiled without humour, and shook her head.

'Well, don't say you wasn't warned.' The man sounded annoyed now. His mission had failed. Another loud thud. 'We'll have you out of there in good time, see if we don't. Then you'll be sorry.'

One set of footsteps retreated across the gravel. Gone to work out their plan of attack, no doubt. But it seemed likely at least one guard had been left on the door. Maybe at a discreet distance, in case they tried to get out some other way.

If there was another way out. Which seemed unlikely.

'Siege,' Kim said softly.

He nodded.

'I'm pretty sure I heard the gates opening again just then,' she added. 'They'll have that digger now.'

'I know.'

Terry paid no attention to their exchange, staring about at the gloomy high-roofed space. 'Why are we here, Savage?' His tone was aggressive, and a touch panicked too. Terry would need careful handling if he was going to be anything but a liability, Savage thought, watching him. 'I only came to get Dani back. But there's no sign of anyone here. So what did we just risk our bloody lives for? You think there's something in here that Barton's been hiding?'

'Hiding in plain sight, yes.'

Geoff straightened, both hands supporting his lower back as though it hurt. 'Terry's right. There's nothing here. And certainly not my daughter.' His deep voice echoed about the hall, thick with frustration. 'Where could the Reverend Barton hide anything in here? Look around, for God's sake. This place is empty.' He nodded to the huge cupboard they'd pushed against the door. 'Except for that, maybe.'

'Not big enough.' Savage studied the bank of light switches beside the door. 'This is meant to be a holy space, isn't it? I'm thinking what we need is some illumination.'

He clicked down all the switches marked Main Hall, one by one, and blinked as sharp white electric light flooded the place from huge globe-like lights strung among the rafters.

'Let there be light . . .'

'Too bright,' Kim said urgently.

'Agreed.'

Rapidly, he flicked the row of switches up again, one after the other. Gloom engulfed them once more, the room now obviously growing darker by the minute. There were marked wall lights too. He tried those switches, with much the same effect, then turned them off as well. For all he knew, Barton might have closed-circuit television set up in this damn hall, and the less light the better.

'What's that?' Terry said, standing at his shoulder.

He was pointing to a separate, smaller panel to the far left of the Main Hall switches. It had a range of different switches, some colour-coded. But what the code meant, he had no idea. The whole panel was marked simply, *Hele*.

Kim came up behind them, shotgun resting casually over one shoulder. 'Hele,' she read out, her voice low. Their eyes met. 'Now I wonder what that is.'

'Barton's hiding place?'

Experimentally, Savage flicked down the main switch.

A light came on at the far end of the hall, on the stone wall behind the metal grille. Except that, now that whole area was lit up, he could see that it was not merely a grille in the wall, but an actual gate. About five foot high and maybe three foot wide, set into the wall with thick hinges. It had narrow metal bars, like a prison gate. And a lock.

Kim had seen the lock too.

She turned, shotgun still on her shoulder, to the key board beside the door. Scanning the keys judiciously, she selected a few, then came back to Savage, jingling three pieces of metal in her hand.

'I'm willing to bet one of these should open that gate.'

CHAPTER FORTY-SEVEN

Sure enough, the third key they tried unlocked the gate. It swung open easily, as though inviting them to explore further, and they both stepped back in surprise. The hinges had been recently oiled, he realised, the metal glistening in the soft yellow light.

Beyond the gate was a brick wall, and immediately in front of it, a set of narrow steps leading down into darkness. Savage wrinkled his nose. The air smelt musty and even a little tainted. Like a faint whiff of the sewers, emanating from somewhere below.

Not exactly enticing.

'Very Crystal Maze,' Kim said, grimacing as she peered down the steps.

'Maybe there's a torch.'

Geoff, somewhere over in the shadows, called out, 'There are some torches here.'

'I think we can do better than a torch,' Kim said. 'Terry? Try some more of those switches on the separate panel, would you?'

About ten seconds later, more lighting came on below, out of sight of the gate.

'Thanks, that's great,' Kim called. 'You two wait there. Let us know if there's any more activity outside. We won't be long.'

'You will come back, won't you?' Geoff shouted back.

'Ten minutes, tops,' Savage said.

Actually, they would probably need fifteen. But there was no need for anyone to panic. Not yet, anyway. Savage reckoned that Barton would be busy working out a plan of attack that would not involve damaging his very well-appointed hall any more than was necessary. And he knew what such group meetings were like. Everyone had an opinion, or thought they knew better than everyone else. Which gave them at least another twenty minutes to discover what was beneath the hall, and if there were any other exits.

Kim looked at him. 'Me first? Or you?'

'Ladies first.' He nodded to her weapon. 'Besides, you've got the gun.'

She grinned, then swung the double-barrelled shotgun off her shoulder and directed it down the stairs instead. 'Stay close behind,' she said in a whisper, and started down the steps.

The stairs were circular, like those in a castle keep, and made of stone, which made it impossible to go down them silently. But Kim was quieter than him, treading down each step warily, her back against the wall, staring into the yellow glow at the end of the staircase.

Their footsteps echoed eerily on the scuffed white stone of the staircase, suggesting a larger open space lay below.

Kim rounded the last corner and stopped, as though surprised.

'What is it?' he asked. 'Have you found a sacred well?'

'Not quite.' She looked up at him, her face curiously blank. 'I've found cages.'

'What?'

'Hang on a minute.'

Kim kept going, her shoulders hunched, tense now, checking that nobody was waiting for them down there. The red furnace of her hair disappeared.

Five, ten, fifteen seconds stretched out intolerably while he waited, listening hard and hearing nothing. Damn, she was good. Soft-footed as a cat. Dangerous, too. He wouldn't want to come up against her in the dark, that was for sure.

I've found cages.

He hadn't been expecting that. Containing what, though? If it was animals, that would certainly explain the unpleasant odour. It wasn't the smell of death though. He knew what decay smelt like, unfortunately.

At last he heard Kim say loudly, 'All clear,' and he continued down to the base of the steps, not sure what to expect.

He was stunned at first by what he saw. Then disgusted. Finally, blazingly angry. A row of cages set into the wall of earth and rock, some with red lights above them, some unlit. All of them dark inside.

Barton had been keeping people in cages down here.

Human beings.

Caged up. Treated like wild animals.

He felt physically sick.

'I counted eight cages,' Kim called back, her voice shaking. She was partway down the length of the underground corridor. 'Four on each side. The numbers are above each cage. Not all are in use. But a couple . . .' Words failed her. She cleared her throat. 'At least a couple of them seem to have double occupancy. Maybe eight prisoners in total?'

They were all women, he realised, taking a few steps along the corridor, looking through the bars in horror.

Young women. Stripped and dressed in some kind of dingy, paper-thin, ankle-length robes, presumably once white, now filthy from the earth floor of their cages. It looked like the kind of temporary outfit worn by patients going into surgery, only intended to be worn for a few hours. But these had been used for permanent wear, in a cage roughly six foot by five foot, with an open pan for a toilet and a few blankets on a ledge as a bed. So of course they were heavily soiled, with rips and tears, pale skin showing through underneath, rust-dark stains here and there that suggested blood.

He met the bleary eyes of one woman, mid-row, who had risen from her makeshift bunk at their approach and now came to the bars, staring out silently.

It was like looking into hell.

'What in God's name is this?' He looked at Kim. 'I knew Barton was hiding something down here. But this.' He shook his head. 'This is . . .'

He did not know how to end that sentence.

Kim looked like she was going to throw up. Not from the foul smell, he was sure, but the sheer depravity of what they had found. The cruelty and inhumanity.

'Monstrous,' she said, finishing for him.

Savage tried the door of the nearest cage. It was locked. He shook the bars, suddenly furious, and they rattled noisily. Some of the women moaned, covering their ears.

'What's your name?' He looked at the woman, trying to keep his voice gentle and unthreatening. God alone knew what she had been through at the hands of Barton and his men. 'How long have you been here?'

She got up, which was promising. But she merely stood there, staring back at him as though mute. Her face was slack, and there was a little drool running down her chin.

'They've been drugged,' Kim said, studying the other women, most of whom seemed to be lying down, unaware of their surroundings. 'Kept sedated to minimise noise, I expect.'

'They're so thin.'

'I guess you don't eat much when you're sedated.'

'We need to get them out of these cages.'

'Copy that.' Kim shouldered her weapon again, starting to

look about the place. 'Only I don't see any keys. Maybe Barton keeps them on him. For safety.'

His hands clenched into fists around the bars, like he could simply tear them out of the earth. He wanted to kill Barton for this. Though killing would be too good for him, of course. Barton needed to be punished for what he'd done here. Punished so that he understood the depth of his evil. And he doubted even a life stretch in a British jail would be enough to satisfy that need.

'There have to be keys around here somewhere. What if there was an emergency and they needed to get in while Barton wasn't here?' He touched Kim's shoulder, aware that she was suffering too. 'You start looking at this end. I'll check down the other end, OK?'

He was interrupted by a high-pitched clicking noise from further down the row of cages, the sound of metal on metal, then something that made the hairs rise on the back of his neck.

'Aubrey?'

It was Faith's voice.

'Look for keys,' he repeated to Kim, then hurried down the row, stopping to peer into each cage in turn. 'Hello? Faith? Where are you?'

'I'm here, Aubrey.' A hand waved through the bars. 'Right at the end.'

A few feet away from what looked like a natural spring, oozing a slimy water out into the earthen passageway, stood the final cage in the row.

To his relief, the cage contained Rose, Dani and Faith.

The three women were cramped together in the narrow space, and still in the clothes he had last seen them wearing. No doubt Barton had not got around to dressing them up in those special, paper-thin white robes. Rose seemed to be asleep or perhaps unconscious, curled up in a foetal position on the earth floor.

All three looked pale and dishevelled. Faith had a fresh bruise across her right cheek, and her lip was dark and swollen where it had been bleeding. But she was smiling, reaching out to him.

'Faith, thank God.'

'Aubrey.' Her grip was strong, and she seemed undaunted by her experience. 'I knew you'd come. I kept telling Dani, but she didn't believe me.'

Savage forced himself to smile, though inside he was boiling with fury at Barton. He squeezed Dani's hand too. 'Hey, Dani. How are you bearing up?'

'Not so good.' Dani met his eyes. 'We should never have left the pub. I'm sorry, that was all my fault. We got a call from Billy.' Her tone became accusing. 'Rose was so shocked. I'd just told her he was dead.'

'Yes, sorry about that. It was a shock for us too. Obviously some kind of misunderstanding.' He grimaced. 'Probably deliberate on Barton's part. He's a trickster. Likes to make people believe one thing so they don't see what lies beneath. It was an undercover policeman who was killed. I believe you knew him. Charlie Petherick?'

'Oh God.' Dani blenched, and glanced at Faith, who looked shocked too. 'Poor Charlie. I thought he was just on the take, you know? But all the time . . .'

'He was undercover, yes, trying to find out what was really going on up here. And I guess Barton found out and disposed of him the same way he disposed of Callum. So how did Billy persuade you to leave the pub?'

'He said Terry had been shot and was asking for me.'

'Your husband's here. With us.' When Dani looked up at him, her eyes widening, he nodded. 'I'll call him down in a minute, so you can see for yourself. Go on, tell me the rest.'

'There's not much to tell. I knew you'd never let us go. So I persuaded Rose to hitch over to Geoff's place with me. That's where Billy said Terry had been taken.' She made a face. 'I was such an idiot to believe him. They took us almost as soon as we got on the main road. I guess they must have known where we were the whole time.'

'Not your fault.' He looked at Faith. 'Sorry it took me so long. But I didn't realise Barton had taken you until I tried ringing you, and he answered.'

'They took my phone when they put me down here. That horrible man, Mike Cooper. He gave me this.' She indicated her bruised face. 'I punched him in the gut.'

'Good work. I hope you hurt him.'

'I think my fist just kind of bounced off, actually. That huge belly . . .' She paused. 'What did Barton say to you?'

'Nothing. He hung up almost immediately. But I said a few things to him. Probably gave him a fright.' He glanced at Rose on the floor. 'Is she OK?'

'They drugged her.' Faith sounded as frustrated as he felt. 'Because she wouldn't stop screaming. I don't know how long it will take to wear off. She's been like that for a couple of hours now.' She looked at him, desperation in her eyes. 'Get us out of here, would you? This place is . . .'

Faith stopped, unable to finish.

'Absolutely, don't worry.' He tried not to sound like he wanted to kill someone, his voice light. 'Kim's on the case.'

'Kim? Who's Kim?'

'The vicar.'

Faith looked blank. 'You brought the *vicar*?'

'She's very handy. Especially with a shotgun.'

Faith buried her face in her hands, then gave a cracked laugh. 'Whatever.' She looked up at him. 'Just get this damn cage open, Aubrey.'

Savage leant back and checked the number above the cage. Then he called down to Kim, who was scanning the walls for another key board. 'I've found my friends. Cage eight. Any luck finding those keys?'

'Nothing yet.'

'You may have to hang on another few minutes, I'm afraid,' he told Faith and Dani.

'It's an automated release system.' Dani pointed above her head. 'I've been watching. The red light means it's locked. No light means it's empty and unlocked.'

Sure enough, there was a red light on the metal gantry above their cage.

'Look for a release mechanism,' he told Kim.

'There's a keypad.'

Savage went down to see what she'd found. It was a small, black numerical keypad attached to the wall near the bottom of the staircase, numbered nought to nine. Beneath it were eight buttons.

'I guess you need to press one of the buttons to select a cage, then enter your key code. Cage eight, right?' Kim leant her shotgun against the wall and studied the keys. But there was no obvious fingerprint pattern left behind to show which ones had been pressed most frequently. She selected eight on the buttons, then paused, her fingers hovering over the keypad. 'Maybe four or six digits? Something quick and convenient.'

'Four or six digits sounds about right. Any clues?'

'Someone's date of birth?'

He called down to Faith and Dani, 'Any idea what Barton's birthday is?'

Silence.

'Sometime in December,' Dani shouted back. 'The sixteenth?'

Kim keyed in one-six-one-two.

Nothing happened.

'Maybe we need the year as well,' Kim said.

'When was he born?' Savage called down the corridor. From above he could hear shouts, and the distant roar of machinery. Something was happening topside. 'We may need to hurry,' he added to Kim. 'Sounds like we've got company up there.'

She nodded.

'Sorry,' Faith shouted back. 'Dani doesn't know. She thinks he might be thirty-two.'

He looked at Kim, but she was already trying that date with the birth data. She input the day, month, and two figures for the year. That didn't work. So she tried it with the full four figures for the year. That didn't work either.

'No joy,' he called out.

There was a sudden commotion from partway along the row of cages. The woman who had wandered groggily to the bars when they first came down was now on her knees, shaking and retching.

Kim met his eyes seriously. 'Aubrey, this isn't working. We can't stand here all evening, trying number combinations. We have to *do* something.'

CHAPTER FORTY-EIGHT

'What do you suggest?' Savage kept his voice low, not wanting the others to know they were at an impasse. 'Unless you have access to heavy duty bolt-cutters, I don't see any other option but to keep trying the keypad.'

Terry ran down the stairs, and had almost reached the bottom when he stopped dead, seeing the cages and their frail, white-robed occupants.

He swore, staring. 'What the hell . . . ?'

'Barton deserves to be kneecapped for this,' Savage said, nodding as his own disgust and anger were reflected in Terry's face. 'This is what he's been hiding. The secret prisoners of the Green Chapel. Is this what you expected to find down here?'

Terry covered his mouth, his eyes guilty.

'Wait, you knew about this?' Kim looked round at him, horrified. 'And you didn't say anything?'

'I only heard whispers, I swear.' Terry swallowed, looking down the line of cages.

'Whispers you ought to have passed on to the police.'

'Barton would have killed me, and you know it. So would any of the others. And I'm no grass.' He made a face. 'Besides, the Reverend made sure we were all right, you know? A few hundred here and there, pushed through the letterbox in an envelope. Sometimes thousands, like when he came for the women.'

Even as he spoke, Savage could see Terry was going back through those decisions in his head, and hating himself for going along with the deceit. Especially when it came to Dani and the way he had allowed Barton to tamper with her. His own wife. No amount of money could make up for that weakness, nor help Dani forgive the abuse her husband had tacitly condoned by not intervening.

'He said it was money for the community,' he finished lamely, 'that the chapel was giving back to the people.'

'Hush money.'

'I always thought they were men Barton was dealing in. You know, cheap labour. Illegal immigrants. Coming in by van from Eastern Europe, processed here, then taken off to where they're needed.' Terry grimaced, and put a hand to his nose, clamping it against the foul smell of human ordure. 'I had no idea about . . . this.'

From the top of the stairs, his voice echoing oddly in the enclosed space, Geoff shouted, 'Hurry up, would you? I'm telling you, I can hear something. We need that shotgun back.'

Terry made no reply, staring at the cages, his expression stricken.

'Look at me.' Savage gripped Terry by the shoulder and shook him. 'What's going on up there? You came down to tell us something.'

'Yes, yes.' Slowly, Terry came out of his daze. 'They came to the door again, with guns. But we told them to get lost. Now they're back. Only Geoff thinks they've brought the digger this time. And they're going to use it against us.'

'To tear open the doors?'

Terry nodded.

Kim had turned back to the keypad and was trying combinations wildly, her fingers flying over the small black keys, her face more tense as each try failed.

'What's that?' Terry glanced from the keypad to the red lights above the cages. 'You need a code to get them out?'

Terry was clearly more observant than him, Savage thought, a little chagrined.

'That's right. And if you want Dani back, you'll help.' He nodded to the row of cages. 'She's locked in one of these hell-holes.' Terry took off down the row at a run, in search of his wife. 'With Rose. And my friend, Faith. And we can't get the cage door to open.'

Kim stopped trying the keys. 'This is useless.'

'You should head back up top,' Savage said, picking up the shotgun and handing it to her. 'If they're coming in with the digger, Geoff's going to need help.'

'What about you?'

'I'll give it another couple of minutes, then I'll be right behind you. Then Terry can keep trying the combination. That's his wife in there, after all.'

He followed Terry down to the end cage. Faith was kneeling beside Rose, who was still on the earth floor but appeared to be stirring at last. Terry was speaking in a low, desperate voice to his wife, who had taken a step back from the bars and was staring at him intensely.

Those two were going to need a good marriage counsellor, if they ever got out of here alive.

'The keypad that opens the cages takes a four or possibly a six-digit code,' Savage said briefly, interrupting them.

Rose whispered something, clutching Faith's sleeve.

'What? Sorry, I didn't catch that. Say again?' Faith bent closer to hear. Then she turned to Savage. 'I'm not sure, but I think she's saying . . . Mayday.'

MAYDAY.

He remembered the scrap of paper he'd found in Dani's hold-all. And the burnt fragment they'd found in the abandoned room at the pub.

Dani stared at him through the bars. 'Of course. That's what it meant. Billy wrote it down on a pad by their telephone, after a call to Mike Cooper. Rose knew it must be important, so she tore it out and gave it to me, told me to keep it safe.' She gave a shaky laugh. 'I didn't realise it was a code though. I always thought it must be a special event they were planning for Mayday.'

'Me too,' Savage said. 'Or a code name for someone or something. An alert, perhaps. Mayday, mayday.'

Dani nodded. 'We tried writing it down in the hotel room, and splitting up the letters. To see if it could be rearranged to mean something different. Like an anagram, you know? Or an acrostic. But we gave up.'

'And burnt the evidence.'

'Yeah, sorry about that.' She looked guilty. 'But Billy said on the phone that Barton knew where we were. That he was on his way and we had to get out of there quick. We should have told you. But Rose wouldn't let me. She didn't want to get caught with Barton's top-secret code on her, but she didn't want to leave it behind either. In case one of his men found it and came after us. So we set fire to it.'

Rose spoke again.

Faith helped her to sit up, though she looked very sick. She glanced round at Savage. 'Rose says it's his mother's birthday. Barton's mother.'

'Mother Barton?'

Dani nodded eagerly. 'That's what she likes to be called. She was the one you had Charlie tie up at the farmhouse, remember?'

'How could I forget?'

'She runs everything round here. I mean, Barton's the boss. But he always does what his mother tells him.'

'How marvellously filial of him.'

Savage went straight back to the keypad, selected cage eight, and firmly pressed the keys zero-one-zero-five. The first day of May in numerals.

Only nothing happened.

He frowned.

Then laughed at his own stupidity, and punched out zero-five-zero-one.

The red light above cage eight blinked out, then they heard the faint clunk of a door unlocking at the far end.

'It's open,' Terry shouted down to him.

Mayday.

The first day of the fifth month. Mother Barton's birthday. The most important day of the year, he imagined, for the Reverend, still tied to his mother's apron strings. Except that Barton was an American, and in the American calendar system, the month came before the day.

Savage selected cage three, where the pale, sickly woman was still swaying in silence, staring at him through the bars. Keying in zero-five-zero-one again, he saw the light go out and heard that cage door click open as well.

The woman stumbled out, falling to her hands and knees. Savage moved to help her. But Faith was already there, dishevelled honey hair falling into her eyes as she helped the other woman back to her feet.

'It's OK, I've got you,' she said soothingly.

The woman said something in Romanian, not a language Savage knew well, despite its Latin roots. But it was obvious she was saying thank you.

Faith looked up at him, a frown in her eyes. 'What's this about, Aubrey? What the hell is Barton doing with all these women?'

'You want an educated guess?'

'I'm drawing a blank here.'

'Modern slavery.' He selected another cage and entered the passcode again. A cage door further down the row swung open. Nobody came out. Probably too heavily sedated even to notice they were free. 'That's what I'd put my money on. I was totally wrong about the babies. The fertility treatments are just his smoke screen.'

'More like his hobby,' she said bitterly.

Terry and Dani were making their way out of the cage, supporting Rose, who seemed unable to walk properly.

He selected another cage. 'It's closer to what Terry thought was going on. I'd guess Barton's been selling people. These women have come in from Eastern Europe, via Russian couriers, to be processed here, then shipped out to various parts of the UK.'

'As what, though?'

'Domestic servants, child-minders, unpaid sex workers. Whatever his clients want.' He punched out the passcode to unlock that cage. 'Orders come in, he sources suitable women from Eastern Europe to fulfil them, receives and processes them here, which includes sedating them to avoid trouble in transit. Then he ships them out again to the waiting clients.'

'Like a depot.'

'Something like that.'

'It's sickening.' Faith helped the pale, stumbling woman towards the stairs. Then her eyes widened. 'So that's what Paglia meant.'

'Paglia?'

'I wanted them to come up here and investigate what was going on. I made a big fuss. Told her straight out that Barton was involved in those killings. I was sure she'd have no choice but to respond to an accusation like that.'

'Except she didn't.'

'That's right. Paglia just went quiet. Then she said her hands were tied, and it was outside her jurisdiction. She sounded pretty hacked off. I thought maybe she'd taken a bribe to turn a blind eye.'

'But?'

'But what if Paglia meant the authorities are already aware of what's going on here? That they already had someone on the inside? You said someone like that was killed by Barton.'

'Charlie Petherick,' he said heavily. 'It looks like Barton must have staged that hunt to flush him out. He probably knew no police officer would stand by while something that barbaric happened under his nose. And it was probably me who set him wondering about Petherick. Because he didn't put up enough of a fight when I took Dani away from the farmhouse.'

'Poor bastard.' Faith shook her head. 'But it made me wonder if the police haven't moved against Barton yet because they're waiting for something.'

'More evidence, you mean?'

'Or the names of perpetrators higher up the food chain. A list of suppliers from Eastern Europe and Russia, perhaps.'

Savage had no time to process that possibility. The sound of faint shots rang out from beyond above, and then somebody came running.

This time it was Geoff, panting and almost incoherent as he shouted down the stairs, 'Need you right now, Savage.'

CHAPTER FORTY-NINE

Leaving Faith and Terry to break the remaining cages open, Savage took the winding steps two at a time. The high-roofed hall was dark now, only one wall spotlight illuminating the double doors. Evening must have fallen while they were in Barton's underground prison block. From outside he could hear the noisy roar of a large diesel engine being revved hard, and a confusion of voices, at least one shouting orders loud enough to be heard from inside the hall.

'Get closer.' The voice was hoarse, raised above the sound of machinery. 'That's it. Keep going, keep going.' Pause. 'Another couple of feet.'

It sounded like Mike Cooper, presumably directing Billy in the digger. Getting their largest agricultural vehicle in position to attack the doors with his massive metal scoop. That's what he would be doing in their position. It might not be the most effective way to get into the hall, but the noise of that scoop crunching repeatedly against the doors would almost certainly frighten those inside.

Kim waved him to join them, then put a finger to her lips. Shotgun at the ready, she had flattened her back against the wall, right beside the entrance doors. There was a wild look in her eyes, yet her face was oddly serene. The calm before the storm.

Definitely enjoying this, he thought.

'I called the police,' she said, and now there was a certain defiance about her. 'I know you said to wait, in case there was nothing here, but—'

'No, that was good thinking. We've got evidence now. More than just evidence. We've got people down there whose testimony would be enough to put Barton away for life. His crew too, I wouldn't doubt.'

She nodded.

'So when will they be here?' he asked.

'I'm not sure.'

'I don't understand. Did you tell the police what's down there?'

'Not just that. Since you'd said she knew about the situation, I asked to be put through to DI Paglia. I told her everything, and told her we would need ambulances too. For those unfortunate women.' Kim looked grim. 'Only it seems there's a slight hiccup.'

'Such as?'

'Some kind of high-level protocol at work.'

'Tell me you're kidding.'

'I wish I was. But I couldn't get her to say more.' She patted her back pocket. 'Paglia said she'd ring back as soon as she got the nod.'

'Protocol?' Savage shook his head, disgusted. 'I think I can guess what that's about. How long ago was this conversation?'

'Ten, maybe twelve minutes.'

'So we wait.'

'That's about it, yes.'

'And try to hold these doors. Bloody typical.'

'My thoughts exactly.'

Savage didn't like their situation. Basically, they were alone out here. Yet what could he do but accept that they were screwed and try to keep this place locked down for as long as possible? Because he'd been in this kind of crapulous position before.

Protocol.

That was just another word for red tape. And red tape was what this bullshit was all about.

Before anything could happen here on Dartmoor, a conversation had to happen somewhere in the dark corridors of Whitehall. Official A had to speak to Official B, and possibly C too, because somewhere down the line this place had been put on a high-level Watch List. Which meant there was probably a veto on local police involvement. Only a special task force could come storming in here to save the day.

And to make matters worse, it was highly possible that none of the officials with the power to activate that special task force were even in the office at this time of the evening. Official A was probably at home by now with his or her family. Official B might be at dinner with colleagues in an expensive restaurant. And if Official C was also involved in making that decision, odds were they were holed up at this very minute in some discreet hotel room or apartment along the River Thames with their latest squeeze, phone turned off to avoid interruption. Because that was his kind of luck.

Behind them in the shadows, Geoff stood with a long metal pole balanced precariously under his arm, like a medieval knight with a lance. It had a curved hook-like structure at the end, like a billhook used for catching boats on the river.

Savage looked at the metal pole, eyebrows raised.

'It maybe opens them top windows.' Geoff had spoken in a whisper. He pointed dubiously to the arrow-slit windows high up on the wall. 'Think so, at any rate.'

Savage nodded. 'Suits you. Just don't fall over.' He looked at Kim, also keeping his voice low. 'Why are we whispering?'

'I don't want to give away our position.'

'Right.'

'They're bringing the digger up. Second time.'

'Tell me.'

'First time was a warning. Digger scoop just banged on the doors a few times. Made the place shudder. Otherwise not much impact.' She met his eyes. 'Then they told us to open up or they'd fire through the door. I ignored them.'

'Because the doors are too thick for that to be a credible threat.'

'Exactly.'

'So, warning over.'

'That's what I'm thinking. They went away to have a little chat. Now they're back, and this time it's the real thing. They're determined to come through the door, and they're using the digger to do it.'

'You think they can do it?'

'It's a blunt instrument, that digger.' She glanced at Geoff, who was sweating and swaying, his eyes closed. *He* was not enjoying this, that was for sure. Her whisper dropped to a mere thread of sound, intended for his ears only. 'But it could shatter the hinges if they come at it hard and fast enough. Or it could make a big enough dent to allow a bolt-cutter through.'

'Or a shotgun barrel.'

'Yes, and pick us off one by one.'

Savage studied the large double doors, bolted three times and barricaded with a heavy cupboard. If the hinges didn't break, they could hold this entrance for a considerable amount of time. Which had presumably been in Barton's head when he had this place constructed. Religious place of worship was probably how he had described it on the planning permission. If he'd even bothered to get planning permission, given the man's propensity for greasing palms to get things done. But fortress was a better description.

Still, the idea of someone able to shoot indiscriminately into the hall made their position more difficult. They could retreat to the area below ground, of course. Those winding stairs were defendable too, though only until they were out of ammo. But that would enable Barton and his men to work freely up here, perhaps with axes or bolt-cutters. In which case, they would simply be delaying their surrender an hour or two.

'Is there any chance of looking outside? I'd like to see what they're doing, and who's out there.'

Kim nodded to the vast cupboard. 'If we move that, you could see through the crack between the two doors. But it's dark out there.'

He glanced up at the nearest high arrow-slit window, where a gleam of pale light was shining through, illuminating a ghost slit on the dark wall opposite.

'See that? They've got lights on outside. Probably vehicle lights.'

She put down the gun. 'Geoff? Give us a hand.' He blinked, but dropped the metal pole to the floor with a loud clatter. Kim gave him an encouraging smile. 'Let's move this bloody great thing again, then.'

Savage grabbed the nearside of the cupboard, beginning to lift with the other two. 'Just stand it upright,' he said. 'Then we can lay it back against the doors after I've had a look outside.'

Once the cupboard was upright, Savage wriggled into the dark space between its back and the doors.

'Don't stay there too long.' Even from the other side of the vast cupboard, he could hear the disapproval in Kim's voice. 'You might get your head blown off.'

'Yes, Sergeant,' he said drily.

Silently, he placed a palm on each of the wooden door panels, leant forward, and set an eye to the narrow gap where the two doors met.

CHAPTER FIFTY

It was only the tiniest of cracks, but wide enough for him to get a feel for what was going on outside. Darkness had fallen, and the rain was beginning to ease. It felt slightly warmer than earlier. The air was misty white with electric light, a battery of torches and vehicle headlights turned in their direction, tiny steel needles of rain clearly visible as they fell past the doorway. The Russian van they had left partly blocking the double doors had vanished. Kim had taken the keys, of course. But it would have been the work of a few minutes to push the van to one side so they could bring the digger into attack position. The compound was a hive of activity, with someone shouting in English just beyond his field of vision, the words too garbled to hear, other men standing about with shotguns trained on the building, the guard up in the gate tower a dark silhouette staring out over the moors, and the entrance gates standing wide open.

The digger sat opposite the double doors, about three hundred feet away, scoop in its upright position. The engine was silent, the driver's cab empty.

Where was Billy?

He leant closer to the crack and studied the farmhouse instead. All the windows were blazing with light, the front door partly ajar. Through the gap he could see people moving about, stick figures against the light.

He wondered if the real Russian courier had arrived, and was now waiting impatiently to collect his next vanload of sedated young women, to be transported wherever his orders took him. Perhaps to another halfway house like this one, or on to their final destinations. Discreet private houses in Birmingham or London, perhaps. Bordellos and brothels, or some wealthy sheikh's household, someone to scrub and sew and make meals, and never need payment or an expensive dental plan.

As he watched, the Land Rover Defender was backed laboriously up to the front door through muddy puddles. *DARTMOOR GUN CENTRE*, the advert on the spare tyre cover proudly proclaimed. *Quality Guns Bought & Sold.*

Mike Cooper jumped out and opened the back of the vehicle.

Then he went inside the farmhouse, leaving the front door wide open. The hall was empty of people, but there were suitcases standing about inside. Mike picked up two cases, one in each hand, and carried them laboriously out to the Defender.

Was Barton leaving too?

Perhaps he had given up hope of recovering this situation and was getting out before the police arrived. As he must know they would eventually. This place was remote. But not on the moon. The police would come in the end, and there would be no explaining away the prison cells hidden beneath his hall of worship, not even if he had cleared out their dazed and drowsy occupants.

'Well?' Kim peered round the cupboard at him. 'What can you see? What's happening out there?'

'Looks like Barton's doing a bunk.'

'He's leaving?'

'It's possible. Hang on.'

Huffing and puffing, Mike had returned for another set of suitcases. These next two cases were as heavy as the first, apparently. Wherever he was going, Barton did not believe in travelling light, it seemed.

But Savage doubted the cult leader would leave before making sure of his secret prisoners. They must represent a considerable investment on his part, after all.

He wasn't sure how much a young woman cost on the slavery market. Not exactly his area of expertise.

But he doubted they came cheap.

As Mike put the last cases into the back of his Defender, a familiar figure came to the front door of the farmhouse. A man dressed in black, with a mid-thigh-length black raincoat over the top and an old-fashioned black umbrella hooked over his arm.

It was the Reverend Barton.

Staying carefully inside the shelter of the doorway, he spoke to Mike Cooper, who was standing beside the Defender. Mike made some kind of reply, slamming the rear door shut. Then Barton turned his head towards the big hall, his gaze piercing even at that distance, as though looking straight at Savage.

Savage stiffened.

Someone else had come to stand beside Barton. A woman, also in black, but with blonde hair. Not a young woman though. She was in her sixties, at least. So the colour had come out of a bottle.

He recognised her at once.

Mother Barton.

MAYDAY.

She spoke to her son, and he turned at once to listen, smiling but with a distinct air of deference. Maybe even trepidation.

She spoke rapidly.

Barton seemed to flinch at every word, bowing his head to listen.

She finished and glared at him.

He replied briefly, and she turned away, clearly dissatisfied.

Savage was unable to hear a word, of course, but he could imagine how the exchange had gone.

'Haven't you got those women out of there yet, Francis?'

'I'm afraid not, mother.'

'What are you waiting for? Good God, do I have to do everything myself? Pull yourself together. Break down the doors, shoot the bastards, and drag the women out. We're on the clock here, you know.'

'Yes, mother.'

Barton watched as she retreated back inside one of the well-lit front rooms. To wait impatiently for the deed to be done, no doubt, pacing the room like a caged panther. Or complaining to the equally impatient Russian courier that her son was useless, and she was constantly disappointed in him.

The Reverend strode across the shining wet compound, black umbrella swaying on his arm, shouting, 'Billy? Where are you?' Billy emerged from behind one of the vehicles, where he had been enjoying a quiet smoke with some of the other men. Barton knocked the cigarette from his hand with the tip of his umbrella. 'What are you doing? Get back in the digger.' As Billy turned and ran back towards the red digger, he yelled after him, 'No more warnings, you hear me? I want that door down.'

Savage wriggled out of the gap between the cupboard and the doors, and said to Kim, 'They're coming. Right now.'

'Right.' She helped him push the cupboard back into position, then stepped back and blew out a breath. Still composed, but excited and nervous beneath that. 'So if they get in, what should we do?'

While he had been gone, more women in paper-thin white outfits had come stumbling up the steps from below the hall. They looked sick. Not much use there. And he needed to consider their welfare too. It might almost be better to surrender than leave them open to getting shot. But that last resort hadn't been reached yet. And with any luck, they would never get there.

He took stock of what they had. Which wasn't much, frankly.

Once the door was down, they would have Kim with her shotgun and him with the Glock. She could get two shots off before needing to reload, though he imagined she would not be slow at reloading if they were coming under heavy fire. He'd fired off six rounds outside. That left eight cartridges in the Glock. Not much against a potential army.

Then there was Geoff with his metal pole. Terry, Dani and Faith with nothing but their bare hands. And a handful of sedated women in various states of undress, huddled on the floor or wandering about looking dazed.

'Do we have anything like an axe? Or a hammer?'

'Only Geoff's pole.'

They both looked at Geoff, who was comforting Dani. His metal pole lay forgotten on the floor.

'Why do we need an axe?'

'I'm thinking of smashing a hole in the back wall.'

Kim blinked. 'OK.'

'I know it's not ideal. But you hear that?' He indicated the doors, and they both listened to the sound of the digger engine roaring into life. 'That's Billy, and he's coming through that door any minute.'

'The bolts will hold.'

'I'm not so sure. Barton's looking like a man under pressure.'

She frowned. 'From whom?'

'His mother, mostly.' He nodded when she stared. 'I saw her just now. She's terrifying. Like a cross between a prison officer and a hedge fund manager. And he's clearly in her pocket.'

'So you think he won't worry too much about destroying the hall, only about upsetting Mummy?'

'I think we've run out of time for other options.'

Kim gazed about the place, scanning the walls. 'I've seen no axes. Or hammers. Only that.' She nodded to a small glass-fronted fire escape box on the wall near the door. It contained a small metal hatchet, maybe a little bigger than his hand. 'That's about it. I doubt you'd be able to make much impact on these thick walls with something so small.'

'I could always bury it in Barton's head, if push comes to shove.'

Kim grinned.

'What's happening?' Dani had come over and was listening, her face taut with anxiety. 'You looking for an axe?'

'Do you know where to find one?'

She shook her head.

'In that case, no, we're looking for another way out of this hall. A rear exit. A low window. Maybe a back door through the cell block. Do you know if anything like that exists?'

She thought hard, rubbing her forehead. 'I . . . I'm not sure. Sorry.'

Outside Billy's digger rumbled into action.

'Get back from the doors,' Savage said, and they all retreated to a safe distance. He touched Dani's sleeve. 'Would Rose know?'

'I'll go ask. Though she's not herself. Still very woozy.'

'Maybe one of the other women.'

'I don't think many of them speak English. Or not very well.'

'See what you can do.'

In the compound, people were shouting over the strain of the engine. Encouragement, perhaps. Urging their hero on. Someone beeped a car horn, perhaps for the same reason.

Billy's digger accelerated towards the hall.

Terry swore, standing in front of Dani and Rose. Geoff grabbed up his metal pole and pointed it towards the entrance. Several of the women clapped hands over their ears and screamed. One crouched down, moaning and shuddering at the noise of the digger's approach, and rocked back and forth, completely out of it.

Kim steadied herself, staring at the doors, shotgun at the ready, cradling the menacing double barrel, stock lodged comfortably in her shoulder. Savage wondered how many shells she had left in that belt pouch. Not many, he expected. It was not a large bag and Kim had fired off quite a few shots when they entered the compound. But she would make every last shell count, that was for sure.

Then the digger struck.

CHAPTER FIFTY-ONE

It was like an explosion going off. The whole building shook. The vast cupboard fell to the ground with a hollow, echoing crash. The double doors bowed inwards under the immense pressure of the digger's impact. Two of the three bolts snapped, and several of the hinges failed on the right side. Dust fell in soft clouds from the rafters high above. Puffs of dislodged white plaster filled the air. The building creaked ominously.

But the door held.

Beside him, Kim sucked in a breath.

'Hang on,' he said.

There was a long moment of silence. No doubt those outside had stepped forward to inspect the damage. More shouts followed.

He imagined Mother Barton watching from the farmhouse, remembering how he had ordered Charlie Petherick to tie her to the bed, and willing the destruction on, eager to make Savage pay for humiliating her. For making her son look weak in the eyes of his men. He imagined that was something Mother Barton could never forgive.

Then the digger shifted, with a low crunch of machinery.

The wood high up on the double doors began to splinter, cracking asunder as the metal scoop tore and ate at them.

Phase Two had begun.

Dani came back to his side. She didn't look well, her face

as white as the paper-thin outfits the other women were wearing.

'Rose says there's a trapdoor under the altar. It leads to an escape tunnel. Billy showed it to her once.'

Savage kissed her on the cheek. 'Thank you.'

'What was that for?'

'Telling me Barton's contingency plan.'

'Sorry?'

'I knew he would never risk being forced into a Wako-style last stand. He's not that kind of man. He'd leave his believers to face the end together while he crawled off to rebuild his own life somewhere else.'

Her gaze on the double doors, Kim spoke urgently over her shoulder. 'That third bolt is about to break. We've only got minutes. Then they'll be inside.'

'Copy that.'

Savage went to the central altar, leaving Kim to guard the entrance. A memory rose in him. Something Phyllis had said about bones being found when the altar was moved one time. But why had they been moving the altar in the first place, if not because it concealed something?

He kicked the altar over, scattering its contents across the floor. Underneath he found no bones, but a grating in the floor and a chill draught rising up through the iron bars. It didn't appear to be secured in any way.

Fast access in case of emergency, he guessed.

Terry came over, supporting Rose, an arm about her waist. 'So much for your plan,' he said bitterly, glaring at Savage accusingly. 'He's going to kill us all.'

'He can only kill us if he catches us.'

Terry stared down at the grating. 'What the hell is this?'

'Our way out.'

Savage grabbed hold of the bars and gave a strong tug. The

grating jerked free of the ground. He threw it aside with a clatter.

Below was a short drop into a tunnel. The tunnel was unlit with dark earthen walls and floor. It smelt dank and putrid. But it seemed to be roughly the height of a man. If you didn't mind bending your head. And possibly your knees too.

'Geoff? Still got those torches?'

Geoff came puffing over with a couple of long-barrel torches possibly left in the hall for this very purpose. He too stared down into the tunnel, apparently not put off by the unpleasant smell. But then, he was a farmer.

'We getting out of here?' He grunted, then handed Savage a torch, before shining his own torch beam into the dark hole. 'About time too. That Billy, he's nearly got them doors down.'

Crouched over the hole, Savage looked up. 'Terry, you want to help? Get these women down there, quick as you can. Those who can walk, at least.'

Terry looked round at the gathered women. 'Most should be OK to make their own way. Only two are too drugged to walk. I can try carrying one of them though.'

'And I'll carry the other.' Geoff shrugged at Terry's look of disbelief. 'What?' He pointed at a young woman lying crumpled in the shadows. 'That girl looks to weigh less than a two-kilo sack of potatoes. I can handle a two-kilo sack of potatoes. Even down in that hole.'

'Good work.' Savage straightened, leaving them to it. 'We'll hold them off for as long as possible.' He strode back to Kim, who did not appear to have moved since he'd left, shotgun still levelled at the entrance. 'How long have we got, do you think?'

'Barely any time at all. He's nearly through.'

She indicated the double doors without taking her gaze from them. At that moment, the doors shook under another forceful impact. Savage saw the gleaming teeth of the scoop bite into another chunk of wood and tear it viciously away from the frame. There was now a substantial hole at the top of the right-hand side door, where the hinge had snapped off and was hanging loose, and through it he could see the damp night air lit up by headlights.

The final bolt, down at the base of the double doors, was still in place and holding. But for how long? Mere minutes, by his guess.

'What's going on over there?' she asked.

'Evacuating the prisoners.'

She glanced round at him at last. Her short red hair was shining in the light that was streaming through from the outside compound. He thought again of a furnace, burning hot and steady all through the night. Lucky Phyllis.

'You found a way out, then.' It was a statement, not a question. She bared her teeth. 'Under the altar. It had to be, of course. How typically irreverent of that charlatan to have built his escape route under the altar. It's like a metaphor for everything that's wrong about this rotten bloody fake cult of his.'

Savage grinned at the vehemence behind her words.

The digger scoop wrenched a huge chunk from the left-hand side of the double doors, leaving most of the top half wide open to the elements, then came back, probing and pushing through the hole. In that instant, it looked like a gigantic metal hand reaching inside the hall, hunting for someone to grab.

He checked over his shoulder. Only Dani remained, shining her torch down into darkness. The rest of the prisoners, and the two men with their loads, had already disappeared into the hole under the altar.

'I'm going to give them some covering fire,' he said, pulling the Glock from his waistband. 'They need to get clear.'

Kim nodded, hefting her shotgun again.

'No, not you. You've done an incredible job holding them off for so long.' He put a hand on her shoulder. 'But you should go with them. I've no idea where that tunnel leads. But it's better than waiting here.'

'Agreed,' she said, and gave him a straight look. 'Which is why I'm not leaving until you do.'

Giving up, Savage moved through the shadows until he was nearer the ruined door, aware of Kim following him. He waited until the toothed scoop of the digger had begun to descend again, and then steadied his aim on the brightly-lit cab, where he could see the driver busy at the controls, his face a mask of vicious excitement.

Billy, doing the work of the Reverend Barton.

For what reward?

A place in the hierarchy, presumably. A young farmer like Billy had a limited future on Dartmoor. Cold dawns on the land and even colder nights, with nothing at the end but grinding debt. By working for Barton, grafting hard for a place by the big man's side, Billy could become an important person in his own right. Someone other people feared and obeyed. Someone who could afford a flash car and a pad in London, perhaps.

But only if Billy lived long enough to earn them . . .

The scoop descended further, fully exposing the cab at last. Abruptly, Savage found the angle he'd been waiting for, and squeezed the trigger.

The first shot ricocheted off the metal frame of the cab.

Billy heard the noise but did not seem to realise what was happening, pausing for a few seconds before continuing his onslaught against the doors.

Savage fired again, straight through the gap left by the digger's tearing scoop. This time the bullet cracked the rain-streaked glass of the cab, missing Billy by a whisker but obscuring his vision.

Barton had to be close by. Savage heard his voice raised in exhortation. 'Keep going, Billy. That's it. You've nearly done it.'

Behind him, Dani was the last to climb into the hole. The powerful beam of her torch disappeared with her, leaving them in semi-darkness.

Revving the engine, Billy retracted the scoop again, its cruel teeth catching on the ragged edges of the hole.

Savage fired twice more, but with the vehicle headlights directly in his line of sight, the shots ricocheted harmlessly off the metal scoop both times. Now he was running out of ammunition as well as time.

'How many cartridges do you have left?' Kim asked, still at his side.

He checked, but it was too dark to read the indicator properly.

'Can't see. How about you?'

'I don't think this will be a very lengthy shoot-out, let's put it like that.'

A face appeared in the ragged hole and stared in at them. Some hairy lout with a sawn-off, who saw them and instantly raised his shotgun with a look of glee.

Stepping instinctively in front of Kim, Savage fired twice again, directly at him, and the man disappeared with a cry.

They fell back against the wall by mutual consent, in case of a retaliatory strike.

'I can protect myself, you know,' she said drily.

'Sorry.' He grinned at her. 'Force of habit.'

There was some frantic shouting from outside now. Voices bounced off the mist. Somebody called out, 'Stop, that's enough.'

Billy crunched the gears and began to back up his digger. After a few feet, he turned off the engine.

Beyond the digger, he could see shadowy figures approaching the hall en masse, threatening bodies silhouetted against the lights. Rain had stopped falling, though the night was misty: a thick, damp mist that clung to everything like a fine coating. As though the whole of the Green Chapel compound was lost inside a cloud.

'We've got to go,' Kim said urgently. 'Now.'

Then her phone rang, loud in the sudden silence.

CHAPTER FIFTY-TWO

Kim answered the call, then handed the mobile phone to him. Her expression was suitably blank, but he sensed disapproval in her tone. Like, *why the hell is someone calling you at a time like this? And on* my *phone?*

'DI Paglia for you,' she said.

He took it with a nod, his gaze on the ruins of the double doors. Someone was firing up what sounded like a chainsaw outside. Now that Billy had moved his digger, a chainsaw would make easy work of what remained of their defences.

'Savage, where are you? I've been trying to ring but there wasn't any answer.' Paglia was breathless. 'We're on our way to you. Five minutes out.'

'My phone's dead. Who is *we*?'

'My team. And the special task force.' Paglia hesitated, a flicker of something like surprise in her voice as she added, 'And someone else too.'

'This special task force ... It wouldn't be modern slavery, would it?'

'I couldn't possibly say.'

'With a man already on the inside at the Green Chapel?'

'Again, I couldn't possibly say.'

Kim dragged on his sleeve. 'We have to go,' she mouthed.

He started walking backwards with her, his gaze still on the broken double doors. The menacing whine of the chainsaw was louder now, close to the entrance.

'PC Petherick,' he said into the phone, 'he's been working here undercover, hasn't he? With the modern slavery task force.'

'I can neither confirm nor deny that, Savage.'

There was a special kind of pain in her voice.

The kind he knew himself.

That moment when you lose one of your own.

The man-hunt he'd seen had been specially organised by Barton to flush out the traitor in their midst. A clever ruse. It would have been hard for an undercover officer to watch Barton ordering a man to be hunted with guns and dogs, chased across the moors like a wild animal. Even a low-life like Billy.

Petherick must have felt tempted to intervene. Or to delay things, at least. And would have betrayed himself in that instant.

So Barton had turned those same guns and dogs on the police officer instead.

'I'm sorry about Petherick.' They had reached the hole. 'He had me fooled. If I'd realised he was only acting the part of a bent copper—'

He was interrupted by Kim. 'There's no time for a chat. We've got company.' She pointed to the entrance, where the chainsaw was swiftly reducing what was left of the doors to wood chippings. 'How long before the police are here?'

He relayed her question to Paglia, who said, 'Five minutes? We can see the gates. They're standing open . . . Wait, there's a Land Rover coming out.'

'That's probably Barton.' Savage indicated to Kim that she should jump into the hole before him. Stubbornly, she shook her head. 'And his mother.'

'His *mother*?'

'Apparently she's heavily involved in this nasty little

operation. Takes special care of the girls for him, you know? I saw one of his men loading their suitcases into the car. I think they're running.'

He caught the sound of a car horn, eerily loud, both on the phone and outside in the compound. Paglia continued speaking through the slamming of doors.

'So you've found women being kept there against their will? Hidden in cells below the large central hall within the complex?'

The detective was running now. He could hear her rapid breathing.

'Yes,' he said.

'Women from Eastern Europe?' Now he could hear police officers ordering the driver of the Land Rover to stop and turn off the engine. 'Is that right?'

'Yes.'

Kim must have seen something, because she suddenly yelled, 'Get down,' and he ducked along with her.

There was a tremendous crack of shotgun fire, a spray of shot burying itself in the wall above their heads. At the same time, Savage saw a vast, shadowy figure step over the remains of the broken door like it was no obstacle at all. Long legs like those of a giant spider, and a towering, spindly body . . .

'Get in the hole.' He shoved Kim. 'Now!'

Paglia sounded confused, her voice in his ear. 'What hole?'

'Sorry, not you. I was talking to Kim.' He jumped down after her, landing awkwardly, phone still clamped to his ear. It was dark in the tunnel, but he could feel Kim moving ahead of him, both of them bending their heads slightly. 'Have you got Barton yet?'

'Negative, he's not here.'

'What?'

'There's some big guy driving the Land Rover. Says his name

is Mike Cooper. Suitcases in the back, like you said. But no sign of the Reverend himself.'

'Barton must have sent the car out as a diversion.'

'We're coming into the compound.' She was breathless, running again. The line crackled ominously. 'Heading . . . through the gates . . . right now. What's your location?'

'We've in some kind of escape tunnel under the hall.'

Kim called back the warning, 'Roof slopes,' and he bent further as the roof did exactly that, still listening for sounds of pursuit from behind.

His position was not particularly promising, he thought, bending over as he shuffled along behind Kim. He had the Glock, with two bullets left by his calculation, but there was no room to turn at that point, so he'd be aiming blind. The last thing he wanted was to get shot in the buttocks.

'We could do with some back-up. We're seriously outgunned.'

'What?' Paglia said urgently, sounding like she was gargling. 'Say again, say again. I missed that last. You're breaking up.'

Then her voice cut off.

He checked the phone signal. It had disappeared. Not surprisingly, given that they had to be at least six feet underground.

He shoved Kim's phone in his front jeans pocket alongside his own, making a sizeable bulge, and hurried after her. To his relief the earth walls of the tunnel widened after another ten yards, ending in a flight of ten rough steps that led up into the misty night. There was a spiky, yellow-flowered gorse bush that had been allowed to grow high and broad, sprawling over the opening, presumably to conceal it, and another iron gate that had pushed open as the others came through.

Gingerly, he began to negotiate the thorny bushes, and almost bumped into Kim, who was standing stock-still ahead of him.

He recognised the place at once as the path that led down to the Green Chapel. The others were there too, Terry and Geoff beside a ragged, pitiful group of women in white outfits, and Faith supporting one woman who didn't seem able to stand unaided. But they were not alone. Barton was standing a short distance away, a shotgun held loosely in the crook of his arm but levelled at Kim, his other hand gripping Dani by the upper arm.

'Drop the gun,' Barton told Kim coldly.

She did not move.

'Don't be stupid,' he said. 'Toss it.'

Kim threw the weapon into the grass behind her.

The shotgun fell near where Savage was crouching, shielded from view by the vast gorse bush guarding the entrance to the tunnel.

Could he reach it without being seen?

Stealthily, he checked the Glock. Two cartridges left. Not a comfortable margin for error. Though it would be an easy enough shot this time, nothing between him and his targets but air. Always assuming he could get a shot off before Barton swung that shotgun in his direction.

Savage peered round the spiky edge of the gorse, hoping the darkness would keep him safe and unseen until he could find the right moment to grab the shotgun. The pouch of shells was still hanging from her belt. Though maybe Kim had used them all.

With any luck, at least one barrel was still loaded.

Beside her captor, Dani looked sick with anxiety. She was frozen, caught terrified and motionless in a beam from a torch, like an animal in the headlights.

Barton's mother, a little ahead of her son on the path, had turned and was blazing her torch hungrily over all their faces in turn, as though searching for someone. Her gaze fell on Faith, standing a little apart from the rest, clearly out of place.

'Where is he?' Mother Barton, as they called her, was hissing out the words, her eyes narrowed and seething with hatred. 'The one who did this to us? I want his blood.'

No wonder she had been the one to 'care' for the newly arrived illegal immigrants down in the cells, grooming and preparing them for a life of slavery in the United Kingdom. She would have shared a language with many of them, and a common culture, a strong enough bond perhaps to keep things running smoothly even when any newcomers were scared or rebellious.

Mother Barton shone the torch around their small circle and watched them shrink away from her scrutiny. 'After that, you will come with us, all you girls. Or my son will shoot you too, one by one. You understand me, you ungrateful bitches? I offered you a new life here in the UK, and how do you repay me? With betrayal. With hard words. With a heart as cold as ice.' She tapped her chest vehemently. 'Me, your country-woman. The closest you will ever come again to your own flesh and blood. You betray me, and disgrace yourselves. So now you must suffer. But first, I want the man they call Savage.'

CHAPTER FIFTY-THREE

As she finished speaking, Savage made up his mind. He thrust the Glock into the front waistband of his jeans, and made a grab for the fallen shotgun. He edged in front of Kim, aiming the muzzle directly at Barton.

Barton froze, staring round at Savage. The sudden move had taken him by surprise, so sure of himself that he'd been looking away at the silhouette of the farmhouse, not expecting a counter-attack.

'Good evening,' Savage said, and nodded to Mother Barton without looking away from the Reverend. 'You were looking for me, I believe? Aubrey Savage.'

'You again!' Mother Barton stared at the shotgun pointed at her son, then sucked in her hollowed-out cheeks even further, looking him up and down. Close-up, she looked much older and more gaunt than at a distance, the smooth mask of her make-up unable to conceal the deep lines about her mouth and eyes. '*You* are this Savage?'

Barton's mother turned away without waiting for an answer, as though disgusted with the sudden reversal of their position.

But her slumped body language was an act.

In a well-practised move, she grabbed Faith by the sleeve and spun her round in front of her body, a stiletto-thin knife appearing out of nowhere – as though concealed up a sleeve, perhaps – to be pressed across Faith's throat.

'Shoot my son and this girl dies.' Mother Barton glared at him over Faith's shoulder. 'Your woman, yes? I will slit her throat like a chicken's, and sleep peacefully tonight. Trust me on this.'

He did trust her.

But that didn't change the situation. He met Faith's eyes silently, and saw her fear. Small wonder too. The knife was pressing deep against the fragile skin of her throat. Scarlet beads of blood had already appeared, one rolling slowly down her neck. But Faith was not hysterical. Which meant she was not without hope.

That was good.

If this was to work out in their favour, he needed Faith to stay calm and focused.

'Do that, and your son will die a few seconds later,' he said, continuing to point the shotgun at Barton, who had neither moved nor relaxed his grip on Dani's arm. 'Have you ever seen what a shotgun does to a man's head, Mrs Barton? It's not pretty. But it is fairly reliable in terms of snuffing out life.'

Mother Barton swore in Russian. Her eyes narrowed on his face in disbelief. 'You do not believe I will hurt her?'

'I believe you.'

'You don't care about your woman, then? Is that it?' Pushing aside Faith's honey-blonde hair, she whispered loudly in her ear, 'You hear that, girl? He will let me kill you.' Faith shuddered but said nothing. 'Your man does not care if I spill your blood.'

He glanced at the knife. The drops of blood.

It was a risk.

Mother Barton looked crazy enough to slit Faith's throat, drop her to the floor, and move on to one of the other women.

But he was gambling on a woman's love for her son.

'So they'll die together.' He shrugged, as though the prospect of Faith's death meant little more to him than an inconvenience. 'Her blood will be on your hands. His brains will be on your face. Poetic justice.'

Mother Barton screamed.

'Let her go,' her son said, his voice cutting through her fury. She stopped and stared at him.

Then, with another grimace of disgust, she slowly withdrew the knife. In Russian, she said, 'This is a mistake.' But she obeyed, and pushed Faith away.

'Drop the gun,' Savage told Barton, 'and release Dani.'

Barton hesitated, then let go of Dani's arm. Another frustrated pause, then he threw the gun to the ground. Kim darted round at once and picked it up.

Savage dragged the Glock from his waistband and handed it to Dani. 'Here,' he said, and grinned at the blonde. 'Next time someone grabs you, point this at them and shoot. Unless it's your husband, of course.'

Dani took the Glock, staring down at the handgun, and then turned in one slow swivel and pointed it straight at Barton's head.

'No!' Mother Barton screamed.

Barton sucked in his breath but said nothing. He stared directly into the muzzle of the Glock as though he could not quite believe what was happening to him.

'Dani, it's not worth it,' Savage said, realising too late he might have made a grave strategic error in giving her the Glock. But since she'd had almost the same gun in her holdall, he'd assumed she could be trusted to handle one now. 'There are many other people with grievances against Barton. Let the police deal with him.'

When Dani did not move, still pointing the gun at the Reverend Barton, Kim lent her voice softly to his. 'That man wanted to imprison you for the rest of your life. You pull the trigger, that's exactly what will happen. He'll have won.'

That argument seemed to get through to Dani, who lowered the Glock and looked round at Kim wonderingly.

From above, Savage heard the wail of police sirens.

Reinforcements arriving.

The modern slavery task force was probably a small team of no more than five bodies. Their primary task would have been rounding up the men with guns. Then instigating a search for Barton and his mother in the complex of buildings, while sealing down the forensics bonanza of the underground prison block. By now, they should have ascertained that Barton and Co. had left the buildings. Soon, the task force would be spreading out in teams of two or three, perhaps augmented by the local police, and searching the rest of the compound.

Kim stepped up. 'Terry, Geoff, I want you to escort these women back to the farmhouse.' When Geoff frowned, she urged him on with the brisk, no-nonsense voice that all capable sergeants seem to develop. 'Come on, get them moving. You'll all be safer up at the farm, trust me.'

Geoff made a frantic 'Hurry up, follow me' gesture to the women near him, then began to walk uphill, looking back over his shoulder. The women stared at Mother Barton as though incredulous that she was allowing them to leave, then stumbled up the slope behind Geoff, heading for the farmhouse. One even turned back and snatched the torch from Mother Barton's hand, then used it to light their way back to safety.

Mother Barton did not say a word.

Dani and Terry took up the rear, herding the stragglers up the grassy sloping path.

Terry asked for the Glock, and then put his arm about Dani's waist. She pushed him away, her expression haughty, saying something under her breath that made him stiffen and look guiltily away.

That was one relationship that would take a long time to heal.

With the torches gone, it was so dark that Savage could barely make out Barton's face, though the man was standing only about ten feet away. But he did not need to see his face to shoot him. Ditto with his venom-spitting mother.

He would willingly shoot both of them if that became a necessity. He'd seen first-hand the damage they had done to those unfortunate women in the underground prison, and what they would do to Faith and Kim, given half a chance. He was not going to drop his guard.

Above them, right on cue, the clouds rolled dramatically away to reveal a large, cold moon, its baleful light burning through the mists.

Now he could see Barton's face. The man was planning something, that was certain. His lips were pinched and his eyes were darting everywhere. Especially sideways to Faith, as though trying to work out how to leverage the friendship between them so he could get away.

Faith had gone back to support Rose, who had been throwing up and was still looking wobbly, on her knees in the damp grass.

'Faith,' Savage said clearly, 'take Rose and follow them.'

'What about you?'

'I'm otherwise occupied right now.'

Faith's eyes were glittering. Unshed tears? She put a hand to her throat, as though she could still feel the imprint of the knife there. Nonetheless, she shook her head.

'Nice try, Aubrey,' she said, her voice husky. 'I'm not going anywhere. Not without you.'

'That was an order.'

'I'm not one of your bloody toy soldiers.' Faith helped Rose to her feet though, her face mutinous. 'You can't order me about.'

'Rose needs medical help. I don't.'

Faith glanced at the other woman, now swaying on her feet, pale as a waxwork. She bit her lip, then nodded reluctantly. 'Very well,' she said. 'For Rose, then.'

'For Rose.'

As the two women passed them, he inclined his head to Kim, standing right beside him, and said quietly, 'You too, Kim.'

'Not a bloody chance.'

'I need you up there. To make sure things get done right.' He lowered his voice to a whisper so only she would hear, 'Tell Paglia where I am, OK?'

Kim made a noise under her breath, struggling against the desire to refuse. Then she too nodded, saying in the same whisper, 'You want my gun?'

'Why would I want a second gun?'

She said nothing, but her gaze dropped significantly to the shotgun he was still pointing squarely at Barton. Her back to the others, she mouthed. 'Empty.'

He almost laughed at the joke.

Not only had he given away his only loaded weapon to Dani, he'd been threatening Barton with an empty shotgun.

Which was when he noticed something odd. Barton was no longer looking at him and the shotgun. He kept glancing nervously downhill instead. He was shuffling that way too, one tiny, barely perceptible step at a time. And his mother with him.

They were edging down the path towards the outdoor Green Chapel.

Why?

Savage had climbed up through that narrow rocky crevice, crowded by spiny bushes, in order to access the Green Chapel. And how he had noted that there seemed to be no guards down there and no fences to keep people out. He had thought it strange that Barton had not bothered to secure that area.

But perhaps it had been a deliberate oversight.

The cult leader might have sensed the end coming days ago, when young Callum foolishly stepped up to challenge his authority. The locals biting back at last. He could have arranged for an off-road vehicle to be parked on the other side of the compound, fuelled up and with the keys in the ignition, hidden somewhere out in that rocky wilderness where it was unlikely any police car would venture. Perhaps he had known about the special task force too. It was possible that he had tortured PC Petherick before the young man died, forcing him to give up what the task force already knew about Barton's organisation.

'Fine,' he said gravely, trying to cover the reason for the switch of guns, 'you can take this one. I'll take yours.'

They swapped shotguns.

Kim gave him a brisk nod and hurried after Faith and Rose, who were almost out of sight at the top of the path.

'OK, now it's only the three of us. And you can stop edging away like that.' He gestured Barton and his mother to stand still, once more pointing the shotgun at them. 'It's time we had a little chat.'

'A chat?' Barton looked at him blankly. 'What about?'

'An old friend of mine.'

'That wasn't anything to do with me. I swear to God. He was already dead when Billy went up to the house.'

'Who?'

'Your friend, Peter Rowlands. OK, I did send Billy up there that night. But only to frighten him. To tell him to keep quiet.'

Savage's hand clenched on his weapon. The urge to blast Barton's rotten head off his shoulders was almost overpowering.

'Keep quiet about what?' he asked through his teeth.

'About his wife, of course.' Barton paused, then frowned. 'He didn't tell you?'

'You tell me, and I'll decide what he told me.'

'There's no time for this,' Barton's mother suddenly hissed. She pointed up the path. In the moonlight, they could clearly see a group of men starting to search the grounds, maybe three hundred yards away, beating the bushes with sticks. 'Shoot us or let us go,' she told Savage, baring her teeth at him. 'But no more of this stupid *chat*. It makes me sick to my stomach to hear you men talking. Chat chat chat. And never any *doing*.'

Somewhere in the darkness above a dog barked, deep and alert. Not one of Barton's, Savage was sure, but a police dog.

'OK,' Savage said to Barton. 'You tell me what you know about Peter's wife ...' He paused, and took a calculated risk. 'And I'll let you have a head start on those men.'

Which was when something hard and heavy, almost certainly a rock, clouted him in the side of the head, and Savage dropped to the ground.

CHAPTER FIFTY-FOUR

He probably only lost consciousness for a few seconds. Mild concussion. But he was out long enough for the man who had smacked him in the head with a rock to drop his improvised weapon and grab up the fallen shotgun.

Advantage gone.

Savage opened his eyes to find an outlandish figure, seemingly tall as a tree, towering above him in the mist, shotgun in hand. He was baffled and not a little annoyed with himself for allowing someone to creep up on him like that.

Then he heard his attacker speak, and knew what had happened. And *how* it had happened too. Almost exactly.

'Aubrey Savage,' the man said in guttural tones, then nodded to himself, as though these words were enough of a statement in themselves. 'Ah.'

Big Swanney.

The last thing he had seen before jumping into the tunnel back at the hall had been the intimidating sight of Big Swanney, climbing in through the remains of the double doors. That had been enough to persuade him to leave at once. He was no coward. But he liked a fair fight. And much as he fancied his chances with any of Barton's other gang members, or indeed Barton himself, maybe even two or three on one, he was less certain of victory against the giant Russian.

Big Swanney could probably pick him up and use him as a back scrubber. Which wasn't a role he was particularly keen to play.

His mind cleared.

There was blood in his mouth, a familiar iron-rich taste. His head must be bleeding, he realised, and blood was rolling down into the corner of his mouth.

Big Swanney had followed them through the tunnel. Though probably only after discovering that the cells below the hall were empty. With his immense height, he must have found the tunnel hard going. It would have taken him some time to negotiate, perhaps on hands and knees. And possibly in the pitch-dark too, since they had taken the torches. And having to keep quiet, given that the police must have been searching for Barton's men by then, right above his head.

'Shoot him, Savanovic. Shoot him dead, right between the eyes,' Barton's mother was saying in swift, furious Russian. 'What are you waiting for? Can't you see the police are coming? This is all his doing, you must punish him for destroying my son's work.' Her voice rose, almost hysterical. 'Do it now, you stupid great oaf. Finish it, I tell you.'

Big Swanney pointed the shotgun straight at his head. The muzzle wavered. His eyes met Savage's. 'Sorry,' he said, the sound rumbling up from deep inside his chest. 'Orders.'

Lying on his back in the damp grass, Savage gazed up into the two perfectly round holes at the end of the shotgun muzzle. Like a pair of dark eyes staring back at him.

There were not many options.

He could roll sideways, of course. Let the big Russian chase his head or temple or even throat in an undignified manner. It might take another shot or two before the job was done. Another precious ten seconds of life. More time on this earth was always worth pursuing. Alternatively, he could simply give it up as a lost cause. Lie there in quiet acceptance and wait to discover what Peter had perhaps discovered once life was finally extinct, ie, if there was something beyond this world. Something better than human existence.

Sod it.

Savage rolled, and heard the loud click of the trigger, and then . . .

Nothing.

It took another second or two to realise why.

That shotgun was also empty.

He scrambled to his feet while Big Swanney was still staring in consternation at the useless firearm, slammed a foot into the Russian's right knee and heard a distinct crack as that long-suffering joint broke under the impact.

Big Swanney gave a groan of agony and fell to the grass, clutching his shattered knee. He groped in a pocket with his other hand and withdrew a knife, steadying himself as though about to pitch it towards Savage.

Damn it.

Apologetically, because it didn't seem very sporting, Savage kicked out again. This time the kick caught him in the jaw, slamming his bald head backwards.

The big Russian grunted. His cadaverous eyes rolled back, bloodshot white.

He'd passed out.

Savage turned, instinctively ready for Barton's first punch.

But the Reverend had vanished.

And so had his mother.

He turned, shouting, 'Down here,' to the men searching the bushes above, and saw a torch beam pick out his face. 'Where's DI Paglia?'

'Who are you? Put your hands up.' The officer began heading his way with the others. He sounded suspicious.

Savage blinked in the torchlight. He did not put his hands up. He hated being told to put his hands up.

'I'm Savage.'

'Wait there. DI Paglia was looking for you just now. But she got a call.'

'From whom?'

'None of your business. Just wait there.'

Savage said nothing in response. But he took a few seconds to consider that not-very-polite order, carefully and judiciously, as he always did when given a command he disliked or disagreed with.

'I did send Billy up there that night. But only to frighten him. To tell him to keep quiet.'

'About what?'

'About his wife, of course.'

Savage came to a decision. Silently, he turned and plunged into the mists, heading down to the Green Chapel in pursuit of the Bartons.

CHAPTER FIFTY-FIVE

In the winding heart of the outdoor chapel, behind an enclosure the height of a man formed by tangled thorn bushes and woodland, the silence was eerie. It wasn't the ordinary silence of the moors at night, punctuated by coughs from sheep and the far-off bark of a dog fox; the unseen rush of water in a brook or stream; a car back-firing on a distant road. It was more a deliberate hush. A sudden and complete absence – or even failure – of sound.

It was the kind of too-quiet hush that made him suspicious. The kind that came with traps and ambushes and unexpected dead ends.

Wary of exactly that, Savage had taken a second meandering path that seemed to lead the same way, only more steeply and circuitously. A rising, pumpkin-round moon had lit his way through rich, twisted undergrowth and across the occasional plateau, made treacherous by swampy marshland. Then, swinging down through a rocky chicane as softly as he could, Savage had finally entered the Green Chapel proper, the wild, boulder-strewn place of natural worship that had given its name to the whole complex.

There, a mist descended again and the silence became oppressive. Tiny hairs rose on the back of his neck, and his breathing sounded loud and laboured to his ears.

Savage slowed his pace, straining to hear . . . something.

Anything.

Except there was nothing else to hear beyond the beating of his own heart. And it felt to him at that moment as though the moors themselves were listening to the night's events. Listening and holding their breath. Waiting for something to happen, in fact. Something out of the ordinary. Something untoward.

Only he had no idea what.

He brushed past a low-hanging tree branch, and suddenly there was a rapid flutter and sweep of black wings past his head.

Bats.

Savage stood still holding back the tree branch, waiting for the bats to swoop past, and in that moment realised something. He was not alone.

'Don't you British aristocrats ever give up?'

Savage pushed the branch aside, and there was Barton, facing him in the misty moonlight, his back to a boulder, a knife in his hand.

Between them was a large uneven patch of ground, the boggy grass pierced by flag irises and thin, tall, brown reeds, the kind that only grow in marshy, waterlogged ground. Here and there, jagged outcrops of rock jutted up through the grass like tiny islands. Some would be useful as stepping stones across the marshier areas; a few were as much as two feet high but tiny, narrow and peaked like spires, making the terrain unpredictable to negotiate.

'You are the most irritatingly tenacious man I've ever had the displeasure to meet,' Barton continued.

'I believe the Classics master at my school would argue against that description. He had trouble getting me to stay awake.'

'Is Savanovic still alive?'

'Yes, he's alive. His knee may be broken though. Possibly his jaw too. Sorry about that. Needs must.'

Barton glanced over his shoulder, his expression wary. A shuffling sound behind the boulder confirmed Savage's suspicion. Mother Barton was there too, hiding.

'There's no point, you know,' he told Barton. 'In running, I mean. The police will have the others by now. And it won't be long before they find you too. Why make things worse for yourselves by resisting arrest?'

'So much concern for our welfare,' Barton said, sneering.

'Not particularly.' Savage reached up and snapped off one of the branches above his head. While Barton hesitated, peering at him through the mist, he rapidly stripped the branch of its leaves, leaving a pointed stick that felt strong enough to inflict considerable damage on a human body, given the correct amount of pressure. 'If you want to fight, that's fine. Let's fight.'

Mother Barton growled in Russian from behind the boulder.

'Stay where you are,' her son said. 'I'll deal with him.' He dragged off his jacket and crouched, passing his knife lightly from one hand to the other. Not entirely unskilled in hand-to-hand combat, then. 'All this because of one dead fool. You English are so sad. Why are you even here? To defend your friend's manhood? It's too late for that.'

Savage kept his gaze on Barton's face, ignoring the temptation to watch the knife instead. 'Are you talking about Maura?'

'We used to joke about it. Peter's wife. The woman who wanted "more-ah". She was quite a little vixen, you know. In bed, I mean. All claws and teeth.'

'You raped her.'

They were circling each other on the treacherous, marshy ground. Savage stumbled on a rocky outcrop, then hurriedly righted himself. He feinted with the sharp-pointed stick and Barton danced away, then came quickly back. Moonlight glinted off Barton's blade as he tilted it, creeping round Savage again, but this time counter-clockwise.

Behind him, Mother Barton emerged from behind her rock, watching them through the mist. Savage briefly glanced her way. He didn't like having to keep an eye on her at the same time as her son. But she seemed to be unarmed.

'On the contrary, I didn't give Maura anything she wasn't absolutely begging for.' Barton licked his lips, his eyes narrowed and fixed on the business end of Savage's stick. 'You still don't get it, do you?'

'Enlighten me.'

'I gave those women pleasure.' He waited, but Savage said nothing. 'Come on, I looked you up. You're a scholar. Anglo-Saxon, Middle English, Latin, all those dead languages.'

'Your point?'

'I gave them *wynn*. Pleasure, like the rune says.'

'I believe a more accurate translation of the Old Norse would be joy.'

'Joy, pleasure, what does it matter? Besides, what could be more joyful than sexual pleasure? As a man of learning, you must understand why I tattooed all the women who came through here. It was my personal brand. They came in bare, and left with my mark on them. Wynn. So wherever they ended up, everyone would know I'd had them first.'

'You branded them.'

Barton shrugged.

'You've probably overlooked this in your enthusiasm,' Savage added, 'but sex has to be consensual for it to be pleasurable.'

'All right, maybe some of the women were reluctant at first. But all they needed was a little . . . persuasion.'

'You drugged them, you mean.'

'Not all of them. Your vicar's girlfriend, for instance. Phyllis. She was desperate for a baby, no strings attached. She came up to the Green Chapel a few times. But there was never any unpleasantness about it.'

'And Maura?'

Barton smiled, as though at a delicious memory. 'Maura was a woman of great sensuality. She wanted what I could give her. She took it willingly, and came back for more. That's what your friend couldn't stand.'

'Peter. He has a name.' Savage corrected himself. 'Had a name. You killed him.'

'He killed himself. Because he knew he wasn't up to the job.'

'Job?'

'The job of being a man.' Barton laughed. 'Peter Rowlands wasn't a real man. Not where it mattered. He couldn't give his wife what she needed. That's what drink does to you.' He smiled, almost smug. 'Impotence has never been my problem. But it was always Peter's. And Maura was desperate for a child. So desperate, she didn't care if everybody knew that her husband wasn't the father.'

'You're saying you got Maura pregnant?'

'Didn't he tell you about that?' Barton was sneering again. 'Well now, that's a turn-up. I thought you two were best buddies.'

'OK, let's say for a moment that you're not lying. That it was consensual, and pure *wynn*, and all that. If Maura was so keen on you, and was having your baby too, why did she leave?'

'Why do women do anything? Maybe she told Peter the truth, or his friend ratted her out, and Peter slapped her about, so she took off. Hard to blame him for feeling put out. Though it was his fault in the first place, of course. If he'd been a proper husband, Maura wouldn't have needed to look elsewhere.'

Savage felt cold inside. 'His friend? What friend?'

'The one who came to threaten me with his Glock. The arrogant Iraqi. He thought he could tell me what to do. Here, in my own place too. I sent Savanovic and the boys after him. Over the moors one night, with the dogs and bikes. They like a good hunt, you see.'

Barton charged him before he'd even finished speaking.

Savage, still stunned by that revelation, only managed to dodge sideways at the last second. He turned early enough to escape the knife, but too late to avoid over-balancing. His right foot twisted and got sucked into what felt like quicksand, sliding out from under him with alarming speed.

He tried to steady himself with the stick, but it snapped under his weight. Savage ended up on his hands and knees, sinking into mud up to his elbows.

Barton recovered, turning lightly on his heel.

He headed back to where Savage had dragged his arms free but was still grappling for a handhold on the marshy ground, his fists full of soggy earth, his knees already forming waterlogged depressions.

'Friend of yours too, was he, the Iraqi with the Glock?' He spun and stamped hard, aiming for Savage's knee but missing. 'I should have known. He had the same plummy accent. Same stupid belief that he could come up here and threaten me. Well, he certainly failed there. As you've failed too.'

Savage rolled, using the springy wetness of the grass for added momentum. Barton was above him, still trying to stamp on him. He got in one brutal kick, aimed at Savage's groin, but thankfully it fell short, connecting with his stomach instead. Not pleasant, but not incapacitating. Savage grabbed the broken stick, now considerably shorter, and thrust it blindly upwards into what he reckoned should be Barton's thigh, putting all his strength behind the blow.

Barton gave a shriek of agony, staggering back with the stick embedded in the back of his leg. The knife hung loose from his hand as he twisted at the waist, staring down in horror at his impaled leg, the black jeans already sticky with blood.

Finally locating a rocky outcrop he could grip, Savage

heaved himself up off the marshy ground. He was winded by that kick, but in reasonable shape to continue.

Unlike Barton.

'What are you waiting for? It's only a flesh wound.' Mother Barton tore at her white-blonde hair in despair, watching them from a rock top on the misty fringes of the bog. Despite her dishevelled hair, she still looked somehow immaculate and coldly beautiful, and almost too young to have a son in his thirties. A look she had worked hard to maintain, Savage guessed. 'You're losing, you fool. You can't lose. You must kill him. Do you hear me? Kill him now. Must I do everything myself?'

Barton looked round at his mother, blank-faced. Then he gave a guttural cry and lunged for Savage with his knife.

Savage was ready for him. He spun round, smashing his foot against the front of Barton's wounded thigh, and heard the man roar. Barton stumbled, and the knife went spinning away into the marshy reeds.

But, infuriatingly, he didn't fall.

Tackling him, Savage fell heavily on top of Barton in the sucking marshland, both men flailing about in the mud. It was the kind of deep, glutinous muck that resisted any attempt to pull oneself free, and trying to wrestle in it rapidly became tiring. Savage gave up the attempt and, setting his palm and wrist edge against Barton's cheek, attempted to thrust his face round into the mud. Barton realised what he intended, and fought back, his fingers digging sharply into his upper arm, then his shoulder and throat, working their way up to his face, while Savage kept up that immense pressure, his whole arm across Barton's throat now, driving him deeper into the bog.

Barton's face was almost under the mud now. He was gasping, gulping at the misty air, struggling to stay out of the mud.

The gasps became tortured, then quietened to hissing

sounds, until at length his grip on Savage's throat began to slacken. Eventually, the Reverend's hand fell back limply on the ground, a bubble of mud sucked back and forth through barely parted lips, his struggles a mere periodic jerk of his limbs.

Then he lay still.

Exhausted, Savage relaxed at last, resting his forehead against the other man's shoulder and closing his eyes.

But not for long.

Behind him, Mother Barton screamed her son's name.

The man did not answer.

Eyes still wearily closed, Savage heard a soft thud-thud-thud at his back, like a series of distant underground explosions, and only belatedly realised what it was. The sound of an enraged mother on her way to wreak revenge for her beloved son's defeat. Though 'trophy' could probably be substituted for 'beloved' in that context without much loss of accuracy.

Savage pushed himself to a semi-kneeling position.

But too late.

White-hot pain skewered between his shoulders.

Barton's knife.

Agony and instinct made him leap to his feet, fuelled by a second wave of adrenalin coursing through his veins like gasoline. He needed to move before his attacker could drive the blade any deeper. Or potentially extract it for a second thrust.

He turned to find Mother Barton right behind him, whole body heaving with rage, her perfect face flushed and distorted like that of a madwoman.

'What have you done to my son? What have you done to my beautiful boy?' She was panting, almost incoherent. She bent to Barton's motionless body, and groped blindly at his mud-black throat for a pulse. But everything was so slippery, it was clear she could not find one. She moaned and cried his name again, rocking mindlessly to and fro, then scooped up handfuls of the gooey black mud and smeared them down both her cheeks, like war paint or camouflage, sobbing, 'Oh, my dearest son. My darling boy.'

Savage hefted one arm over his shoulder, struggling to feel for the knife in his back.

He was dizzy, losing blood.

Somewhere through the thickening mists he could hear shouts. Then he caught the ghostly reflection of blue lights bouncing off fog.

'Over here,' he shouted.

Mother Barton staggered to her feet. She dragged her muddy hands over her chest, pushing the black gunk deep into the fabric of her clothes. Then she turned towards him, staring with mad eyes.

He stumbled backwards but one foot sank into the marsh and refused to release him. She caught up with him easily. Her slender hands came up, grappling with his throat, squeezing his windpipe with surprisingly strong fingers.

'I'll kill you. You deserve to die.'

'No.' He was choking. 'I don't. Actually.'

'Die, die, die,' she began to chant in Russian.

Savage clamped his hands around her hands and tried to tear them away. Every movement sent jolts of searing agony through his back and shoulders. He was a butterfly on a pin having his antennae squeezed. He stared back at her through a reddish mist.

Mother Barton was a woman, and he'd been brought up not to hurt women. Even when the woman in question was a deranged psychopath who was attempting to throttle him.

But he also liked the idea of staying alive.

He head-butted her.

Mother Barton fell back with a strangled gasp, then crumbled slowly, almost like an afterthought, knees giving way, her face blank in the moonlight.

She didn't move again.

Paglia reached him roughly three minutes later, decked out in wellington boots and armed with a powerful torch. She picked her way gingerly round the edge of the bog patch, pausing beside the special task force officers who had been first on the scene. Three men in matching brown suits and deeply unsuitable black leather shoes, also armed with torches, who had come swiftly down through the trees as Barton's mother was collapsing in the mud. They had cast him a hard sideways look, then stepped carefully over the marshy, waterlogged grasses, concentrating on Barton and his mother.

'Well?' Paglia snapped.

Two of the men ignored her. Deliberately. As though she had already made herself unpopular with them tonight.

Ranking officers, probably.

'Both still alive,' the third man said, turning away to make a call on his phone.

'Well,' Paglia said, 'that's something, at least.'

Paglia continued on round the fringes of the bog and stopped in front of Savage. Her torch beam moved up and down his body, apparently in disbelief, taking in his gunk-coated clothes, then half-blinding him as she studied his bruised and muddied face.

'Savage.' She shook her head at the state he was in. 'Why didn't you wait?'

He said nothing.

More police arrived, this time with large, muscular German Shepherd dogs. The men stared at him first, then at the other two. The dogs stared too. The muddy clearing began to feel crowded. Green-jacketed paramedics appeared out of the mist with astonishing rapidity, cleaning Barton's airways of mud, checking his mother's vital signs. Someone appeared with a mobile phone and handed it to Paglia. She had a brief conversation with someone, sounding annoyed. Then nodded the phone away, and came back to him.

'Seriously, Savage, why didn't you wait?' she repeated. 'You knew we'd get here eventually. You shouldn't have interfered. Now I have to arrest you.'

He did not feel too good. 'What for?'

'How about obstruction? Illegal possession of a firearm?' She glanced round at Barton, who was being lifted onto a stretcher. 'Malicious wounding?'

'It was a citizen's arrest.'

She raised her eyebrows. 'And his mother?'

'She was trying to kill me.'

'Oh, come on. His mother?' Paglia made an impatient noise under her breath. 'You should have waited.'

'I didn't want any evidence shipped off while you were kicking your heels back at the station, waiting for a warrant. Face it, you'd never have found those women again if Barton had managed to get a replacement van here in time. Besides, my friends were down there.' He paused. 'Is Faith OK?'

'She's fine. Blankets and a hot drink. Same as the rest. Then she'll be asked to give a statement to one of my officers.' She paused. 'As will you.'

'I wouldn't say no to a hot drink. Or a blanket, to be honest.' He made a face, trying again to reach the knife in his back. 'Look, could you possibly . . . ?'

Savage turned to show her the knife still embedded in his back.

She shone her torch beam across his back while he swayed, not sure how much longer he could remain standing. Dimly, he wondered how much blood he'd lost.

Paglia said, 'What in hell's name is that?' in a rather different tone.

'A present from Mother Russia.'

'Why on earth didn't you say you'd been wounded?'

Paglia swore under her breath, and turned, urgently calling a paramedic over to assess him. While the two women discussed whether the knife could be extracted safely, not even asking his opinion on the situation, one of the officers came over. He was bearded and grim-faced, dressed all in black. Determined to look hard, in other words.

'Aubrey Savage?'

'Who's asking?'

'I'm Gibbons.' The man looked him up and down. 'You're Viscount Chiche?'

'You should lie face-down while this is done,' the paramedic said.

'Actually, I'd rather you just did it. Get the damn thing over with. If it's all the same to you.' He breathed shallow as the woman cut gently around the knife, removing his clothes. Soon he was standing bare-chested in the misty moonlight. Not exactly an ideal way to answer questions, he thought. But if it kept his mind off what the paramedic was doing, he was OK with that. Then he turned his head and glanced at the bearded man calling himself Gibbons. 'Yes, you've got the right man. How can I help you?'

'I work for . . .' Gibbons cleared his throat, glanced at the other officers working around them, then finished in a lower voice, 'the government.'

CHAPTER FIFTY-SIX

'Is that so?' Savage looked him up and down. He was preoccupied with what was happening at his back, which was an exquisite agony. But he had a fair idea who the man was, and what he had come to ask him. 'You're here about the Glock I found in Dani Farley's holdall.'

'Yes.'

'It showed up during the police search. Raised a flag in your database.'

'Something like that.'

'I had nothing to do with the murder of that boy, Callum.'

'So we understand.'

'Or this business with the Reverend Barton. Wrong place, wrong time. That's all. I came here visiting a friend of mine.'

'Peter Rowlands.'

'That's right.' Savage felt a sudden urge to be sick, and fought it. 'I had nothing to do with his murder either.'

'Suicide, the police report said.'

Savage shrugged, but said nothing.

'You don't agree?'

'Peter was left-handed,' Savage said, taking the tiniest possible breaths as the lacerated skin around the knife blade was cleaned with something that stung like hell. 'Yet apparently he shot himself in the head on the right side. Does that seem possible to you?'

'Yes, that was flagged up in the initial crime scene report. There were indications that he was left-handed.' Gibbons shrugged. 'They made some enquiries among the locals, and apparently, Rowlands was ambidextrous. It was well-known that he could use either hand equally well.'

Savage frowned. 'I'd never noticed that. Besides, there was bad blood between him and Barton. I only just learnt that the Reverend fathered a child with Peter's wife, without Peter's knowledge or consent. When he found out, it broke up the marriage and left him very bitter. He . . .'

'Go on.'

'Peter drank. A lot.'

'Duly noted.'

Savage didn't like Gibbons's tone.

'Ready?' The paramedic looked round at him. She had an open, smiling face, lit up by the beam of Paglia's torch. 'Feeling brave?'

'Not particularly.'

'OK, hold still a moment.' She put one hand against his back, pressing down with a pad of some kind, then slowly withdrew the knife. 'That's perfect. Nearly out . . .'

Savage gritted his teeth against the pain, glad that he'd always had a higher threshold for pain than most people. 'Insensitive,' his sister had called him when they were younger. Particularly when he barely felt the drill at the dentist's. Maybe he was on the insensitive side at times. But it was a useful thing to be after a stabbing.

'There you go. All done.' The paramedic patched him up with some kind of tight bandaging, which took another few minutes, crisscrossing his chest and right shoulder. Then she told him to make his way up to the ambulances once he was ready. 'You need to have that checked and stitched up at the hospital. It's not deep, so I doubt there's any lasting damage. But you've lost some blood.'

'Thank you.'

She smiled and bustled away to help with Barton's mother, who had revived and was being handcuffed. Mother Barton looked defiant and far from beaten. Though the vivid bruising across her forehead made him feel a little guilty.

He focused hard on Gibbons, aware that he was close to fainting. Never a good look, lying face-down in mud. He was also very cold. But again, he didn't like to ask for a blanket.

'Why are you really here?'

'I told you, we're here about the Glock. Just a routine enquiry, of course. But we wondered what you know about the whereabouts of its owner.'

Savage met the man's eyes.

Just routine.

The British government didn't scramble agents to the wilds of Dartmoor for a routine matter. They made coded phone calls. Sent secure emails. Maybe risked a few texts to someone already on the ground nearby. But to send a man on a few hours' notice . . .

We wondered what you know about the whereabouts of its owner.

Jarrah.

They didn't even know where their own man had gone. He had suspected as much before. But couldn't quite believe it. This, though, was a tacit confirmation of his suspicions. *We wondered what you know about the whereabouts of its owner.* He thought of Barton's taunting description of the hunt, and how he had left Jarrah to be torn apart by his men and dogs, like PC Petherick.

He could share that information. But something told him to be careful with this man. Circumspect, even.

'I don't have a clue what you're talking about.'

There was a flicker in Gibbons's face. Incredulity. Then scorn. He didn't believe him. Gibbons knew who he was and that he was looking for Jarrah. But clearly he wasn't prepared to say so aloud. Not out here in this wild place, anyway, and certainly not in the aftermath of this business with the Reverend Barton.

The man changed tack instead. A threatening tone. 'Your fingerprints were all over that gun. Why?'

'It was hidden inside a holdall that was left in my van.'

'Whose holdall?'

'A young woman. I gave her a lift.'

'This . . .' He consulted a pocket book. 'Dani Hoggins?'

'That's right.'

'So you stole her holdall.'

'She left it there. I didn't steal it. I had a quick look through, hoping to find something that would help me contact her. I found the Glock, but put it straight back in the holdall. I didn't shoot anybody with it.'

'You didn't report it to the police either.'

'I forgot.'

'Forgot?' Gibbons was incredulous.

'It was a difficult day.'

'So how did it end up in Peter Rowlands's hands?'

'I left my stuff at his farm when I was arrested. The Glock was still in the bag.'

'And how did this Dani Hoggins get hold of it in the first place?'

'You'll have to ask her that.' He grimaced, his chest and back an icy cold now, the bandaged wound aching. 'Meanwhile, I've got a hole in my back, and rather think I need to go to hospital to have it stitched up. And I imagine the police will want to ask me some questions.'

Paglia had been standing a few feet away, pretending to talk to a fellow police officer but no doubt secretly earwigging on their conversation.

'I'll get someone to help you up to the ambulances, Savage,' she said at once, coming over. 'Before you fall over.'

She looked sharply at Gibbons.

The man shrugged, and then turned away, disappearing back into the misty darkness. Presumably returning to London to make his report in some shadowy office in Whitehall.

Once he had gone, Paglia raised her eyebrows at his bare chest. 'The Tarzan look suits you. Except for the goose bumps, maybe. Do you need that paramedic back?'

'Maybe in a minute. And yes, I could do with a blanket. I'm bloody freezing like this. But first, I wanted to ask you something.'

'Go on.'

He had decided to take Paglia into his confidence.

She seemed as frustrated as he'd been about the interference of the special task force, and then the arrival of Gibbons. A government man, for God's sake, out here on Dartmoor, getting underfoot and asking questions. And leaving Savage with a burning question of his own, still as yet unanswered. Where the hell was Jarrah?

'Once I've been checked out at the hospital, will I get my camper van back?'

'If you're fit to drive, then yes, I suppose so.'

'Tomorrow?'

'I expect that can be arranged. Though only with the doctors' say-so. It's quite a large vehicle, after all.' Her smile was lopsided. 'Can't have you mowing down the good people of Devon because you've fainted at the wheel.'

'Agreed.'

'You're planning on leaving Dartmoor soon, then?'

She sounded almost disappointed.

'Most probably.'

Savage felt bone-tired now that it was all over. Ready for a hot shower to wash all this mud and sweat off, once his wound had been seen to at the hospital, and then a long sleep. That pub should have a free room he could use. He'd speak to Faith about it.

Unless the hospital insisted on keeping him in overnight. Though the wound in his back didn't feel so bad now the knife had been removed.

Barton and his mother had been taken away, leaving only the forensics team, who had moved in already with their white suits and bags of kit. The female paramedic was waiting for them on the edge of the clearing, talking to a police officer. Blue lights were still bouncing off the mist in the compound above, though the air seemed to be slowly clearing.

He tried to read Paglia's face in the glimmering darkness, but failed.

'Unless you're planning to arrest me?'

'Like I said, not under such extenuating circumstances. Besides, I had a call shortly after we arrived here. From a very senior officer. Once you've given your statement, I'm to let you go. No questions asked.' Her smile was curious. 'Seems you have friends in high places.'

Savage said nothing.

'Anyway, I think we can mostly cover this as self-defence. Though I'd feel happier if you could stick around for a few days, at least. You'll need to give us a full statement and some contact details. You may be required to return as a witness later. We've arrested a number of local men tonight, as well as Barton and his mother. I'm guessing your evidence will be key in the case against them.'

'No problem. Though there is something else. Will you go out with me?'

Paglia blinked. 'Sorry?'

'Back to Peter Rowlands's farm. There's something I need to show you.'

CHAPTER FIFTY-SEVEN

Paglia was late.

Savage checked the clock on the dashboard again, then gave up waiting. Taking the spade from the passenger bench seat, he swung down out of the camper van and locked it up behind him.

It was late morning, and there was no wind today. The recent rains were a distant memory too, only the occasional puddle still lying shallow in the shadow of boulders, the weather suddenly glorious. The sun was high over the wild expanses of Dartmoor, tiny birds like bright jewels darting from tree to bush or skimming above pooled water. Lichened rocks glinted like distant treasure in the sunshine, a carpet of rough grasses and heather springing underfoot for as far as he could see, tough and wiry, its fragrance intoxicating him with every step.

On a day like this, he could understand why Peter had come home to Devon after university, why he had chosen to live in this desolate place while his two best friends wandered the world. Dartmoor in particular had an edge of raw sweeping beauty, vital and uncompromising. And the high moors held their own dangers, as he knew now.

He had said goodbye to Faith early yesterday morning, before she set off home to Oxfordshire. She had embraced him outside the pub, though gingerly, taking care not to start his wound bleeding again.

'If you ever get yourself arrested again, Aubrey,' she said, smiling up at him, 'don't call me, OK?' Then she jingled her car keys, slid into her Mercedes, and drove away without even a wave backwards.

She couldn't stay mad at him forever. But it would probably take at least a couple of years for her to calm down.

His phone buzzed in his pocket, and he hooked it out.

It was Kim.

Sorry we didn't get to say goodbye properly. Have a safe trip home. Keep in touch. And thanks for the adventure. It was fun! K xxx

He grinned, then tucked the spade under his arm and texted her back, still walking. It took a few minutes as he kept typing the wrong letters.

Ditto. And good luck with the baby. Love to Phyllis.

He could hear the stream now, bubbling away in the sunshine. He was nearly at the ruined cottage. Slowly, he picked his way through the tangle of undergrowth, bramble thorns snagging on his jeans, until he was inside the cottage itself.

Everything was just as he remembered it, except that it was nearly midday now, not night or early dawn. He stood there and looked about at the ruins, spade in hand. The fallen slate roof and chimney, the collapsed walls, the blue sky above seen high and breathless from what would have been the heart of the house. It was still and quiet here. At peace, Peter might have said, if he had been standing here too, a spade in his own hand.

In his dream, Jarrah had been pointing out of the window.

He crunched over brambles and loose stones to the window, and once again stood there, examining the wild altar left behind on the sill by person or persons unknown. Pebbles, catkins, withered snowdrops, the crumbling petals of a flower . . . And two shards of black slate, lying aslant each other, forming the shape of a makeshift cross.

He leant the spade against the wall, and pulled on his leather gloves. Time for a little gentle excavation work. Taking care not to pull any stitches.

He had not given up hope of Paglia appearing. Perhaps by the time he had cleared this debris under the window sill, she would have arrived to bear official witness to his findings.

Whatever they might be.

He found the old mangle again first, and wrenched it free of its entanglements. Then he dragged out five splintered sections of a rotten roof beam, originally about ten foot in length, that had presumably fallen in during a storm, along with numerous slate tiles, broken pieces of brick and rough stone, jagged glass shards, and occasional odds and ends of plastic rubbish, blown across the moors in the high winds of winter before being trapped here and then buried by undergrowth.

Eventually, he had cleared the ground, cut down or beaten back the intricate living knot of brambles, removed all evidence of flooring, and finally hit soft earth.

He straightened up for a breather, and saw DI Paglia heading for the cottage. She had left her Volvo parked up beyond Rowlands Farm, its bonnet just visible, glinting darkly in the sunshine, and walked across the heather the same way he had come. She was now about a hundred feet from the tumble-down remains of the garden wall, dressed in black again and looking very stern and businesslike.

Savage raised a hand, and she saw him, waving back after a slight hesitation.

Perhaps Paglia had guessed why they were there.

Experimentally, he set the spade against the cleared square of ground, put a foot on the right tread, and pressed its sharp blade into the soil. He hit a large rock, and had to stop while he excavated it. Then he started again, pushing down, digging deep into the stony earthen ground beneath the cottage.

'Sorry I'm late,' she said a few minutes later, standing in the doorway. 'What is this place?'

He gave her a brief version of the story Peter had told him about the unfortunate Agnes, her failed marriage and eventual demise. Murdered by her husband for having taken a lover. The story felt strangely resonant now.

Her gaze fell to the hole he had already dug out beneath the window. 'And what's that?'

'A hole.'

'Clearly.' She came inside and stood a moment in silence, watching him dig. 'I meant, why am I here?'

'To bear witness.'

'To what?'

'To whatever this is.'

DI Paglia sighed, and shrugged out of her jacket. 'You think this is a grave. That someone's buried under there.'

'It's the likeliest explanation.'

'Who?'

He paused, breathing heavily. 'I'm not sure. A friend of mine, perhaps.' There was sweat on his forehead. He wiped it away with the back of his hand. 'The friend I came here looking for.'

She threw her jacket aside onto the heap of oddments he'd excavated from under the bramble patch. 'OK, give me the spade. Let me do it.'

'I'm sorry?'

'I'll do the digging. Two nights ago, you got stabbed in the back. Or have you forgotten? You'll open your wound, going at it like that.'

'I'm fine.'

She wrestled the spade from him, her frown severe. 'Go,' she said, pointing outside the ruined cottage. 'Take five minutes, at least.'

Savage saw it would be pointless arguing with her. Some people were like that. They couldn't take no for an answer. He left her to keep digging, and stepped outside. The air was cooler in the shadow of the cottage. He closed his eyes and took several deep breaths of fresh, moorland air.

His back was aching.

The doctor who stitched him up had assured him the wound wasn't as serious as it could have been. As if he had needed to be told that. But he'd thanked her anyway. It was useful to be sure that infection was the worst he needed to watch for. And he'd had two hot showers since that night, keeping his wound dressings dry as best he could, but scrubbing the rest of his body with plenty of strongly scented soap, trying to get rid of the stench of that horrendous bog mud.

The best moment of all had been getting his camper van back. He had climbed back into the silent cab, glanced over his shoulder at the bunk and table, the sink and fridge, the WC at the back and the dusty blinds over the side windows, and felt instantly at home again. They had turned the place over, of course. But it had all been put back together, and was now in the same comfortable state of disarray as ever.

'Savage?'

He went back into the cottage.

DI Paglia was standing in the hole itself, at the end furthest from the window. She was looking sweaty now too, her face flushed. She wasn't digging though, but bending into the bottom of the hole. The excavation was roughly four feet in length now, and coming up to what looked like three feet deep.

'What is it?'

'I've found something.' She looked up at him oddly. 'A bone.'

'Human?'

'No doubt about it.'

He crouched at the edge of the hole, looking down as she

took one of his discarded gloves and began to clear dirt gently away from the partly exposed bone.

'A radius,' he suggested. 'Or perhaps an ulna.'

She stopped, peering closer at the human remains.

'It was broken,' she told him, her voice crisp. 'There's a clear fracture line. And something else.' She straightened, and then nodded to her jacket. 'Can you get my phone? Inside pocket.'

Savage hesitated.

'I'm sorry,' she said more softly, 'I know you came here looking for your friend. But this is as far as we go without alerting the forensics team. We could be trampling all kinds of evidence here. I need to call this in.'

CHAPTER FIFTY-EIGHT

Some hours later, DI Paglia knocked on the window of the camper van. Savage, who had been resting as best he could without being able to lie flat on his back, got up wearily and opened the side door. He'd moved the camper closer to the moors so he could watch the police arrive, the dogs, and the police doctor, and the white-suited forensics team. It had been a hot afternoon, but now clouds were beginning to roll in from the east, along with a fresh, whippy breeze, and already there was a cooler feel to the air.

Paglia looked rather grubbier than before, sleeves rolled up, jacket still missing, a smear of mud on her cheek. He liked that she got stuck in, that she was such a hands-on detective. But he also knew Paglia wasn't popular with the rest of her team, that they considered their relatively new DI an interloper from upcountry, and constantly rubbed her the wrong way. She wasn't smiling, which could have meant anything, under those circumstances. But he could tell from her expression that she didn't have good news for him.

'Well?' he asked, looking down at her.

'It's not your friend.'

That surprised him. And didn't feel right.

He came down the steps into the sunshine, searching her face. 'How can you be sure? It's early days yet, you've only just found the body, and—'

'Savage, the body belongs to an adult female. Not a male.' Paglia took a handkerchief from her trouser pocket and wiped her hands with it. 'And she was pregnant when she died. Substantially pregnant, in fact. Maybe as far along as seven or eight months, according to the forensic officer on site. Though we'll know more after the post-mortem.' She made a face. 'Not a nice discovery.'

He stared.

Then closed his eyes in horror.

'Maura.' Savage pushed away the sickness rising inside him, and forced himself to look at the matter dispassionately. To consider the facts as he knew them. 'Peter did kill himself. I've been a fool.'

'Tell me.'

'When I turned up on his doorstep, asking about Jarrah, Peter must have guessed that I'd find out about Maura eventually. About her and Barton, and Jarrah's visit to the Green Chapel. The Glock, the fertility cult, the man-hunt, the whole sorry business.'

'I don't follow, sorry. Who is Maura?'

'Peter's wife. He told everyone she'd run away. But when he found out about the baby, he must have lost his temper and killed her.'

'Why, in God's name?'

'Because it was Barton's child she was carrying. Not his.'

Paglia looked aghast.

'She was desperate to have a child,' Savage said. 'They'd been trying for years. I imagine she lied to Peter when she first got pregnant. Told him it was their child. Peter would have known it couldn't be true. He was a heavy drinker, and even admitted to me that they'd had trouble conceiving. In fact, he pretended that was why she'd left him. But he was desperate to keep Maura. He loved her, you see.' Savage looked out over the moors towards the ruined cottage, and thought of the haunting regret in Peter's voice as he told the tale of Agnes and her disgrace. Perhaps he had been close to confessing that day. Only they'd met Barton's boys on the ridge, and then the police had arrived. And the next time he'd seen Peter, his friend was dead. 'So when she claimed it was his baby, Peter probably went along with the charade at first. Anything to hold their marriage together.'

'But something changed.'

Savage nodded, feeling an intolerable sadness for his friend. 'Seeing Maura getting bigger every month, and living in such close proximity to the father . . . It must have been hell. Maybe Barton rubbed his nose in it. He even boasted to me about it. Said Maura "went back for more". And maybe she did. Maybe she'd fallen a little bit in love with the man who'd got her pregnant. Who knows?'

'But to kill his own wife . . .'

'I guess Peter just snapped one day.' He looked across the desolate moors, trying not to imagine what had happened. 'He probably panicked, and buried Maura's body in the ruins of that cottage where he knew nobody was ever likely to find her.'

'Except you guessed where she was.'

'I should have spotted the inconsistencies earlier. There were clues right in front of me. Only I didn't see them. Too busy, too focused on finding Jarrah. There was her laptop, for a start. What woman leaves her laptop behind when she runs away from her husband?' He thought of Maura, her vibrant, sensual beauty, and found it hard to continue. 'It's my fault he died.'

'What?'

'Peter knew it was only a matter of time before I worked it out. He shot himself rather than face me.'

He remembered the way Peter had torn down and destroyed

the sign to the Green Chapel, the bitter venom in his voice. He should have realised then that his friend's anger was personal. Deeply, intimately personal. And forever inescapable.

'I was so sure Barton did it. I kept coming back to the fact that Peter was left-handed. That he couldn't have shot himself on the right side.'

'He was ambidextrous, not a true leftie,' Paglia said quickly. 'His drinking partners at the pub confirmed it. Everyone knew.'

'He mostly used his left when we were friends at university.' He grimaced. 'But that was years ago. People change, don't they? Peter changed. And I didn't even notice until it was too late.'

'You can't blame yourself. If your friend murdered his wife, as seems likely, it was never going to end well for him.' Paglia frowned. 'But what about your other friend? The one who's still missing. Where does he come into all this?'

'Jarrah.' Savage drew a long breath. 'He was my brother-in-law as well as my friend. He came here to visit Peter. Maybe he guessed Peter was in trouble, or Peter told him, and that's why he came to Dartmoor in the first place. Jarrah took himself up to the Green Chapel. Threatened Barton with a gun, and told him to stay away from Peter and Maura. And Barton killed him for it.'

Paglia's gaze narrowed on his face. 'You know that for sure?'

'Barton said they drove Jarrah over the moors, then let the dogs tear him apart.' The horror of that image almost destroyed him. To hide the tears, Savage put a hand to his face as though shielding his eyes from the sun. 'His body's still out there on the moors, scattered in a thousand pieces. We may never find him.'

'I wouldn't bet on it.'

He lowered his hand, staring at her. 'Sorry?'

'Did you ever come across a huge Russian guy up at the Green Chapel? Over seven foot tall, bald head. Like something out of a nightmarish Slavic folk tale.'

'Savanovic?'

'That's the one. When we were interviewing him, Savanovic claimed Jarrah got away.' Paglia met his eyes. 'That the dogs never managed to track him.'

Savage was astonished. And incredulous too. 'If that were true, he'd have shown up by now. He'd have let Peter know what happened.'

'Maybe. Or maybe something else happened to him.' She paused. 'This Jarrah worked for the government, didn't he? That's why that guy Gibbons came hurrying down here at such short notice. It was the Glock. Your friend's gun.'

'Yes, it sent up a red flag at MI5. Though according to Gibbons, they don't know what happened to Jarrah either.' Savage wanted to believe Jarrah was still alive. But he had to be realistic. He frowned. 'But if he isn't dead, why stay silent all this time?'

'Have you never wanted to disappear?'

He gave a wry grin at her expression. 'Yes, maybe. Or he could be in trouble.'

'So go find him.'

'I wish I could.' Savage shook his head wearily. 'The trail went cold two years ago. Dartmoor was my only lead. I've got nothing left to go on.'

'Perhaps this will help.' Paglia held up a see-through plastic evidence bag. Inside was what looked like a USB memory stick. 'It was in Maura's pocket. And we think its placement was deliberate. That it was intended to be found with the body. It's even wrapped in cellophane to protect it from damp.' She paused, looking at him. 'But here's the real kicker. It's got a label. Just two words.'

He waited.

'Aubrey Savage,' she said.

CHAPTER FIFTY-NINE

Peter had been his best friend for years. Along with Jarrah, that was. The Three Musketeers. It was not the easiest thing in the world to consider Peter's guilt, that he had killed his wife for betraying him with their neighbour, Barton. And then, when that first murder looked like it was about to be discovered, had shot himself rather than face the consequences. But of course that had been why Peter had drunk so much. Because of the guilt, all of the gnawing, body-heavy, soul-darkening guilt . . .

Now all he had of his friends was what remained on the memory stick.

Paglia took him into an interview room at the police station and allowed him to access the USB memory stick. But only while she looked on.

'I shouldn't be doing this, of course.'

'Of course.'

The memory stick contained only two items. Both files were marked with Savage's name, clearly intended for him in the event of Peter's death. Yet they'd been left with Maura's corpse in her makeshift grave at Agnes's cottage two years ago.

At the time he killed his wife, Peter must have known that Savage had started looking for Jarrah, that he might return to Dartmoor eventually and start asking awkward questions. But decided that he'd either be dead by his own hand or have disappeared long before that day came. Later, of course, he must have thought he was off the hook completely. That Savage wouldn't bother to find Jarrah once Lina was dead. Because of what Jarrah had done to his family. The unforgivable nature of his betrayal.

So Peter had kept drinking and brooding, and had thrust that dark deed to the back of his mind. Until the day Savage drove into his farmyard ...

The first item was an audio file.

It was three minutes twenty-one seconds long, including hesitations, which were lengthy and at times filled with a horrible sobbing that wrenched at his soul.

Savage listened to the recording through three times, while Paglia discreetly waited by the door. But he knew she was able to hear every word.

Hey, Aubrey, old thing, it's me. If you're listening to this, then you already know what I've done. The awful, unforgivable thing I've done. But maybe not why. And since I don't intend to be around to do the whole twenty-questions thing, I thought I'd leave this for you, or for whoever finds Maura. If anyone ever finds her. You know, it's a funny thing, love. While everything's OK, you think it's going to last forever, and you can't imagine ever hating that special person enough to ... But you can hate someone that much, of course. You can hate them enough to end them. Just like that. Maura made a fool of me, Aubrey. She behaved like an animal with that man, like she couldn't control herself. And when I said I wasn't going to put up with it anymore, that I was throwing her out, do you know what she did? She laughed at me. Laughed right in my face. She told me it didn't matter. That Barton was a better man than me. That she was going to live with him and his other women. That she'd never ... Never enjoyed being with me. Not since before we got married. And something just snapped, you know? Jarrah had gone up there to tell Barton to lay off. But he never came back, and then Maura ... She just laughed again. Said Barton had known how to deal with a limp Oxford type like him. Like me, she meant. I grabbed her by the throat and shook her, and then I squeezed . . . I'm not sure I meant to kill her. Not at first. I only wanted to shut her up, to wipe that smile off her face. I'd had enough of being laughed at behind my back. Of being sneered at in the village. Because they all knew. All of them. Even before I did. And Jarrah guessed as soon as he turned up. I only wish he'd never offered to speak to Barton on my behalf. I still don't know what they did to Jarrah. Though I can guess. Perhaps I should have gone up there with him. But he had a gun, and what did I have? Nothing. Story of my bloody life. I've never had anything. Only Maura. Maybe the baby too . . . But it would have been Barton's, and I couldn't have faced that. Anyway, I'm not asking for forgiveness, because nobody can forgive what I've done. But I am sorry, Aubrey. Sorry about Maura, and about Jarrah. I messed things up, and I know what I have to do. There's a photo with this. Happier times. Goodbye, old friend.

The second item was a JPG file.

It was a photograph, presumably scanned into Peter's computer and then added to the memory stick. He studied the photograph in silence for several minutes, trying to work out why Peter had stuck it on the memory stick alongside his audio file.

The file was dated two summers ago.

Jarrah's final visit to Dartmoor?

The photograph was of Jarrah leaning against the bonnet of his car, a standard bottle-green Mondeo, a typically low-profile vehicle for an MI5 spook, being ordinary to the point of invisibility. It had been taken in the yard at Rowlands Farm. A black-and-white sheep dog sat beside him, tongue lolling in the sunshine, and perched next to him on the car bonnet was a vibrant, sun-tanned Maura. Jarrah had his arm about her shoulders, and both were smiling cheerfully into the camera lens.

The photographer had presumably been Peter himself.

So why was it important?

Guilt, again.

Look at what I destroyed.

'What's that?' Paglia said abruptly, leaning past him. She was pointing at something in the Mondeo windscreen. A small white rectangle.

'Some kind of parking permit?'

'Here, let me.' She played with the mouse, cleaning up the image, and then zooming in on the white rectangle on display in the windscreen.

At that resolution, it was mostly a blur. Only five words were distinguishable, and even they were faint.

Visitor Pass. Dstl, Porton Down.

Paglia stepped back, reading each word out. Then she said slowly, 'Porton Down. That's the military research facility in Wiltshire. Chemical weapons?'

'Jarrah must have been there immediately before driving on to Devon. *Visitor Pass.* I wonder what took him there.'

She looked at him. Then carefully disengaged the USB memory stick from the police computer, replaced it in its see-through evidence bag, and whisked it out of the room.

'It's evidence,' she told him. 'I'm sorry.'

Savage waited about ten minutes in the interview room before it occurred to him that Paglia did not intend to return. Or perhaps had been waylaid. She was a busy woman. Lots of claims on her time. Not that it mattered.

He didn't need to wait for Peter's post-mortem. He'd made a mistake there.

It had been suicide.

He had failed Peter though. Failed to help him when his need was greatest. Just as he had failed Lina that day in the marketplace in Kabul.

It was time to break the pattern.

When we were interviewing him, Savanovic claimed Jarrah got away that day. That the dogs never managed to track him.

He persuaded the friendly duty sergeant to let him out of the back door, then crossed the police car park to where he'd left the camper van parked precariously on a low kerb. It was dark, there was no moon out yet, and a light rain was falling once again. It felt almost refreshing on his face. He climbed into the cab, started her up, and gently swung the camper van onto the road. There was nobody about.

Minutes later, Savage was heading north-east and upcountry, Dartmoor and its dark secrets behind him, the whole of England before him.

Acknowledgements

I still can't quite believe it's happened. This was always my dream book, the secret story lurking at the back of my mind for long years before it ever made it onto paper as a reality. I often talked about writing it, and even made copious notes about my aristocratic protagonist, Aubrey Savage, and his pet obsessions like Anglo-Saxon and poetry, not to mention the rackety camper van he lives in.

But Aubrey Savage's story, while fascinating, didn't fit with the kinds of novels I usually wrote, so the project kept being shelved. Finally, determined to bring him to life, I forced a gap to appear in my writing schedule, and thought, this is it, now or never.

So in late 2017, I began to write my dream book – and *In High Places* is the result.

For continuing to believe in me and support my writing for nearly a decade now, I'd like to thank Luigi Bonomi, Alison Bonomi, Danielle Zigner and all the agency team at LBA. And a big thank you to my editor Emily Yau for offering *In High Places* a home at Quercus Books. It's been a long journey, but here we are at last!

As always, I give loving thanks to my partner-in-crime, Steve, for his patient beta-reading of my various drafts and his encyclopaedic knowledge of cars and guns. Also, many thanks to my five long-suffering children – Kate, Becki, Dylan, Morris and Indigo – for washing up, making me endless cups of tea and enduring my 'absentee parenting' (their words, not mine) during writing retreats and research trips to Dartmoor etc. Honestly, it will all be worth it come Christmas.

And lastly, thank you to Aubrey Savage, for springing so effortlessly and fully-formed from my imagination, and always knowing what to do next. May I be permitted to accompany you on many more adventures in the future!